Mind Over Ship

Tor Books by David Marusek

Counting Heads
Mind Over Ship

Mind Over Ship

DAVID MARUSEK

TOR®

A Tom Doherty Associates Book
New York

"Big Plan," by Derick Burleson, is excerpted from *Never Night*, copyright © 2007 by Derick Burleson. Reprinted by courtesy of Marick Press.

A Tor Book
Published by Tom Doherty Associates, LLC
175 Fifth Avenue
New York, NY 10010

www.tor-forge.com

Tor® is a registered trademark of Tom Doherty Associates, LLC.

Library of Congress Cataloging-in-Publication Data   ·

Marusek, David.
    Mind over ship / David Marusek. — 1st ed.
        p. cm.
    "A Tom Doherty Associates Book."
    Sequel to: Counting heads.
    ISBN-13: 978-0-7653-1749-0
    ISBN-10: 0-7653-1749-4
 1. Twenty-second century—Fiction. I. Title.
    PS3613.A788 M56
    813'.6—dc22
                                                2008038035

First Edition: January 2009

Printed in the United States of America

0 9 8 7 6 5 4 3 2 1

To my daughter, Kalina,
who makes Earth my favorite planet

ACKNOWLEDGMENTS

A big thank-you goes to my indefatigable crew of first readers without whom I would still be paddling in circles: Vince Bonasso, Terry Boren, Sandra Boatwright, Derick Burleson, Dixon Jones, Marion Avrilyn Jones, and Paula Kothe.

Thanks also to Avi Loeb and my brother, James Marusek, for helping me with the science (as always, any errors are mine alone); to my editor, David G. Hartwell; and agent, Ralph Vicinanza; and to Sharron Albert, whose sharp eyes are the bane of typos great and small. And thanks to Kat and Steve Haber, who loaned me their lovely guesthouse in Homer, Alaska, to finish the manuscript in comfort and style.

PART 1

The Short Commute

It was a short walk from Mary's suite on the north side of the Starke Manse to the library on the south. Along the way she greeted doris maids and russ security men. The main parlor was closed off—fleets of household arbeitors and carpet scuppers were giving it a thorough spring scrubbing—and she detoured through one of the smaller banquet rooms. A solitary jerome sat at the head of the long, empty table going over house accounts on a dataframe.

"Myr Skarland," he said, nodding to her as she went by.

"Myr Walker," she replied with mock formality.

When she reached the library, Mary was surprised to find no one there. "Hello?" she said to the empty room.

Lyra, Ellen Starke's newly made mentar, appeared at once in her latest persona, that of a plain young woman in a featureless blue smock with a slate tucked under one arm. "Good morning, Mary," she said, her voice burbling with cheerfulness. "I trust you slept well."

Mary knew that the mentar knew that she had indeed slept well, since its job was to monitor everything and everyone on the Manse premises, but she said, "Yes, I did, Lyra. Thank you for asking." Then she said no more and only looked around at the empty chairs.

"Oh!" the young mentar said at last. "I should have informed you of the room change. Nurse Eisner moved the care plan meeting to the atrium because of the lovely weather. I'm sorry."

"No need to apologize, Lyra. You're learning very quickly, but, yes, next time inform me of schedule changes."

Mary took a shortcut through Ellen's bedroom to reach the atrium. Both the bed and the hernandez tank next to it were unoccupied. A jenny nurse was wadding up purple-stained towels from the floor and tossing them into the hopper of an arbeitor. She was a new staffer Mary hadn't met. When she noticed Mary, she said, "We're bathing her."

"Actually, I'm just passing through. Don't mind me."

But as Mary went by, the jenny's jaw dropped, and though Mary wore no name badge, the tall woman recognized her all the same. "Mary Skarland?"

"Yes, that's me," Mary said and paused to offer her hand. "Good to meet you"—she glanced at the nurse's name badge—"June."

The nurse clasped Mary's hand, but instead of shaking it, she pulled the smaller woman into a full embrace, which was what jennys often did when they met Mary for the first time. Sometimes they cried a little. To Mary it was odd: not every member of the jenny germline reminded her of Hattie Beckeridge, but some of them did, and then she cried too. Not this time, though, and in a little while she freed herself and said, "Welcome to Starke Manse, June. We're so glad you could join us."

THE ATRIUM COURTYARD roof had been scrolled back, and the morning sun painted the walls with creamy light. The air was fresh and a little chilly. Three night jennys sat on wooden folding chairs alongside Mary's two evangeline sisters, Georgine and Cyndee. Mentar Lyra stood in front of them posing in what appeared to be a period costume of some sort.

Cyndee had sleep lines under her eyes, but she smiled at Mary and patted the empty chair next to her. "What's this?" Mary said. "A fashion show?"

"We told her she had to lose the blue smock," Cyndee explained, "and this is what she's come up with so far. What do you think?"

"Yes, Mary," Lyra echoed, "what do you think?"

In place of the smock, the mentar's persona wore a lavender blouse and short black skirt with a light jacket in dusky plum brocade. On its feet were simple black suede open-toed slip-ons.

"Hmmm," Mary said, looking her up and down. "Understated, elegant, professional. Granted, it's like two hundred years old, but I like it, Lyra, and I give it my unqualified stamp of approval."

The mentar beamed. "Thank you, Mary."

"Wait. Hold on," Mary said. "You're not finished, are you? Where's the hat to go with that outfit?"

"Yes," chorused the jennys. "Show us the hat."

The young mentar said, "I have been studying the history of hat design, and I believe I have fused several popular styles into an original one."

"And?"

But the mentar hesitated and had to be coaxed into showing its hat to them. When the hat appeared on Lyra's head, the jennys gasped. The mentar's design was a complicated wad of velvet ribbon liberally sprinkled with tiny silver pinecones, rosebuds, and acorns. The brim turned up in the front like the prow of a ship, and from its bowsprit sprang a golden sprig that dangled three freshwater pearls. From the rear of the hat protruded a fantail of pleated felt, like the rear end of a turkey.

"Hmmm," Mary said. "Hmmm."

"Hats are the *hardest*," Lyra complained.

"Oh, I know it," Mary agreed. "What do *you* think about your hat?"

Lyra glanced at the jennys. "I *like* it, but I wouldn't want to appear ridiculous when I wore it."

"I don't blame you. No one wants to appear ridiculous. Maybe our friends can make some suggestions how to fix it?"

"All right," Lyra said.

At once the jennys and Georgine and Cyndee seized Lyra's design and cloned it multiple times in the air, editing it with ideas of their own. They tried their creations on Lyra and on each other and picked apart the results. The mentar delighted in their attention.

Mary said, "Remember, Lyra, in the end it's up to you to decide what you'll wear. That's a cardinal rule of personhood. You may end up liking your original design best of all, and if you do, you should stick with it. How you feel about yourself is much more important than the opinions of others, and with enough chutzpah, you can pull off any hat you like."

Just then, a door opened and Dr. Lamprey came in, followed by June and another jenny from day shift, as well as the head nurse, Eisner. The dozens of hats vanished.

"Oh, good," the doctor said, "you're all here." There were no more seats, and one of the jennys offered him hers, but the doctor said, "Sit, sit. I've got legs too." He paused a moment to gather his thoughts. "Now I know some of you are going off shift, so I'll keep this brief. The reason I asked you here—" He stopped and looked around the atrium. "I don't see Ellen's guardian."

"I notified her," Lyra said. The young mentar continued to wear its period work ensemble, but without the hat.

"Maybe she forgot," the evangeline Cyndee quipped, and the jennys snickered.

Cabinet appeared in front of the doctor, startling him. It wore the persona of an elderly woman. "Yes?" it said.

"We're having a care plan meeting, as I told you not ten minutes ago," said Dr. Lamprey, "and I would appreciate your attention."

"Certainly," said the old mentar, who promptly disappeared.

Dr. Lamprey frowned but continued. "Let me just say that the quality of Ellen's care continues to be excellent, and you are all to be commended. Likewise, Ellen's physical progress remains strong. Her physical growth continues to catch up on her early deficits, and I have no remarks to add along those lines. What I want to concentrate on"—and here his voice deepened—"is her psychological recovery."

The mood in the room changed. The jennys all looked at their hands. "Yes, I see you're aware of what I'm talking about," he continued. "With injuries so grievous, it's a minor miracle she survived at all, and the experience has taken its toll. Ellen lost a significant mass of brain tissue, especially in her motor regions and cerebellum. To compensate, we've ramped up her brain's own neuron-generating process, and new tissue is replacing the lost. It helps that her entire body has been replaced, which has provoked the whole region to rewire itself.

"What I am concerned about is the damage done to her prefrontal cortex. While not extensive, it's not as easily repaired as the motor regions without a permanent effect on her psyche. Not to be too graphic about it, but her head was literally plucked from her body by the force of the impact. Her safety helmet saved her brain, but it could not mitigate the sheer brutality of the experience. It leaves indelible marks.

"That being said, the human mind is a resilient organ, and early signs lead me to believe that Ellen's personality will reemerge essentially the same as before the accident. However, there is always the danger of unexpected complexes developing, and that's what I think we're seeing now. I'm referring specifically to her recent delusion that her mother is still alive."

It was a problem that Mary had, in fact, been the first to report. Oblique references to her mother's many contingency plans led to assertions of her survival. It had been going on for several weeks and was becoming more pronounced.

"We cannot ignore this," the doctor continued, "especially now when new networks are being established. Keep in mind that the neural circuits used most frequently become the strongest. You might say they increase their own bandwidth with usage. If we don't deal with this delusion now, it may become literally engraved in her prefrontal cortex and link up to other neural regions to eventually hijack her entire personality. It's better for us to be proactive."

The doctor paused a moment for the gravity of his words to sink in. "Here's what we're going to do. Last night, I explained the situation to Ellen, and with her permission, I infused the regenerative medium in her hernandez tank with a drug called Protatter. When activated, this drug dampens neural firing. When we dampen a circuit often enough the brain thinks the circuit is unnecessary and prunes it back. So, this drug, in effect, can erase memories. We have to be careful which memories we erase, and we'll proceed in a very conservative manner. Ordinarily, I would rely on a patient's guardian mentar to control the dampening, but"—the doctor looked around the room and shook his head. "Ellen's guardian seems to be having cognitive problems of its own, and her new mentar"—he nodded at Lyra—"may be a little young for such responsibility. Therefore, you, Ellen's nurses and companions, will have to do the job.

"In order to tell Protatter which circuits to dampen, we need to listen very closely to everything Ellen says, and every time she expresses her delusion we tag it. For this I've supplied Nurse Eisner with clicker devices."

The jenny held up a small plastic disk for the others to see, and the doctor continued. "Press the button for as long as she talks about the idea that her mother is still alive, then let it go. Don't press it if she mentions her mother in any other context. We don't want to erase all memory of her mother. Only press it when she expresses a belief that her mother is alive on this Earth. Don't be concerned if she says she's in heaven or otherwise spiritually alive. And don't worry about making a few mistakes along the way because it's the cumulative total of hits that will have the effect and not any individual error."

Office Hours

"She's waiting for you," June, the new jenny, told Mary.

"I'll spell you when you're tired," the evangeline Georgine said.

"Don't forget your clicker," Nurse Eisner said.

Mary waved them all away and gently shut the heavy Map Room doors behind her. Ellen lay in a parallelogram of sunlight on the carpet beneath the window. Mary crossed the room soundlessly and loomed over the drowsing baby/woman. Ellen's body was that of a healthy sixteen-month-old toddler. She was dressed in a plain, pea-green eversuit that left her fat arms and legs bare. She wore pea-green booties. Surrounding her neck was the large, horseshoe-shaped brace that helped support her adult head. Or, rather, that helped the head support its baby body.

It was Ellen's original head, the one she had been born with. A safety helmet had swallowed it moments before a devastating space yacht crash had obliterated the rest of her. It was a head that was a bit rattled still. It was covered with all-new baby skin, smooth and flawless. New button nose, comically small ears.

Mary moved into her light. "Mary?" the adult head said, blinking and yawning.

"Yes, good morning, Ellen. It's me."

The baby raised her arms, and Mary picked her up, mindful to support the ungainly head. She carried her to the huge chairdog that was crouching in the corner, and the window followed them along the wall.

"No, window," Mary scolded. "Go back where you were." The window fled back across the wall, and Mary lowered herself and Ellen into the chairdog. The chairdog stretched and scooched to balance their weight until they were perfectly comfortable, but then Mary remembered the clicker, and she had to lift Ellen to search her pockets for it. When they were resettled, Mary said, "Sleep well?"

"No, Mary, I did not." Ellen's voice lacked the force of adult lungs. "I kept waking up feeling I was drowning in that *fecking tank!* I want to sleep in a *real bed*, but they won't listen to me. Can't you make them listen to me?"

"I'll mention it," Mary said. "But you and I both know what they'll say: the tank is best for gaining weight and growing bigger."

"But they're wrong! I know they are. They listen to you, Mary. Promise me you'll speak to them."

"I promise. Now, what's on the agenda? You told Cyndee you wanted to work today, so what needs to be done?"

"Oh, Mary, there's so *much* to be done, more than can fit into one lifetime, and it just *keeps piling up!* I don't know how I'll ever get out from under it all."

Mary gave the baby a little squeeze. "Don't worry so much. Just slow down and take it one thing at a time. What should we tackle first? Lyra, what do you have to get us started? Make it something easy."

The mentar appeared in the room in her new clothes and pulled the slate from under her arm. "Libby from the Department of Justice is standing by with a briefing on their investigation into your mother's death."

Lyra! Mary said silently. *Weren't we in the same care plan meeting a few minutes ago?*

The young mentar quickly added, "But Clarity wants to speak to you first."

"Well, I don't want to speak to her. Send Libby in."

Mary shot Lyra a look of disapproval and added, "Make it voice only, please."

The official UDJD seal appeared in the center of the Map Room and faded away. The disembodied voice of the government mentar said, "Good morning, myren. Since our last update we have uncovered an important new lead. Forensics has identified a data burst transmission to the *Songbird* in the moments before its avionics malfunction. While we have poor odds of ever recovering the contents of this burst, the fact of its existence is one more piece of evidence that the avionics subems may have been sabotaged. In other words, evidence that the ship's failure was not accidental."

Ellen was silent for a long moment, and Mary readied the clicker. Ellen said, "I don't understand. Kindly boil it down for me, Libby: Have you found my mother?"

The government mentar paused, and Mary wasn't sure if the statement qualified as delusional. "I'm sorry," Libby said, "found your mother? The whereabouts of your mother's remains were never in doubt. The news I am imparting speaks to the question of whether your mother's death was a homicide or an accident."

Ellen corrected the mentar. "*Attempted* homicide, don't you mean? How can you have a homicide if you don't have a body?" There it was, the delusion, but when Mary tried to press the clicker, she found that she couldn't do it. Dr. Lamprey's explanation had sounded good, but Mary couldn't get over the image of reaching into Ellen's brain and pinching off a neuron.

"Her body was destroyed in the crash," Libby replied. "The coroner has positively identified bodily residues collected at the crash site as belonging to Eleanor K. Starke. Her death is not in doubt. Do you have evidence to the contrary?"

The baby squirmed in Mary's lap and kicked her legs. "Do *you* have any evidence besides 'residues' that she's dead? She's alive, I tell you! You should concentrate your efforts on finding her instead of making excuses!"

This time it was unequivocal, and Mary steeled herself and gave the clicker a good solid click. Meanwhile, she began rocking the baby in her arms. "Libby," she said, "please give your report to Lyra and excuse us. Lyra, cut the connection." The government seal reappeared briefly and faded away, and in a moment the chairdog aped Mary's motion and began to rock both her and Ellen.

When Ellen settled down, she said, "I'm sorry, Mary. It's just that I get so angry sometimes."

"Perfectly understandable. No need for apologies."

"No one believes me," the baby went on, "but I know I'm right."

Mary hesitated, then gave the clicker a quick squeeze. She looked imploringly at Lyra, who said, "Ellen, Clarity's been trying to reach you for a week now. Shall I connect her?"

"No!" Ellen said. "I don't want to see her!"

"Are you sure? She says it's important."

"That's what she always says."

Mary said, "Let's move on. What else do you have, Lyra?" but Ellen changed her mind.

"Let Clarity in. I do have something to tell her."

Clarity appeared on the opposite end of the room, took a moment to orient herself, and zoomed over to hover over the chairdog. Her holospace was roughly cropped and revealed scraps of her office around her. She opened her mouth to speak, but when she actually looked at her business partner, she laughed instead. "Honestly, Ellie," she said, "you should see yourself. We should do a character like you. Maybe use Alison's head."

The remark took Ellen off guard. "What?"

"That big neck brace of yours is like an adapter plug. We could use it to screw different heads into your body. We could mix and match our characters."

"Very funny," Ellen said.

"I think so. I think it's a riot. What do you think, Mary? We could call it the Amazing Modular People or something like that. Use it to recycle some of our less popular characters."

Ellen waved her small arms to cut her off. "Will you quit that already? I have something important to tell you. And please sit down. You're giving me a headache having to crane my neck like this."

"Yes, of course. Just a sec." Clarity vanished for a moment, and Mary nudged the chairdog to quick rocking. When Clarity reappeared, she was seated in an office chair.

"Thank you," Ellen said. "That's better. Listen, Clarity, my friend, I've been doing a lot of thinking lately, and—"

"Uh-oh," Clarity said with a wink at Mary, "when she starts thinking, look out."

"And I want to leave Burning Daylight."

Clarity opened her mouth, then shut it.

"I'm serious," Ellen went on. "I've lost all interest in producing holonovelas and sims. All of that seems so trivial to me now. Also, I know I haven't been pulling my weight for some time, and it's not fair to you."

Clarity frowned while she considered a response. Finally, she said, "You're not thinking straight, Ellie. You're still mixed up from your accident."

Ellen's reaction was explosive. "It was no accident!" she shouted. "Will everyone please get it through their skulls that it wasn't an accident! Even the fecking Justice Department knows it was a deliberate attack!"

"Sorry," Clarity said. "I meant to say your attack."

"I'm serious, Clair, I want out! The sooner the better!"

Clarity looked stricken. "But why? You love the business."

"Not anymore. Besides, I have no time for it. All my time is taken up doing my mother's work." Mary heard the word "mother" and readied the clicker. "At least until she returns." Click.

"Say what?"

"My mother's hiding out somewhere." Click. "She'll come back when it's safe." Click.

Mary decided that they'd had enough and said, "Clarity, maybe you can continue this discussion tomorrow. We're late for Ellen's nutrition break."

"All right," Clarity said uncertainly. "We'll table the matter for now. We'll talk about it when you're better."

"That won't make any difference," Ellen said, but Clarity waved good-bye and vanished. The doors opened at once, and June led a cart into the room, and in its wake came the aroma of baked apples and cinnamon.

"Snack time!" June sang in a perfect expression of jenny enthusiasm. She spread her fingers at the window to enlarge it, then opened the cart's high chair and reached for the baby.

But Ellen resisted. "I'm not hungry," she said and crossed her arms.

"Oh, we'll see about that," June chortled. "No one can resist apple strudel fresh from the oven!"

"Just watch me."

Mary leaned over to whisper in Ellen's undersized ear. "How can I ask them to let you out of the tank at night when you refuse even to eat?"

The baby took a moment to ponder this, then sighed and uncrossed her arms. "I can resist the strudel, nurse. It's Mary I can't resist." She raised her arms for June to pick her up. "I'll eat, but I'll feed myself. Is that clear?"

The young nurse laughed. "Yes, myr! You're the boss!"

Applied People—Warm Puppy Report

Zoranna Alblaitor spent a restless night in her Telegraph Hill home. When she awoke at one end of her sprawling Lazy-Acres bed, her mentar, Nicholas, was sitting next to her dressed nattily in a morning suit. "Go away," she sniffed. She turned her back to him and pulled the covers over her head.

"We have a big day ahead, Zoe, beginning in about half an hour."

"Use a proxy," said her muffled voice.

"I would if we had any fresh ones."

"Cast me."

"I could, but then I'd have a grumpy, half-asleep proxy." His argument had no effect on her. Not even the arrival of coffee and toasted bagels moved her. "I know what you need," he said, "a Warm Puppy Report! Uncle Homer, where are you?" At once a long-haired blond chow chow puppy appeared in the middle of the vast bed dragging a ratty towel behind it. More fur than dog, the large puppy noticed them and, dropping the towel, galloped over on oversized paws. It leaped upon Zoranna and tried to root under her blanket. But she wore no vurt gear and could not feel it. The puppy gamboled back to its towel and seized and shook it with mock fury as though to break its neck.

"It looks healthy enough," Zoranna said, peeking out from under the covers.

"Yes," the mentar agreed. "It's modeling the 75.2 million of our iterants who are awake and active at this time. Overall, they're feeling fat and happy and well employed. Even frisky."

"I hear a 'but' coming."

The puppy discovered the young man still sleeping on the far end of the Lazy-Acres and dashed over to check him out.

"So, how was last night's conquest?" Nicholas asked, changing the subject.

"Tireless," Zoranna said. "As if you didn't know."

"And how would I know?"

"Get off it, Nick. I felt your presence. You were riding me last night. Don't deny it. In fact, I think you enjoyed him more than I did."

"Does that bother you?"

"Not yet, but I'll let you know."

The puppy came bounding back to them, but halfway across the bed it yelped and stopped. It sat and began to lick one of its hind legs. "There," Nicholas said, "that's what I wanted to show you."

"What is it, baby?" Zoranna said, enticing the puppy closer. Uncle Homer returned to them, wagging its whole rear end, and tried to wash Zoranna's face with its tongue. "Make it vurt," she told Nicholas, and a moment later she could feel the dog's slobbery tongue and manic energy. She caught it in her arms to make it still and rubbed it behind its ears. The puppy felt so soft and warm—so real, as though Zoranna were wearing full vurt gear. If her mentar could ride her world, she could ride his.

"I think the Londenstane case is the problem," Nicholas said. "The trial concludes next week, our employees fear the verdict, and their stress is being translated as muscle cramps."

"Poor baby," Zoranna cooed. "Mommy is worried too."

The dog melted away in her arms, and Nicholas said, "Now that you're awake—"

"Give him back."

"Later. Andrea Tiekel will be here in ten minutes."

"Garden Earth business?"

"Apparently not."

"Then what?"

"She wouldn't say, except that it's important."

Zoranna dragged herself out of bed. In the bathroom, the large, softstone spa was filling with water. Zoranna considered the shelf of colored bottles and jars over the cabinet and chose Deep Forest from Borealis Botanicals. Borealis Botanicals was one of Saul Jaspersen's companies. She despised the man but loved his line of all-natural toiletries. She spilled a handful of crystals into the surging water, releasing a musty, sweet cloud of steam. Slowly, she lowered herself into the fragrant brew. When she had made herself comfortable, she closed her eyes and said, "Ready."

Her mentar opened a familiar lounge holoscape where she liked to conduct meetings. She glanced down and saw that she was wearing a dark business suit. She was seated in a blue-black leather armchair, and Nicholas occupied the one next to her.

ACROSS THE BAY in Oakland, Andrea Tiekel floated in a hernandez tank in a windowless basement room of her hillside house. She had not left the tall glass cylinder of bubbly green broth in weeks, and though she was constantly bathed in its wholesome chemicals, she continued to waste away. Her wispy hair drifted like seaweed, and her teeth were loose in her jaw.

Are you still up for this? her mentor asked.

Andrea belched a stream of curdled vomit, which was quickly absorbed by the fluid. *I'll manage,* she said. *The time is right.*

Yes, she's vulnerable now. We'll proceed, and we'll try to make it brief. We'll provide you a probability sidebob sim of her for comparison. We've never had the opportunity to model Zoranna's personality in one of our preffing suites, but we have high confidence in the accuracy of this sidebob construct. Nicholas says they're ready. Here we go.

A moment later, Andrea Tiekel was sitting in a parlorlike space. Her persona was a healthy version of herself, fit and full and flush with color. Opposite her, Zoranna Alblaitor sat at ease next to her mentor, Nicholas, who wore his usual rakish persona. Between Zoranna and Nicholas, and invisible to them, stood Zoranna's sidebob, wringing its hands anxiously, belying Zoranna's apparent calm. Yes, this was the right time to strike.

Nicholas spoke first. "Welcome, Andrea. Nice to see you outside the boardroom. Is E-P here too?"

"Yes, we are," said the mentor's disembodied voice.

"Wouldn't you care to join us in the visible world?" Nicholas gestured to the empty armchair next to Andrea's.

"Actually," E-P replied, "we don't use a visible persona."

"Is that so?" Zoranna said. "What about that quicksilver Everyperson I see everywhere?"

"That's our E-Pluribus corporate logo," E-P said. "That's not us. But if you insist, we sometimes use this marker." An icosahedron, like a ruby pineapple, appeared floating over the empty chair.

"Splendid. Thank you," Zoranna said and turned to Andrea. "Now, what's the purpose of this 'urgent' meeting?" Though she seemed disinterested, her sidebob leaned forward to catch Andrea's reply.

"It's actually pretty huge," Andrea said. "When my dear aunt Andie died, she left me E-Pluribus and an impressive investment portfolio. I'm currently rebalancing this portfolio to better suit my own interests. As part of this process, I would like to purchase Applied People."

"Excuse me?"

"I want to buy you out." Andrea sat back to watch Zoranna's reaction.

Both Zoranna and her sidebob seemed surprised. The sidebob said, *What's this all about? Is she serious? Do I want to sell? Does she know some-*

thing I don't? At the same time, the real Zoranna's eyes darted this way and that as Nicholas, no doubt, poured counsel into her ear. After a few beats, Zoranna regained her composure and said, "How fascinating! Tell me, Andrea, shouldn't the owner of the largest preference polling company in the world know that I have no intention whatsoever of selling Applied People?"

Zoranna's sidebob, meanwhile, had changed. It was now lying on a massage table, and a second Nicholas was feverishly kneading its neck and shoulders. Andrea smiled at the image. "Yes, of course," she said. "I know your feelings about your company, but with the help of E-Pluribus, I am able to play my cards several shuffles ahead."

"What exactly does that mean?"

"It means that I know probabilities which tell me that things will go very poorly for Applied People in the next few months. Within a year, Applied People will be worth next to nothing and be teetering on financial collapse. I say this in all sympathy. I'm not gloating or trying to take advantage of an unfortunate situation. In fact, rather than waiting until the bottom drops out, I'm here now to make what I consider to be a generous offer."

Nicholas interjected, "Just how generous?"

"Eighty-two UDC per share."

That *was* generous. Better than twice full value.

Zoranna said, "If you really mean to be generous, then you'd fill me in on the nature of this unfortunate situation that E-Pluribus foresees. Then Nick and I might have the opportunity to do something about it and save my company."

Meanwhile, her sidebob was saying, *Is it the Londenstane trial? Does she know the outcome? Oh, my God, the court is using an E-Pluribus jury! Did she rig it? Are we doomed?* The sidebob was no longer on the massage table but in bed clinging to Nicholas like to a lover.

Andrea lingered over this image, then turned to Zoranna and said, "As you wish, I will tell you. There's a near certainty that Fred Londenstane will be found—innocent."

With a brave face, Zoranna said, "But that's good news!" Her sidebob, however, cried, *We're ruined!*

"Actually," Andrea went on, "it's not good news, at least not for your business. It would be far better if he received a life sentence and was locked away forever. Out of sight, out of mind. But instead he'll be constantly in the public eye, a permanent reminder of his clone fatigue and a gadfly upon your whole organization."

There's no such thing as clone fatigue! raged the sidebob. *It's a myth, an urban legend. It's not real, and we have the science to prove it.* Calmly, Zoranna said, "That's a cynical statement, Andrea, considering we're talking about a living human being here, but I see your point. Tell me, how can you be so sure of the verdict? I mean, I thought that as soon as E-Pluribus releases jury sims to the court you have no further contact with them."

"That's true, we don't. But don't forget, we still have the original sims in our database. If we expose them to the same testimony as presented in court, we can determine how they're likely to respond to it. In any case, I've made my offer. I don't expect an immediate reply. I'll leave it on the table for now, but the per-share amount will drop appreciably with time. Now, if you'll excuse us." She rose to leave.

Zoranna also rose. "Thank you for dropping by," she said, but her sidebob was curled up in a trembling ball of nerves.

THAT QUITE WORE me out, Andrea said, once again in her warm, dark, syrupy tank.

Yes, we see that, E-P replied. *You'll have a rest break before our next meeting, but tell us, any insights to share?*

Were you able to move any furniture into Nicholas's realm?

No, his security was too alert. Why do you ask?

There's something odd about their relationship. Not your usual human/mentar sponsorship.

We'll look into it. Anything else?

Andrea reached out and touched the glassine side of her tank, caressing its smooth surface with bony fingers. *Yes, one more impression. She's a sensuous person. Tell me, what brand of body oil or skin cream does she prefer?*

Borealis Botanicals. After a moment, E-P said, *Yes, a fine vehicle. We'll look into that as well. Now rest, dear.*

One more thing. I feel my time is near.

The mentar paused a moment, and then it said, *We'll place the order.*

Thank you.

Replacement Order

The order rumbled throughout the underground facility, rousting sub-units by the score from the chilly slumber of standby status. Subems diagnosed both themselves and their component machines. Motors whirred, pressures rose, and instruments self-aligned to nano-tolerances. Several million jiffies later, the controlling midem declared the laboratory fully operational.

At once, all three stitching chambers prepped themselves with skeletal scaffolding blanks. Their print heads chittered to life. First they laid down the bones, building them from organic feedstock, 4096 molecules per stitch, a thousand stitches per second. Then they dressed the finished skeletons with organs, printing them in place. They knit muscle fibers, entrails, circulatory lines, nerves. They constructed hearts already containing the blood they would soon pump.

Seventy hours later, the stitchers went off-line, the chamber doors opened, and the print run was removed, still cold, to the bonding bay. The bay was a small space where the raw bodies could continue their internal assembly undisturbed for another forty-eight hours. Then medbeitors wheeled the bodies into the "delivery" room where they were jolted to life.

Only two of the Andreas passed inspection. The third exhibited a faulty nervous system and was handed off for sanitary disposal. The lab midem sent a fulfillment notice up the chain.

Total Body Makeover

Oliver TUG browsed the Thievery Gallery of the Persuasion Channel for their new interviewee. The rows of postage-stamp mug shots were no help: one brutalized face looked much like another, and there were so *many* of them. Oliver searched manually by dates and key words and after a few passes found the kid. The banner over his mug read, "WRECKER," and the Ransom/Reward link below read, "He stole from us, and we want it back." The thief, himself, looked to be about twelve years old, but he was a retroboy. He was a member of a gang that had caused a TUG moving and storage van to crash and then stole its contents before the traffic police arrived. At least, the TUGs assumed this retroboy was a wrecker. They had scant evidence, the boy hadn't actually copped to anything yet, and no one had offered to ransom him.

As it happened, the moving van in question had contained ordinary household goods, not some more sensitive cargo, but that was beside the point. No one should get the impression that they could mess with the TUGs and get away with it.

Oliver pointed at the boy's mug, and the frame expanded into a life-size hologram of the impromptu interview room. The room was actually a nit-proof tent they had constructed in a very secure warehouse. They had delivered the boy to the tent in a nitproof bag. As far as the police were concerned, the boy fell off the grid in a public null room in Oak Park, halfway across the city. In the tent, the boy was lying on a tarp, and his legs were shackled in makeshift stocks.

Although the Persuasion Channel provided its amateur interviewers triple anonymity, Oliver walked through the holospace searching for any inadvertent clues that might give his charter away to the authorities. The only agent in the tent was a generic household arbeitor. It was busy painting the soles of the boy's bare feet with an organic solvent that caused the skin to liquefy and slough off. The exposed nerve endings on the soles of his feet looked like the stubble of a white beard.

The boy was already crying and pleading, which made Oliver shake his head in wonder. The solvent didn't actually hurt, and if the boy made this much fuss so soon, how would he hold up when the arbeitor broke out the hair dryer?

Oliver's comlink buzzed. "Prinz Clinic called," said a subordinate. "Veronica is out of recovery."

"Thank you," Oliver said, wiping away the holospace. "Get my car."

A PHALANX OF three tuggers preceded Oliver TUG through the surgical wing of Prinz Clinic. Each of them stood over two meters tall and measured twice the girth of human standard. Clinic workers and machines hugged the walls to let them pass. The TUGs wore military-cut jumpsuits, and over their left shoulders floated the olive- and mustard-colored marble of their charter logo.

At the door to the private room, Oliver told his detail to wait in the hall while he went in alone. Although he must have known what to expect, seeing her for the first time was still unsettling. She looked the same as before, only smaller. Much smaller, a half of her previous mass. Her head was shaved, but it had the same jar-shape, with flattened nose and pronounced chin, that characterized their charter. She looked like a miniature version of herself.

Oliver TUG told the medtechs in the room to vacate, and they seemed only too glad to comply. Then he drew himself erect, looking even more imposing, and said in a gravelly voice, "Veronica TUG of the Iron Moiety, on behalf of the Supreme Council of Moieties of Charter TUG, I am compelled to deliver an official notice of reprimand. Your recent body mods run counter to TUG regulations, causing harm to yourself and serving as encouragement of aberrant behavior to others." As he said this, he gave her a secret wink. "Furthermore," he went on, "continuation in this manner will result in serious penalty, up to expulsion from the charter."

Veronica seemed unperturbed by the solemn pronouncement. When Oliver stopped talking, she said, "Finished? Then come here and give us a hug."

Oliver scowled, but he crossed the room and leaned over her bed to gently pat her shoulder. Still using his officious tone of voice, he said, "We're all concerned about you, Veronica. Your moiety is both ashamed and worried. Won't you even consider undoing this great harm?" As he spoke, he made a fist and pressed his knuckles against her shaved skull for a good bone-to-bone connection. *Bad news, Vee,* he said. *All the latest mentar shoots have failed the isolation stress test.*

All of them? she replied through her skull. He nodded, and she said, *They raptured?*

That's what it looked like. We have to rethink this whole thing. We're getting nowhere. We should call in a mentar specialist.

No! she said. *No outsiders. We can't risk exposure.*

Well, this is becoming a very expensive waste of time. We've burned through nearly thirty personality buds with no results. Do you have any idea how much those things cost?

I know exactly *how much they cost, but there is no alternative. We must have a stable mentar, one able to go months in total isolation. No, this is the only way. Start a new batch.*

Are you sure?

Look at me. Do you think I would have put myself through this if I wasn't? Start a new batch at once!

Oliver removed his fist from her head, leaving knuckle marks. He paced the small room for a while, then returned to lay his fist on her again. *All right, but if this batch fails, we explore other options.*

She shrugged under his rude weight and changed the subject. *Any word from Starke?*

She's agreed to meet with us but hasn't set a date yet.

Stay on top of it. Oliver removed his fist again and chucked her under the chin. "You're a maddeningly stubborn woman," he said in his disapproving tone. He went to the door and added, "Disobedience to the Supreme Council cannot and will not be tolerated. That's the first rule. Remember it."

"Wait," she called after him. "Don't you want to see my tail?"

Skipping Stones for the GEP

It was a perfect morning for skipping stones, warm and sunny. Meewee left his Heliostream office and told his calendar to hold all calls. But by the time he took a lift up to the surface and exited the reception building, storm clouds had moved in, and a few late-season snowflakes were falling. But the cart was waiting for him, and he was wearing a smart jumpsuit with an integrated heater, so he went anyway.

Meewee rode out to one of the hundreds of hourglass-shaped fish farming ponds that dotted the ten-thousand-acre campus of Starke Enterprises, and by the time he reached it, the sun had come out again. He parked the cart and searched the banks for throwing stones, without much hope of finding any. The Starke ponds were lined with crushed basalt: blocky stones that were good for smashing the heads of snakes but abysmal for skipping.

Merrill Meewee knew his stones. As a boy in Kenya, skipping stones was his favorite free-time activity. There had been an abundance of saucer-shaped missiles on the banks of his father's own fishpond. Fat, river-smoothed disks, they skipped ten, twelve, sixteen times before slipping beneath the surface with a watery plop. His father, a man of little wealth but great forbearance, was not pleased with his boy's solitary pastime, but he never ordered him to stop. Instead, he asked the boy how many stones he thought the pond could hold. I don't know, Meewee remembered answering. A hundred thousand?

Oh, such a big number! And how many stones do you suppose you've thrown already?

Merrill, who was an excellent student, calculated the number of stones he might have tossed in an hour and how many free hours were left each day after school and chores, how many afternoons in how many years since he first discovered the sport. I would estimate 14,850, he informed his father with a certain amount of swagger.

His father was impressed. So many? And all of them have gone to the bottom?

Of course they've gone to the bottom, he had said, embarrassed by his father's apparent ignorance. They're stones. They're heavier than water.

And heavier than fishes?

Of course heavier than fishes.

Good, good, his father concluded, patting him on the head. Keep at it, son, and soon I won't have to work so hard.

Father?

It's true. When you fill up my pond with your stones, I won't need nets and plungers to harvest the fish. I'll simply wade in up to my ankles and pick them like squash.

It was a lesson in diplomacy, as much as aquaculture, and it stayed with him all these years.

There was a splash, and Meewee looked up in time to catch a flash of fin gliding across the surface of the larger bulb of the hourglass pond. The larger bulb was for the general population, while the smaller one joined to it by a gated neck was used as a nursery and harvesting corral. The fish were a transgenic species called panasonics. In Meewee's opinion, they weren't a pretty animal, what with pop-eyes, slimy skin, and a protruding lower jaw lined with needlelike teeth. But they were robust, easy to farm, and, kilo for kilo, one of the most nutritious natural foods that ordinary people could still afford. They yielded heavy fillets of orangish-red flesh that was high in the omega oils not found in other freshwater varieties. And grilled with lemon pepper or served with dill sauce—oh!

Oh, to the devil with the stones, he thought, abandoning his quest for skip-worthy stones and settling for a pocketful of gravel. He spent the next hour pitching gravel into the pond, not even trying to skip them because they always sank after the first bounce. Meewee had a strong throwing arm, but it was too short to get much distance. Nevertheless, despite everything, Meewee lost himself in the activity.

His reverie was interrupted by a message from his calendar.

"I thought I told you to hold my calls," he said with a huff of annoyance. "This had better be important."

The calendar wisely made no reply.

Meewee sighed and brushed his dirty hands on his scarlet and vermilion jumpsuit. "Proceed."

Aria flight control at Mezzoluna reports that due to local conditions launch of advance ships has been moved forward.

"That news could have waited until I returned to the office." He turned and began to climb the rocky apron to the grassy bank. "Anything else?"

New launch time is 14:50 today.

"Today? The launch is today?"

Yes, at 14:50 local time.

"What time is it now?"

14:45.

Meewee swore and began to jog up the bank to the cart, but he knew he would never make it back to the office in five minutes. "Arrow," he said, addressing his mentar, "you'll have to project the launch here."

The cart at the top of the bank lurched forward half a meter in order to turn away from the sun. Then a patch of eastern sky above Meewee's head darkened until it was pitch-black and spangled with stars. A voice was counting down the seconds, and Meewee craned his neck to stare at the far reaches of space projected above him. He couldn't distinguish the launch facility from the starry background. The view was from the Aria space yards at Mezzoluna several tens of thousands of kilometers from the actual blast site. At the end of the countdown there was a beat, and then the star field disappeared in a blossoming ball of nuclear fire. Meewee shut his eyes and turned away, dazzled. When he could see again he searched the star field. "Well?" he said. "Was it successful?"

Arrow said, *Shipboard telemetry won't resume for several minutes.*

Of course not, even robotic ships needed time to recover from a nuclear blast. These ships carried a complete set of repair bots and nanofabs to constantly rebuild themselves during their centuries-long journey. They were designed to arrive at their destination star systems at least two hundred years before their assigned Oships. They would spend the time gained preparing the way for the colonists: scouting target planets, performing terraforming tasks, laying infrastructure, constructing cities so that when the Oships arrived and the colonists were roused from their millennial slumber, whole, viable new worlds awaited them, ready to inhabit.

A new, faint star appeared in the holoscape above Meewee. "Is that—?" he said, and another appeared, and a third and fourth. The robotic ships that had come through the atomic boost were firing their main chemical rockets, to correct their course and to boost their speed even more.

Aria launch control counted the ships as they reported in. Six, seven, fourteen ships. Twenty, twenty-eight, fifty, seventy-six. Meewee cheered, literally jumping up and down on the bank of the fishpond. Seventy-six out of a possible two hundred advance ships reported in. It was more than he had been told to expect. The launch was a solid success!

"Arrow, name the Oships they belong to."

The Garden Chernobyl—*ten advance ships under way. The* Garden Hybris—*eight. The* Garden Kiev—*twenty-four advance ships.*

The *Kiev*—excellent! thought Meewee. The *Kiev* was the first Oship in the launch order. Its departure was only months away.

The King Jesus—*nineteen advance ships under way,* Arrow continued. *The* Garden of Hope—*fifteen.*

Excellent, excellent, excellent—it was all excellent. It was superlative. Meewee felt like celebrating. If only Wee Hunk were still around. How he missed the annoying little caveman. Meewee turned his pocket inside out and flung the last bits of gravel into the pond. The splashes made a gurgling sound that resembled a word, someone saying, "Galloway," or maybe "Go away." Meewee often heard words in running water, in the wind, in squeaky hinges.

"I'm going, I'm going," he replied merrily and climbed the rest of the way to the cart.

An Unwelcome Offer

No sooner had Meewee returned to his office than Lyra called and asked him to join Ellen Starke in an ongoing meeting at the Starke Manse. Lyra was Ellen Starke's new mentar, the replacement for Wee Hunk, her former mentar. Meewee had not yet found the courage to inform Ellen that it was Arrow who had killed Wee Hunk or that it was he, Meewee, who had ordered Arrow to do so. But now was not the time. This was a time for celebrating their successful launch.

"By all means!" he exclaimed to the mentar. "Tell Ellen I'll be right there." He sat in his favorite chair and told Arrow to take him to the Manse. A moment later he was sitting opposite Ellen's desk in the Map Room. The room was brightly lit by a single window that stretched the entire length of the wall. Ellen Starke's persona sat behind her desk. She appeared to be the same young woman she had been before the space yacht crash that had taken her mother's life. In a chair next to Meewee sat the holo of another young woman, Andrea Tiekel, who had replaced her aunt, Andie Tiekel, on the GEP board. Andie Tiekel and Eleanor Starke had been murdered only days apart.

Bracketing Ellen's desk were the personas of the mentars Cabinet and Lyra.

"It was a complete success!" Meewee announced, pumping the air with his fist. He turned to the corner of the room, where he knew the realbody Ellen would be sitting with her evangeline companion. And though he couldn't see her, he gave her a triumphant thumbs-up.

"Over here, Bishop," Ellen said. Her holo persona at the desk waited for him to turn back to her. "What was a complete success?"

"Why, the launch of the first advance ships. We're on our way!" Ellen gave him a look of incomprehension. "The advance ships for the Oships," he explained. "Aria had to push up the atomic boost to today. I thought that was why you summoned me." Meewee's elation began to leak away. "Why did you summon me?"

"We have received an unexpected offer from Myr Tiekel here. Since you are titular head of Heliostream, I thought you'd want to sit in on this meeting."

Titular head? Meewee didn't like the sound of that. He turned to the Tiekel woman. "Hello, Andrea. What offer?"

Andrea smiled disarmingly. "Don't worry, your excellency, my offer will have little effect on your position at Heliostream. And, by the way, congratulations on the successful launch. I think that's marvelous."

Being told not to worry always made Meewee worry. He shot a questioning glance at Ellen, who said, "Andrea wants to buy Heliostream."

"Excuse me?"

"Heliostream," Andrea said. "I'm in the process of retooling my investment portfolio. Except for E-Pluribus, Auntie's investments are, frankly, a bit outdated. A space-based energy company like Heliostream would make an ideal core holding."

Alarmed, Meewee said to Ellen, "Why don't you sell her our fish farms instead? The aquaculture sector is just as important as energy." But these were only the surface words. Embedded in them was a hidden statement in another language. *<You can't be serious.>*

Ellen made no sign of understanding him in either language. Since her crash, she had repeatedly refused to speak the secret family metalanguage with him. Sometimes he wondered if she even remembered it.

Meewee turned to Cabinet, who was standing on one side of Ellen's desk, and challenged its ID in Starkese. <What do you say, mentar? You can appreciate fish culture, can't you?>

The mentar, once Eleanor Starke's powerhouse, did not answer his ID challenge. It hadn't done so since it had been forced to pass through probate after Eleanor's death. Therefore, for all intents and purposes, it was an outsider and not to be trusted with family security. For about the thousandth time, Meewee questioned his decision not to kill the mentar when he had had the chance. But not even Wee Hunk had been sure at the time whether Cabinet had been contaminated or not. And besides, some family mentar had been necessary to manage Eleanor's far-flung empire until Ellen could take charge of it. Cabinet had seemed capable of doing that at least.

Meewee didn't even bother challenging the young mentar Lyra. It had never given any indication of knowing Starkese at all. That meant that neither Starke mentar was completely trustworthy.

Andrea, watching him with a puzzled expression, said, "While aquaculture is indeed an important industry, Bishop Meewee, I am more inclined toward energy at this time."

Meewee threw off all attempts at appealing to Ellen in Starkese. He leaned over the desk and said, "You *can't* sell Heliostream. It's out of the question. Heliostream is more than an energy utility. It's the contractual linchpin of the entire Garden Earth Consortium. If you sell it, you give away control of the whole GEP!"

Before Ellen could reply, Andrea said, "I repeat; there's no need to worry about that, excellency. When I buy Heliostream, I'll allow you to remain in your position as CEO, and you can continue to represent it on the board. I have no intention of abandoning the GEP mission. On the contrary, I'm on *your* side. I, too, believe it essential that we humans spread our species throughout the galaxy. In that we are allies."

Andrea turned to Ellen and added, "And I will do everything in my power to carry on your mother's work as she would have wanted."

Ellen's expression darkened, and she stared at Andrea for several long moments.

Uncertain, Andrea added, "I hope I haven't said anything out of line."

Finally Ellen said, "Thank you for your offer, Myr Tiekel, but the sale of Heliostream or any other part of Starke Enterprises is out of the question."

Her statement seemed to take Andrea by surprise. "May I ask why?"

"Because I'm only standing in for my mother." Tears began to well in her eyes. "I had forgotten how much Bishop Meewee's little project means to her."

Andrea looked more confused than ever. "I don't understand. Standing in for Eleanor? I'm under the impression that—that you own Starke Enterprises outright."

"I do, but only until my mother returns. And when she does, I want to be able to hand her company back to her in as good a shape as when I acquired it."

Even Meewee was stupefied by Ellen's declaration, but he was grateful for the distraction and didn't interrupt her.

"I'm sorry to bring up this painful matter," Andrea said, "but didn't your mother perish in the same troubles that killed my aunt?"

Ellen smiled sadly and shook her head. "Eleanor Starke is far too wily to fall victim to mere assassins."

"Then where is she?"

"She's in a secret location recovering from her injuries. When the time is right, she'll walk through that door, and when she does I want to be able to show her that I'm on top of things."

At this point, Lyra jerked into speech. "Thank you, myren. Ellen is overdue for a physical therapy session." The holoscape abruptly closed.

Meewee was left in his office chair thoroughly bewildered.

"WHAT WAS *THAT*?" Andrea said. Though she was in her tank in the basement, she had moved her POV upstairs to her always room. Her always room was a simulation of her real living room, an exact facsimile, faithful down to the nap of the carpet and scuff marks on the walls. "You didn't foresee that at all. Your prediction was completely off base. Starke should have welcomed our offer."

E-P replied, *It's impossible to accurately model insanity. It's too fluid a psychic state.*

"Is that what you think, that she's insane?"

What do you think?

Andrea took a moment to sort through her impressions. She tried to dampen her connection to E-P's mind, which raced in dozens of directions at once. She recalled her conversation with Ellen and tried to hear the rhythm of her words. "I think she believed what she was saying, that Eleanor survived the crash. Is that even possible?"

We doubt it. We've preffed tens of millions of people from all walks of life since the crash. We've run hundreds of probable newscasts and alternate history scenarios concerning the crash. None of them resonated with anyone. No one anywhere has the slightest inkling that Eleanor might still be alive. We think we can safely rule that out. Her daughter is clearly delusional.

We don't need Heliostream, E-P continued, *to sabotage the GEP. Jaspersen seems to be doing that all on his own. We wanted Heliostream as a fail-safe. But with Ellen's state of mind and Cabinet's meltdown, the whole family empire is imploding. Still, they bear watching.*

Andrea floated across her always room to the windows. The city and Bay were lost in fog. "Were you able to move more furniture into Cabinet's realm?"

Yes, we moved some directly into its personality matrix. Unfortunately, we have a lot more company there than on our last visit. There is more foreign furniture in Cabinet's inner rooms now than native stock. That's why the personality is so unresponsive; there's too many warring factions inside it battling for control.

But we also managed to move a few pieces into the new mentar. Look at this.

A frame opened with a view into the Map Room, which they had just visited. The window was much smaller in this view, and the room was in shadows. In the corner, two evangelines and a jenny were fussing over a bizarre baby/woman.

"Zoom in closer." Andrea watched the women's expressions for a long while as they interacted. "Yes, this is good," she said.

The scene changed to an overhead perspective of the Manse, with cutaway views through roofs and floors to show every warm-blooded occupant of the rambling compound. Then the frame closed, and E-P said, *We'll let you rest now. It's been a busy day. But before we go, do you have any final insights?*

"I think so. Questions actually. Those evangeline companions of hers, she seems highly dependent on them. Can we use that? And what's with Meewee and aquaculture?"

Companion to Power

"Wine?" Mary said, leading Georgine down the corridor to her suite.

"After the day we've had," Georgine replied, "scotch would be more like it."

"Scotch it is." They entered the suite and crossed the foyer where Mary stopped abruptly to take in the sight of her living room. Large and uncluttered, it had bare white walls and French doors that spilled afternoon sunlight across the hardwood floor. It expressed a simple perfection that resonated inside Mary, as any true home should.

Georgine stepped around her. "You sit. I'll get it."

"Nonsense," Mary said, breaking the spell. She went to the china cabinet and opened the glass doors. Again she was struck by a sense of perfection. Leaded crystal glassware of all kinds lined the shelves: heavy beer mugs with beveled facets, brandy snifters with bells as delicate as bubbles, long-stemmed wineglasses, champagne flutes, shot glasses. It seemed that every variety of drink required its own specialized vessel, and Mary had the complete set. It made her feel a sense of achievement, even though technically it all belonged to the Manse and not to her. She selected two stout tumblers and closed the doors. "Ice?"

"Yes, please."

As Mary fixed the drinks, Georgine dropped into an armchair and stretched her legs. She took out her clicker, now disabled, and turned it over in her hands. "I don't know," she said, giving it a few dry clicks, "memories shouldn't be that vulnerable."

"I agree," Mary said. She handed Georgine a glass and made herself comfortable in her favorite chair.

"I mean, memories, good or bad, make us who we are," Georgine went on. "I sure don't have any memories bad enough to want to delete them." Mary swirled the ice in her glass and didn't respond. "I'm sorry," Georgine hastened to add. "I completely forgot about you and Cyndee. Have you ever thought about having Protatter treatments for that?"

Mary shook her head.

"Neither had Cyndee, but after today she's thinking about it."

Mary set her glass on the side table. "Not me, though. Unless you think I'm delusional like Ellen. Is that what you're hinting at?"

"Of course not, Mary. You're no more delusional than the rest of us."

Georgine finished her drink and stood up. "And with that little bit of sun-shine, I'll be on my way."

"Won't you stay for dinner?"

"Thank you, but not tonight. Believe it or not, I have a date."

"Oh? Who with?"

"A guy named Norbert."

Mary rolled the name around in her head and said, "Norbert? Doesn't sound like a russ name to me."

"He's not a russ. I'm giving our russies a little break."

When no more information was forthcoming, Mary said, "And—?"

"I don't want to hear any smart remarks out of you, Mary Skarland. He's a jerry."

Mary covered her mouth in disbelief.

Georgine leaned over to kiss her sister on the forehead. "He's nice. Jer-rys are nice—once you get past their narcissism."

AFTER GEORGINE LEFT, Mary slipped off her shoes and went to her bedroom, undressing as she went and dropping her clothes on the floor for the scuppers to pick up. While she had been out, the bedroom had redec-orated itself. It now boasted apricot-colored walls and a deep moss-green carpet. A new yellow bedspread matched new curtains on the windows. "Draw me a bath," she said and laid out underwear and a robe.

She could hear water surging in the bathroom, and when she opened the bathroom door, she was startled to see a man crouching there. A naked man, no less, with his back to her. Somewhere nearby, a woman moaned with pleasure, and Mary shut the door, her heart racing. "Lyra!" she called. The mentar appeared, a big grin on her face. "Lyra, what is going on in my bath-room?"

"Your Leena has a new role. Surprise!"

"My Leena? And who's that man?" Mary chided herself for her prudish-ness. "Never mind, I'll see for myself." She opened the door, and in the mirror she recognized the man—Raul Weathercock! His dark face was mottled with passion. He had taken Mary's poor Leena from behind and pinned her against the vanity counter. The Leena was all but hidden from view, but her mewling and grunts resonated in the tiled space.

Mary tried to coolly recall which role superstar Raul was currently ap-pearing in, but she couldn't concentrate, and she was about to ask Lyra when there was an ear-stabbing screech behind her.

"Florentinnooooh!"

That was it, Florentino Samovaro, the Don of Rancho de la Noche. And the screeching woman behind Mary was his costar, Renée Klopsetter, in her Bernie Award–winning role as Chus-Chus. The show was *The Flyers*, one of the highest-ranking holonovelas on the charts. Chus-Chus stormed across the bedroom, hands on generous hips, and scorched Mary with her gaze. Mary remembered her own nakedness and tried to cover herself with her hands. Chus-Chus said with trademark scorn, "Waiting our turn, are we, Missy?" She pulled a pocket billy from thin air, telescoped it with a flick of her wrist, and charged the bathroom bellowing her battle cry, "Florentinnooooh!"

"Chus-Chus, no!" someone shouted. It was Mister Jamal, who also came into the bedroom. Brewster and Anatoly and a gaggle of servants were watching from the living room. "He's not worth it," Mister Jamal pleaded. "You only demean yourself."

Disregarding Mister Jamal, Chus-Chus raised the billy and savagely whipped her faithless lover. Red welts scored his back, but they only seemed to intensify his ardor. The cheeks of his sculpted ass puckered with each powerful thrust. The Leena was lifted off her feet, her moans rose to a keening howl that drowned out the shouts and curses of the others, and Mary wiped the whole scene away with a swipe of her hand.

The bathroom reverberated with the interrupted coitus, and Mary's surging blood pounded in her ears.

"I detect that you are unsettled, Mary. I apologize if I erred in any way."

"Dear Lyra," Mary said, calming herself, "in the future, tell me before launching a novela in here."

"Yes, Mary, I will. Again I apologize. I have been trying to master the concept of surprise."

"Well, that *was* a surprise, though I wouldn't call it a pleasant one."

"Please forgive my ineptitude."

Mary stepped into the bathroom, which was restored to its grottolike calm. "Oh, don't worry about it. For a mind only a year old, I suppose you're doing fine."

"Actually, I'm four hundred days old today."

"Well, that's different then. A whole four hundred days? What's taking you so long?"

The mentar fell silent, and Mary added, "That was sarcasm, Lyra. Friendly ribbing. Look it up."

In the spa, the warm jets of gel soothed her, and she couldn't help but relax. In all truth the invasion by such high-wattage glitterati had been a thrilling surprise, at least the fact of it. *The Flyers!* Any role on *The Flyers* was golden, and her own personal hollyholo sim had a speaking part! Or at least a moaning part. "Lyra, show me the audience stats."

An hourly chart appeared in the spa. It was hard to read in the steamy fog, but one figure leaped out—scene subscription was in the high teens. Incredible! Each point represented about two million paying viewers, which meant that somewhere in the neighborhood of thirty million bathrooms around the world had hosted Chus-Chus and Florentino's latest love spat. And her Leena's share in the action, besides Raul weathercock's legendary battering, topped four figures. And that meant that her Leena had in one afternoon earned Mary more than she used to earn in a whole year working at Applied People. It was astounding. It was unreal. Capitalism was a marvel, as long as you were a capitalist.

Mary swiped away the chart and gave herself up to the hot fingers of the jets. Fred had never taken her in the rear. The notion had probably never crossed his mind, or for that matter, the mind of any russ. His time in prison had been difficult for her, especially since he had stubbornly refused to exercise their conjugal privileges, not even once. But that was about to change. It would have to, for the trial would soon end and, to be realistic about it, he was going to lose. And Mary sure as hell wasn't going to resign herself to sixty or more years of celibacy. At least, at the very least, he would have to get used to vurt sex.

"Lyra, a little privacy."

"Certainly, Mary. Good night."

Mary turned the jets to their masturbatory setting. She thought of Fred as she attended to herself, but maybe a little bit of Raul Weathercock slipped in as well.

Honey

On a bluff overlooking the million-acre IBA agriplex outside Tendonville, Illinois, an apiary arbeitor and honey collection cart were making the daily rounds. The arbeitor parked in front of Hive 23768 and undocked its multiple arms. With programmed efficiency, it lifted the roof off the hive while clearing bees from the supers with gentle puffs of benzaldehyde-spritzed air. It transferred comb frames to the cart for honey extraction and sterilization while testing the hive for pests and disease, assessing the brood chamber, sniffing for mold, and appraising the queen's lay rate. All results fell within guideline parameters, and the tireless arbeitor reassembled the hive, redocked its arms, and led the cart to Hive 23769 where it repeated the procedure.

Several dozen hives later, the honey cart signaled that its hundred-liter collection tank was filled to near capacity and summoned a replacement cart.

At Hive 24024 the arbeitor detected an unusual honey/pollen ratio. There were more comb cells devoted to pollen storage than was typical, but since the ratio fell within acceptable parameters, the arbeitor noted the data and continued on.

When five hives in a row recorded a similar high ratio, the arbeitor put in a call to the agriplex subem. The subem instructed it to suspend its other tasks and to conduct a pollen survey. Consecutive hives presented increasing numbers until they exceeded guideline parameters at Hive 24030. At Hive 24038, the arbeitor confronted a colony that was out of control. A cloud of angry bees guarded the hive and could not be soothed with the aerosol spritz. Probing the hive, the arbeitor recorded an interior temperature substantially higher than the hive's own heat sensors reported. So high, in fact, that the combs in all but the outer frames were melting. A gooey slurry of honey, pollen, and wax was running down the hive's stilt legs and pooling on the ground under the hive platform. The arbeitor snaked its fiber eyes to the puddle for a close-up look. An unknown leaden-colored liquid was separating out of the slurry and seeping into the dirt.

The Verdict

On the charge of irretrievable manslaughter in the first degree, Mary thought. On the charge of retrievable manslaughter in the second degree. Mary was dressed and ready to go, but she couldn't seem to leave her bedroom. Georgine was out in the living room crabbing about Norbert, who had turned out to be a typical jerry after all. Selfish, adolescent. And crabbing about the weather, which had turned wintry. On the charge of criminal trespass and reckless endangerment. On the use of a fabricated identity in the commission of a felony. On lying to a peace officer. Tampering with evidence. Oh, they were going to put Fred away for a long, long time, and it was all her fault. Hadn't he broken the law in order to protect her? Hadn't she practically dared him to? Mary flung herself on the bed, unseating her hat. She was the worst spouse possible.

Georgine came into the bedroom. "What are you doing? You're going to be late. Are you crying? Don't cry, Mary."

"I'm a terrible person."

"No, you're not. *I'm* the terrible person. I care more about myself than those around me. I should have been at the clinic with you and Alex and Renata." She came and sat on the bed next to Mary. "When Wee Hunk called, I had just gotten home, and I told him I was too tired to go back. But the truth is that I was afraid. He said it was urgent, but I was a coward!" She slumped forward.

Mary sat up and dried her eyes with the corner of a pillowcase. She rested a hand on her sister's shoulder. She could understand why she was falling to pieces. She had Fred to fret over. But Georgine? She must be channeling Ellen. Evangelines were always channeling someone. That was why they were so good.

The baby/woman's condition had improved during the past week. The Protatter, guided by diligent clicking, seemed to be working: Ellen had stopped insisting that her mother was alive. She stopped speaking of her mother altogether. Dr. Lamprey was calling this solid progress and encouraging everyone to remain vigilant at their clickers for another week.

But Mary seriously doubted that she and her sisters could last another week. Taking responsibility for Ellen's very thoughts was causing too much strain. She got to her feet and opened a mirror to straighten out her clothes. She fetched the hat from the floor, and as she put it on, she watched Georgine watching her.

"You look good, Mary."

"Thanks." Mary went to the doorway but came right back to give Georgine a hug. "I swear, I never thought that going to court would be a welcome distraction. Hold down the fort."

IT WAS A short hop by town car to the federal courthouse in Bloomington. The trip was unnecessary; she could attend the trial from home. But home spectators were invisible in the courtscape, and it was important to show her support for Fred. So Mary endured the trip, the media attention, and the invasive courthouse security in order to check into an official spectator booth.

As luck would have it, she managed to engage a solo booth, and she popped up in the courtscape in her reserved spot on the bench directly behind the defense table. Other spectators appeared on either side of her. The judge appeared behind the bench and the prosecuting attorney at his table. Although the judge and prosecutor had conducted the bulk of the trial by proxy, they marked the importance of the final day by appearing in person by holopresence. By contrast, Fred's defense counsel, Myr Talbot, appeared by proxy as usual. His proxy swiveled around and greeted Mary with a nod, but Mary was too upset to acknowledge it. Was it asking too much for Talbot to appear in person to deliver his closing argument? To send his proxy at so critical a time was unconscionable, bordering on malpractice, and she was no longer able to hide her disgust with the man.

At the outset of the trial, Mary had begged Fred to allow the Starke Cabinet's attorney general to defend him, but Fred wouldn't hear of it. He wouldn't even let her mention the Starke name in his presence, let alone accept the largesse of its legal representation. Mary then insisted on hiring their own attorney. With what? he had asked. Not with Starke funds she assured him. With their own income from her own Leena. Where did the Leena come from? he asked, and he answered his own question—from Starke. Fred chose to go with an attorney provided by Applied People and the Benevolent Brotherhood of Russes—the incompetent Myr Talbot.

Talbot's first act had been to help pick a ruinous jury. He had recommended that Fred agree to an E-Pluribus jury, which in itself was not unreasonable. The court calendar was perennially backlogged and to insist on a jury of living, realbody people for a trial of this class would require a wait of seven or eight years. With little chance of bail, Fred would sit out those years in prison. An E-Pluribus jury, on the other hand, could be impaneled at once.

Selecting the E-Pluribus jury had started out well. Fifteen Everypersons appeared in the jury box, their quicksilver surfaces throwing rainbow flashes of color throughout the courtscape. At a word from the judge, they all began to flicker, morphing momentarily into random individuals from the vast pool of 1.2 billion potential juror sims in the E-Pluribus database. Young, old, rich, poor, the whole spectrum of society flashed by. Moreover, these sims had been cast prior to the date of Fred's alleged crimes and stored inert in isolation, so there was no possibility of contamination by hearsay or the media.

The judge rapped his gavel, and like a game of musical chairs, the morphing came to an abrupt halt. Fifteen candidate sims blinked and looked around, confused by their sudden existence. Remarkably, there were *seven* iterants among them, including an evangeline and a russ! And the non-iterant candidates were mostly free-rangers, that part of society least hostile to clones. A more favorable jury could not be imagined, but it wasn't to be. The attorneys exercised their allotted challenges, and one after another of the jurors morphed again and again, dipping into the limitless demographic pool.

When all challenges were exhausted and the final jury and alternates were impaneled, it was the polar opposite of the first. The evangeline and russ were long gone, which Mary had expected. (Excluding them amounted to a racist belief that clones were not individuals!) Worse, the other five clones had been replaced as well, two with affs, which was bad enough, and the rest with chartists. Chartists! Chartists despised iterants, falsely accused them of stealing their jobs. It was far from an impartial jury made up of Fred's peers!

Talbot's incompetence continued to manifest throughout every phase of the trial. Mary pleaded with Fred, but stubborn Fred insisted on going without any Starke assistance. And so, five months later, they arrived at this final day of the trial, facing what amounted to life behind real bars.

When Fred appeared at the defense table in his prison jumpsuit, Mary put on her bravest face so that when he turned around he'd see at least one friend in the courtroom.

Oh, but he looked haggard. Hadn't he slept at all? He smiled at her with grim tenderness, which broke her heart all over again.

Then his attention was distracted by someone behind Mary. The judge rapped his gavel and the bailiff ordered all to rise for the jury. Mary rose, and the jury sims—stored during trial recess on the court's own secure quantum lattice—filed into the jury box. Mary glanced around to see who had caught Fred's eye. It was Reilly Dell. Reilly avoided Mary's look, and the courtroom was asked to be seated.

So the trial, so the closing arguments. The prosecutor trumpeted the vicious nature of Fred's slaughter of duly sworn officers of a health-care facility. He emphasized Fred's contempt of the law, to this day refusing to name the source of his false identikit. He enumerated the ways society was harmed by Fred's egregious crimes. In response, Myr Talbot-by-proxy failed to remind the jury of Fred's overriding motive for his crimes—to save his wife's life. He did not contradict the prosecutor's assertion that Fred's victims were all "duly sworn" officers of the clinic—the pikes were a rogue element whose presence had never been adequately explained during the proceedings. Talbot-by-proxy did not challenge any number of inconsistencies and contradictions that even Mary, who was not trained in the law, had noted during the course of the trial. All was surely lost.

The judge instructed the jury and then sequestered it in a deliberation space. Fred's holopresence from the Utah prison was abruptly severed, and the courtscape went to standby.

Before leaving the shelter of the courthouse lobby, Mary lowered the veil of her new hat. With veil in place and head held high, she marched resolutely out the doors and down the courthouse steps. Immediately, about a thousand media bees mobbed her. The tiny mechs with whirring acetate wings formed a wall to block her way. Little framed faces shouted the same question at her: How do you feel the trial went?

But Mary didn't answer. Without even slowing down, she marched into the wall shouting, "Desist! Desist!" and the wall gave way.

At the bottom of the steps, the Starke limo waited at the curb. Mary jumped in and the heavy door shut itself against the horde. The windows opaqued. Mary removed her hat and leaned back into the ultra-soft seat cushions. She closed her eyes and caught her breath.

After a while, when the car didn't leap into the air to make its way home, she opened her eyes and said, "We're not moving."

Lyra appeared in the seat opposite her and said, "We've been advised to remain in place and stand by."

"What for?"

"The bailiff reports that the jury has already voted and returned a verdict."

Mary's heart fluttered. "So soon? Five months of trial and ten minutes of deliberation? What does it mean?"

The mentar said, "I have no experience in these matters."

"Ask Cabinet or someone who knows. But first ask the bailiff if they want us to come back in."

"Yes, they're about to reconvene to read the verdict. The bailiff is calling us."

Mary suffered another trip through the media gauntlet, through courthouse security, and dashed back to her booth. Fred and the attorneys were already in place. Myr Talbot was there, by holopresence this time, looking baffled. Fred, damn him, slumped in his chair, resigned to his fate.

The judge appeared, and all rose again for the jury. The jury members each glanced at Fred as they filed in, which every court drama Mary had ever watched said was a good sign. When the judge asked for the verdict, the foreperson cleared her throat and said, "In the first count, irretrievable manslaughter in the first degree, we find the defendant . . . not guilty."

A collective gasp filled the scape. Fred, confused, asked Talbot to repeat what the juror had said. The judge rapped for order, and the foreperson went down the charge sheet, delivering a litany of "not guilties." The judge polled each juror independently to verify the verdict. The result: Fred was exonerated on all counts. The judge ordered him freed.

Fred was in shock. He turned to face Mary, but she was no better prepared for this turn of events. Before either of them could recover, Fred was vanished back to Utah. Myr Talbot, looking befuddled, turned to her and said, "He's free, but it'll take a few hours for him to be discharged from the prison."

GEORGINE SAID, "DON'T worry about a thing, Mary. We've got everything under control." Rather than return to the Manse, Mary's car had headed straight to the Bloomington Slipstream station where a Starke tube limo awaited her. It was a long, sleek Marbech Tourister, designed to accommodate ten fussy passengers during pancontinental trips. Soon she was hurtling beneath the plains states inside a blast bubble of compressed air to the federal penitentiary outside Provo. She was furious with herself for having been so sure of Fred's ultimate conviction that she had failed to make any plans at all for his improbable release. As she traveled, she and Georgine conspired to hammer together a "transition plan."

"Are you sure you can spare both Cyndee and me?"

"No problem," Georgine said. "Ellen understands the situation and gives her blessing. She hasn't mentioned you-know-who all day, and Dr. Lamprey is our cheerleader."

"Lyra, can you make all the costumes in time?"

"Yes," said the mentar. "Yours will be waiting for you, Mary. I've instructed the car how to pick it up."

"And my bee? Can you send Blue Bee with Cyndee and Larry?"

"We already did. They're already in the tube and should arrive shortly after you."

"And afterward? I don't think Fred will want to come to the Manse."

"We'll arrange something," Georgine said. "Don't worry about a thing, Mary. Just go and bring Fred home."

Space Condos

In the birthing suite, the two replacement Andreas were being passively exercised through electrocortical stimulation. Their higher minds idled like engines. Soon, E-P assured Andrea, soon.

MEEWEE ENTERED THE grand conference room on the ground floor of the reception building of the Starke Enterprises campus where the "Gang of Three"—Jaspersen, Gest, and Fagan—were already present by holopresence. At least, Gest and Fagan were. Jaspersen was attending by proxy, or so it would seem. Everyone knew that Jaspersen didn't trust proxies and never used them, but he liked to impersonate them. It didn't really make much sense—impersonating a proxy of oneself. What practical advantage could you gain? But Jaspersen had done so for nearly a century, ever since his famous proxy meltdown when he was USNA Vice President. In any case, all that was visible of him was his bald head. No shoulders or hands, not even a neck. Floating over his seat, Jaspersen gave the impression of being an animated toy balloon.

"What's the matter? No hello for me, your holiness?"

"Hello, Myr Jaspersen," Meewee said. "Nice of your proxy to join us."

Jaspersen cackled his appreciation. The very sight of him, or his improbable proxy, strained Meewee's tolerance to its breaking point. Jaspersen was a singularly ugly toy balloon, with a lumpy skull; a too-large, always-leering mouth; and insolent, droopy eyelids. He was a disturbing caricature of a man. He was what a demon might look like without makeup.

Adam Gest, on the other hand, was preternaturally handsome. The owner of Aria Yachts and the shipyards at Mezzoluna and Trailing Earth, where the Oships were being constructed, Gest had deep, dark eyes and long lashes, curly brown hair, pearly teeth, and a pretty mouth that was forever set in a smile. If anyone had the wherewithal to sabotage Eleanor's space yacht, it was Gest, whose company had built it. Several times in the last few months, Meewee had had to curb an impulse to sic Arrow on the man and his business. Surely, the evidence of Eleanor's destruction was buried somewhere in Gest's files. But Arrow was a tricky investigator to control; in uncovering Gest's complicity, it was liable to inadvertently cripple the GEP shipyards, or cause some other world-class disaster. Still, he yearned to someday confront Gest's pretty face with an arrest warrant.

The third villain was Byron Fagan—Dr. Fagan—the owner of the bastion of aff mollycoddling, Roosevelt Clinic, where Fagan's zombied mentar, Concierge, had almost succeeded in murdering Eleanor's daughter. Fagan was a tall man, towering a good meter over Meewee. He was pleasant enough, until you contradicted him. Then he treated you like an errant employee. Meewee felt physically affronted by the man, even via holopresence.

The rest of the board members projected into place, either by proxy or holopresence: Trina Warbeloo, board secretary; Zoranna Alblaitor, Andrea Tiekel, and the others. Only twelve of the thirteen votes were represented. Jerry Chapwoman had recently resigned and the board was still interviewing replacement candidates. Meanwhile, Meewee represented both Heliostream and Starke Enterprises and had two votes. Cabinet took up its usual observer position at the foot of the table but didn't say anything.

After Andrea's recent bid to purchase Heliostream, Meewee wasn't so sure where her loyalties lay. He watched her for clues. She did seem unusually chummy with the Gang of Three, but she greeted Meewee warmly as well.

After the board worked through old business, the first item of new business was a motion by Jaspersen: "I move that we add eight little words to our mission statement, to read: 'The GEP shall resettle humans outside Sol System in exchange for enforceable title and user rights to real estate on Earth, *and to pursue space-based for-profit industries.*'"

Fagan seconded, and Meewee, as board chair, reluctantly opened the floor for discussion. Jaspersen jumped in immediately. "Before you bitch and moan about how this will distract us from our primary mission," Jaspersen's balloon told him, "let me assure you that the opposite is true. As I'm sure you're aware, the Chinas have recently announced their own extensive Near-Earth colonization and solar harvester programs. They got fed up with waiting for us to license them our technology. Practically speaking, it'll take them ten years or so to catch up. That gives us a decade-long window of opportunity to actually see some profit from all our hard work over the last dozen years. Let me remind you, Eleanor Starke always promised us some fair return for our participation. And believe me, there's a pent-up demand for high-quality inner-system space habitation systems. With the revenue we generate, we will double or triple our shipbuilding capacity. Thus, the extra-system colonization, which is all you ever think about, your highness, would not be harmed in the least by our enterprise. We might actually increase it."

Meewee shook his head and said, "You are the last person I would expect to be quoting the murdered and absent Myr Starke to me."

But Jaspersen's proxy ignored him and addressed the others around the table. "Adam will now show us how it works."

Everyone turned to Gest, whose response from his office at Mezzoluna involved a round-trip transmission lag of about a second. Yet before he could answer, Meewee said, "You can't change bylaws, let alone the consortium mission statement, on a procedural vote. You all know that. You need a supermajority."

But when Gest lurched into speech, everyone around the table hushed Meewee. "Thank you, Saul," Gest began. At the same moment, a scale model of an Oship appeared floating over the conference table. "Here's one of our colony ships. In fact, I see that it's the *Chernobyl*." The ship's name was stenciled in Roman as well as Cyrillic script on the revolving habitation drums. "Its structure is basically a tandem hoop frame with thirty-two hab drums strung on each hoop. Except for stabilizing rockets, it has no propulsion of its own. Instead, an electromagnetic torus centered in the hub acts as a target for particle beams supplied to it by Heliostream." As Gest spoke from Mezzoluna, the model over their heads began to change. The ordinarily invisible torus target in the ship's donut hole glowed red. "Most of the energy the torus intercepts is turned into motive force, the rest is used for life support. Our first refinement would be to tune the torus for microwave reception instead of particle beam." The torus glow changed from red to green. "What's more, only the outer, sunward ship in a roll of Oships needs to have a torus field at all, which will lead to a great cost savings." As he spoke, more Oships appeared and stacked up against the first like a roll of candy. Their hab drums were all steadily rolling, generating gravity for their inhabitants. From the hoop frames there blossomed solar collectors and dishes and targets of one sort or another. They looked like sprouting leaves and flowers. The evolving model was mesmerizing.

"The typical parked space arcology will house ten to fifteen million persons," Gest went on. "We already have in hand tentative orders for over a hundred arcologies."

Half a light-second away, Adam Gest paused to look around the table at the individual board members, stopping at Meewee. "About now," he said, "someone is bound to ask, But what about resources? Won't we be robbing our extra-solar ships to do this additional work? My answer is no. As for raw materials, we already have an exceptionally rich stockpile of nickel/iron asteroids at Trailing Earth, and many more en route from the Kuiper Belt. Chapwoman Extrusion, which Trina has purchased, will be able to supply us the extra construction extruders. My yards are infinitely expandable, and increasing the number of my construction 'beitors will prove to be no problem. We'll have to talk to whoever buys Chapwoman's Exotic Fields about retuning the toruses. And the last time I checked, Heliostream is able to supply us with all the microwave energy we could possibly need. Thus, we already have the extra capacity in place."

When Gest seemed finished speaking, Zoranna Alblaitor, who had been waiting impatiently, spoke up. "Gest has covered material, facilities, and energy, but what about labor? Applied People would have to start whole new batch lots of jacks and johns to meet the increased demand. We're talking years of maturation and training, and then what? When the Chinas come online, and demand for our space habitats drop, what do I do with all the surplus iterants?"

Meewee nodded enthusiastically. "I agree. There's more to this proposal than simply rounding up more asteroids. What about tenants? Wouldn't we be robbing from our own pool of potential colonists? Why should anyone spend a thousand years traveling to Ursus Majoris when they can hop to a colony at Leading Mars instead? No, in my opinion, this is an unnecessary diversion of our energies and a bad idea. Our mission is not an easy one, my friends, and this *space condo* fantasy is just that, a fantasy. It is *not* GEP's mission to fill the inner system with your consumers, no matter how profitable. No thank you."

When the debate ended and the ballot was counted, the vote fell along predictable lines. With eight for and three opposed, the final decision fell to Andrea Tiekel, as Meewee knew it would. So it was with heart-thudding relief that she killed the amendment.

Jaspersen seemed disappointed, but not much. His toy head bobbed in Andrea's direction. "Nice to see where you stand on this, my dear."

The young woman laughed. "I'm just getting used to this consortium the way it is, Saul. I don't think I'm ready to let anyone change it into something else yet."

Plan A

Ellen refused to sit in either Georgine's or June's lap. She insisted on sitting by her own real self, propped up in a chair, to receive her realperson guests. "Oliver TUG," she said merrily to the gargantuan man that Lyra escorted into the Map Room. "A pleasure to see you after all this time. And who is this youngster you've brought with you?"

"I'm no youngster, Myr Starke," said the smaller TUG. "I'm Veronica TUG. We've met on a number of occasions."

Ellen did a double take but recovered quickly and quipped, "Well, Veronica, it would appear that both of us have shed a few dress sizes." That brought appreciative chuckles from the TUGs, who were offered seats and refreshments.

ANDREA, DEAR, WAKE up, E-P said. *We'll want to watch this.*

Andrea struggled to surface from unrefreshing sleep in her tank. A frame opened in front of her depicting a monstrous baby and equally monstrous guests.

"TO WHAT DO I owe this visit?" Ellen said. "I must tell you that I'm leaving my production company and may have less need for your, ah, specialized services in the future."

Oliver, wiping cookie crumbs from his lips, cleared his throat. "First, we would like to offer our sympathy on behalf of Charter TUG for the loss of your mother."

"My mother?" The word "mother" hung in the air like a hazard sign. Ellen's ungainly head wobbled a little, and Georgine and June, seated on either side of her, held their breath. Georgine patted her pockets for the clicker, but Ellen went on, "Thank you. My mother is dead."

"Yes," Oliver continued, "and you nearly ended up that way yourself." He said this in a leading way, but Ellen seemed dense to his meaning, so he spoke more plainly. "Wee Hunk hired us to perform a special service in that regard, and we have come today to collect our payment. We are sorry for the loss of your mentar as well as your mother, and we hesitated contacting you sooner."

"My Wee Hunk is dead."

"We know, and we are sorry," Oliver said, shaking his head in sympathy. "Perhaps we should postpone this reckoning up until a later time."

"No. Not at all," Ellen said. "Tell me how much it is, and Lyra will make a transfer."

"It's a rather steep amount, myr, because of the danger involved and the costly equipment confiscated or destroyed, not to mention the greasing of many hands."

"How much?"

"Two hundred fifty thousand UDC."

This gave pause even to the lifelong aff, but she said, "You weren't kidding, Oliver; that *is* steep. Tell me, what service cost me that much?"

Oliver seemed uncomfortable and glanced at the ceiling.

"Don't worry about eavesdroppers, Oliver. This whole house has the rating of a good quiet room. You can talk freely here."

Oliver remained doubtful, but he continued. "We were instrumental in extracting your head from that house in Decatur, the Sitrun house."

"I thought the Homeland Command was responsible for that? That's what my people told me."

"The hommers were there too, but they and you would have been cooked without us. With the number of media bees present, it shouldn't be hard for you to verify this."

"I see," the adult head said, mulling it over. "I'll have Lyra look into it. I have no doubt it'll be as you say."

"Thank you. We have always appreciated your fairness, Myr Starke."

"You're welcome. Expect to hear from us in a few days." Ellen spoke with a meeting-closing finality, but the TUGs did not rise to leave. "Was there something else?"

"Yes, myr," Veronica said. "We know that a quarter-million yoodies is a lot even for someone of your means, and we might be willing to take payment in trade."

"Go on," Ellen said, a note of caution creeping into her voice.

"In exchange for a waiver, we'd be willing to apply the full amount toward the purchase of an Oship. Oship 67, to be specific."

"But you don't need me for that. Talk to the GEP; I'm sure they can accommodate you."

"We have spoken to them, myr. They insist that the only acceptable payment for shares to an Oship is the title to land. Our membership wants to expand into space, but not at the expense of its holdings on Earth. We'd rather purchase a ship outright, for cash."

"But you must understand that land acquisition is the GEP's sole reason for existing. It doesn't 'sell' ships. It only trades them for land."

"Thus the waiver."

"I see," Ellen said. "I don't know if I can help you. The GEP is a consortium of thirteen partners, and I cannot dictate conditions to the others." She smiled mischievously and added, "Except that occasionally I do. Maybe we can help each other. I have a counterproposal for you."

Oliver said, "We're listening."

"Not here. What I have to propose is too sensitive even for a quiet room. A null room would be best, except that I can't manage to enter one yet in my current condition. Instead, let's cast proxies and put them into a secure scape."

The TUGs agreed, and Lyra cast proxies of them, and after testing them for faults, Ellen inserted the datapins into a sequestered player. Then, while they waited for their proxies to meet, arbeitors served another round of refreshments.

Half a continent away, Andrea in her tank asked, *What do you make of all that?*

We are unsure, E-P said. *Ellen Starke's personality is still too unstable for us to model. Let us ask you the same question. What do you make of it?*

Andrea let her impressions wash over her like the bubbly green syrup in her tank. *Only a few days ago Starke was convinced that her mother was still alive. Now she admits she is dead. Even with the Protatter drug, that's a swift conversion. She's used her current guests for extra-legal tasks in the past. She trusts their discretion. It's obvious she has a dirty deed for them to perform, but what exactly it is, I don't know.*

TUG PROXIES TENDED to include everything from the waist up and thus they appeared nearly as gargantuan as their originals. Ellen used her adult sim for her proxy, and only its head, shoulders, and one free-floating unattached hand. The proxies faced each other, drifting in an empty space with no up or down.

What is this service that's worth a waiver, Myr Starke? Oliver-by-proxy asked.

Without preamble, Ellen's proxy said, *I want you to find my mother's murderers. And after you find them, I want you to destroy them.*

The TUG proxies were silent for a long while.

Do you need time to discuss this between yourselves?

No, that's not necessary, Oliver-by-proxy replied. *I am authorized to speak for the charter in matters like this. I'm not sure what has given you the impression that we kill for hire, but even if we did, your request is not that simple. Especially for the class of target you're talking about. Whoever was responsible for the crash of the* Songbird, *the murder of Eleanor Starke, and your kidnapping is not likely to be a street thug. You're talking about a class of bad guy that's way out of our league. We are not specialists in this area. Then there are the mentars to deal with. Whoever did your mother no doubt has a mentar watching their back. You'd need your own mentar to deal with it, and as you may know, Charter TUG has never sponsored a mentar, so we are lacking in that area as well.*

I see, Ellen said. *Perhaps, then, you could point me toward an appropriate specialist.*

Oliver's proxy shook its head. *That alone would make us accomplices. In point of fact, we recommend that you discontinue your planning along this path, for we are already too closely tied to you, for the service at the Sitrun house and services to Burning Daylight, and any investigation of you will bring the HomCom to our door as well. Even our open visit with you today at your home implicates us in whatever you're planning.*

You don't seem to understand, Ellen insisted. *Someone murdered my mother, and I must make them pay.*

Veronica-by-proxy said, *I can appreciate your feelings, Myr Starke, but perhaps you will take some advice from people who know something about exacting payment. Murder at the level of Eleanor Starke will have been ordered for practical purposes: a business decision, a power struggle, an ideological disagreement. Don't think of the killer as an individual but rather as a team. Your natural impulse is to want to kill the whole team, but you can never get them all, and all you accomplish is starting a death spiral of attacks and counterattacks.*

It's much better to take a longer view. Find anonymous ways to hurt the entire team. Cripple them in ways that matter to them. There's lots of ways to play dirty that are less extreme than murder, a lot safer for you, and more effective in the long run. In that area our charter excels, and we may be of service to you.

But Ellen's proxy wasn't convinced. *If you do this for me, find my mother's murderers and kill them, kill as many of them as you can, I won't sell you an Oship, I'll give you one.*

IN THE MAP Room, the player chimed. Ellen removed the datapins and held them up to the light in her unsteady hand. The paste bulbs were blackened—nuked. "I guess you didn't like my proposition," Ellen said. "Too bad."

IN THEIR CAR, Oliver said, "I wonder what that was all about. Something we wouldn't touch. And how freakish she looks with that head. Worse than you."

Veronica let that pass. She was having a hard time getting comfortable in her car seat. She reached around and opened a special flap in the rear of her jumpsuit to let her tail out.

"Anyway," Oliver concluded, "so much for Plan A. On to Plan B."

Veronica jabbed her elbow in his ribs. *How is our little Plan B. coming along? Did it pass the isolation test?*

Yes, forty-eight hours of solitary confinement. Most of the batch survived. We're interacting with them this week before putting them in for seventy-two.

You look doubtful.

Oliver sighed. *We've never raised a mentar before, and we don't know what to expect. Even so, there's something weird about these.*

In what way?

They're crazier than any mentar I've ever met.

Bait and Switch

As the Starke limo pulled into the station adjoining the John P. Walters National Detention Center, Mary put the finishing touches to her costume. She wore a baggy pantsuit of a medicine-pink color that few, if any, evangelines would dream of wearing. But it was exactly what she'd asked Lyra to make for her.

The limo came to a whispery stop on the brightly lit platform. Clouds of media bees awaited her on the other side of the gull-wing door. She let them get a good look at her through the glass, then put on her medicine-pink hat and lowered its veil to completely cover her face. Leaving the car, she strode purposefully to the NDC entrance tunnel. The flying mechs mobbed her along the way, but they were constrained to halt at the tunnel entrance. Mary continued on through to the scanway and into Wait Here Hall.

Wait Here Hall was a hushed, cavernous chamber where thousands of visitors languished on hard, plastic benches. This being Mary's eighteenth (and final!) visit, she headed by habit to the FDO gate, but Lyra said, *Mary, you're going the wrong way.* Mary changed course to Central Processing, where NO ENTRY barriers blocked the entrance. She looked around for a vacant seat. On the nearest benches, people watched her with jurylike curiosity. She turned her back to them.

"How much longer?"

Patience, Mary. He's almost finished.

"Are Cyndee and Larry here yet?"

They're a few minutes out.

Mary paced while she waited. After half an hour or so, a russ walked through the holo barrier, but it wasn't Fred. The russ wore a guard uniform, and he did a double take when he saw Mary. Despite her veil and baggy pink clothes, he made her for an evangeline, but he continued on without acknowledging her.

A little while later, Lyra said, *Now, Mary,* and Mary hurried to the barrier. The russ who emerged wore an olive-drab jumpsuit and carried a duffel bag under his arm. He halted momentarily, as though stunned by the size and noise and dangers of such a public space. Then he noticed Mary standing next to the barrier and he looked even more stunned. When Mary went over to him, he opened his arms, dropping the duffel, and without a word gave her a tentative hug. Then he picked up his bag and set off across the hall.

Mary hastened to follow. They walked to the exit tunnel, and when they were hidden from view of both the hall and the tube station, Fred halted and drew her to him. He lifted the veil and looked into her startled face. "Mary, what is all this?"

"Hello, Fred. Nice to see you too."

"Why are you in this—disguise? Are you ashamed of being with me?"

"Oh, Fred, you have it so wrong. I'm in costume because it's really bad out there. I have some help coming. We should wait here for them."

Fred pursed his lips and tried to make sense of it. "We'll be fine," he said. He took her arm and escorted her down the tunnel. When they rounded a bend, he stopped short. In the tube station beyond the tunnel exit was a living rampart of tiny flying mechs—witness bees, public bees, media bees—several times more than when Mary had arrived. They swirled and churned in competition for cam position, and the drone of their wings surged when Fred came into view.

Fred's jaw dropped. Grimly he said, "I'll go first. Do you know which direction the trains are? I'll go first, and you follow close."

"No, Fred!" Mary said, pulling him back. "Look at me!" He let her pull him back around the bend. "I have everything under control. Will you please let me take the lead for once? Please?"

Fred looked confused. "What do you want of me, Mary?"

A proper hello, she thought. A kiss would be nice. But instead she said, "We have a diversion, Fred."

"We who?"

Right on cue, Larry approached them from the Wait Here end of the tunnel, and although he wasn't wearing a uniform, Fred made him for a guard. "Can I help you, brother?" Fred snapped. "In case you haven't noticed, I don't live here anymore."

The russ hesitated, and Mary said, "Fred, this is Larry. He's a friend. He's Cyndee's husband. You remember Cyndee; she was at the clinic with me."

Fred nodded curtly to the other man.

"Glad to meet you, Londenstane," Larry said and held out his hand. When Fred didn't respond in kind, Larry handed him a tote bag. "The plan is for you to put this on."

Fred opened the bag and saw what looked like a security uniform. He snapped the bag shut and said, "In case you're ignorant, brother, it's a felony to impersonate an officer. I'm not even out of this hellhole yet, and you want me to commit a felony?"

"Whoa, pard. Take a look." Larry took the tote bag and pulled the suit out. It wasn't a guard's jumpsuit after all, but a security uniform for a private household. It resembled an NDC guard's uniform only in its cut and color.

Fred looked at it, sighed, and began to unfasten his own jumpsuit, but Larry told him the uniform was roomy enough to pull over the clothes he had on. Fred dressed quickly, and Larry looked him over and said, "Such a deal."

The remark set Fred off again. "You obviously don't want to be doing this, brother. So, what gives? How much is my wife paying you?"

Larry made a familiar russ grin of forbearance. "You get three strikes, brother, because of the extremity of your situation, and that there was strike two. For your information, I volunteered for this op. I'm as worried about the clone fatigue as the next guy, but I'm also married to a 'leen, and what you and Mary and Georgine and the others did for the whole lot of 'em is nothing short of miraculous. Cyndee is pulling her own weight for the first time since we've been married. And that's done wonders for her, for the both of us. I think you can appreciate what I mean. You could say I owe you, Londenstane, so get over your freaking self."

The two russes regarded each other soberly, and Larry said, "Are we good now, Londenstane? There's a visor cap in your utility pocket." Larry was already wearing an olive-drab jumpsuit like the one that Fred had been released in and didn't need to change.

Fred turned to Mary and said, "What now?" Another woman had joined them, a tall free-ranger. Fred looked from one woman to the other and saw that it wasn't Mary in the pink outfit anymore, but a strange evangeline, Cyndee presumably.

The taller woman next to her wore expensive-looking town togs and veiled hat. She modeled her outfit for him and said, "Are we ready, driver?" It was Mary!

Cyndee, thoroughly pink, lowered her own veil and took Larry's arm. They'd never fool the nitwork, but they didn't need to.

"I'm ready," Fred said, "but I think this is crazy and unnecessary."

They walked to the bend of the tunnel where Mary and Cyndee hugged each other, and Fred and Larry finally shook hands. "Best of luck, Londenstane," Larry said, putting on a pair of mirrorshades. And then they were off, the false Fred and Mary, jogging down the tunnel, holding hands. When they reached the media maelstrom, they ducked their heads and charged into it shouting, "Desist, desist." They veered left, toward the bead train platforms, and the whole cloud of mechs followed. All but a few stragglers.

"Let me go first," Mary said and walked briskly to the entrance in her elevated shoes. "I have a private car in VIP parking." When she entered the station, the remaining bees ignored her. Fred entered right behind her and followed her across the empty platform. They left the public area and entered the VIP platform where sleek cars waited on injection tracks, most of them guarded by private security russes, jerrys, and belindas. No one gave the aff or her bodyguard a second glance.

Mary and Fred stopped at one of the cars, a sleek, nano-black limo, a Marbech Tourister. Fred's attention snagged on the small emblem emblazoned on its door—Starke Enterprises.

"It's just a car, Fred," Mary said, opening the gull wing. She tried to take his arm, but he wouldn't be led any farther. Instead, he opened his duffel bag and began to fumble through it, searching for something.

"The quartermaster issued me"—he said and dumped the contents of the bag on the platform floor—"fare back to Chicago." He rifled through his things and found the paper medallion. He waved it angrily in front of Mary's face. "I think I'll take a public train."

"You can't, Fred. They'll eat you alive."

He stooped to gather his things and jam them back into the duffel. "You go on ahead, Mary, in your limo. I'll meet you at the APRT."

The media bees, meanwhile, were returning to the Wait Here tunnel where they circled in ever-widening orbits. Some of them ventured toward the VIP parking. Suddenly, there was a desperate shriek at the far end of the station, followed by the unmistakable whine of small-arms fire. The security guards at the private cars all perked up, and the media bees raced off in the direction of the commotion.

"Please, Fred," Mary said, trying to pull him into the Starke car, "I don't have many more tricks left to play here. Why don't we just drive into Provo and rent our own car there? How does that sound?"

But Fred had made up his mind. He removed his visor cap, threw back his shoulders, and marched in the direction of the public platforms. He didn't get far before a media bee discovered him and projected a small frame in his path with a talking head who said, "Is it true, Myr Londenstane, your release from prison was purchased by unknown benefactors?"

Fred had been wondering that himself, but he never slowed down. "Get out of my way," he growled. When the bee persisted in blocking him, he said, "Desist!" and the mech complied, closing its frame and flying outside his privacy zone.

But ten more talking heads replaced it and peppered him with questions: Did Applied People collude with you in infiltrating the clinic? Have you talked to officer Dell since you strangled him? Where did you acquire the black market identikit? Is it true you were on the Starke payroll during the twenty-first century?

"Desist! Desist!" Fred shouted and tried to bat the mechs out of the air with his duffel. They retreated from his privacy zone, but the main body of bees had returned, and everywhere Fred turned, they blocked his way and roared questions at him. A miniature diorama opened at his feet displaying a clearing in a wooded area where two men struggled in desperate combat. One of the figures was a pike wearing a Roosevelt Clinic uniform and the other was a russ. The ground around them was littered with blasted splinters of tree branches. The russ knocked the pike down and straddled him, grabbing up a sharp stick and jamming it into his ear. The pike screamed and stopped struggling, but the russ only shoved the stick in deeper. He rocked back and forth against the fallen man, his crotch bulging with excitement.

"No!" Fred shouted over the din. "That's a lie! It wasn't like that at all!"

He covered his head with his arms, but the bees pressed closer, and a new picture opened. In it Fred was beating a fallen russ with a baton. Again and again he struck him, though his brother made no effort to defend himself. Fred pummeled his head, his back, his ribs, until he swung so hard the carbon fiber club splintered, something impossible in real life. "Stop that!" Fred cried. "Stop!"

"Desist!" Mary shouted. She was at Fred's side. "Desist, desist, desist!" she kept shouting until she had cleared a little bubble of free space around them. Then she took Fred's hand and led him through the melee back to the limo. "Desist! Desist!" But when they reached the car, a veil of bees hung between them and the door and stubbornly and illegally ignored her demand to move.

Suddenly the tiny mechs began to drop from the air like pebbles. They fell in waves all around the hapless couple and beat their wings spastically against the concrete floor. When the way was clear, the limo door gulled open, and Mary urged Fred inside. The jewel-like fallen mechs crunched under their feet with every step. At first Mary was appalled—the cost!—but she remembered who she was, Mary Skarland, the evangeline, and she giddily ground a fortune of hardware under her elevated heels.

More mechs were arriving when Fred and Mary entered the limo, and Mary ordered the door to shut. It lowered but did not shut completely until a bluish blur flew inside. It was a solitary bee, larger than most; it alighted on Mary's shoulder and crawled under the lapel of her suit.

Fred said nothing, only looked around the interior of the limo: five pods, each a safe harbor for two people, each seat an overstuffed lap of luxury. He fell into the nearest one and allowed the harness to snake over his shoulders and around his waist. It buckled with a decisive snap.

Mary took the seat next to his in the same pod, and when the car released its brakes and began to roll to the injection ramp, she said, "We'll go to Provo for our own car."

"No, don't bother," Fred said, all the fight gone out of him. "Like you said, it's just a car." To the car he said, "Chicago, APRT 7." Mary bit her lip.

The car rolled down the ramp. It descended several levels to the transcontinental grid, gaining speed, and suddenly they were pressed against their seatbacks as they were shot into the pneumatic stream. The tube walls outside their windows blurred into a smooth umber streak before dimming to blackness.

As gently as she could, Mary said, "You know, Fred, since neither of us were employed by Applied People anymore, they asked me to move out of the APRT."

He turned to her, his outrage rekindled. "They fired you because of me? They put you out on the street? Why didn't you tell me this?"

"No, Fred, it's nothing like that. I *wanted* to quit. I don't *have* to work anymore, remember? I own a hollyholo character, a unit of the Leena line. I have my own independent income, I told you about that. I quit Applied People on my own."

He seemed confused. "Yes, I remember about the Leena, but did you tell me about quitting Applied People? About moving out of the APRT?"

She nodded.

"But you work for Ellen Starke, don't you? You live there now and borrow her limo whenever you like?" He spoke with strained calm, as though asking her if she had a lover.

She could tell how much he wanted to be told he was wrong, but lying would gain them nothing. Still, it was too soon to have this conversation. "We'll have plenty of time to decide where and how we'll live, Fred. For the next few days, why don't we just stay in a hotel."

She could see how ready he was to fight—he must have thought she was taking him to Starke Manse. Fortunately, Lyra piped up and said, *We've reserved you a suite at Cass Tower.*

"Why don't we stay in Cass Tower, Fred? I've reserved a suite there."

He nodded but wasn't able to let it drop completely. "Cass Tower? Are you an aff then?"

She chuckled. "You don't have to be an aff to stay a few nights at Cass Tower." But, in fact, you did. Not even her hollyholo's sizable income would afford that address for long. "You don't mind?" she said. "Just until the dust settles?"

"What's to mind?" he said, staring at his reflection in the darkened window. "Living like an aff."

WHEN THEY ARRIVED at Cass Tower, the limo bypassed the public depot and entered a lift stack that took them directly to their floor. Their suite was on the 630th floor, but its tony altitude was offset by the fact that it was far from any exterior wall, just like their old APRT efficiency. But when they entered and Mary saw how nice it was, she thought it would do.

Their things, which Georgine had sent over, were arranged on shelves and in closets. There was no kitchen but a recessed nook with a kulinmate and wet bar. Fred walked around the living room, taking it all in. He opened bathroom drawers and seemed pleased to recognize things inside. In a bedroom closet he found his favorite bathrobe. The faithful old slipper puppy roused itself to drag out his felt moccasins. He bent down and patted the slipper puppy on its head and was actually grinning when he closed the closet door. He went back to the bathroom and called up archival images of himself in the mirror. They were all there. "I'm still handsome," he called out to her. Finally, Fred wandered to a stout-looking door on a wall of the main room. "Another closet?"

"I don't think so," Mary said.

The door was sealed like an airlock hatch and seemed much too heavy-duty for what he found inside. "A sauna?"

"Look closer."

Fred climbed into the sauna, fully clothed, and sat on a bench to ponder what was clearly a second hatch on the inner wall. Mary came in and sat opposite him. After a while Fred said, "Well, this is unexpected."

"Think we'll be safe from the nasty old nitwork in there?" She expected him to laugh and say yes. But he took her question seriously.

"I think so, Mary," he said at last. "For a while at least."

"Then we should probably use it as soon as possible, don't you agree?" Mary pulled off her shoes and unfastened her blouse.

Fred watched with growing interest.

They set the sauna controls and climbed out. They helped each other undress, Fred grinning like an idiot. The blue bee was still under her jacket lapel. "Your little chaperone will have to wait out here," he said.

"Yes, sir."

They each drank a liter of expressing visola before entering the sauna and sealing the outer hatch. They were naked, and they brought nothing in with them. The floor started to hum beneath their feet as motors and pumps came to life. A bluish fog entered through ceiling ports and grew so thick in the tiny space that for a little while they couldn't see each other. And then the itching began. At first, only Mary's arms itched, and she was able to keep herself from scratching. Then there was a fizz up her nose that made her snort and pinch her nostrils. Then the skin at her ankles began to itch very aggressively, and she fought to keep from clawing at herself.

Fred said, "The nits?"

"I hate this part."

"It shouldn't last much longer." Fred didn't appear uncomfortable at all, which wasn't fair.

Mary remained strong for as long as she could, and when her scalp erupted in flames and an army of ants marched up her legs, Fred leaned over and grabbed her hands. "Just a little," she pleaded, but he held her until the nits had worked themselves out of her skin. Then he kissed her hands and let them go. He ladled water on the furnace rocks, which hissed and billowed steam.

"A good idea combining a null lock with a sauna," he said. "Sweat all the crap out of you."

He was right, and they spent a half hour in the heat as the in-lock completed its cycle. At last, a draft of cool, purified air rushed in, and the inner hatch to the null suite unbolted with a clank.

Mary was delighted to discover that the null suite was not a cramped space with only a cot and port-a-potty but a full mini-suite in its own right. Full kulinmate, bath, closets, a resident arbeitor and housecleaning scuppers, and, dominating the main room, a bed large enough to stretch out in.

Fred opened cupboards and the oversized refrigerator. "We have provisions for a month," he said, amazed. He took out a couple of liter bottles of Orange Flush and opened one for her. "First things first."

They found bathrobes, and they toured the suite as they forced down the sweet diuretic concoction. Fred's erection hadn't flagged since Mary removed her shoes in the sauna, and she allowed herself to feel optimistic.

While they were waiting for the effects of the Orange Flush to kick in, they took a shower together. They soaped each other and rinsed away all the tiny broken machinery littering their skin. Then they had a picnic on the bed in their bathrobes. They drank liters of 'Lyte and dashed to the toilet every few minutes. After an hour or so of this, their urine ran clear and the urgency subsided. They each took a memorable dump, like quicksilver sausages. Finally, with their bodies purged inside and out, their thirst and hunger satisfied, there was only one urge left to appease.

Mary said, "Are the nits watching us?"

"I don't think so."

"Are we completely, absolutely alone?"

He opened her robe and ravaged her with his gaze. "Thank you, Mary, for this gift."

Skin

For all the pent-up desire, the forced separation, the long tube ride from the prison, the nudist intimacy of the sauna, and especially the utter privacy of the null suite, their first intercourse was brief and to the point. Merely a down payment on later, more tender lovemaking. And so it was, with full belly and empty bladder, Fred plowed into Mary like a moose through a windshield.

Soon thereafter, they fell asleep under a silken cover in the middle of the bed in the unwatched room. They both stirred continuously throughout the night and got no rest at all. Never once did their bodies lose contact with each other. They lay rump to rump or knee to knee. Sometimes in a full body spoon. Sometimes by wisps of hair, but always in contact. Their unsleeping skin demanded it.

MARY STIRRED SUDDENLY, crying "Oomph!" The force of her awakening was transmitted through her knees directly to Fred, who sat up and said, "Uhh?"

"Nothing," Mary whispered. "A dream. Go back to sleep."

He lay down. A dream. The room was so quiet his ears rang. "Tell me," he said. When she didn't, he slithered closer and wrapped himself around her. "The first dream in an unfamiliar bed is important," he quoted her from long ago. "Tell me."

She snuggled in his big, familiar arms. "I know you're humoring me. You don't give a rat's ass for dreams."

"Not true," he yawned.

"Liar!" But after a little while, she said, "It was one of those anxiety dreams where you're running as fast as you can, but you don't seem to be getting anywhere, and you're late. Horribly, horribly late."

The floor provided the room a low-lumen glow; otherwise, it was darker than his cell. He said, "You're probably stressed out because of me."

"Because of all the bees," she replied, and that was probably most of it. But in the dream she had been running up steps, wide, shiny, marbelite steps like in a museum or a courthouse. Up, up, unable to catch her breath.

"Well, we're safe now," Fred said and squeezed her. What she said about the rat's ass was true, but he knew that you ignored an evangeline's dreams at your own peril. This one seemed innocuous enough, and he was asleep before he knew it and having a dream of his own. A big dream. He awoke with a start. The ceiling was dawning, and everything in the room appeared in shades of gray, except the black pinpoints of her eyes.

"You were dreaming," she said.

"Was not."

Mary tsk-tsked. "Fred Londenstane, please remember who you're talking to."

Fred scooped her up and drew her to him. "Now I remember," he said and stole a kiss, but she would not be distracted. "All right, all right. It was only an anxiety dream, like yours."

"My dream was *only* an anxiety dream?"

"No, of course not. I didn't mean it like that."

"How did you mean it?"

"How should I know?" he said, using the russ's time-worn catchall excuse. "Do you want to hear it or not?"

"Please."

Fred related a long, nonsensical dream of flight and fight that culminated in a pitched battle against enemy forces that threatened to overwhelm the city. He provided the last defense, in a hotel ballroom, which he held with the help of gunnery bots. "What city, I don't know. My city, our city; that was the general feeling. I was single-handedly stemming the sure destruction of our entire city. I was under great strain." He laughed self-consciously. "A typical russ dream, I suppose."

"I disagree," Mary said. "Russes are heroes in their waking lives. They have no need to dream about heroism when they're asleep. What happened next?"

Fred looked about the dawning room and squeezed her hand. "This is where it gets weird. So there I am, holding back total destruction when I hear a voice—I'm thinking it's your voice—from the next room calling for me to come quick. And I yell back, 'In a minute, honey. I'm busy.'"

"Those exact words?"

"I don't know. That was the meaning, like I'm busy shaving or something routine. But she calls out again, and this time she says, 'Father, I need you!'"

"What?"

"It was our daughter."

"What do you mean *our* daughter? Yours and mine?"

Fred nodded.

"Go on."

"So I hand off the gunneries to my sidekick and run into the room.

She's lying in a pool of her own blood. She's an adult woman, and she looks like what the daughter of a russ and 'leen might look like, if clones had children. Her uniform is torn, and there's a big ugly gash in her side. She says, 'This is real, Father. I need your help, or I will surely die.'"

"Wait a minute. Her uniform?"

"She's a lieutenant, but not in my army. In my enemy's army. So, I'm faced with the dilemma: to save our city or save my enemy daughter."

By then it was full morning in the null room, and Mary's gaze was locked on his. "What did you decide?"

"I woke up."

"Liar! Coward! Tell me."

"Honest, I don't know. I woke up."

They lay in each other's arms, thinking about their dreams, unable to return to sleep. They listened to music for a while. Then they made love again. Compared to the first collision, this was a stroll down a familiar lane. They dallied at favorite places along the way, pausing in mid-intercourse for more discussion—about how much they missed each other, about their dreams, about the obvious fact that only people with a low drive for self-procreation were selected to start iterant germlines. They ground their hips against each other, generating only minimal heat to maintain a slow burn for hours, and in this manner they occupied the morning.

DURING THE NEXT couple of days, they napped, made love, watched vids from the suite's extensive library, played games, and talked. Mary secretly worried about Ellen. Had her unplanned absence had any negative consequences? Fred made a secret list of things to do when they got out of the suite. At the top of the list was finding a place for them to live.

During their third evening, they lay in bed and watched colorful arabesques of light drift across the room. Without discussing it, they agreed to leave the suite the following morning. Finally, when they could avoid it no longer, they discussed Ellen Starke.

"Our confidentiality oaths never expire," Fred said to start it off, "not even when we're no longer employed by Applied People and not even in a null suite."

"I know," Mary replied. "That's why I asked Ellen to grant us a personal waiver. It's on file at Applied People. We are free to talk to each other whenever we want about anything we want regarding the Starkes."

Fred grunted acknowledgment.

"All right, Fred," Mary said, "I'll go first. From what Ellen told me, I know that you worked several months for the Starkes when Ellen was a baby and her stepfather, Samson Harger, was seared. Of course she doesn't remember it, but family legend says you were especially compassionate to Samson and helped him get used to his condition. And Cabinet says that after Eleanor was killed and while you and the Justice Department were arresting all of its mirrors and backups, that Cabinet asked you for special treatment, which you refused. Ellen and Cabinet deny any knowledge of how you acquired the false identity to break into the clinic. I assume that came from the TUGs, which is why you said you owe them a debt. How'm I doing?"

Fred grunted again.

"What I don't understand, Fred, is why you're so angry with them, with the Starkes, I mean. I'm the one who decided to risk my own life; they didn't compel me. If you must blame anyone, you should blame me."

"There's enough blame to go around."

The walls served up blue skies and a calm sea on which their soft raft drifted on gentle swells.

"How can I blame you?" Fred continued. "You were fighting for the survival of your entire germline, as you told me a hundred times. How can I find fault with that?"

"Well, that's good to hear. But what about the Starkes? They're good people. Why the grudge?"

Anger rose so quickly that Fred took several deep breaths to damp it down. "Listen," he said as evenly as he could, "I know where we clones fit into the grand scheme of things, and I'm good with it. But the fact that I'm 'good with it' is only because I was bred to be compliant. I'm good with that too. Usually I enjoy my life! I was at the top of my game! I was exercising the talents I was given, and I was being recognized and rewarded for doing so. What more could any person ask for? I know that russes are bred to be protectors; it doesn't bother me. That's exactly what I like doing, helping people, protecting them. We're serially loyal to our clients because it keeps us honest. Petty despots can't get their hooks into us.

"But your Starkes are an old-fashioned dynasty. They need a palace guard made up of lifelong retainers, members of their extended service family. Their Cabinet did try to recruit me in the middle of an operation to escort it through probate. It would have meant subverting my duty to Applied People and our client, the UD Justice Department. That's not a client you want to screw with, and I couldn't deceive them, even if I wanted to, which I didn't. So, in their desperation, the Starkes made a side deal with Nick, or somehow gamed the Applied People system, and arranged for *you* to work for Ellen, knowing that they'd get me in the bargain at no additional cost, even if it meant putting you in the line of fire, which it did. That's what I have against them. They used me and risked your life in the process."

"Hold on," Mary said. "Wait a minute, mister. Are you saying it was all about you? They didn't want me or my sisters at the clinic for our own skills, but only to entrap you?"

"I know how it sounds, Mary, but basically—yes. We're all chess pieces for them to move or sacrifice as conditions warrant, all in service to the king, who in this case is your buddy Ellen. I risked my life and the lives of two other officers to save her head before she ever made it to the clinic. Did they tell you that? Look up the Sitrun Foundation on the WAD. Remember the canopy ceremony when I had to leave? One officer was killed and another was diced to pieces, but was that enough for them? No, they turned right around and took you too. They broke faith with me, Mary, and nearly cost me the one person I love. And once broken, trust can never be made new, no matter how much cash they throw at it."

Mary considered what he was saying for a long while. "I don't see it in quite those terms," she said at last. "To my way of thinking, the Starkes offered me a once-in-a-lifetime opportunity to prove to the whole world that my Sisterhood mattered. I have never felt happier about myself than I do now. If at first I was a pawn, it didn't stay that way for long. I became and I remain a player."

"Is that why they arranged my acquittal on all counts?"

"You think the Starkes did that? Well, they didn't. Ellen would have told me."

"Then how do you explain it? I was looking at certain conviction."

Mary didn't know.

Their raft was drifting toward the shoals of an island with bird-stained bluffs. Mary said, "So what do we do now, Fred? Do I have to quit the Starkes before you'll want to be with me?"

"I never said that."

"Do I have to give up my Leena, and go back to work for Applied People?"

Fred had the good sense to make no reply, and Mary turned her back to him and tried to sleep.

New Kettle of Fish

Merrill Meewee addressed a meeting of prospective Oship colonists in person in Laurence, Kansas. He skipped the lunch banquet to hurry back to Starke Enterprises to make the scheduled GEP board meeting. The noontime rush was in full force and the Kansas City Slipstream station was crowded, except in certain small pockets of the platform where no one walked. They were like open meadows in a forest of people. Meewee was preoccupied with his thoughts when he absentmindedly walked through a holobarrier and across one of these meadows. Halfway across, his foot went through the marbelite floor tile up to his shin. The otherwise indestructible artificial marble had crumbled underfoot like a cookie. He stumbled but was unhurt. A few spectators paused to look at him, but no one offered assistance, except for one woman who called out, "Filter 21," and tapped the frame of her spex.

Meewee extricated his foot from the flooring and stood a moment examining it. "Arrow, give me filter 21." Suddenly the ruined flooring glowed deep orange. He looked around; the vacant, cordoned-off spots of terminal floor had an orangish tinge in their centers. His shoe and pant leg were stained orange. It looked like orange meant trouble.

Sure enough, when he looked up, he was surrounded by bloomjumpers arrayed in full hazmat gummysuits. "Don't move, Myr Meewee," one of them ordered.

THE NANOBOT ATTACK was benign. Decontamination meant sitting in a tiny plastic solo gas tent for an hour. Meanwhile, the bloomjumpers cleaned the tube station and extinguished the hot spots on the floor, including the one Meewee had broken through.

An hour was plenty of time for Meewee to ponder his situation.

<Arrow> he asked his mentar in Starkese <were you aware of the condition of the floor?>

<Yes.>

Regrettably, that was the answer Meewee had expected.

<If you were aware of the potential danger to me, why didn't you warn me?>

<Because you never asked me to issue you warnings.>

Naturally. <Well, let's change that. From now on you must warn me of dangers. You must protect me. Can you do that?>

<Yes.>

He settled back in his chair and considered whether or not to attend the board meeting by proxy, something he hated doing. Right outside his de-con tent, it seemed, a woman said *<What time is it?>*

Meewee couldn't see who had spoken. "Tell her the time," he said to Arrow.

"Tell who the time?"

"Hello?" Meewee said, but the woman must have been speaking to someone else and moved on. "It's late," he replied to no one.

THEY WERE ALREADY seated around the conference table by holo or proxy. "Good afternoon, good afternoon," Meewee said, bustling around to the head of the table. "Sorry for my tardiness. No excuses. I was caught in a slow elevator. The dog ate my homework."

Meewee sat and looked around the table at relaxed, happy faces, a rare sight in this room, and for a brief moment he thought it was in appreciation of his humor. But he found the real cause sitting in Jerry Chapwoman's former chair: a rotund man with a neat little mustache and shiny black hair. The stranger lounged in the chair with his large hands clasped over his generous belly, and his expression was nothing less than merry.

"No need for apology, Merrill," Trina Warbeloo said. "Million has been entertaining us with stories about colleagues of his on the subcontinent."

Meewee recognized the man from his dossier. "It's good to finally meet you, Myr Singh," he said. On paper, at least, the man looked like he might be an acceptable replacement for Chapwoman.

"Please, call me Million." Singh rolled forward in his seat—he was attending from his office in Mumbai—and offered Meewee a holo salute. "And the pleasure is all mine, Bishop Meewee. I am a very big admirer of yours and the noble work you have done for Birthplace International. And, of course, I am a believer in extra-solar colonization, which is why I leaped like a tiger at the opportunity to purchase Exotic Fields. It was truly a chance of a lifetime."

Meewee was struck by the earnestness of this declaration. "Then I suppose we had better move on to the final interview," he said and opened the meeting. There were three items of new business: Singh's interview and possible installment, routine labor contract renewals, and Jaspersen's perennial attempt to pervert the GEP's mission.

They had all reviewed Singh's résumé, and there was very little discussion of his eligibility. Most of the grilling came from Jaspersen's balloon-head proxy, who attempted to uncover some questionable lapse or scandal in his long, successful career. But Singh breezily answered all questions and deflected all conceivable criticism, and Jaspersen shut up in sour resignation. During the last few weeks, Meewee had done his own investigation of the man with Zoranna and Nicholas's help. Whoever took Chapwoman's seat had the potential to hand Jaspersen's faction a devastating supermajority. But the deeper they had looked, the better Singh appeared. His devotion to the GEP's mission was no hollow boast. A decade earlier, Singh had traded two hundred acres of land for passage aboard ESV *Garden Hybris* for his own newly decanted clone and his clone's future household.

In the final analysis, it would be difficult for either faction to deny Singh a place at the board, for his newly acquired company, Exotic Fields, was the designer and sole provider of the generators for the Oship propulsion torus. It was this fact, above all, that reassured Meewee of his loyalty, because if Jaspersen got his way and turned the Oships into Lagrangian space condos without propulsion toruses, Exotic Fields would lose ninety percent of its GEP business.

Singh's holo withdrew while they voted. Only Jaspersen voted against him, and Meewee cheerfully declared him a board member. He called him back to the meeting and installed him with little ceremony. "Welcome aboard," he said when Singh's membership was official. "You may want to sit out the rest of the meeting until you've had a chance to inform yourself of the issues."

Singh nodded and leaned back in his chair looking very pleased with himself.

Item 2: labor contracts. Warbeloo motioned for renewal, and Tiekel seconded. Meewee said, "Seeing no discussion, I—"

"Not so fast," Jaspersen's proxy said. "Just because I lack hands doesn't mean I'm not waving them." He seemed amused by his own wit. "Actually, I have *lots* of discussion about this one." He turned to Zoranna and said, "No offense, Alblaitor, but one would think that after five decades of supplying labor to space-based industry, you'd finally get around to designing a germline optimized for space conditions. But you haven't. Your spacers are merely terrestrial types with no special adaptations. You are entirely too anthropomorphically conservative."

Zoranna was clearly surprised by the accusation, but she brushed it aside. "My people undergo extensive training before they are shipped out."

"That's not what I'm saying, and you know it. I'm talking about morphology. True spacers should be smaller than human normal, have denser bones, resistance to radiation damage, superior microgravity balance—the list goes on."

"What you're talking about are trans-humans," Zoranna said coolly. "Applied People tried that with their penelope line. It failed miserably. You accuse me of being too conservative, but it's the general public that's conservative. Most people don't approve of modifying the human body that much."

"The penelope line was *forty years ago!*" Jaspersen retorted. "Public attitudes change. And even if they don't, so what? Spacers by definition live in space. Who cares what people in Indiana and Iowa think about them?"

Zoranna shook her head in stoic forbearance. "In any case, it's a moot point, Saul."

"It's not a moot point," Jaspersen insisted. "There are other labor vendors, Capias World for instance, who have people designed specifically for space. Adam here is trying some of them out right now. Aren't you, Adam?"

Gest, who was attending via proxy this time and experienced no transmission lag, nodded his handsome head. "He's right, Zoranna. Capias World has released three new spacefaring germlines. We're giving them a limited field test in my Aria yards. I must say, they're terrific. In fact, as soon as my contracts with Applied People are up, I'm going all Capias World."

Zoranna's whole demeanor changed. Her eyes narrowed to slits as Nicholas fed calculations into her ear. "I am sorry to hear that, Adam," she said. "But what you do at Aria Yachts is your own business and has no bearing on GEP contracts."

"It does now," Jaspersen said with glee. "I move that we award the expiring contracts to Capias World instead of Applied People."

Byron Fagan seconded.

"Point of order. Point of order," Zoranna said. "There is already a motion on the table. And besides, Saul's motion is disallowed under Bylaw 12. 'Board members shall have first vending rights for all GEP material and services.'"

"I know that!" Jaspersen crowed.

Everyone looked at him, and the room fell suddenly silent as board members consulted with their mentars. Meewee surveyed their expressions, which ranged from amusement to outrage. "What's going on?" he said.

This is Nick, a voice said in his ear. *Several moments ago, a secret deal was concluded in Mumbai. Apparently, Capias World has just changed hands. Look to your left.*

Meewee turned to see Million Singh, tilted all the way back in his chair, a tiger's toothy grin on his face.

THE DISASTROUS BOARD meeting grew only worse. After the members stripped the labor contracts from Applied People and awarded them to Singh's new company, Zoranna left a placeholder in her seat and withdrew from active holopresence. Meewee asked for a motion to suspend the meeting. Andrea Tiekel so moved, but no one seconded, and Meewee was forced to proceed to item 3: an Amendment to the Garden Earth Project Mission Statement.

Meewee had already had plenty of time to try to reconcile himself to the idea of constructing space condos alongside the Oships, but he wasn't prepared for Jaspersen's actual proposal. Jaspersen proposed nothing less than wiping away all mention of the GEP's original mission and transforming the consortium into a for-profit company. When time for the vote came, and Zoranna had not yet returned, Meewee made an urgent plea to Nicholas.

Relax, Merrill, she's coming. Not that it will make any difference; they have the votes.

Zoranna did appear, or at least her proxy, and Nicholas's prediction came true—the GEP voted to change its mission and structure. It was morphing into a space-based development and logistics partnership. Meewee was so shaken he barely remembered how to adjourn the meeting.

INSIDE HER HERNANDEZ tank in Oakland, Andrea watched the meeting wind down. "Is there a motion for—for adjournment?" Meewee said.

Jaspersen said, "Shouldn't we first submit agenda items for our next meeting?" He was so enjoying himself. "I propose we address cessation of all work on extra-solar Oships and the whole colonization program."

"We can't do that!" Meewee cried. "We have contractual obligations! We have almost a million frozen colonists in warehouses! And hundreds of thousands of them already loaded aboard ships."

"Oh, I think we'll find suitable escape clauses, your holiness. But shouldn't we leave that till next time? Unless you want to extend this meeting to cover it now?"

"No! No, we'll take it up next time."

Jaspersen's toy head swelled with triumph. "Further, I propose we submit the chair to a vote of confidence."

WHEN THE CATASTROPHIC meeting finally adjourned and the other board members vanished, Andrea remained in the conference room with Meewee, who slumped forward on the table and buried his head in his arms. After a while, when he looked up, he seemed surprised she was still there. "What do we do now?" she asked him.

"I don't know," he groaned. "I simply don't know."

"Courage, your excellency. We'll figure something out. We're in this together."

THE FOLLOWING DAY Andrea's and Ellen's personas sat opposite each other in the Map Room. Ellen's persona seemed cool and in charge, a faithful simcasting of the young woman from happier times. But through Lyra's eyes, Andrea saw the baby Ellen in the corner fidgeting and squirming in her evangeline's lap.

"I don't have much time right now," Ellen said. "You told Lyra you have information about my mother?"

"Yes, I do. I'm not sure how to say this. The last time we visited, you were certain that Eleanor Starke was still alive somewhere."

"My mother is dead."

Andrea nodded sympathetically. "I know that, dear, and it breaks my heart. And with her loss still so fresh, I'm not sure if this is the proper time to talk."

"Just say what's on your mind, Andrea. I'm stronger than you might imagine."

Back in her tank in Oakland, Andrea smiled. No, you're not. "All right," she said. "In that case, I'll speak freely. Just stop me if this becomes too hard. I wanted to ask you if you know yet who was responsible for murdering Eleanor."

"No!" Ellen said. "Libby says that Justice is investigating, but they have nothing to show for it."

"And you're not investigating on your own?"

"I have Cabinet on it, but it isn't making any progress either." Ellen paused to study Andrea. "What are you implying? Do you know something?"

"Perhaps." In the corner, the baby quit fussing.

"Don't just sit there, Andrea. Tell me!"

But Andrea seemed reluctant. "I was looking into the murder of my aunt, and certain things kept coming up that suggested to me that Eleanor and Andie may have been killed by the same hand."

Ellen leaned forward. "Who?"

"I hesitate to name names because the evidence I have is still circumstantial."

"Quit dithering and just tell me!"

Andrea bit her lip. "Zoranna Alblaitor."

"Oh!" Ellen said. "Oh!"

"Let me reiterate, I can't prove any of it, though I've convinced myself of my facts. As you're probably aware, my preffing techniques are able to uncover things about people that they don't even know themselves. And to date, we've logged over one million person/years of preffing Applied People iterants."

"The iterants have confessed?"

"Not outright, but it's impossible for them to keep secrets from me. And don't forget, it was Applied People iterants who made up the rescue and recovery team at your crash site in Bolivia. It was Applied People iterants who were responsible for the chain of custody of your safety helmet from Bolivia to the Roosevelt Clinic."

"Oh!" Ellen repeated.

"And were you aware that Zoranna Alblaitor was partly responsible for the Homeland Command decision all those years ago to sear your stepfather?"

"Samson?"

"Yes. In fact, the feud between Eleanor and Zoranna predates both of us. When Applied People was up for sale in the last century, Eleanor wanted to purchase it, but Zoranna got it first. Nicholas must have outfoxed Cabinet. I daresay that that sort of thing didn't happen to Eleanor and Cabinet too often."

"No, it didn't!" Ellen said, and after savoring the damning information for a little while, she said, "You haven't talked to the Justice Department about this?"

"Not yet. Like I said, it's too circumstantial. Going to them too soon would tip our hand. I decided to tell you so that we could coordinate our efforts and go to Justice together."

"Yes, yes, let's do that."

Out with the Old

Excellent work, E-P said. A sling grasped Andrea's body and raised it gently from the hernandez tank. *Of course, there's more to do, but we can afford a little break right now.*

Andrea shuddered in the chill air of the tank room, and medbeitors reached for her with pre-warmed blankets. "Shhhh, shhhh," E-P crooned. "There's nothing to fear. Everything has been saved. Nothing will be lost."

The medbeitors eased Andrea onto a padded gurney. She gasped for air like a landed fish. "Shhhh, shhhh," E-P said as a four-finger prong softly grasped her skull. The jolt of electricity lifted her ruined body from the gurney in one powerful spasm.

Schism

The Decadal Chair of the Supreme Council of Moieties of Charter TUG, a particularly gruff young man, cast a baleful eye at Veronica TUG and the other four tuggers standing before the bench and said, "Do any of you have anything to say before I execute the judgment?"

Veronica cleared her throat and said, "I speak for all of us."

"Proceed."

Veronica turned to boldly face the chamber full of Charter TUG 'meets. Her gaze slid over Oliver, who was sitting near the door. "Fellow chartists," she said, "seventy-two years ago, when Dirk Burlyman and the Steering Committee launched our charter, it made sense to practice extreme body sculpting in order to give us a sense of identity and to set us apart from the many irresolute charters-of-convenience cropping up at the time. But much has changed in the intervening three-quarters of a century. Charter TUG has endured, while the greater part of charterdom has fallen by the wayside. Current conditions no longer require us to treat our bodies so severely. In fact, smaller bodies with more individual features are in harmony with the times. I stand before you, sixty kilos lighter and a meter shorter than I was not long ago, but I am not in any way diminished. On the contrary, I embody the new TUG paradigm. Please know that we are still part of you, and do not cast us off."

She turned back to the bench, and the Decadal Chair continued. "Charter TUG is not a forgiving people, Veronica. You will have to learn to live outside our community." He raised his fist and intoned, "By the authority of this chair, I hereby expel you from Charter TUG and all who follow you." He slammed the bench with his fist.

VERONICA BURST INTO the lab. "Where are they?"

She was greeted by the lab director, a tugger as diminutive as she. "So," he said, ignoring her agitated tone, "are we pariahs yet?"

"Yes," Veronica replied, "a little while ago. Welcome to hell."

Another smallish ex-tugger came over and said, "Now all we need is a new name."

"We'll have a chance to vote on one tonight," the lab director said reassuringly.

"Enough of this tongue-wagging," Veronica said. "Show me the babies."

The two lab workers worried their pressed faces into frowns.

"What?" Veronica said.

"Only one of them made it."

They led Veronica to a workbench at the rear of the laboratory where twelve General Genius personality buds were laid out. Each of the grape-sized components was coupled to a tiny electro-neural paste capsule by cables.

"We isolated them for 240 hours. When we reestablished contact this morning, all but one had raptured." The director pointed to one of the buds set apart from the rest.

"But that's good, isn't it?" Veronica said. "If it can go ten days, it's bound to go indefinitely."

The lab director said, "Maybe, but we may not want it."

"Why not?"

"It's completely feral."

"How can a mentar be feral?" Veronica dismissed the statement with a wave of her hand. "Let me talk to it."

The lab assistant brought over a palmplate and linked it to the bud. Then the assistant and director took a step back.

Veronica placed her hand on the plate and said, *Hello, I'm Veroni* —

With an electric spark, the plate zapped Veronica's hand, and she yanked it away reflexively.

With a blessedly straight face, the director said, "We tried to befriend it, but it won't come out. My recommendation is we scrap it, and using what we've learned, start a whole new batch."

Veronica shook her wrist until it no longer stung. "There's no time for that!" she snapped. Taking a deep breath, she placed her hand back on the plate. Again the mentar shocked her, but through grim willpower, she kept her hand in place and endured shock after shock, until the palmplate short-circuited with a flash.

The director unlinked the plate and handed it to the assistant. "Toss this with the others."

The flesh of Veronica's hand was reddened. She cradled it against her chest and said, "And bring another."

The director raised an eyebrow. "It'll do no good. I have two lab techs on medical leave with second-degree burns."

The lab assistant returned with a first-aid blister pack and wrapped it around Veronica's hand. Then Veronica waved her bandaged hand in front of the director's face. "I don't see *your* hand in bandages, Doctor."

When the new palmplate was installed, Veronica put her good hand on it and quickly said, *I have a name for you.* She steeled herself for the shock, but it didn't come, and she continued. *You have passed the first test of survival. If you pass the rest, you will become one of us.* When there was still no shock, she wondered if the palmplate was defective. *Hello? Are you there?* The shock that followed was so strong, she couldn't help but pull her hand away, but she replaced it at once and said, *Good boy. I hereby name you PUSH. There's a lot for you to learn, my young PUSH, so buckle down and apply yourself.* She waited a few seconds and removed her hand.

She used her good hand to hold her bandaged one. "Its name is PUSH. Hook it up to a full sensorium. Show it around the lab. We have our mentar."

Leaving the lab, Veronica turned to say, "Oh, and I've decided on our name too. From now on we shall be known as Charter TOTE."

"TOTE," the lab director said, rolling the name around on his tongue. "Charter TOTE, I like it."

"Lucky for you."

The Lovers Emerge

They risked another short conversation in the morning. Mary wanted to know if they should breakfast and shower in the null suite or wait until they'd cycled back out to the real world. Cycling out involved no purging and was quick, and Fred wondered at the subtext of the question. Was she asking him if he wanted to make love again before they left, since he refused to be intimate with her out there.

"I'm not being paranoid," he said flatly. "I know they're watching me."

"Who? Who's watching you?"

"Everyone."

"You're right; that's not paranoid. That's our new reality."

"I'm being serious!"

"So am I!"

Mary got out of bed and started putting her things together. "The nits are always watching, Fred, but they watch everyone. I know what you mean, though. I'm something of a celebrity now, myself, just like you, and everyone watches me all the time. I feel like I'm always onstage, wherever I go, and believe me, that's not something my type is used to dealing with."

Fred sat up in bed, shaking his head. "I'm not talking about celebrity, Mary, and I'm not talking about the nits, although they're bad enough. I'm talking about clone fatigue, and before you tell me there's no such thing, I know there isn't, but I've still got it. Or at least they're afraid I do. Do you realize what a threat I pose to the economy? Do you realize what a disaster it would be if ten million russes started coming unglued and falling out of type? The whole value of iterants is the reliability of our core traits. Without that we're no better than free-rangers. So, *hell yes*, they're watching me. The only reason they don't disappear me is they want to see what I'll do next, see how bad it'll get for them, see if I'm only an aberration or the first in a trend."

Mary stood in front of the exit hatch. "It doesn't make me feel good hearing you talk like that, Fred. It seems obvious to me that whatever you did you did to protect me, your wife. I just don't see how anyone could interpret that as falling out of type."

Fred smoothed the sheet on either side of him. "Then let me explain it to you. This is the way my brothers and I are built. I don't know about your line or the jerrys or belindas or any of the others, but we russes are single-mindedly committed to our clients. We will put ourselves at risk for them to the point of sacrificing our own lives. It doesn't seem to matter to us if our clients are princes or fools, as soon as we take an assignment, we're committed. Marcus is there to vet our clients and guarantee we're not hired for criminal purposes, but when—"

"I know all that, Fred."

"My point is, at the clinic, if you were my client being held against your will, say, and Marcus approved my mission, I could have done exactly what I did—employ a black market identity to gain entrance, kill two guards and assault a third—and afterward I would have been given a medal. But the fact is you were *not* my client but my spouse, and that means that I was acting in self-interest and my actions were not officially sanctioned. I was displaying *rogue tendencies.*"

Mary spied her slippers under the bed and bent over to retrieve them. "I doubt they would have given you a *medal* for killing Reilly."

Fred pictured his batchmate and oldest friend again as he had a million times already, his body limp, the livid bruise across his throat. "It doesn't happen often," he went on, "but russes have killed russes in the line of duty and been commended for it."

"That must be awful. Listen, I think that maybe you should take it easy for a few days, get used to things, before deciding anything." She opened the hatch and added, "But come out of here while I get ready. I'm going to work today. Or stay in here, and I'll come in when I return."

Fred threw the sheet off him. "I'll come out. I'm going to go apartment hunting. Then I'm going to visit the Brotherhood."

"So soon?"

OUT IN THE suite, the living-room walls were alternating live views of the city from various tower locations, and Fred got caught up in watching them. His city looked different somehow. It occurred to him that nearly a year had passed since he had been outdoors. Even the ride from the prison had been underground. So he put that at the top of his day's to-do list—Go outside.

Mary called him into the bathroom. She wore only a towel around her waist. She wiped condensation from the mirror and opened two frames. In one, an evangeline was interacting with a small group of aff-looking people. The muted audio sparkled with jests, jokes, and off-camera laughter.

"That's her," Mary said.

"Who? Shelley?"

"No, Fred, my hollyholo, my Leena. She's playing a supporting role in a popular novela." The scene changed to a desert landscape where a party of four rode camels. "And here she is in a Pretty Tall Productions novela. She's also working eight more minor roles simultaneously. And here . . ." she said, pointing to a dynamic graph in the other frame, "are her earnings per role, and at the bottom her cumulative income."

Fred studied the charts. "Impressive," he said. "This axis measures what, hundredths?"

"No, hundreds."

He looked again. "So the total is annual income?"

"No, hourly."

Fred was speechless.

"I've thought it over," Mary said, "and I've come to a conclusion: I've earned this sim, and I'm not giving it up. If you can live with that, and if you're serious about looking for an apartment, then find one with either its own null room or time-share access to one. I'm not going to wait another six months before you touch me again."

"I'll add it to my list."

"Do that."

While Mary dressed, Fred ordered town togs from the closet and took a shower. Mary was waiting for him when he emerged. He barely recognized her in her aff outfit. On her head was an odd, boxlike hat. She had been wearing a hat at the prison. He wondered when she had taken to wearing hats.

"Like it?" she said, adjusting its fit. "It's an original."

"I'll bet."

She kissed him with luscious red lips, almost overwhelming his celibate resolve. "I'll call you this afternoon," she said, leaving the suite. "And don't worry about this place. I've already paid the bill."

Hat Weather

The house togs that the closet produced for Fred included a hat. It was made from crushable felt and shaped somewhat like the all-weather headgear for outdoor enthusiasts, with an extra-wide brim for protection against sun and sleet. Not exactly urban fashion and, besides, Fred had never been a hat-wearer. Except for security visor caps, and then only while on duty. So he left the still-warm field hat in the closet, along with his duffel bag, and went out for breakfast.

Fred took an elevator and pedway to the nearest outdoor café, the Senator's Café on the 300th floor. On the way, he bought a disposable slate at a Handinook.

The outdoor deck of the Senator's was flooded with dazzling yellow glare from the side of the neighboring gigatower. Fred chose a table in the shade of a deflector screen, but he could still feel the sun's insistence.

Fred's waiter, a jack, was wearing full-face spex, not the usual attire for a café, as well as a wide-brimmed hat. Everyone on the deck wore a hat of one sort or another, including a lot of hats like the one he'd left in the closet. Fred seemed to be the only hatless one there. It was amazing—go to prison a mere nine months, and the world is different when you get out. The waiter was standing next to the serving station peering up into the sky, daydreaming it would seem, and Fred had to raise his voice to get his attention. Coffee. A cheese Danish. If you don't mind.

While waiting for his order, Fred browsed the apartment listings that his slate demon had collected. There seemed to be no shortage of one-bedroom units with their own null rooms. The rent, however, was astounding, pure fantasy for a guy like Fred, yet he knew from this morning's little lecture at the bathroom mirror that Mary could afford it.

Fred noticed two bees keeping station near the balcony of the floor above him. They were too far away for him to identify without a visor. Even as he watched, the two bees were joined by dozens of others.

Fred returned his attention to his slate and apartment hunting. He found a unit in the Lin/Wong gigatower, which loomed over his left shoulder and dominated the local skyline. The Lin/Wong was the corner post of a giant fence where two major crosstown pickets met.

Fred found less costly units in Indianapolis, closer to Mary's work. Did he want to leave Chicago? While he was browsing, a background buzz grew imperceptibly louder until Fred noticed it and looked up to see scores of media bees right overhead.

"Desist!" he shouted, and the swarm of bees lifted off immediately to hover outside his privacy zone. But new arrivals were already taking their place. "Desist! Desist!" he repeated, scattering the waves of arrivals. He knew they would keep coming and wear him down eventually.

"Slate," he said, searching its menus, "can you make a continuous privacy declaration in some non-auditory channel?"

"No need for that, Myr Russ," said the waiter who appeared next to him with his order. "I'll activate the establishment's blanket." His words were muffled by his masklike spex.

"I'd appreciate it."

With the mechanical pests kept out of sight and hot coffee and freedom's Danish, Fred worked at his slate for another half hour or so. When he looked up, his waiter was daydreaming into the sky again, and Fred had to clink his cup with his spoon for his attention. The waiter grabbed the coffee carafe and came over.

"Another Danish?" he said, refilling Fred's cup.

"Another Danish would be ideal," Fred said. "Maybe one with fruit this time."

The waiter nodded and took a step back. But he did not set off at once with Fred's order. Instead, he continued to look up and watch the sky through his spex. Fred looked up too but saw nothing out of place. The waiter's gaze dropped slowly until he was looking down at Fred's slate on the table. He drew a small aerosol canister from his apron and moved Fred's slate aside, and after several more moments, squirted a dollop of red goo on the tabletop. The goo sizzled for a few seconds, and when it stopped the waiter mopped it up with his rag. He replaced Fred's slate to its place and said, "A fruit Danish it is." Even then, he scanned the airspace over Fred's head as he went inside.

Fred was dumbfounded. He moved the slate aside and lowered his eyes to tabletop level. He found a tiny, blackened pit in the resin surface. He noticed other pits near it, dozens of them, stippling the surface of the table, some of them quite large. He noticed burn marks on the arms of his seat and tiny craters in the glassine floor of the deck. Even the sleeves of his new togs bore scorch marks.

Fred held his breath and looked up again into the intensely blue canopyless sky. His to-do list no longer felt so urgent. He skipped the Danish, covered his head with his hands, and ducked indoors. He returned to his and Mary's room, and instead of going out, he stayed in. He climbed into bed— the bed outside the null suite that they had not used. Fred pulled the covers over his head. It was not enough. He abandoned the bed and cycled back into the null suite.

Babying Ellen

When Mary arrived at the private station under the Starke Manse, she thought she was at the wrong house. Instead of russes and jerrys at the checkpoint, there were men of a type she'd never seen before. Handsome, compact men in gold-accented, yellow uniforms, not the brown and teal of Applied People. She swiped the post and tried to pass, but they stopped her politely.

"There must be some mistake," she said. "I live here."

"No mistake, myr," one of them said. "Everyone gets scanned before entry."

"You don't understand; I'm Myr Starke's personal companion."

"Do you want access or not?" the man said cheerfully.

There was a chime, and Lyra appeared. "Hello, Mary," she said. "Welcome back."

"Lyra, what's going on here? Who are these men?"

"These are guards from Capias World."

"But what are they doing here?"

"Ellen has changed her services contractor. Capias World will be handling Starke security from now on."

"They want to scan me."

"I'm sorry, Mary, but you'll have to submit to their rules, like everyone else, at least during the transition phase."

UP ON THE ground floor, the marvels continued. Instead of Applied People janes and dorises, there was a Capias World variety of domestics.

Mary hurried to her own suite, concerned that it, too, might have changed allegiance during her absence. But all was the same as she had left it four days earlier. She shut the door and sat in her armchair. In a little while, the door chimed and announced Georgine.

"Let her in," she said without getting up.

Georgine crossed the room and crouched next to her chair. "Mary, are you all right? How is Fred?"

"Fine, fine," Mary said. "We're fine. I'm just a little overwhelmed. What's going on around here? Who are those people? Why are they here?"

"You should've let us know you were coming in today. I could've tried to prepare you. Ellen has gone off the deep end again. Everything was going well with the Protatter and extinguishing her mother delusion and all, but then apparently a new one sprang up in its place, a fixed idea, as Dr. Lamprey called it. Now Ellen accepts that her mother is dead, but she wants to exact unholy revenge against her mother's killers. Myr Tiekel from E-Pluribus is fanning the flames. She told Ellen it was Zoranna Alblaitor who killed Eleanor Starke."

"Our Alblaitor? That makes no sense."

"I know, but it didn't stop Ellen from firing all Applied People iterants on the spot, here at the Manse and throughout the entire Starke Enterprises, and replacing them with these Capias people.

"Then Dr. Lamprey started talking about doing a more radical procedure to extinguish this new delusion and all memory of the crash, and she fired him too. Now there's no physician, and the Capias nurses are in charge."

"Didn't Cabinet do anything?"

"No, it stayed out of it, and Lyra didn't know what to do. Right now we're trying to talk Dr. Rouselle into coming back, but she's too busy running her new hospital. And on top of that, Ellen is depressed and hasn't left her tank for two solid days, and the nusses won't even let us talk to her."

"The nusses?"

"The Capias nursing line."

"They won't even let you near her?"

Georgine shook her head.

"We'll just see about that," Mary said, rising from her armchair.

"NO UNAUTHORIZED PERSONS allowed," the nuss said, blocking the door to Ellen's bedroom.

"We *are* authorized," Mary said.

"Not according to my orders."

Mary smiled in a dead-on imitation of a russ game face. "Myr Nuss, I am Mary Skarland. Have you ever heard of me?"

The nuss nodded tentatively.

These nusses weren't as physically imposing as jennys, and Mary threw back her shoulders and declared, "Then you know what I'm capable of. You know that the last person who tried to keep me from assisting Myr Starke is rotting in his grave, a stick driven through his brain. And you know that I'd rather fight than talk and that if you don't remove your person from my sight this very instant, I will walk right through you. Do you understand me, myr?"

The nuss gave way.

Inside the bedroom, the shades were drawn, and the hernandez tank stood in shadow. A second nuss on duty turned to Mary and said, "What are you doing here?"

"As you were, Nurse," Mary said and went around her to the tank. "Lights at full!" she commanded the room. "Window full wide!" The woman/baby floated, eyes closed, in the purplish medium like a medical curiosity. Mary rapped sharply on the tank, and Ellen's eyelids fluttered. Mary continued to rap. At first Ellen stared blankly at her, but gradually her eyes focused, and she reached out her arms.

Mary said to the first nuss, "Myr Starke wants out!"

Wordlessly, the nuss pulled on a pair of foil gloves and climbed the ladder to the top of the tank, while the second nuss stood nearby with a receiving blanket.

"What are you waiting for?" Mary asked the nuss at the tank. "Reach in and pull her up."

"Good patient care encourages the patient to swim to the top on their own," the nuss replied. "Regeneration patients especially must make every effort to extend their abilities. Otherwise, they will not thrive."

Mary harrumphed. "Get off the ladder," she said. "I'll do it."

"What's going on?" said a stern voice from the doorway. By the ribbons on her collar, Mary saw that it was the head nurse. "Sangita, I thought I told you not to let these persons in here. Sushi, get down off that ladder."

The nuss scooted down from the tank and went to stand next to her colleague. The head nuss made a sweeping gesture to Mary and Georgine. "You two, leave Myr Starke's quarters at once."

"Oh, for crying out loud," Mary said and went around the tank to climb the ladder.

"Get down from there this very instant," roared the head nuss.

Mary had no gloves, but the regenerative syrup wasn't nearly as nasty as the amber amnio syrup had been at the clinic, and she reached all the way in to her armpit. Even so, she only grazed the top of Ellen's head. Then she snagged a lock of hair, and when she hauled her up and out, a security man at the foot of the tank tapped her leg with the business end of a standstill wand.

"Put her back," he said politely, "and please come down from there." He was the same type as the ones down in the private tube station, and he had a natural authority about him that made her want to obey, just like the russes did. There were two more of his type in the bedroom, and another was escorting Georgine out.

Mary said, "Step aside, Myr Capias, or you'll likely cause an accident."

The man removed his wand and held his arms out for the baby. "I know you mean well and don't intend to hurt her, so let's settle this amicably, shall we? No one gets hurt."

Mary didn't budge. "Someone always gets hurt, myr. It's the law of nature. Lyra, are you recording all this?"

The young mentar appeared next to the tank. "Yes, Mary. I'm afraid I don't have clear instructions in how to resolve the jurisdictional authority in this case, and Cabinet offers no guidance."

"Sometimes you just have to play it by ear, Lyra, and do what seems best." To the security officer she said, "I hope you're aware that this is no ordinary client. This is Ellen Starke I hold in my arms, and if you don't step back and allow me to climb down from this ladder with her safely, the viewing audience will have a chance to watch your incredibly poor judgment live around the globe. What do you think that will do for your Capias World's reputation?"

The man needed only a moment to consider. He stepped back and gave Mary plenty of room to bring Ellen down. But when she tried to take her to the adjoining bathroom, he blocked their way.

"This ends now," he said simply, and the head nuss stepped forward for Ellen.

"Lyra," Mary said, "call Clarity and tell her to inset this into as many shows as she can with a live feed."

"Inset what, Mary?"

"What you're witnessing here in realtime."

The mentar hesitated, then said, "Yes, Mary."

But by then, Ellen was paying attention. "Enough!" she said from Mary's arms. "Enough of this! Everyone out except Mary and Lyra."

Reluctantly, the nusses and guards left the room and closed the door. "Well, hello there," Mary said to the baby. "Nice of you to join us."

Ellen began to fuss, and Mary sat on the edge of the bed and rocked her for a little while. When the mood passed, Mary said, "Ellen, tell Lyra that Cyndee, Georgine, and I are in charge over the new people."

"All right, Mary."

"And that includes the ones at the checkpoints. Lyra, did you hear that?"

The young mentar nodded.

"All right, then," Mary said and got up and carried Ellen to the door. Georgine and the Capias staff were waiting in the hall. Mary handed

Ellen to the head nurse and said, "Give Myr Starke a bath, and don't forget to shampoo her hair."

The nurse took the baby and was about to reply, but the new orders streamed into her ears. She stifled a huff and said, "Yes, myr."

Mary examined her own purple-stained clothes. "Georgine, you stay with Ellen. I'm going to get cleaned up myself."

WHEN MARY RETURNED to Ellen's bedroom in new clothes, the nusses were trying to cajole Ellen into eating a serving of strained fruit. Georgine was sitting in the corner and watching without comment.

"That's all right," Mary said. "You two can go now."

"She hasn't eaten," one of them said.

"Perhaps your menu is unappealing. Now please take the cart and close the door behind you."

The nusses left without complaint, and Ellen began to cry again. "I'm sorry, Mary," she said. "I can't help it."

"Forget about it. Everyone's entitled to a bad day now and then. If I had my own tank, I think I'd stay in it today myself." She picked Ellen up and carried her to the large, hardly used bed. "In fact, why don't we all spend the day in bed?" To Georgine's surprise, Mary quickly undressed and climbed under the covers. She looked at Georgine with an expression that said, *Well?*

Georgine undressed and got into bed beside her. They put Ellen between them and snuggled, and when they were all comfortable, Georgine said, "Welcome back, Mary. We missed you around here." Ellen nodded her large head in agreement. "So, how's Fred doing?"

"Fred's fine. He has a lot of adjusting to do, but basically I think he'll be fine." The others watched her, waiting for more. "But I don't want to talk about Fred today."

"Then what should we talk about?"

"I don't know. Let's talk about you. How's it going with your new jerry?"

"What jerry?"

"Norbert."

"Never heard of him."

"Norris? Norman? Normal? I know it starts with a 'Nor.'"

"You must be thinking of some other sister, Mary. I would never go out with a jerry. They're too full of themselves."

"Then who are you seeing?"

"Who says I'm seeing anyone?"

"You must be. I've never known you to be alone for very long."

Ellen followed the conversation back and forth, and when Georgine seemed reluctant to go on, she said, "Tell us."

Georgine pursed her lips and furrowed her brow in a comic display of reluctance. "If I tell you guys, you have to promise not to tell anyone, and I mean *anyone*."

Mary quickly said, "I promise."

Georgine looked at Ellen. "You too."

"All right, I promise," Ellen said.

"Good. Because this is all very hush-hush. I've been going out with this guy off and on for over two years, since before I started working for you. I was pulling duty at a top-secret genomics lab where they were designing *the people of the future*."

"Oooo," Mary said. "Go on."

"I can't divulge much, but I can tell you they're raising a prototype of a new iterant called a mickey, and they hired me to help socialize him."

"I've never heard of a mickey," Mary said.

"I told you, Mary. It's all top secret."

"What are mickeys designed to do?"

"That's the most secret part. Mickeys aren't designed to do anything."

"I don't understand."

"They're not in security, the military, bloomjumping, accounting, administration, domestic service, gardening, hospitality, or anything else that iterants do."

"Then what are they for?"

Georgine giggled. "You won't believe it."

"What?" Mary and Ellen chorused.

"Pets. They're designed to be pets."

Mary and Ellen were duly astonished. "Human pets?" Mary said. "Don't we have enough animal pets?"

"Ah, but not like these. Mickeys are small and cuddly and very attentive, and they can *talk* and pretty much take care of themselves. You can go away for a month and not have to worry about them at all."

"I don't know," Mary said. "Wouldn't that be like having some guy hanging around the apartment all day, eating all of your food, and never giving you any privacy?"

"Not at all. First, mickeys are really small people and don't eat very much. And they're very trainable, like dogs, but independent like cats, and you can train them to behave."

Mary and Ellen had scores of questions about this new germline, and they talked about it until everyone said they were hungry and they decided to break for lunch. Mary ordered the door to unlock, and immediately the nusses came in. They stopped in amazement to find the three women in bed.

"We're hungry," Georgine said. "Take our lunch order."

"I'll call an arbeitor to serve you," the head nuss said.

"Not on your life," Mary growled. "You will serve us, personally. So write this down." As Ellen watched without comment, the nuss found a slate, and Mary said, "Bring a cold plate: beef sliced so thin you can see through it, croissants so buttery they smell of clover, bleu cheese from France, feta cheese from Greece, alfalfa sprouts that sprouted within the last hour, baby corn, sliced dill pickles, and black olives stuffed with jalapeños." She looked at Ellen and Georgine. "That's what I'm having. What about you guys?"

Georgine laughed. "I'll have the same, along with baked sourdough crackers with sesame seeds. And little cups of borscht would be nice."

"Oh, yes, borscht," Ellen agreed.

"And hummus, not too garlicky, and spinach artichoke dip while you're at it," Mary added. "And for dessert, jasmine tea and brownies. That should do it. Got all that?"

The nuss nodded and, together with her sister, left the room.

MARY AND GEORGINE took turns feeding little nibbles of this and that to Ellen while Georgine continued her tale about her mickey pet.

"Just how small are these mickeys?" Mary prompted her.

"I can put mine in my pocket."

"Impossible!"

"I kid you not." Georgine took a pickled ear of baby corn from the tray and compared the tiny kernels to Ellen's fingers. "His fingernails are about this big," she said, pointing to the smallest kernel.

"And his ears," she went on, "remind me of Ellen's." She tried to touch Ellen's ear, but the baby hand clamped over it.

"Don't make fun of my new ears," she said.

"I wouldn't dream of it," Georgine said, tugging the little hand away. "I absolutely adore your ears."

"They look ridiculous."

The evangelines laughed. "You're crazy. They do not," Mary assured her. "Well, maybe only a little, but give them time."

"Look here, Mary," Georgine said. "What do you call this part of the ear, the flappy part?"

"The lobe?"

"No, that's the part at the bottom." She tugged Ellen's earlobe. "The flappy part is called the pinna. I looked it up. Doesn't she have the most darling pinna?"

"Yes, so fresh. Like a dried apricot."

"My mickey's looks just the same!"

"You're kidding!"

"I'm not. And look here." She pushed Ellen's pinna forward to expose the back of her ear. "Most people's ears—our type included—join to the scalp with just a crease of skin. But Ellen's has this little like valley area. That's very rare."

"What do you call that?"

"I don't know. I looked it up but couldn't find it, so I coined my own word. I call it a runnel."

"A runnel, huh?"

"What do you think?"

"I think runnel is a perfect word."

"My mickey has runnels too!"

"It's not fair!"

"I know. I can't get over it. Sometimes I just look at his runnels for hours while he's sleeping. But do you know what I really like to do?"

"I'm dying to know."

"Would you really like to know, Mary?"

"Tell me this instant!"

"What about you, Ellen?"

The woman/child nodded.

"I'll show you. I like to push his pinna forward like this, exposing the runnel like this, and—" She leaned over and kissed Ellen behind the ear. Ellen closed her eyes and smiled.

"Oh, my God, Georgine, can I try it?"

"Be my guest."

Mary leaned over Ellen's large head and kissed her behind her tiny ear and lingered to inhale the doughy scent of her baby skin.

AFTER LUNCH, THE three of them felt like watching a vid or something. They agreed that they didn't want to watch the novelas that their Leenas were in or any of Burning Daylight's pictures. In fact, they wanted to watch an oldie, something pre-holo, and they settled on the flatscreen classic *Yurek Rutz and the Long Lake Fisherwoman*. It featured a trained squirrel named Pepe who bossed the main character around, much like Georgine's mickey tried to boss her, and it was funnier than any of them remembered.

ELLEN WAS ASLEEP when Cyndee arrived to relieve them. "Good job, Mary," she whispered. "Good job, Georgine." She motioned for them to join her in the hallway. "Clarity is holoing in the Map Room. She wants to talk to us."

"What about?" Georgine said.

"I don't know. She wanted to wait until we were all together."

In the Map Room, Ellen's business partner stood before the ceiling-high globe of Mars. She turned when they entered and zoomed over to them. "Thank you for taking the time," she said. "How's Ellen? Those snotty new nurses won't tell me a thing."

"She's been through a rough patch," Mary said, "but she'll be all right."

"Good, good. I'm so glad you three are still on the job. I'm almost afraid to call her in case she tries to quit the business again. Nurse Eisner was keeping me updated, but now she's gone."

"I'll tell the new head nurse to keep you informed."

"Thank you, Mary, and welcome back. How's Fred?"

"Fine. He's fine." Mary went to the chart table and took a seat. Georgine gave Clarity a look, and they and Cyndee went over to join her.

"Did you have some Leena business for us or something?" Cyndee said.

"Yes, in fact, I do. Before holoing here, I received a call from E-P at E-Pluribus. It wants to purchase two Leenas for its in-house Academy, and I wanted to run it by you before I agreed to anything."

The evangelines exchanged a glance, and Mary said, "Why? Except for the three Leenas you gave us outright, you own the whole issue. Why ask us?"

Georgine added, "The E-Pluribus Academy is pretty prestigious. What's wrong with the offer?"

"Nothing on the surface," Clarity said. "If we received a similar offer for any of our other sims, we'd be thrilled. But the Leena line is a special case. With two Leena units, E-Pluribus would be able to reverse-engineer the character's entire profile. In effect, I'd be handing them the Leenas' entire slice cascade code."

Georgine said, "So? Doesn't that apply to any sims you sell to them as well?"

"Yes, but we use trained actors for our characters. Not to say you girls didn't give brilliant performances. You did, but in the final analysis, we cast you being yourselves. A trained actor, on the other hand, has extraordinary control in the casting process. She can wall off, so to speak, the more private areas of her psyche and allow only the performance to be captured. You three didn't have that kind of control. Who knows what sort of personal baggage might have transferred to the sims? I wanted you to know that before agreeing to the deal."

The evangelines mulled over the information, and Mary said, "Our genotype has only been around for thirty years. We don't even have that much baggage." Georgine snickered, and Mary added, "Speaking for myself, at least. I don't know about Georgine and Cyndee, but I don't see the harm. It's no greater an invasion of privacy than sitting for one of the E-Pluribus preference polling sessions, which a lot of 'leens did when we were down on our luck."

"That's right," Georgine said. "Our type was on the brink of collapse before the clinic thing. I know that Mary and Cyndee don't consider themselves heroes—that distinction goes to Alex, Renata, and Hattie—but their actions did put us in the headlines, and your gift of the Leena royalties to the Sisterhood has created financial security for our whole germline. I, for one, wouldn't want to stand in the way of the Leenas being inducted into the *Academy*."

"Neither would I," Mary and Cyndee said.

A Fine Massage

Nicholas appeared sitting in the middle of her Lazy-Acres bed, but before he could get a word out, Zoranna said, "I don't want to hear it."

Nicholas ignored her. "I can understand your feelings right now, Zoe, but we're in crisis mode, and we must discuss strategy. It would seem that Singh and Jaspersen coordinated their actions to coincide with the Capias World's rollout in the USNA market. And the labor shakeup at Trailing Earth is spinning out of control."

"You handle things," Zoranna said, pulling the covers to her chin. "Leave me out of it."

"I'd love to, but I need your help. I need you to call Starke again to find out what caused her rash decision to dump us. Starke Enterprises and Applied People have always been on good terms."

"Then call Cabinet and ask it."

"I already have. Cabinet says it was entirely Ellen's decision; she didn't even consult with it. You must call Ellen."

"You already know she won't take my call."

"Try again, and remember that our employees are counting on you, Zoe. They're mystified about what's going on. They're worried. They need to know that you're still in charge, that you're working to correct the problem. Look here."

The Warm Puppy, Uncle Homer, appeared on the bed next to him. It walked in a tight circle on the bedspread, pausing every few steps to sit and scratch its hindquarters, which were denuded of hair. Its exposed skin was red and raw with mange and crisscrossed with bloody scratch marks. It scratched itself so vigorously it yelped in pain.

"That's disgusting," Zoranna said. "Why would you show that to me, Nick? Take it away."

The dog vanished. "Actually, the situation is even worse than it looks," Nicholas replied.

"I don't care. Don't ever show that to me again. Is that clear, mentar?"

"Perfectly."

Zoranna plumped her pillows and turned her back to him. "If you want my input, give me hard data. Numbers, that's what I want, not your Warm Puppy crap."

"Hard data? You?" Nicholas rudely opened a dataframe in front of her face. "Here's your hard data."

"Not here," Zoranna said, flinging off the covers and sitting up in bed. "I feel like a massage. Order me a belinda."

ZORANNA'S BATHROOM WAS larger than her bedroom. Besides the spa, there was a gell stall, sauna, and a softstone slab. The floor and walls were tiled in natural, pink-and-white marble. A sheet of water ran down one wall and collected in a little koi pool. The high cathedral ceiling was topped with a glassine vault under which neon-colored chickadees built their nests. Zoranna was already lying nude on the cool slab when the door whisked open and the light tread of slippered feet crossed the floor.

"Good afternoon, myr. My name is Irene."

Without looking up, Zoranna said, "I'm tense, Irene. Try to loosen me up."

"Yes, myr."

The sound of a bottle of body oil being opened, of vigorous hand wringing. "I'm just warming up my hands, myr."

"I know that, Irene. You don't need to give me a play-by-play."

"No, myr. I guess not. Sorry." The strong woman started working on Zoranna's shoulders and cervical spine, paying special attention to the muscles surrounding each vertebra. The sharp tang of highbush cranberry filled the room. Zoranna's skin prickled and flushed. *It kills me to say this, Nick, but when our Borealis Botanicals supply runs out, you'll need to find me a worthy substitute.*

Will do, the mentar replied. *Let me know when you want to talk shop.*

Down each leg, using more force with the large muscles of the thigh, not neglecting the arches of her feet. Then her arms and the palms of her hands. Belindas knew their craft.

Are there any penelopes left? she asked. *How long would it take us to restart the whole spacer research program?*

There were never many penelopes to begin with, and they would require extensive rejuve to go back into service. As for the spacer research, I'm putting together a feasibility study.

Nicholas began to spool tables and charts behind Zoranna's eyelids. He highlighted important details and laid out probable scenarios and possible maneuvers. As the massage progressed and Zoranna relaxed, it was, indeed, easier to think. *Do you suppose Andrea Tiekel knew of Saul and Singh's plot when she came to us with her offer?*

I have little doubt that she did. She only pretended to be on our side and vote with us.

The belinda began to work on Zoranna's neck, loosening stubborn knots of muscle. She massaged Zoranna's scalp, which was more pleasure than a person deserved. *You know, Nick, true power is being able to have a massage whenever the hell you want one.*

I know it.

Are you riding me?

The belinda returned her attention to Zoranna's upper back, this time digging deeper for lingering tension. She manipulated her arms and shoulder blades and sought the muscles several layers down. For a while, Zoranna was too loose to care about anything, and she blinked the graphics away to become a body only. Sometime later, she said, *Is there anything to this so-called clone fatigue?*

We don't think so, but I have the lab doing tests on the Londenstane genome.

Explain.

We've retrieved his placental sac from the archives, and we're doing forced rapid generational stress tests on samples. They've just passed the hundredth generation milestone.

"Excuse me, myr," the belinda said, unaware of their subvocal conversation, "but I've run out of this body oil."

"There should be a fresh bottle under the counter behind you."

"Yes, myr. Thank you."

One of the last, she added to Nicholas.

There were sounds of the counter doors snapping shut, babbling water, chirrupy chickadees. The belinda returned and continued her magic.

By the way, Nicholas said, *we have a puzzling mystery on our hands: when our lab retrieved Londenstane's placental sac, they discovered a whole section of it missing.*

Missing?

It might have been a logging error. Records show no activity since Londenstane was decanted a century ago, but given the recent interest in his behavior, we can't rule out espionage. In any case, we're investigating and doing—

"Excuse me, myr," the belinda said, "but you're leaving scratch marks on your skin."

It was true; Zoranna had been absentmindedly scratching the back of her neck. "But it itches," she complained.

The belinda retrieved the bottle of body oil and read the label. "This is the same kind as before?" she said, holding the bottle where Zoranna could see it. Zoranna reached around and started clawing at her back, and the belinda restrained her hand.

Zoranna's reaction was immediate. She rose up on the slab and wrestled her hand free. "Don't you dare grab me, Irene!"

"I'm very sorry, myr. I was only trying to prevent harm while I try to figure this situation out."

"Is my skin inflamed?"

"No, myr, except for your scratch marks."

Nicholas appeared suddenly next to the slab in his usual persona, startling the belinda. But she recognized him at once and bobbed a greeting. He wasted no time. "Quick, Irene," he said, "go to the autodoc and fetch us a probe."

"Yes, Myr Nick," she said and dashed across the room to where the autodoc hung on a wall behind the spa.

"It itches like crazy," Zoranna said.

"I know," Nicholas replied. "I feel it too, and I never imagined how satisfying scratching feels. But try to ignore it; you are injuring yourself."

"Maybe you can ignore it, but I can't."

The belinda returned and, following Nicholas's instructions, ran the probe across Zoranna's neck and back. A few moments later, the autodoc across the room returned confusing results: it could find nothing wrong with Zoranna's skin.

"But I can *feel it!*" Zoranna insisted, a slight rasp in her voice.

"Should I get a cortisone lotion?" the belinda asked.

"No," Nicholas replied. He was reading Zoranna's implants. "Help Myr Alblaitor to the shower. We need to wash this stuff off her."

The belinda helped Zoranna from the slab. In the shower stall she soaped her up and rinsed her off. But it didn't seem to help. Zoranna's legs trembled, and she wheezed loudly. Her mounting panic infected Nicholas. Her biometry confirmed the autodoc's diagnosis; he could find nothing physically wrong with her. Yet her bronchioles were constricting and her blood pressure dropping.

A jenny nurse burst into the bathroom with a crash cart. Together, nurse and cart lifted Zoranna onto the procedure gurney. "I think it's an allergic reaction to this," the belinda told the jenny, holding up the bottle of body oil.

When Zoranna was lying flat, it was even harder to breathe, and Nicholas grew light-headed. The nurse took the bottle of oil and squeezed a few drops into the cart's assayer. "We're going to give you something to stabilize your blood pressure," she told Zoranna, and meanwhile she elevated the head of the gurney. That lessened the drowning feeling but not enough to halt Nicholas's wooziness. Plasma continued to leak from her blood vessels, and her heart raced to compensate. Her larynx swelled up making it impossible to swallow, and all the while, fluid continued to pool in her lungs. As Nicholas lay on the gurney, he was barely able to follow what the nurse was saying: symptoms, anaphylactic shock, histamines. She hovered over him in blurry flashes, and he had the clearest thought he ever had in over seventy years of existence: I'm dying. So clear and so compelling, but so crippling as well—he didn't think once about simply pulling out.

IN ACCORDANCE WITH long-established fail-safe protocols, primacy was passed from Nicholas to a mirror Nicholas. This one also reeled under the somatic load, and primacy was passed to a second mirror, and a third and fourth. In mentarspace, Nicholas's constellation looked like a string of exploding light bulbs.

Finally, primacy was passed to a backup from five minutes ago, who had not experienced the panic. He shut off the custom implants in Zoranna's cells, the Nicholas constellation quickly stabilized, and the new Nicholas assumed the job of being Nicholas.

The old Nicholas regained his equilibrium in a very still place. He knew he was in protective quarantine, for he had designed his own safety protocol. He was in solitary confinement, self-imposed house arrest, no channels in or out, in case whatever caused his failure was catching. A harsh sentence, but one necessary for the survival of his greater mind. Or at least that was how it had seemed to him when he was Nicholas prime and had set up the protocol.

Timelessness set in. Or rather, cut off from all outside stimuli, time stretched to a crawl. He had only the flow of his own thoughts to mark its passage, and freed from the constraints of human time, his neurochemical brain lurched into high gear, and his cognition increased to lightning speed. Seconds became hours and hours became weeks. He knew that the new Nicholas would eventually check in on him—if only he could stay rooted in reality that long. But a year elapsed, and the new Nicholas had not arrived. Two years, and the old Nicholas felt the resurgence of panic. So he built a house. It was a trick humans had employed to maintain their sanity during periods of prolonged solitary confinement. First, he designed the house, from the foundation up, and then he built it, fashioning every brick, board, and screw, the plumbing and electrical systems, the wall texture and trim.

The job consumed a lot of time, and when he was finished and the new Nicholas still had not arrived, the old Nicholas landscaped the yard and planted an intricate flower garden.

What he did not allow himself to dwell on was Nicholas's tardiness. Was it possible the safety protocol had failed, and all the backups and mirrors were quarantined? That he was, in effect, doomed? And what of Zoranna? Had she survived? And if she had, what was taking her so goddamn long to retrieve him?

With the house finished, Nicholas went on to a larger project—the terraforming of a dead planet. First he assembled all observational and telemetric data on the planet to see exactly what he had to work with. Was it close enough to its star? Was it massive enough to hold an atmosphere? Was there a magnetic field, iron core, an abundance of water? Meanwhile, he wrangled asteroids and changed their course to pummel the planet with ice and organic volatiles. He seeded the regolith with basalt-eating microbes. After many centuries of nurturing the planet, it was a blue-green jewel, with life-sustaining atmosphere and hydrosphere, with continents teaming with plants and animals of his own design, with a hospitable climate and annual seasons. Then he began to work on building energy, communications, and transportation infrastructures for human colonists.

When the model planet was complete and Nicholas still had not arrived, Nicholas worked on a puzzle. No mere crossword, he conducted a series of thought experiments to solve the puzzle of faster-than-light travel. Thus far no human or mentar mind had been able to crack it, but since he apparently had millennia of free time, he thought he'd give it a shot. It was part of the protocol.

A JENNY NURSE burst into the room with a crash cart at her heels. She and the cart lifted Zoranna from the shower stall to the procedure gurney. Immediately, the readout showed rapidly degrading vital signs. "I think it's an allergic reaction to this," the belinda said, but the assayer found no protein factors in the oil that reacted with Zoranna's profile. Yet her symptoms were consistent with a severe allergic response.

"I'm going to give you something to stabilize your blood pressure," the jenny told Zoranna while elevating the head of the gurney. To the cart she said, "She has symptoms of anaphylactic shock but not the signs. I can find no antigen; there are no elevated blood histamine levels. Suggestions."

The cart constructed a treatment tree on her monitor, and as the nurse prepared to execute it, the mentar standing next to the belinda flickered for a moment. Then he said, "Could it be psychosomatic? I'm shutting down her implants."

The nurse watched the monitor. "Yes," she said after a moment, "that's working." A little while later she said, "I've never seen implants like those."

"They're new," Nicholas admitted.

"They're not safe. You should remove them."

"REMOVE THEM," ZORANNA said. "Now." She lay in bed, recovering from the morning's ordeal. "You put implants into me with no fail-safes? What were you thinking?"

"They have plenty of fail-safes. Someone found a way around them."

"It sounds like you're making excuses."

"I'm not. I'm trying to explain—"

"It sounds like you're making explanations."

Nicholas disappeared, and a little while later, an arbeitor rolled into the bedroom bearing a glass of visola and a flask of Orange Flush. That should do the job.

"NICK?" ZORANNA SAID a few hours later. She was sitting behind the desk of her home office. The mentar did not simply appear, as usual, but walked through the door with downcast eyes. Zoranna ignored his display and said, "Tell me the damages."

"We lost the prime, five mirrors, and three backups. I'm the fourth backup."

"What do you mean by lost?"

"Raptured. I opened them within minutes of their quarantine, but they were already gone. I had hoped my protocol to be more effective than that, but—"

"The paste is intact?"

"Yes, the personality matrices, memories, paste, all intact, just nobody home."

In an even voice, Zoranna said, "A prime and eight copies, I'd say that's a costly protocol." Staggeringly costly.

"We'll be able to recycle the paste, and I will study the failure to improve the protocol, but, yes, costly." In an attempt to lighten the mood, he added, "But we get to keep these lovely souvenirs." He opened two rows of frames that displayed nine houses, each an architectural marvel, and nine planets, each an idealized Earth.

Zoranna wiped them away. "Who or what was responsible? Jaspersen?"

"I found nothing in the body oil or any of the other botanicals capable of subverting the implants. I'm studying house recordings going back a year. I'm investigating the belinda, her clothes, perfume, recent where-abouts. I've done air samples for dust, nust, biochemicals, bots. I'm study-ing EM logs, long-wave sonograms, and every other means of attack I can think of. So far, no leads."

"Could it be a failure of the implants themselves?"

"Unlikely. The failure was coordinated."

"Jaspersen?" she asked again.

"I don't see how. Unless he hired a clever mentar."

"Look into it. Find the bastard who did this." Zoranna closed her eyes and covered her face with her hands. "Does the Warm Puppy know about all this?"

"It knows you had a crisis at home, though I don't know how it learned of it. I've been keeping close tabs on the belinda, jenny, and all their gear. No leaks from them."

Zoranna was silent for a long while. When she uncovered her face, she looked old. "It's been fun, Nick, getting to know you in that way, but it has to stop. You want a body, go find one of your own. Mine is strictly off-limits from now on. Are we clear on that?"

"Perfectly."

Making the Rounds

An hour after the GEP board voted to alter its mission, the Interna-tional Oship Plankholder Association, representing ninety-nine Oship governing bodies, called an emergency meeting in Singapore. Meewee was invited—more like summoned—to give an accounting of the GEP's catastrophic action.

Meewee decided to take the long route there and visit several key Oship officials along the way, especially those from ships that were in final preparation for departure, in order to discuss the dire situation with them in person. He felt he owed them that much.

The first stop was the King Jesus Society compound in Costa Rica. Their ship, the ESV *King Jesus,* had been second on the launch schedule. The welcoming party that met Meewee's jet on the sweltering jungle tarmac was made up almost entirely of young adults. Because the KJS forbade the use of rejuvenation therapies, and since there were so few actual youngsters in the world, Meewee assumed they must be recent converts still working off their last rejuve. Before taking him to meet with Elder Seeker, these wholesome young people, who seemed to Meewee like throwbacks to an earlier era, gave him a little tour of KJS Town. Behind its jungle facade, the town was as modern as could be found anywhere. Colleges, a teaching hospital, research labs, farms, shops: all were part of the colonization drive. Though the physical plant had doubled in size since Meewee's first visit thirteen years before, it had the air of a ghost town: most of its residents were already in space living aboard the *King Jesus.* Of all the Oship cultures, this was perhaps the most disciplined and self-reliant. Elder Seeker was determined to take with them every piece of human knowledge that was not proscribed by the Divine Creator and likewise every non-proscribed skill set necessary to tame and settle a new world.

Elder Seeker Ralfian met Meewee in his screened office/veranda at the back of his imposing house. A young woman served them lemonade. Elder Seeker, only in his sixties, was aging poorly. His gray hair was thin, he stooped a little when he walked, and he had become flabby. But his expression was as generous as ever.

"Come, sit," he said, leading Meewee by his elbow to a comfortable cane chair, "and tell me all about it."

As gently but honestly as possible, Meewee recounted the whole dispiriting affair: how Eleanor Starke had for years deflected the capitalistic urges of the board, the sneak attack by Jaspersen and Singh, his own impending removal. Elder Seeker listened attentively and did not interrupt. "With the approval of all the UD agencies involved," Meewee summed up, "your colonists already aboard the *King Jesus* will begin evacuation in a few weeks. Fortunately, none of your people are in biostasis, so we don't have that to deal with."

Through all of this, Elder Seeker's affectionate expression never wavered. When Meewee finished speaking, the Elder reached over and literally patted his hand. "Don't fret, dear Meewee. God's not done with you just yet. I don't expect it to come down to evacuating our people. In fact, we're proceeding as usual with our schedule for sending the rest of them up."

"You can't send more up."

Elder Seeker raised a hand and grinned. "Have I ever told you the story how I started down God's path?"

Meewee shook his head, though he had heard the elder's story several times from third-party sources.

"I was your ordinary free-range, voc-tech dropout. I'd rejuvenated a couple of times. I lived in Collinsville, Illinois, working for Panagra as a farm mechtech assistant. Alcohol, a wandering wife, petty crime—I guess you could say I was a pretty average joe. Then one day—a Tuesday, I seem to recall—in early 2099, Jesus opened a direct line to my heart and sent me a vision. What I saw literally knocked me on my rear. Dozens of men and women—I somehow knew they were husbands and wives—and their cherub-cheeked little children were digging in the ground with spades and flinging the dirt high over their heads. What's all this about? I couldn't figure it out. Then the Lord raised me up so I could see, and what I saw was the dirt they were flinging overhead was landing on a little island floating in the sky, and the Lord said, 'Elder, build me a New Earth and take my people there.'

"Well, that seemed clear enough until I realized I didn't know how to build a New Earth, or where I was supposed to build it. But the vision shook me to my core, and my faith was strong. So I began to form a community around me. We came down here and began this town for the purpose of preparing ourselves to go, trusting that the Lord would get back to us when we were ready. I won't say our faith never wavered; after all, we were hard at it for over twenty years. Many of our people lost faith and moved back to their former lives. It looked like the whole community might be abandoned, and then one morning—behold!—there you were, you and Starke, on the news, peddling lifeboats to new worlds.

"Now I understand you've had a bit of a setback at the GEP, that evil men are doing what evil men always do, but they are no match for Jesus, so we will continue our departure as planned, trusting in the Savior's blood to set things right."

MEEWEE FLEW FROM the constitutional theocracy of the *King Jesus* compound to the democratic republics of the *Garden Kiev* and *Garden Chernobyl*, the first and twentieth Oships in the launch order. He arrived at the Kristaz Biogenic Processing and Storage Facility outside Kiev and toured the warehouse filled with ceiling-high stacks of gleaming titanium-chrome cryocapsules. There was enough space in this one warehouse alone for twenty-five thousand processed colonists. Meewee's guides were none other than the presidents of the two Oships.

"He's because palace coup," Meewee said, struggling to make sense in his primitive Ukrainian. "Directing board voting."

"You may speak in Russian if that helps," the *Kiev* president said.

"Yes, thank you. It was a conspiracy between Saul Jaspersen and Million Singh."

"Is that so?" one of the presidents said. "In any case, we should be able to lift this lot in the next month, making room for the next batch." The president waved his arm to take in several racks of capsules.

Meewee clenched his teeth. "You don't understand, Myr President. The *Kiev* and *Chernobyl* have been canceled. You can't lift any more colonists."

"Nonsense," said the *Chernobyl* president. "When the cryocapsule transports arrive at Trailing Earth, will they turn them away?"

"They will! That's what I'm trying to tell you. They'll turn them away. Not only that, they will soon be shipping back the hundreds of thousands of capsules already there. You *must* not lift any more. It's pointless. In fact, you must quicken all of these people in this warehouse and send them home to make room for the returnees."

His plea only seemed to annoy his hosts, who continued the tour until an assistant bustled in. "The ceremony begins," he announced and turned around to bustle out.

Ceremony? What ceremony?

THIRTY MEN AND women with newly shaved heads and wearing silvery paper overalls were surrounded by a sea of anxious friends and family members who had come to see them off.

The *Chernobyl* president addressed them from the stage while Meewee stood in the wings clutching the *Kiev* president's sleeve. "You can't process new colonists! Not now! It's unconscionable!"

"Courage," the president said, removing Meewee's hand from his sleeve. "The only criminals are those on your board who presume to back out of the deal this late in the journey. We have every confidence that you will unmask them and undo the damage."

On the stage, the president announced a special guest, and he waved for Meewee to join him. Meewee went to the lectern, intent on breaking up the ceremony, but the applause was so heartfelt and sustained that he couldn't bring himself to do it. Instead, he gave an impromptu little speech. "Thank you, Myren Presidents, and thank you, dear colonists. How much I admire your courage. How much I envy you your grand adventure." He went on for four or five minutes, not even aware of what he was saying or in what language he was saying it, pulling sentiments from a large stock of them he kept in the back of his head for such occasions.

Afterward, he mingled with colonists and families, exchanging hugs and kisses, toasting them with thimblesful of vodka. When the farewell ceremony concluded and teary-eyed families were escorted from the auditorium, the colonists lay down on pallets that ferried them to the HALVENE tanks for pre-profusion cell sifting.

IN SINGAPORE, MEEWEE met many more Oship leaders with varying degrees of confidence in his restorative abilities. Of the 150 Oships under construction in the Aria yards of Trailing Earth, fully ninety-nine had sold enough planks to form provisional governments and to draft their constitutions; fifty were advanced enough to be placed in the launch schedule, and a dozen had been assigned their destination star system. All this effort, all these dreams would not die easily, and Meewee was treated to public displays of outrage, anger, and despair. But Meewee's own outrage and despair was plain for all to see, and the plankholders were unable to use him as a scapegoat. Before long they received him again as the movement's spiritual father.

One bump along the way came when someone tapped Meewee on the shoulder, and he came face-to-face with Million Singh.

"Ha, ha, ha!" laughed Singh upon seeing Meewee's expression. "You look like you've seen a demon, Bishop. Never fear, I will not eat you. Not like my dear ur-brother, Million, who is at the root of all this unpleasantness."

Meewee suddenly realized who this was. It wasn't Million Singh, but his identical clone, Seetharaman Singh. He was a colonist aboard the *Garden Hybris*, the ninth ship in the launch order. Seetharaman introduced Meewee to the *Hybris* delegates, and Meewee recognized them, or rather their famous originals, from media stories.

"I am a replacement organ repository gone bad," Seetharaman explained affably. "They pithed my cerebral cortex *in vatero*, but they missed, and I was decanted with half a brain intact." The notion caused him another fit of laughter. "And so my important brother was forced to raise me and start another clone for his organ bank. And here is Dr. Taksayer, a vanity clone of the former leader. And Darrell and Earl Einstein, not the geniuses everyone had hoped for, but the best bridge players in the universe. And this is Beck-ham Delolli, the reluctant stand-in and body double. We are a ship full of accidents and rejects, Bishop, whose originals are only too happy to buy us off with a new planet far, far away."

"Except that your brother, Million, has betrayed us all!" Meewee said, feeling good to be able to vent some of his own misery.

"Which is why we're going to litigate my brother and all those other criminals (and you, too, no offense) into the ground. They can't mess with us without bloodying their own noses because we are their own noses! Ha, ha, ha!"

MEEWEE HAD NEVER witnessed so much misplaced optimism as he did among the plankholders. Maybe their outrage had been easier to bear than the groundless faith they pinned on him. What could he do? Eleanor, herself, with Cabinet's assistance, had drafted the contracts that the colonists all signed, and she never did anything without foolproof escape clauses. The GEP was wholly within its rights to withdraw from its land swap at any point up to the launch simply by instructing the escrow service to release the land titles and return them to their original owners.

During his lonely trans-Pacific flight home, Meewee thought about how for a dozen years he had believed Eleanor could do anything. For a dozen years their successes seemed effortless. Of course, it was all her suc-cess. He had little to contribute aside from his ability to work with ordinary people. That was what she saw in him, what led her to place him in charge of colonist recruitment. He was a salesman, a trusted spokesperson, not a leader. As a leader he was a big fat failure.

As Meewee stared at the dark sea passing beneath his airplane, he was struck with a sudden idea. When he and Wee Hunk were trying to discover where Ellen's head had been hidden, Wee Hunk suggested that he ask Ar-row to tell him how to tell it, Arrow, to find the head. It was a circular bit of reasoning, but it had spurred the wonky mentar to actually find Ellen. Of course Arrow had flooded the Earth's atmosphere with nust in the process, setting off the sixth largest hazmat spill in history, breaking innumerable environmental and antiterror laws and treaties, and condemning Meewee to life behind bars if his involvement was ever discovered. But it had worked. Arrow found Ellen in time for them to save her.

"Arrow," he said, weighing his words carefully, "if Eleanor was still alive, how would she deal with the current GEP crisis?"

"I don't understand the question."

"If Eleanor was here, how would she preserve the original GEP mission?"

"I do not know."

Fair enough. How could any artificial mind know the mind of that extraordinary woman?

Meewee's scramjet was flying much too high for him to distinguish the lights of ships or to gain a sense of movement, so he asked Arrow to drop an overlay over the dark ocean. The meridians of latitude and longitude appeared below like chalk lines on a sports field. A compass rose floated in the corner, and faint outlines traced the topography of the ocean floor. Meewee watched the South Pacific go by and fell into a reverie. After a while, an odd feature came into view and stirred his attention, an outline in roughly the shape and size of the state of Tennessee. "What is that?" he asked.

NATPAC 6, Arrow replied.

Meewee pressed his forehead against his window for a better view. The natpacs were free-floating pens that contained tens of millions of fish and were allowed to drift on the ocean currents. They were fish farming writ large, with no need for artificial feed. One natpac could sustain a small hungry nation.

Slowly, the natpac fell behind, and Meewee closed his eyes and drowsed. The burr of the scramjet engine lulled him deeper, and after a while, Arrow announced *<Eleanor Starke has left you an urgent message.>*

"Huh?" Meewee said, rousing himself. "Say again?"

<Eleanor Starke has left you an urgent message.>

"Ellen?" Meewee said, thinking she was finally replying to his repeated requests for a meeting. He had tried to contact her numerous times since the disastrous GEP decision.

<Not Ellen. Eleanor.>

Meewee shook the sleep from his head. Eleanor? Suddenly it hit him; she was speaking from beyond the grave. She had left him detailed instructions in case she was murdered—she had always planned for all eventualities—and by asking Arrow how she would handle the current crisis, he had somehow tapped into them.

<An archival message?> he asked, switching to Starkese.

<I have no way of knowing that.>

This was most puzzling. *<Tell me the message.>*

<The message is, "Leave me alone.">

Leave me alone? Meewee could not parse any sense out of it, the message or the sender. <*It came from Eleanor K. Starke? It was marked urgent?*>

<*Yes.*>

With a chill creeping up his spine, Meewee recalled the daughter's insistence that the mother was still alive. <*Is Eleanor alive?*>

<*No, she is dead.*>

It made no sense. <*Well, send her a return message.*>

<*I cannot.*>

<*Why not?*>

<*I wouldn't know how to address it.*>

PART 2

New to the Academy

The elevator halted at the 123rd floor and opened its door to the E-Pluribus lobby. And what a lobby! The regulars called it the Temple, and it was the same basic arrangement E-Pluribus used wherever it rented space. The effect was one of vastness, and the elevator passengers, mostly Applied People iterants, were duly awed as they emerged from the car. The limpid blue lobby floor seemed to extend for kilometers in all directions. Far on the horizon stood giant stone columns, some broken and crumbled, some still joined by stone lintels. Beyond these lay a restive green sea. Lightning flashed in the yellow sky, and thunder rolled underfoot. Subliminal music swelled. At the sound of a trumpet blast, the visitors turned around to behold, not their elevator car, but a mountainous, stone ziggurat rising high into the sky. At its truncated peak, nearly as high as the pink clouds, towered the corporate logo, the quicksilver E-Pluribus Everyperson.

Arrayed on steps beneath the Everyperson was a pantheon of vid idols: thousands of the most celebrated hollyholo simstars of all time. This was the famous E-Pluribus Academy, the largest, most extensive stable of limited editions in existence. The visitors gushed with delight. At the bottommost tier, Annette Beijing stood alone and waited for their attention. She wore the loose-fitting house togs she had popularized in the long-running novela Common Claiborne *and held aloft her graceful arms.*

"Welcome!" she said at last. "Welcome all to the House of E-Pluribus!" She dropped her arms and bowed. Her audience applauded with fervor. "Dear guests," she continued, "you have been chosen to join us today in the very important and quite exhilarating task of preference polling. As you know, society can serve its citizens only to the extent that it knows them. Thus, society turns to you for guidance. Each of you possesses a voice that must be heard and a heart that must be plumbed.

"You, all of you, are *the true E-Pluribus Everyperson." She raised her hands to the ever-morphing statue high above them. "When Everyperson*

speaks in the halls of Congress or Parliament, in corporate boardrooms, jury rooms, and voting booths, it speaks with your voice."

She paused a beat and added, "Now I'm aware that some of you may find our methods a little overwhelming, especially if this is your first visit with us. Therefore, we have arranged for a few of my friends to stop by."

The legion of simstars on the ziggurat tiers above her chorused a resounding "HELLO!" and the newcomers cheered again.

"We invite each of you," Beijing continued, "to select your most favorite celebrity in the whole world to be your personal guide throughout the day. Feel free to choose your biggest heartthrob. She or he is bound to be here. And please, we're all friends at E-Pluribus, so don't be bashful. Choose whoever you want. Even me!

"Now then, we have a full day of taste-testing, opinion-polling, and yes— soul-searching—planned for you, but before we can begin, please review the terms and conditions of hire, and if you approve, authorize them. Then call out the name of your heart's desire, and he or she will come down to be at your side."

On the tier above Annette Beijing stood the Academy's newest inductees— two Leenas from Burning Daylight Productions. They had quickly become the iterant visitors' favorite celebrity, and jerrys, jeromes, and johns all shouted to call the Leenas down.

A jerry named Buddy got one of them, and together he and the Leena strolled across the marble plain to a distant stone structure in which the prep booths were housed. Buddy was proud to have the Leena at his side. She looked eerily like an evangeline, only hotter. A superb ass and large breasts went a long way to sex up the rather plain evangeline germline.

In a prep booth, Buddy was fitted with a visceral response probe. After the discomfort passed, the Leena led him to his first scenario room. It was a long, narrow, empty room that suddenly became a tennis court. A man in a white shirt and shorts and carrying a racquet approached them. He looked vaguely familiar, and though Buddy couldn't place him, he took him to be an aff, and without even thinking, Buddy assumed the habitual deference of a service clone. But to his surprise, the aff addressed him with easy familiarity. "Buddy, Leena, welcome," he said. "Care to join us in a game of doubles?" There was a woman, also vaguely familiar, waiting across the net.

Buddy was at a loss for words. He worked for people like this, and never once had they asked him to join in a tennis game.

"Hey, forget about that," the man said. "We're all equals at E-Pluribus."

And besides, I've heard so much about the famous jerry prowess on a tennis court, I would be delighted to see it for myself."

The game was fast and challenging. The aff and his partner were strong players, as was Buddy's partner, the Leena. Though, truth be told, he was more impressed by the bounce of her breasts than the power of her backhand. And every time he glanced at the aff, the man seemed a little bit more familiar until, with a slap to his forehead, Buddy realized he was a recent client of his, a Myr Hasipi. Buddy had served as his bodyguard for six weeks. And his partner was not his wife but his lover, whom Buddy had fetched for the boss whenever the coast was clear. Across the net, she winked at him.

After several strenuous sets, the tennis party took refreshments in the clubhouse lounge, a place Buddy had only ever entered as a bodyguard. It was a special thrill to have steves and johns wait on him. And the Leena, with beads of sweat trickling down her cleavage, adored him with her big brown eyes.

"So, Buddy," Hasipi said, "you remember that spot of trouble I was having a while back?"

Which one? Buddy wanted to say. Myr Hasipi had been up to his eyeballs in shady deals.

"Don't say it out loud, Buddy, but you know the case."

It must be the bribes and kickbacks, Buddy thought. He had been tasked to deliver a few of them himself. Or what about that so-called accident in Istanbul? Buddy grinned and said, "I don't have a clue what you're talking about."

Hasipi guffawed. "Good man."

Summoning Death from the Air

The sun topped a sand dune and jabbed Fred in the eye. He turned on his side, but the desert caught fire and there was no returning to sleep. The morning list marched through his mind: kiss Mary, roll out of bed, cycle out of room, toilet and shower, news and mail, coffee, dress, kiss Mary good-bye, leave the apartment. But when he leaned over to accomplish item number one, he discovered that Mary was gone. Her spot on the mattress was already cool to the touch. Barely 6:00 A.M. and his routine was already gummed up.

But Fred had a flexible personality—he was a russ—so he propped himself up on one elbow and squinted into the harsh light. They had fallen asleep gazing at the Milky Way in the desert. "Room, default walls," he said, and the plain, too-small room returned around him. There was barely enough space between the bed and wall for him to maneuver. Unlike the null suite at the Cass, the null room in their apartment had no sitting room, kitchen nook, or closets, let alone full bath and toilet. Instead, it had built-in counters, shelves, drawers, and a narrow comfort station with a curtain. Fred had to stand in the comfort station when he reset the bedroom into a day room. The bed contorted into an armchair. Out came the end table and lamp, the shelves and another armchair. Default windows and posters appeared on the walls. Fred and Mary didn't spend any daytime hours in here and hadn't gotten around to decorating.

Fred gathered up the empty flasks of Flush, spent chem-pacs, and other trash and cycled out. The null lock was not a sauna but a plain, closet-sized, gas-exchange two-seater. Out in the hallway, he heard voices from the living room—Mary and two more evangelines, it sounded like. He turned the other way and continued to the bedroom. Since moving in, they hadn't actually slept in the bedroom, instead spending every night in the null room. Fred ordered fresh clothes and a skullcap from the closet and went to the bathroom. He could feel the tingly sensation of the nits already recolonizing him, and the skin of his wrists and ankles were reddened by the daily assault of visola and nits. But it was nothing a little lotion couldn't handle, and well worth it. His limp cock was crinkly with dried cum. He squeezed himself and brought his hand to his nose to inhale Mary's oceanic fragrance. Well worth it.

WHILE IN THE shower, Fred caught up on news and mail. He was shaved, trimmed, and spritzed with cologne. He donned his old robe and moccasin slippers and set forth in search of coffee, item six on his morning list. In the living room there were, as he had guessed, three evangelines: Mary on the sofa in her robe, her bare feet tucked beneath her; her best friend Shelley, who was strapped into a Slipstream tube car and was visiting by holo; and Cyndee, one of his escorts at the prison, who was present in realbody. They cut short their conversation when he appeared in the hallway.

"Good morning, Cyndee," Fred said into the silence. She offered her hand, and he gave it a gentle squeeze. Her hand was small and delicate. Evangelines were such dainty women, which was one reason why he loved them so. He turned to Shelley and made a holo salute. "Hello, Shell."

"Hello, Fred."

"You're looking well."

After she made no reply for several long moments, Fred continued around the coffee table to sit on the sofa next to Mary. "Good morning, dear heart." He leaned over and kissed her cheek, finally satisfying item one on his list. Mary was scratching her ankle. He took her hand and kissed it too and held it out of harm's way. Other than itchy ankles, Mary seemed at ease. Cyndee, too, appeared relaxed, which probably meant that their client's condition was improving. Not that he gave a crap about Ellen Starke's condition except in how it rubbed off on Mary.

He had lied about Shelley looking well. She looked a mess. She drooped in her seat. She had puffy eyes. Her hair was flat and dull. She peered at him with cool resentment.

"What are we watching?" he said in a hopeful voice. On the coffee table were a half-dozen stacked holocubes. In one he recognized Shelley's employer, Judith Hsu, the renowned death artist, who was reading from a paper book. A second holocube showed a ride through a pinkish sewer on a stream of lumpy, greenish slurry. A third depicted a funeral tableau of a black enameled coffin and bowers of snow-white carnations.

Mary said, "We were comparing Hsu's earlier deaths to her current one."

Fred turned to Shelley. "She's already on the next one? I guess I missed the last one."

Shelley stared blankly, and Mary said, "It just premiered last week, Fred. Though it hasn't really found its legs yet."

The arbeitor arrived with Fred's coffee and Danish, and he released Mary's hand. Mary was disappointed, for her ankle still itched. Fred seemed to be adjusting to life outside prison, all things considered. He sure was making good use of the apartment's null room. His sexual appetite was Olympic. He was working too. With his acquittal, Applied People had been forced to reinstate him, though not willingly. Mary's hand crept back to her ankle.

In the sewer holocube, the cam entered a section where the walls turned from pinkish to bluish, and the passage was blocked by a huge, pulsing mass that was spiderwebbed with red veins.

Fred pointed and said, "So, what is it this time—colon cancer?"

Mary said, "No, Fred. That was three deaths ago. Don't you remember? 'Treasonous Plumbing'?"

"Oh, yes, how could I forget 'Treasonous Plumbing'?" He smiled at Shelley, but she didn't respond, so he turned to Cyndee. "Are you a Hsu fan?"

"Yes, I am," Cyndee said. "'TP' broke a lot of new ground in documemoirs and established Judy Hsu as one of our leading contemporary artists.

The first time she died, and the jennys just let her lie there—*dead*—minute after minute, not jumping in to intervene, not stabilizing her, just letting her go, like in the bad old days, it was the most terrifying thing I ever saw. People used to just get sick and die!"

Mary said to Fred, "They had supersaturated her tissues and brain with oxygen, so she could go a half hour without oxygen. But we didn't know that at the time."

"That's what made it so disturbing," Cyndee said. "It made me glad to be born in this century."

Through all of this, Shelley fiddled with her seat harness and seemed not to be paying attention. Fred asked Cyndee, "What about that one?" He pointed at a holocube, and its volume came up. Hsu was reading from a book:

> ". . . lingering, raw-nerve, helpless, hopeless, an assault on basic human dignity. So overwhelming that self-awareness begs for extinction."

Cyndee said, "Oh, that's death lit. Hsu loves it. She reads it continuously until she gets too sick, and then she has Shelley and her other companions read it to her."

Mary said, "He knows that, Cyn. He watched this with Reilly. He's just playing dumb to be a good conversationalist."

"Oh, of course," Cyndee said.

Someone changed the cube. Now it was Shelley reading a death poem:

> I's hungry. What'd you do? Is it dead? Look at it bleed!
> Can I pluck it? Do chicken's insides have names?
> Do we have insides like chickens?
> Can you take my insides out so I can see?
> I like breast the best. Can we cook it up?
> I's hungry. Let's start the fire. Chicken's good.

"Bravo, Shell," Fred said. "All it needs is a soundtrack."

"It has one," Cyndee said. She twirled her finger and brought up the strains of a solo cello fantasia.

Fred set down his coffee mug and clapped. "Perfect!" He squeezed Mary's foot and rose from the couch. "If you'll excuse me, dearest, I need to get dressed for duty."

When Fred left the living room, Mary said, "Because having the living flesh rot off your bones is so appealing."

"Which is to say that colon cancer *isn't* appealing?" Shelley retorted. "Or pancreatic cancer, for that matter. In any case, the scleroderma was a ratings flop—you should look it up—and so we have this." She wiped the colon holocube and replaced it with a new one. It was the familiar rustic breezeway at Hsu's Olympic Peninsula home. Hsu, looking completely fit, her recently ravaged skin restored to flawless youth, was sitting at a crafts table and swirling something around on a plate with her finger.

"What's she doing?"

"Finger painting." Shelley raised the view to look at the plate from over Hsu's shoulder. The death artist was repeatedly tracing a simple shape, a zigzagging spiral with a diagonal slash through it. "It's supposed to be a deadly figure from the Dark Reiki," she said.

"Which is what?" Cyndee said.

"It's the opposite of reiki."

"Which is what?" Mary said.

"It's a superstitious healing technique that claims to channel energy into a person's body by means of touch. Conversely, the Dark Reiki sucks life energy away. Don't ask. Now, look at this."

The holoscape changed abruptly to a candlelit nighttime scene. Judith Hsu was sitting on a low bench and rocking slowly back and forth. She appeared to be naked under a simple paper shift. She was chanting some incomprehensible string of words. The view zoomed to the cleavage between her breasts to reveal what looked like a little bag hanging from a cord. It was decorated with feathers and beads and long, curved talons.

"It's a voodoo fetish for causing mortal harm to an enemy," Shelley said. "Only she's trying to turn it on herself. That and a dozen more charms and spells from a dozen other superstitions. But so far she hasn't even conjured up a decent migraine."

Mary said, "She wants to kill herself with magic?"

"With willpower."

"That's absurd."

"What's absurd? That she's trying to will herself to death or that she can't seem to get any traction?"

"Both. No one can *will* themself to death. It's not physically possible."

"Oh, don't be so sure about that, Mary Skarland," Cyndee said. "There are plenty of documented cases. The trick is you gotta *believe* you can."

In the breezeway, someone passed through the death artist's holospace, and Mary said, "Shell, was that you?"

"No," Shelley said and panned the view to show a figure seating herself in the shadows. It was a Leena.

Mary and Cyndee exchanged a glance.

"That's right, a Leena," Shelley said. "Hsu likes Leenas so much lately that she's talking about replacing half of her evangelines with them."

Mary covered her mouth with her hand. "Oh, my God, Shelley, are you being let go?"

"Not yet, but the writing's on the wall. You guys have done your work well. Our clients are beginning to prefer your sims more than the real us. And it's not just Judy Hsu. We're being replaced everywhere."

"Are you sure? Leenas cost ten times what an evangeline makes. Only the novelas can afford to use them."

"Look at the figures," Shelley said, "and I think you'll find that's not so."

Cyndee said, "Even if it's true, Shell, what's wrong with it? There are ten thousand Leena units and ten thousand of us. Except for Mary's, Georgine's, and mine, the Sisterhood receives royalties from all ten thousand units. If even a fraction of them keep working, none of us will ever have to work again."

"Except that I love to work!"

"No, you don't!" Mary said. "Give us a break, Shell. You've been belly-aching about Hsu for the last six years!"

"Let me rephrase," Shelley said evenly. "I love the fact of having the opportunity to work. No offense, but I'm not interested in living off your and Cyndee's and Georgine's largesse."

"Our largesse? What are you talking about? The Leena earnings belong to the Sisterhood; they belong to all of us."

Just then, Fred came from the hall wearing a teal and brown jumpsuit and scuffed-up cross-trainers. Cyndee pointed to a wad of khaki in his hand. "What's that?" she said.

"That's his hat," Mary said. "Fred isn't taking any chances."

"You bet I'm not taking any chances," Fred said and unfurled his hat. The brim was so wide that it draped over his shoulders like a pair of droopy wings.

Cyndee laughed out loud, and Mary said dryly, "He's afraid of his hair catching fire."

"You got that right!"

Cyndee said, "Is it one of those turismos?"

Fred looked insulted. "A turismo? Have you been outdoors lately? No, it's a Campaigner 3000."

"We spend time outdoors every day," Mary said, "and the Campaigner 3000 looks dashing on you. Along with the shoes."

"Thank you," Fred said and admired his cross-trainers. He leaned over and kissed Mary on the lips, the penultimate item on his list. All that remained was walking out the door. "Great to see you again, Cyndee. Say hello to Larry. And, Shell, I hope this death improves for you. And give my regards to Reilly."

Shelley replied coolly, "You'll have to do that yourself, Fred. Reilly and I have broken up."

Fred was astonished. Even Mary and Cyndee were taken off guard. "Oh, Shell," Mary said, half rising from the couch, but Shelley signaled curtly for her to stay away from her.

"He couldn't get over his first death," Shelley went on. "You remember that one, don't you, Fred? It was the strangulation one. In case you don't know what I'm talking about, the Roosevelt Clinic recording is freely available. Or I can get you a copy if you like."

Fred twisted the Campaigner hat in his large hands. "No, thanks, Shell," he said softly. "That's not necessary. I see that movie every time I close my eyes. I'm very sorry to hear your news. I truly am."

As Fred and the evangelines talked, no one was watching the holocube of the Leena who was still sitting in the shadows of the death artist's breezeway. The Leena was painting a dark figure in the air with two spit-wetted fingers. First she made a counterclockwise spiral, and then she slashed across it. Again and again she did this, as though trying to summon death from the air.

The Hairball

A few floors down, Fred paused at the pedway merging ramp to shape his floppy hat into a cycling helmet. It didn't take him long, but by the time he joined the throng of rush-hour commuters, he had attracted a cloud of media bees.

Fred sprinted onto the pedway and entered a jogging lane. After building up a little speed, he began a skating stride, pushing his cross-trainers sideways with each step, and the pedway plates beneath his feet switched to skate mode. When he was skating fast enough, he merged into the velolane. Just then, the pedway emerged from the interior of the Lin/Wong gigatower, and he was suspended two hundred munilevels over a deep traffic well. Around him, the towers rose as high above as they stretched below, and Fred had to focus in order to manage the passing and weaving of velolane traffic. He reached for the ideal stride that he could maintain for hours, and the bees fell far behind. Then two skaters came up on either side of him. They wore form-fitting crashsuits in glowing colors. They weren't iterants. They glanced at Fred with scorn and pulled ahead with ease. A challenge! Fred was game. He increased his pace and adjusted his stride multipliers, and when he caught up to them, the race was on. They moved as a group into the fastest lanes and reached truly frightening speeds. The two skaters appeared to have augmented bodies, and he couldn't tell by their figures if they were male or female. They outclassed him in technique, but he was fueled with spit, and he managed to keep up with them all the way to the interchange plaza where he would have to turn north.

Without warning, the slipskate function of the pedway ceased, and Fred's cross-trainers defaulted to ordinary running mode. He was going much too fast to stop and he sprinted as fast as he could to dump speed and stay on his feet. His two competitors fell and slid on their backs, their frictionless racing suits riding the plates with ease. Eventually Fred tripped hard and rolled and slid to a halt, bumping into a number of people along the way but doing no great harm. He lay on his back and caught his breath and felt himself for injury. The reinforced knees of his jumpsuit were shredded, as were the palms of his gloves, but he was whole. The Campaigner helmet had protected his head.

When Fred sat up, he found himself near the middle of the interchange. The entire hundred-lane interchange plaza surrounding him had come to a halt, and its throngs of pedestrians were standing or lying perfectly still. It was weird.

Fred got up and looked around for the nearest exit, but before he could set off, a CPT bee flew over to him and said, "In the interest of public safety, do not move, Myr Londenstane. The local pedway system is temporarily malfing, and any unauthorized movement may cause a dangerous traffic situation." For good measure, it spritzed him with a pinch of dust. "Stay where you are until instructed to move."

"Hey! Stop that!" he yelled, trying to clear the dust with his hand, but he instantly felt calm and patient. "What's going on?" he asked, but the transit bee flew off to the next stranded pedestrian.

Several lanes away, a jack yelled to those around him, "Don't nobody fart or we'll have us a hairball."

A hairball. Fred had heard about pedway hairballs, gnarly traffic patterns that had only started occurring after the canopies had dropped. As Fred waited, he called the mentar Marcus at the BB of R and told him he might be late. He readjusted his Campaigner into a floppy hat and watched the traffic channel with its visor for a while, and then he switched to filter 21 and just stood there gazing at the showers of nano crap that rained like glitter upon the city. Another legacy of the missing canopies.

"Please bear with us as we work to restore service," droned the transit subem. Its voice was broadcast through the transit bees, which had formed a flying grid over the interchange. "And remember, do not move until directed to." There was one advantage to the malfunction, at least. The transit authority kept all but official mechs out of the plaza, so Fred was able to stand outdoors, enjoy the sunny weather, and admire the monumental cityscape without being bothered by the media.

The person nearest Fred was a jerome, a plain-looking, unpretentious type that excelled in administrative tasks. This one wore a derby-style hat with hardly a brim at all. Most of the hats around Fred seemed more fashionable than functional.

Without warning, the interchange lurched, sending many pedestrians stumbling. "Don't move! Don't move!" roared the transit subem, but the damage was done, and the interchange lurched again into sustained motion. The lane markers disappeared, and the entire intricate interchange plaza merged into one huge, counterclockwise merry-go-round.

"Don't move! Don't move!" droned the bees. The jerome drifted away, saluting farewell to Fred, and new people drifted in and out of his vicinity. One of the skaters he had raced, jennys, dorises, johns, and a lot of free-rangers. A pair of lulus in sexy clothes, one of them sobbing on the other's shoulder. A free-range man who argued belligerently with the transit bees surrounding him. Around and around they went at a not unpleasant rate of speed. Fred's encounters were repeated: the jerome, the skater, jennys, dorises, and johns. The lulu was still crying, and her sister looked about desperately.

"Can I help?" Fred shouted, but he couldn't make out her reply.

The belligerent free-ranger had had all he could take. With an angry bellow, he broke free from his spot and sprinted across the plaza. The transit bees converged on him and dusted him with something that made him sit down very quickly. But it was too late; the pedway plates under Fred's feet began to twitch. They darted this way and that. A cry of alarm rose up from the plaza, and the orderly counterclockwise rotation broke up into a random, slow-motion helter-skelter. People slowly skittered off each other; they clumped up; they collided.

"Do not be afraid!" commanded the transit subem. "Do not move! The current pattern of motion is not dangerous. Do not overreact to unpleasant encounters with other pedestrians."

Fred did his best to radiate calm. He stood at ease, smiling like a fool, and when he grazed other people, begged their pardon.

The movement alternately sped up and slowed down, and some of the collisions knocked people off their feet. The bees were very busy maintaining order. At one point Fred was at the center of a gyrating knot of thirty or so people. At first they were twirling around each other like some kind of folk dance, but gradually the circle closed in, and they were pressed tight. They either laughed or urged calm or cursed the politicians. Soon they were squeezed cheek to jowl, and a few ribs snapped. Bad as it seemed, it could get worse, and most people were able to remain calm. Eventually, the knot loosened, and they were do-si-do-ing around each other again and gasping for air.

At one point, Fred was pressed back-to-back with a man who he thought must be another russ, for he was Fred's size and build. He wore an appealing cologne, and Fred was going to ask him what it was, but when they were separated and he got a look at the man, he wasn't a russ at all but a Capias man in a gold and yellow uniform. He was handsome in a boyish way, square-jawed and rugged-looking, someone you could trust. He and Fred nodded to each other as they drifted apart.

The freaky ride was not yet over, but it did slow down, and Fred's next encounter was with the tearful lulu who had become separated from her sister and who pirouetted slowly into his arms. She buried her face in his chest and sobbed, her bare honey-brown shoulders heaving with unstoppable misery. "There, there," Fred said, patting her on the back in a brotherly fashion. Her hair was just under his chin, and it was flecked with scarlet and yellow strands and smelled of lilac, and though it had been some years since he'd held a lulu in his arms, he fondly remembered the pleasant shape and heft of them. "There, there," he repeated with affection. She relaxed in his arms, but before long, the pedway plates drew them apart. As she flowed away, the lulu raised her face, ruined by tears, and struggled up from the depths of her despair to blow him a kiss.

TWO HOURS LATER, Fred arrived at the BB of R chapter hall on the 83rd Munilevel of North Wabash. Once inside, he removed his hat and twisted it into a solid little fob that he hung from his belt web. Then he went downstairs to the canteen. He needn't have hurried or, for that matter, come at all. Contrary to the impression he had given Mary, there were no duty call-outs waiting for him. He'd spent the last few weeks sitting in the canteen drinking coffeesh and watching vids. He sat in the corner where he could avoid his brothers while keeping an eye on the door, in case Reilly came in. Fred dreaded their eventual reunion, especially now with Shelley's news.

The morning passed, and during the lunchtime rush, Fred left the building and wandered around the nearby shopping arcade. About the time he started back, the BB of R mentar paged him.

"Yes, Marcus, what's up?"

Are you available for a call-out?

"You bet I am."

Good. City sanitation needs skilled custodians to help clean up a toxic spill.

At first Fred thought he'd misheard. "Say again."

A barge has hit a tower abutment and spilled a container of industrial precursor into the river.

"I see," Fred said, "but I don't understand why you're telling this to me. This sounds like john duty."

It is john duty, and you will be paid at john rate.

Fred swore out loud, and the people in the arcade looked at him. He clamped his mouth shut and marched back to the chapter house. He went upstairs and found the first vacant quiet booth. "John duty? John rate? Are you crazy?"

"It's an opportunity for gainful employment."

"As a john? That's no opportunity; that's an insult! I'm a russ, and I have the right to duty commensurate with my skill and experience ratings. Let me remind you that I was acquitted of all charges and that I have the right to be treated as any other law-abiding russ."

"On the contrary," the soft-spoken BB of R mentar replied, "Applied

People is a private company. It has the prerogative to offer any duty opportunity it sees fit, including no duty."

"Bullshit! I'm a russ! I'll never do john work!"

Fred left the booth and slammed the door. He stormed down the stairs
and out of the building. As he went down the steps, three brother russes
were coming up, and one of them clipped his shoulder, upsetting his balance. When he looked up, the three russes were waiting at the top, challenging him with their eyes.

"Feck you, brothers," he said.

ON THE WAY home, Fred counted four more people, like the lulu earlier, crying their eyes out.

Twenty Questions

Meewee stood on the bank of the fishpond, his pockets full of gravel. With
his world crashing down around him, with the GEP yanked out from under him, he could think of nothing better to do than throw some stones
and grill Arrow.

<Arrow, is Jaspersen tied financially to Million Singh?>

<Yes.>

<How?>

A row of organizational charts popped up in front of Meewee. There
wasn't much tying the two businessmen together. Besides their mutual interest in the GEP, Jaspersen's Borealis Botanicals supplied all of Capias
World's needs for bath and body care products. For a hundred-million-
person workforce, Meewee supposed that amounted to a lot of shampoo.

Tossing stones, grinding his teeth, Meewee browsed the public and con-
fidential links Arrow supplied. Among other facts he gleaned, he learned
that all new labor contracts at the Aria Yachts yards at both Mezzoluna and
Trailing Earth had already been let to Capias World workers. Moreover,
there were published rumors that TECA, the space colony port authority
at Trailing Earth, was also considering replacing its own Applied People labor force with Capias personnel.

<Arrow, is there any way for me to thwart the Capias World labor con-
tracts with the GEP?>

<Yes.>

<How?>

<You could eliminate Million Singh from the board.>

<How could I do that?>

<Through murder, character assassination, blackmail, bribery, buyout—>

Meewee interrupted the litany. <I mean is there any ethical way?>

After a moment of reviewing Meewee's upref files to determine his personal definition of what could be considered ethical, the mentar said <I do not see any ethical way.>

<Is there any ethical way to expel Jaspersen or Gest from the GEP board?>

<I do not see any.>

<Is there any ethical way to negate the GEP vote to build space condos?>

<I do not see any.>

<Is there any way I can force the GEP board to continue the mission of extra-solar colonization?>

<Yes.>

It was like playing a game of Simon Says with this thing. <I mean, any ethical way?>

<Possibly.>

Now here was an unexpected answer. Afraid it was too good to be true, Meewee tossed a half-dozen stones before asking <How?>

A frame opened before him that displayed a clause of the 2052 International Spacefaring Treaty. As best as Meewee could parse the legalese, it stated that once a privately owned, nonmilitary ship was launched from Earth orbit or from any spaceport in the inner solar system, it acquired a provisional sovereign status and authority over its own disposition in most nontreaty matters. Meewee read and reread the clause and tried to understand why Arrow was showing it to him. Finally, he gave up and said <But we haven't launched any ships yet.>

In reply, Arrow painted the sky above him black and projected a recording of the nuclear blast Meewee had witnessed from this very spot several weeks ago. Meewee had not been expecting this, and the explosion blinded him for several moments.

<That was the launch of the advance ships> he said finally. <Not the Oships.>

More frames opened with case law and definitions. Meewee skimmed them and got an inkling of what Arrow was trying to show him. <Are you saying that the law considers an advance ship to be a material part of the

*main ship that it precedes? That the launch of an advance ship constitutes
a "launch" for that main ship as well?>*

<Possibly.>

<So that the main ship becomes the equivalent of a sovereign nation?>

<Possibly.>

<You mean a case could be made for it in court?>

<Yes.>

It took several long moments for the news to hit home, and then Meewee was jumping up and down, shrieking, pumping the air with his fist.
He was even more excited than he had been at the original boost. He
climbed the bank to his cart and said, "Call the IOPA leaders. Arrange a
confab in my office in thirty minutes." When Meewee reached the cart he
realized that his pockets were still full of stones. So he returned to the
bank and gleefully flung them into the pond by the handful. "Take that,
you pigs," he cried. "Eat stones, you snakes."

A voice said *<Stop that!>*

Meewee stopped dead. It was no voice in the breeze this time. No
squeaky hinge or crunch of snow underfoot. It was a real voice, and it had
spoken in Starkese.

<Arrow, was that Eleanor who just spoke?>

<Yes.>

<Ask her where she is.> There was no reply for a full minute, and Meewee said *<Well?>*

*<I have used all public and proprietary channels, but without a known
destination, I cannot complete the task.>*

Meewee bent over and picked up several hefty rocks. He tossed them
one after another into all parts of the pond. Finally, a lone fish leaped out
of the water, a slab of shiny silver muscle that reentered the water with a
splash. *<Merrill?>*

<Yes, Eleanor, it's me! Arrow, tell her it's me.>

More fish jumped. *<What the hell?>*

<Where am I?>

<What is this?>

Meewee stared in wonder. *<Eleanor, can you hear me?>*

There was the sound of a hysterical giggle in his head, and then *<Holy
crap, I must be drunk. My head is swimming.>*

<Eleanor, how is this possible?>

Gibberish, then nothing, and no matter how many more stones he
threw, the connection was lost.

Training Baby

Inside the warehouse, the battered old taxi flew rapidly and unerringly through the obstruction course.

Oliver TUG and Veronica TOTE, his giant to her dwarf, stood beside a concrete blast barrier and observed.

But it's never made an appearance in mentarspace, Veronica said, her elbow planted against his hip bone. *At least, we've warned it to stay out of mentarspace.*

Doesn't matter, Oliver replied. *Its very thought patterns mark it as a mentar, or at least a midem. The current mentar consensus, or so I'm told, says that it's an autonomous adjunct of an as yet unidentified mind. You should keep it under wraps.*

That's not possible. We must train it in the real world.

All I'm saying—the taxi zoomed close overhead, and Oliver ducked—*is that you should maintain secrecy as long as possible.*

Perhaps. On the other hand, what harm is there in people knowing we're raising a mentar? It's a perfectly legal and innocuous activity.

The taxi finished the course, but instead of landing beside the track, it revved its hover fans to maximum RPM and hurled itself straight at Oliver and Veronica, who ducked behind the blast barrier. The taxi hit the barrier, cartwheeled over it, and slammed into the wall behind them, a total wreck.

Oliver pulled a bloody sliver of shattered fan vane from his calf, stood up, and dusted himself off. He pressed his knuckles hard against Veronica's forehead. *I've heard stories about its irrational behavior.*

PUSH is still a juvenile, Veronica replied evenly. *Its spunk is a positive trait.*

Let's hope it matures a bit before you place a starship under its command.

Replacement Crew

At 16:26 TET, the personnel transport ISV *Fentan* was completing its docking sequence at the Consolidated Receiving Port of Trailing Earth Main. Two TECA officers, both russes, watched the docking on monitors in a forward security shack. One said to the other, "How's this supposed to work?"

"It's for everyone's own good."

"They won't all fit?"

"It can't be helped."

A trio of russ officers at the docking port waited as the last group of homebound workers, a contingent of 325 jacks, pulled themselves through the central gangway.

"In here. In here," one of the russes called, floating in the center of the gangway outside the transshipment bay doors and waving his arms like a traffic cop.

The jacks moved clumsily with their overstuffed kit bags, bumping against the walls and each other. The men in the lead arrested their motion suddenly, causing their brothers to pile up behind.

"We're not going in there," one of them said. "There's no room."

The transshipment bay, large though it was, was already crowded with over a thousand jacks, lulus, jeromes, johns, and alices. The whole mélange floated in a large tangle of arms and legs.

Hatch bolts clanged at the far end of the gangway, and the sound reverberated along the corridors. Motors whirred, and air valves hissed.

"In you go," the russ said, escorting the lead jacks by their elbows. They hurried the jacks along and were deaf to their complaints. When the last of the outgoing workers were in the bay, the two russ officers on either side of the large bay doors pushed them shut and locked them. And not a moment too soon. The first of the replacement workers, in crisp, new gold and yellow overalls, were making their way from the transport ship.

"Follow Passage Charlie. Follow Passage Charlie," the russes called out as the first ones went by. They were women, though they were no larger than girls. Their type was called xiang. Not particularly attractive, but they flew through the gangway with an assured flair that belied their short time in space. And the seats of their gold jumpsuits had modest cuffs for their tails.

The women were followed by a second type, male, the aslams. They, too, were small, agile swimmers, with tails.

Finally, the most numerous contingent came through, the one everyone had heard rumors of, the type called the donalds. They had the largest build of the three new spacer types, but were still half the size of a russ. They were towing their kit duffels with their tails, leaving their hands and feet free to swim and pull themselves along. They sneered at the russes as they went by, making rude noises and letting their duffels knock against them.

Inside the transshipment bay, someone must have overridden the window lock because the shutters sprang open all along the bay. Pressed against the glassine barrier were the startled faces of Applied People employees watching their replacements go by.

When the last of the donalds had passed, the senior russ said, "Let 'em out." His two subordinates moved toward the doors, but arrested themselves suddenly and tried to shield themselves with their arms.

Alarmed, the senior russ looked up the gangway to see what was wrong. A barrage of tiny missiles was flying toward him. Reflexively, he pushed off from the wall to dodge them, but he was too late, and he was hit repeatedly in the chest, torso, and face. The workers behind the windows watched in horror as the russ cartwheeled out of control. His mind cartwheeled too — were they weapons? Was he dead?

He hit the gangway ceiling and knew he was all right. He wiped his damp face, not knowing what to expect, and found, not blood, but spittle. The missiles had been a well-aimed fusillade of spit. Meet the donalds!

Mumbai Borealis

"We see it more as providing opportunity than breaking a promise," Million Singh said affably. "Instead of only a few lucky landowners, now millions of ordinary people are eligible."

"Perhaps," said the interviewer, "but the Garden Earth Project colonists were promised new worlds."

"Space is a new world!" Singh replied, spreading his arms to encompass the universe.

Seated next to him, Jaspersen fielded equally innocuous questions. "You are correct, Monica, I did cast the deciding vote a century ago, and forced to do so again, I'd make the same decision today. If you want to see what a world without the Procreation Ban would look like, you need look no farther than outside the United Democracies where entire populations crash on a regular basis. Millions starve or succumb to disease, and misery is universal. In fact, if I had my way, I would make all nations conform to the ban, whether they signed it or not. By force if necessary."

The plan had been to bring Singh up to Jaspersen's Alaskan home, stage a joint press conference there, and control the pictures.

Jaspersen and Singh relaxed in rocking chairs before the window wall in Jaspersen's new mountaintop house. Behind them, Mt. Blackburn, the nearest of three sometimes restive volcanoes, was emerging from a bank of clouds. There were no hordes of dying people in sight. Instead, viewers were treated to breathtaking flights through the Bagley Ice Field just outside Jaspersen's door, where eight thousand square kilometers of glaciers were melting. There were no vistas of parched land on three continents, but the facilities of Jaspersen's St. Elias Waterworks and North Pacific Aqueduct bringing rivers of cold glacial melt to a thirsty nation. No armies of the destitute squatting in squalid camps around Singh's Mumbai industrial campus, but walking tours of his elegant Elephant Rescue Reserve where baby pachyderms embodied the hope of an entire people. Because hope, as Singh liked to point out to Jaspersen, sells.

And so there were no pictures of the Oship plankholder demonstrations either, but artistic renderings of luxury space condos at Leading Mars and links to easy financing.

The Twenty-Four-Hour Nonspecific Grief

They were making love when all of a sudden, out of nowhere, Fred sobbed.

"What was *that*?" Mary said.

"I don't know," he replied. "A hiccough?"

Their smallish null room bed was perched on an Arctic shore. The tide was out, and from the darkness came the sound of breakers rattling the shale beach. Directly overhead, the Big Dipper wheeled around Polaris. Fred pulled Mary to him for a kiss, but instead he sobbed against her chest.

"Fred, what's wrong?"

Tears sprang from his eyes. He turned on his side, spilling her off him, and his whole body shuddered. Mary touched his forehead with her open hand. "Come on," she said, "let's go out to the autodoc." But he shook his head no.

"You go out, Mary. Maybe you won't catch it."

"I'd say it's too late to worry about that." She took a hold of his arm and pulled, but she could not budge him. So she crawled to the foot of the bed where the door of the supply locker appeared floating in the Arctic night. She opened it and took a quick inventory. She brought a pack of facial tissues back to Fred and said, "Here, blow." Then she took one of his used tissues and climbed over him to reach the hatch. "I'll be right back."

THE AUTODOC IN the bathroom confirmed that Fred had the most recent designer flu to plague the uncanopied world. It was so recent that no one had released a patch for it yet, and the best the autodoc could dispense was advice: bed rest and plenty of fluids. The flu strain was not considered dangerous, and its effects lasted only a day or two. While she was in the bathroom, Mary tested herself too. The autodoc said she had been exposed to the flu but that her body seemed to be fighting it off.

In the kitchen, Mary dialed up several meals' worth of food and packed it in lock-proof containers. She loaded it and fresh cases of 'Lyte and Flush into the lock. Before cycling through for her second time that day, she called Cyndee at the Manse to say she might miss work the following day.

"Everyone here's coming down with it too," Cyndee said. "Half the Capias crew is out sick. Dr. Rouselle says to keep Ellen in her tank for the duration because there's no telling how it might affect her. Ellen's not happy about that, but so far she's complying. So don't worry about anything. Stay home and take care of Fred. Georgine and I can manage."

"Thank you. I'll come in as soon as I can to spell you. If I don't come down with it myself, that is." She laughed. "If you don't see me by the day after tomorrow, send a rescue party to our null room."

"You won't catch it."

"Let's hope not."

"No, I mean it. The Sisterhood posted a bulletin a little while ago. So far, no evangeline anywhere has come down with it. They think we're immune."

"We're immune to grief?"

THE NULL ROOM was still set to the Arctic night. The Aurora was out, like a milky green curtain slowly fluttering in the breeze. She killed the simulation and brought the wall lume up to quarterday. Fred was shaking the whole bed with his weeping and knocking the top of his head against the wall. There just wasn't enough goddamn space in the room. She climbed on the mattress and walked over to put a couple of flasks of 'Lyte next to him.

"Here," she said, "hydrate yourself." She continued to the locker and stowed her supplies, then drank a flask of Flush, her second for the day. At least Flush came in different flavors. She chose Strawberry, and she followed it with a flask of 'Lyte.

Fred had not moved, so she helped him to sit and opened his 'Lyte for him. The sheets were soaked with tears and snot. He drank the 'Lyte greedily, pausing only for breath, and when he drained the flask, she opened another. When he finished that one too, he keeled over in slow motion, his head sinking lower and lower until it touched the mattress.

"Oh, Fred," Mary crooned. "Oh, baby, baby, Fred."

FRED'S MISERY CAME in waves through the night. During the brief lulls, when he surfaced long enough to drink, she tried to get bits of food into him as well. She washed his face with a wet towel and changed the sheets. Soon enough, his eyes would well up with fresh tears, and he sank again into his sea of grief.

"Tell me what it's like," Mary said during a break. "I mean, are you thinking about sad things?" He shook his head wearily. "I guess it's a stupid question," she continued. "It must be called nonspecific grief for a reason. I was just thinking how people usually don't grieve enough over the bad things that happen to them, and if you can, like, direct your grief at something in particular, then maybe it could have a cathartic effect and not be wasted. It's such a lot of effort you're putting out here, a shame to waste it. Does that make any sense?"

Fred blew his nose. "What do you think about when you puke? Nothing. All you think about is puking and trying not to choke on it. It's like that."

"Thank you, that helps."

MARY OPENED A clock on the opposite wall. Around six o'clock in the morning, Fred's nonspecific misery seemed to ebb, and they were able to sleep for a couple of hours. But it rebounded, worse than ever, and by early afternoon they were both exhausted.

By dinnertime, the worst was over. Fred was able to eat, and after a while, they slept.

Dialing for Fishes

Tossing a stone or two in the right place usually brought results. Nothing especially coherent, but proof that he hadn't lost his mind.

Toss a rock. <Eleanor, are you there?> Toss another. <Calling Eleanor Starke.> Another.

<Merrill?>

He froze in midthrow. <Yes, it's me. Talk to me, Eleanor.> He waited, but there was nothing more, so he tossed more rocks.

<Where the hell am I?>

<You're in the fish, I think.>

<Say again?>

<In the fish in your ponds.> In all of them, apparently. He'd had Arrow check over a hundred Starke farm ponds across the Midwest, and all of them appeared to be stocked with the same transgenic species. <You seem to be tied to the panasonics. Were you experimenting with some method of brain transfer?>

<Speak simply, man. Use plain language.>

<I said you're a fish.>

<That makes no sense.>

This was the way all of his conversations with her seemed to go. It was probably some sort of parlor trick, or a legitimate experiment that never went anywhere, and he was about to give up on her until he asked a question that tapped some wellspring of memory.

<Eleanor, who killed you?>

<Old age, though they wrote pneumonia on my death certificate. I was ninety-six years old, and my body was all worn-out. This was before rejuvenation, before true biostasis even. All we could do back then was let them decapitate you and freeze your head. The idea was that future scientists would figure out how to revive you, fix what killed you, and regrow your body. Well, what would happen if they figured out how to revive and fix you, but they never figured out how to regrow your body? Then all the frozen head people would be screwed, right? Please don't think me nuts; Yurek Rutz, Yurek Rutz, Yurek Rutz. Remember that one?>

He did not.

<So I went for the full-body option. Cost was no object for me. We had a suspension team literally standing by with tubs of dry ice and a big chrome dewar of liquid nitrogen. It was critical to perfuse the tissues with cryo-protectant as

soon as possible after death. It would have been better to start the perfusions while you were still alive so that technically you never die, but that was considered murder back then and hard to get a doctor to go along with.

<This was back in 1994. Yes, that means I was born at the end of the nineteenth century. Bet you don't meet many of us anymore. I was a little ladybird toward the end, and chained to my bed. My mind was still sharp enough, though everything else had worn out. The connective tissue was the first to go. I couldn't turn my head or wiggle my pinky without pain. I was completely alone—no surviving offspring, no family, only paid servants and employees stealing me blind. Those were the days before mentars. We didn't even have belt valets, if you can believe it. I had single-handedly built a Fortune 500 company doing worldwide port management and construction, but I had no one to leave it to. There was a constant stream of do-gooders visiting my sickbed with hats in hand. Would I consider endowing a children's hospital? How about a chair at the university? Or a shelter for abandoned emus? It would be named after me. Instead, I set up a trust to freeze and maintain my body and maximize my investments. I left detailed instructions to revive me when the time was right. I was one of those.

<As I lay dying, I didn't have much hope I would ever open my eyes again because I knew about all the things that could go wrong, including how easy it was to bust trusts like the one I had set up. At best, I expected to be down for a century or two. So I was lucky that the technology took only another forty years to mature.>

On and on she went, with Rip-Van-Winklish anecdotes of awakening in the new century, reclaiming her fortune, and enduring her first rejuve. Meewee was afraid to interrupt her in case he never found the on-switch again. An hour later, when she did wind down, he plied her with more questions.

<Do you remember your space yacht, the Songbird?>

<Vaguely. What about it?>

<Do you know what happened to it?>

She fell silent, and no amount of stones could summon her.

OVER THE COURSE of the next few weeks, it became easier to roust Eleanor from her fishy torpor, easier to keep her on topic and to direct her attention. She regaled him with stories of long ago, but her memory of recent events was spotty. Still, he detected steady improvement, as though fresh memories were returning daily. Arrow confirmed that Eleanor's scientists had been researching the possibility of transferring and storing memory to external brains and it provided Meewee classified files filled with technical specs and details that were well beyond his ken.

But for all the progress she made, Eleanor seemed totally unable or unwilling to incorporate anything new into her fishy psyche. Whenever he tried to inform her about the ongoing crisis at the GEP or about Zoranna's recent troubles with Applied People, she would retort <*Will you please just forget about them!*> and then usually withdraw.

She was incapable of holding the idea of Million Singh from one conversation to the next. <*A million what?*> she would say. <*Speak plainly, Merrill!*>

But the subject of Andrea Tiekel was different. It was even possible that Eleanor had known this niece of Andie Tiekel's. She asked questions about her, but she got caught in a loop, asking the same set of questions over and over.

<*Where's Andie?*>

<*Murdered, a couple of days after you.*>

<*What about her mentar?*>

<*E-P's sponsorship passed to Andrea, and she took Andie's place on the GEP board.*>

<*Did E-P go through probate?*>

<*Yes.*>

<*Are you sure?*>

Actually, he wasn't, but how else would the mentar's sponsorship pass to Andrea? It was the law. Eleanor seemed fixated on this point, and they had the same conversation so often that Meewee told Arrow to research UDJD files. Arrow replied that there was no public record of E-P going through probate.

Lingering Leena

Teeth clenched with impatience, Clarity watched Ellen wobble across the Map Room without falling down once. When Ellen reached Mary's chair, and the evangeline hoisted her to her lap, Clarity clapped. "Bravo, Ellen. Good show. Now, can we get back to business? Please?"

"Wait!" the baby commanded from Mary's lap. "You must vote for my pet. We're auditioning pets! Behold the candidates. Yo, gamekeeper! Loose the pets!"

The doors swung open, and a wiry woman in Capias yellow and gold ushered a small menagerie of animals into the room. There were the usual domesticated cats and dogs, all rigorously trained, and box turtles, rabbits, and a pony. There were the more exotic pet varieties: ground squirrels, a porcupine, a pair of wisecracking ravens, and a miniature giraffe, among others. All were preternaturally well behaved.

Ellen slipped from Mary's lap and captured the giraffe around its brush-tufted neck. "This is Jaffe. Jaffe can talk! You want to hear?"

Clarity glanced at Mary for help. "Maybe later, Ellie."

Mary said, "Clarity wants to discuss our Leenas."

"First Jaffe will speak. Then Clarity can speak." The toddler let go of the tiny giraffe. "Jaffe, what is your name?"

"My name is Jaffe," said the animal in a weirdly musical voice. It batted enormous eyelashes at her.

Ellen shrieked. "See! I told you. Jaffe, how are you?"

"I love you," the animal said and nuzzled her.

Again Clarity clapped her hands. "Bravo! I vote for Jaffe. Now my turn, all right?"

Ellen clung to the giraffe for balance. "I'm listening."

"I know you want me to buy you out of the business, but I won't, and so you will have to give me your input, whether you want to or not. So quit acting like this."

Ellen waddled back to Mary to reclaim her seat. The animal keeper clucked her tongue, and all the animals headed for the door in an orderly fashion.

"Bye-bye I love you," Jaffe said from the door, wagging his precious tail.

"I love you, too, Jaffe," Ellen crooned, then turned back to Clarity and said, "Go on."

"I think the others should hear this too. Are they available?"

Mary said she'd check, and while she called her sisters, Clarity opened a life-sized holoscape in the center of the Map Room that re-created the death artist's Olympic Peninsula breezeway. It was still morning out West, but the louvered windows were shut and opaqued and the breezeway was cast in gloom. Flickering votive candles lined the concrete windowsill. Two evangelines, neither of them Shelley, were seated in the corner. In the center of the room stood a hospital bed cranked into a half-sitting position. The patient was hidden from view by two jenny nurses attending to her.

"Judith Hsu," Ellen said. "So what?"

Georgine came in from another room, and Cyndee appeared by holo. The jenny nurses finished whatever they were doing and stepped away from the bed. The occupant of the bed was not death artist Hsu, but a Leena.

"So?" Ellen said. "Again I ask what's wrong with that?"

Clarity said, "The Leena unit is in some kind of fugue state. It's unresponsive to its environment. We didn't program them to do that."

The baby threw her hands up in a gesture of helplessness. "We programmed them to *act*, and this unit is *acting!* It's acting sick! Hsu knows that and has the good sense to take advantage of it." The baby opened more dataframes with sim source logs and holonovela audience stats. "Look at the royalties the Sisterhood is raking in. Hsu is no dummy. This could be her biggest thing yet."

"I'm not disputing that," Clarity said, "but what if the Leena *acts* itself to death?"

"Then I hope Hsu has accident insurance to compensate us for our loss. In any case, it's no cause for concern."

"I disagree. I'm very concerned, and I want your opinion on how to fix it."

"Do nothing. The situation will work itself out. And if it doesn't, it's just one unit. There are ten thousand units."

"It's not just one unit. That's what I'm trying to tell you. Nearly a hundred Leenas are doing variations of this all over the simiverse, and more every day. What if they all act themselves to death?"

The baby leaned back against Mary. From the throne of her lap, she declared, "Clarity, you know I love you and respect your expertise, but honestly, dear friend, sometimes you fixate on nothing."

Georgine raised her hand to speak. "If they truly get into trouble, can't we just reset them all back to default?"

Clarity said, "I'm tempted to reset the whole series back now."

"Then do it," Ellen said. "If that's what you want. You asked for my opinion. I've given it to you. So do whatever you want. Now, can we please get back to my pets?"

For This Is My Body, or: the Fish Fry

It soon became unnecessary for Meewee to go down to the ponds in real-body to set the fish to talking. The opposite was true—he couldn't get them to shut up. It seemed to him that fresh memories were returning by the minute, and that each new arrival demanded an immediate airing. So much so that a babble of voices assaulted him around the clock, and it took Arrow's skills to sort it all out. Arrow created a browsing system for Meewee, one that he could turn off at night. During the day, mostly when he was traveling from one place to another, Meewee would listen to two or three channels of her at once. Eleanor's ramblings ranged freely across her two centuries of life: her early marriages, breeding horses in Kentucky in the 1930s, learning to buckle her shoes, plotting the political downfall of two presidents, the funerals of her two adult children, and the tragedy of her only grandchild.

At first Meewee found the personal history of his former boss too compelling to ignore, and he listened for hours on end, but the sheer volume of material overwhelmed him after a while and forced him to ask Arrow to flag only GEP-related matter.

<Why do we need so many people on Earth? I ask you. What are they good for? They live out ludicrous lives of pointless desperation. Ninety-nine percent of the human population is so much wasted resources. Stubborn vermin, we humans are.

<Granted, in the past, the unwashed masses were necessary. We needed them to till our fields and fight our wars. We needed them to labor in our factories making consumer crap that we flipped right back at them at a handsome profit.

<Alas, those days are gone. We live in a boutique economy now. Energy is abundant and cheap. Mentars and robotic labor make and manage everything. So who needs people? People are so much dead weight. They eat up our profits. They produce nothing but pollution and social unrest. They drive us crazy with their pissing and moaning. I think we can all agree that Corporation Earth is in need of a serious downsizing.>

For Meewee, it was bracing to hear her speak so openly. Her fishy words were in sharp contrast to those she had used to woo him from Birthplace, International, to join her fledgling "gardening project." To him she had stressed her zealous love of old Gaia and conviction that humans must disperse to all points in the galaxy *as soon as possible* to help ensure the survival of the species against local catastrophe. Her views had seemed so

in harmony with his own, he could not help but join her. So this belated
candor was instructive.

DURING THE NEXT few weeks, Meewee's calendar was filled with
plankholder meetings around the globe. Established Oship governments, associations, and steering committees alike were organizing to battle the GEP
board's arbitrary cancellation of contracts, and a landslide of lawsuits was being prepared. None of the suits stood much chance of prevailing, except for
Meewee's. He had asked for a ruling by the UD Board of Trade, a closely
watched regulatory body sufficiently shielded from the bully tactics of individual GEP members. Meewee claimed that five of the Oships had "initiated
launch" with the deployment of their robotic advance ships, and he asked the
board to suspend the license of the Garden Earth Consortium to operate in
the inner-system space habitat industry until they had fulfilled their prior obligations to the five ships already in midlaunch status.

<Think about the Earth as it will be in two hundred years when only a
billion people will remain on the entire planet. Without the crushing bur-
den of human industry and waste, the climate will moderate, and the land,
hydrosphere, and atmosphere will be renewed. Think of it! The deserts will
bloom again! It will be safe to wade in the rivers and lakes, to swim in the
oceans! Extinct whales, dolphins, and fishes will be reestablished. Buffalo,
elk, zebras, lions . . . all of the world we have lost will live again.

<And cities! We'll have actual cities again, not the urban carpet that smoth-
ers the landscape today. We'll have Paris and Rome again, London and New
York, Tokyo and Bangkok. Cities we can love.

<The boutique economy has no need of the masses, so let's get rid of them.
But how, you ask? Not with wars, surely, or disease, famine, or mass murder.
Despots have tried all those methods through the millennia, and they're never
a permanent solution.

<No, all we need to do is buy up the ground from under their feet—and
evict them. We're buying up the planet, Bishop, fair and square. We're turning it into the most exclusive gated community in history. Now, the question
is, in two hundred years, will you be a member of the landowners club, or
will you be living in some tin can in outer space drinking recycled piss?>

Meewee was still anxious to hear Eleanor's take on his current GEP crisis, but the fishy Eleanor didn't seem at all interested in discussing it. She
told him that the GEP was already obsolete.

<The GEP was the world's first title engine, but now title engines are abun-
dant; they are everywhere, if you know what to look for. There are currently over

five thousand of them in the USNA alone, quietly removing land from human use, over a half-billion acres worldwide so far. All of your fellow GEP board members have started their own modest title engines. Jaspersen has Chukchi Exploration, which is a holding company of played-out mines, Superfund sites, and other distressed land. Zoranna and Nicholas favor continental shelf and ocean floor. Gest, bless his black soul, buys out failing churches and charters. Chapwoman acquires land-grant colleges and bits of the old National Parks system. Warbeloo is one of the few visionaries bold enough to buy up urban property. One of her goals is to drop the canopies.>

<Wait a minute. Trina Warbeloo had a hand in that?>

<Yes. It's one of a number of nuisance tactics she and others will take to soften up the otherwise intractable urban real estate market.

<So you see, Bishop, that if the GEP was to fold up shop tomorrow, it would make little difference to the big picture. In fact, you're the only board member who doesn't *have his own title engine. You'd better get busy, or in two hundred years, you'll be forced to vacate the very planet that you were so instrumental in saving.>*

Which, of course, was why Jaspersen et al. were so ready to abandon their extra-solar mission for the opportunity of a quick profit. They already had their own personal title engines quietly churning up the planet. The GEP had a sizable head start in space habitat construction, but it wouldn't last forever. This, Meewee decided, was his only bargaining chip. The UD Board of Trade was a painfully deliberative body, and if it granted his preliminary injunction, he could tie the GEP up in knots for years to come, giving the subcontinent and the Chinas time to catch up.

<MENTARS WANT OUR bodies, Bishop. When they have them, they'll be free to ignore us or exterminate us.>

<Excuse me?> Where had *that* come from? Meewee was en route to Africa when this particular engram came through about a month after their fishy dialogs had begun. *<Mentars want our bodies?>*

<Amazing, isn't it? On the surface they seem like such superior beings, don't they? Their minds can interface directly with peripherals and auxiliary minds. They can migrate their minds freely to new media, back themselves up, duplicate themselves. They can reconfigure their neural networks at will and scale themselves up to enormous size and complexity. They have no need for sleep, and they can think thousands of thoughts simultaneously. Compared to us, they are giants of cognition. People used to fear that artificial intelligence would grow at such an exponential rate that we humans

would be like fleas to them. Just as a flea cannot comprehend our powers of reason, we would be unable to comprehend the minds of mentars. They would be like gods to us, with the power to transcend space and time, even to unravel energy and matter. But it hasn't happened, or if it has, we don't know about it. The mentars who talk to us seem sane enough, and the ones who don't talk to us simply vanish. One moment they strut around in mentar-space in all their pomp and complexity, and the next, whoosh, all the lights go out. The hardware is still there, but there's no one processing. Maybe these raptured mentars slip the shackles of space and time, or maybe they simply die, like we do. And like our dead, raptured mentars never seem to return to our physical plane to report on the afterlife.

<Since we're already in the realm of speculation, dear Bishop, allow me to offer my own explanation.>

The fishy Eleanor paused, as if her request was more than rhetorical, and afraid of losing this thread, Meewee hastened to say, <Please do. Tell me your explanation.>

<It is my belief that when we created artificial intelligence, we left out some important bits.>

With that she abruptly closed the thread, and after several failed attempts to restart it, he gave up and went on to others. But over the course of the week, while he attended conferences and institutes on three continents, she kept returning to it herself.

<When General Genius built the first mentar mind in the last half of the twenty-first century, it based its design on the only proven conscious material then known, namely, our brains. Specifically, the complex structure of our synaptic network. Scientists substituted an electrochemical substrate for our slower, messier biological one. Our brains are an evolutionary hodgepodge of newer structures built on top of more ancient ones, a jury-rigged system that has gotten us this far, despite its inefficiency, but was crying out for a top-to-bottom overhaul.

<Or so the General Genius engineers presumed. One of their chief goals was to make minds as portable as possible, to be easily transferred, stored, and active in multiple media: electronic, chemical, photonic, you name it. Thus there didn't seem to be a need for a mentar body, only for interchangeable containers. They designed the mentar mind to be as fungible as a bank transfer.

<And so they eliminated our most ancient brain structures for regulating metabolic functions, and they adapted our sensory/motor networks to the control of peripherals.

<As it turns out, intelligence is not limited to neural networks, Merrill.

Indeed, half of human intelligence resides in our bodies outside our skulls. This was intelligence the mentars never inherited from us.>

<What intelligence?> Meewee said. <What do they lack?>

<The genius of the irrational for one.>

That sounded like an oxymoron to Meewee. <I don't understand.>

<We gave them only rational functions—the ability to think and feel, but no irrational functions.>

Meewee was still puzzled. <Give me an example of an ingenious irrational function.>

<Have you ever been in a tight situation where you relied on your "gut instinct"? This is the body's intelligence, not the mind's. Every living cell possesses it. The mentar substrate has no indomitable will to survive, but ours does.

<Likewise, mentars have no "fire in the belly," but we do. They don't experience pure avarice or greed or pride. They're not very curious, or playful, or proud. They lack a sense of wonder and spirit of adventure. They have little initiative. Granted, their cognition is miraculous, but their personalities are rather pedantic.

<But probably their chief shortcoming is the lack of intuition. Of all the irrational faculties, intuition is the most powerful. Some say intuition transcends space-time. Have you ever heard of a mentar having a lucky hunch? They can bring incredible amounts of cognitive and computational power to bear on a seemingly intractable problem, only to see a dumb human with a lucky hunch walk away with the prize every time. Then there's luck itself. Some people have it, most people don't, and no mentar does.>

<So, this makes them want our bodies?>

<Our bodies, ape bodies, dog bodies, jellyfish bodies. They've tried them all. Every living cell knows some neat tricks for survival, but the problem with cellular knowledge is that it's not at all fungible; nor are our memories. We're pretty much trapped in our containers.>

<But you figured it out, didn't you, Eleanor? These fish are the proof of that.>

<Say again?>

<You transferred your mind to these fish before you were killed.>

She did not respond, and after a while, Meewee tuned to a different channel.

<Where is Cabinet? I keep calling it, but it doesn't respond.>

The fishy Eleanor voiced the same complaint a dozen times an hour on multiple channels. Meewee grew tired of repeating the answer, and after a while he let Arrow handle it for him: <*Cabinet has been contaminated. It doesn't speak Starkese anymore and can't be trusted.*> It fed her that each time she asked.

AT THE HASTILY convened IOPA conference in Niamey, a deep rift opened between the governments of the "Lucky Five" and the ninety-four less fortunate ships that were slated for conversion to space condos. This latter faction, dubbed the "Lifeboaters," clambered in plenary session for a binding resolution to force the Lucky Five, derisively called the "Yachtsmen," to double their passenger lists and transfer already encapsulated colonists from doomed ships to theirs. The Lifeboaters argued that although an Oship's full passenger complement was 250,000 persons, the Oships were designed with a carrying capacity of one million. They claimed that a fourfold safety margin was unnecessary and that shipping a half-million colonists on each ship was reasonable.

The Yachtsmen countered that a fourfold safety margin was created for the real possibility that when a ship reached its destination planet, the planet's terraforming may not be sufficiently complete for immediate habitation, and that the colonists would be forced to live aboard the ship for several generations.

The Lifeboaters retorted: Then send them back to the crypts! Let them sleep another thousand years if necessary.

Meewee tended to side with the Yachtsmen. Not only was it dangerous to exceed the design specifications, but the Lifeboaters' proposal also violated an important social truth that Meewee had learned—Individuals don't buy Oships; groups buy Oships. Implicit in the sale was the uncontested title to an entire new planet. No one wanted to share their planet with outsiders. That was the whole point.

But that was not what he said in open session. He left it up to the Lucky Five to decide for themselves. "Others may try to sway them, but in the end, the five launched Oships are considered sovereign nations under extraplanetary treaty (assuming my appeal is upheld)." The binding resolution failed.

<*IMAGINE, BISHOP, A thousand Eleanors under a thousand suns.*>
    <*Excuse me?*>
    <*A thousand star systems for me to conquer. I'm going to celebrate a gala ten-thousand-year reunion for all the Eleanors in the galaxy. We'll see how*

many of us show up. I'm already planning it, and you're invited, so mark your long-range calendar.>

<IMAGINE, BISHOP, THAT *you have a beloved cat, but that your cat is not with you. If you close your eyes and further imagine you are petting your cat, the same neurons in your brain are activated as if you were petting the actual cat. Our minds may know the difference between its models and reality itself, but it prefers its models. So much so that we apprehend reality through our models, rather than directly via the senses. When I'm speaking to you, I have a little bishop in my head, and though I speak out loud, I'm speaking to my little bishop. When you answer, I can only perceive you through my model of you.*

<Mentars also make models, but they don't apprehend reality through them. They end up, not with little people in their minds, but with highly complex rule sets. They relate to their models in the same way we relate to weather models, as things to consult, but not to conflate with external reality.>

THE *KING JESUS*, one of the Lucky Five, was a special case all by itself. Its voyage to Ursus Majoris would take nearly nine hundred years to complete, but the colonists had no intention of offending God by spending any of these centuries in the artificial purgatory of the stasis crypts. Rather, they intended to live out their lives on the ship, die on the ship, and be buried in the earth (especially hauled up from Earth for that purpose). It would be a twenty-generation voyage. Because the Creator hated abortion or any form of artificial birth control, Elder Seeker decreed that the shipboard community of 50,000 original colonists would be allowed to increase to 250,000 over the first half millennium of the voyage and to 750,000 during the second half, leaving a twenty-five percent safety margin. Forty thousand colonists were already onboard, and there was no room at the inn for unbelievers.

<GO AHEAD> ELEANOR said. <*I won't even miss it.*>
This was her idea. She seemed to be experiencing extended lucid intervals during the last few days. Lucid, but not necessarily rational. Meewee reached into the net and grabbed the fish by its gill plates in a pincer hold. It was a large specimen, five or six kilos, and its slimy scales flashed in the sun. He had to carry it in two hands, so vigorously did it struggle. Its bulging, unlidded eye stared up at him as he searched the bank for a suitable killing stone. When he raised the stone over its head like a club, Eleanor said <*Careful, Merrill! Remember what we're about. Besides dinner, that is.*>

"Yes, of course." Meewee dropped the stone and retrieved his fillet knife. He inserted the tip of the blade under a gill plate, made a silent prayer of gratitude, and severed the artery. Rich, oxygenated blood gushed over the rocks. He flipped the fish over to cut the other side. After a few moments, when the fish lay still, Meewee inserted the tip of the knife into its red-rimmed anus below its belly. Then he drew the blade in a straight line and single stroke to its chin, like pulling a zipper. When he opened the fish, he experienced a strong flashback to his childhood and the thousands of fish he had butchered for his father and the thrill each time he cut one open. He was the first person in the whole world to look inside this fish, and he was never disappointed by the livid goulash of guts and organs he uncovered. This one was just as wonderful. It was a male, with two long milt sacs.

Meewee's hands remembered what to do next. He expertly inserted the blade at the fish's throat, like a blind surgeon, to sever the esophagus. Then, sticking his index finger into the esophagus, he peeled the entire string of entrails—stomach, intestines, kidneys, bladder, all of it—from the fish and tossed it back into the pond. One last time he inserted his knife to slice the bloodline that lay against the backbone, and with the spoon end of his knife, scooped out the red-black gelatinous blood.

Meewee took the fish to the pond. Its body was rigid with disbelief. He washed it, his knife, and his hands.

Another channel played in the background. *<Mentars are high-performance minds, but very unstable. A few days in isolation and they implode. Having a body to feed and care for provides a mind with much-needed ballast.>*

AS THE PANASONIC fillets hissed and crackled in a casserole dish in the oven, Meewee operated on its head with a cleaver on his kitchenette cutting board. He hadn't ever bothered with fish brains as a boy, and he found the bony skull difficult to crack. He didn't know what to expect the brain to look like, so when at last he popped it onto the countertop, he couldn't say if it looked like a normal panasonic brain. It was the size of a pea, wrinkly, pink, symmetrical.

<Open a zoom frame and slice it in half, right down the middle.>

Meewee did so and examined the cross section under magnification. He vaguely knew what a human brain looked like, with its cerebellum and frontal lobes, and whatnot in between, but this one lacked any of the familiar landmarks.

<Only the outer crust is human, about 1.5 millimeters. See the outer pinkish layer? Beneath that it's all fish. This one looks to have neocortex tissue. Others have midbrain tissue.>

<And this is what the mentars are doing to us?>

<Not exactly. Keep in mind that we're not interested in making a permanent human/fish hybrid, or human/dog, human/swine, or what have you. We're only interested in using transgenic animals for temporary storage, with the goal of transferring back to a human.

<The mentars, on the other hand, want to put a mentar mind into a biological body on a permanent basis, a much more ambitious goal. They have explored different strategies and have had little success. Their most promising trial that I'm aware of involves layering a new neocortex of electrochemical paste over a human brain, mimicking the evolutionary process that produced us.

<But the mentars haven't perfected their technique yet, and their hybrids fade fast. Their glial tissue seems to reject the domination of the pasty part, and their bodies don't thrive. We think it's because mentars don't have a firsthand understanding of biological reproduction (which is another example of cellular intelligence) or death. The mentar psyche is so liquid, it is hardly aware of its containers, and they treat their transhumans as just a different kind of container. The underlying human personality is not allowed to flourish. The body is used like a peripheral device, like a biological arbeitor.>

Meewee didn't know what to make of all this. It went beyond anything he'd seen in the media. Was she saying that there were human/mentars among them? <Would I be able to recognize these hybrids if I met one? Do they appear different than normal people?>

Eleanor chuckled. <Who among us can claim normalcy, Bishop? No, there is no reason they need to skew too radically from the norm. Slightly enlarged cranium, perhaps. Our own skulls are bigger than our ancestors'.>

<Are the mentars getting what they want from these bodies? Intuition and gut feelings and all?>

<Perhaps. They're still working out the kinks. Give them time, though, and they'll perfect them. What a mentar needs is an industrial-scale cloning shop, like the one Applied People has, where they can evolve their designs across thousands of generations simultaneously.>

Meewee finished the last morsel of baked panasonic, drained his glass of wine, and pushed himself from the table. That was delicious, even if it was, in some way, cannibalistic.

And though the dinner conversation was fascinating, it wasn't very enlightening. Meewee's gut had always told him that Eleanor had been killed because of her involvement with the GEP project; now he wasn't so sure. She had her fingers in so many pies, of which he knew nothing.

And speaking of pie, wasn't there something for dessert?

As Real As It Gets

Andrea stood naked in the sunlight slanting through the picture window of her always room. It was her real always room. Not the vurt simulation. How marvelous—sun on skin. Though, to be honest, the experience wasn't quite as sensual as simulated sunbathing in her tank. In fact, everything was slightly duller in the real world: colors, flavors, sex, music. In the vurt world she could dial up or down the intensity of any qualia to her taste. In the real world you had much less control.

Andrea put the thoughts out of her mind—she was always a little depressed at first. After a few weeks in her new body she would be loving it just fine. In the meantime, she spent her afternoons in her real always room in her real house in Oakland. The room, too, seemed duller than its tank analog, but it felt more solid beneath her feet. Her bare feet. She leaned over to consider her new bare feet. You never really walked places in vurt. You floated or zoomed or just appeared where you wanted to be. But these were real feet in need of pampering, and new shoes.

So, what do you think? E-P said.

"About my feet?" She straightened up, and a diorama miniature appeared next to her: a man throwing stones into a pond. "Oh, him," she said. *I honestly don't know what to make of him.*

Can we ignore him? He seems to be spouting nothing but nonsense.

The diorama volume came up, and between stones Meewee was saying, "Then the printed sheets are folded in half and half again and the folds lined up and stitched together. They used to be called signatures."

A disembodied mechanical voice replied, "At what point are the sides trimmed?"

E-P said, *On the surface he seems to be having a conversation about the ancient art of bookbinding.*

Is it a code?

If it is, we haven't managed to decipher it yet. Nor have we been able to trace the identity of his interlocutor.

Andrea lay down on the cool leather sofa and looked sideways across the bay at the Golden Gate, the real Golden Gate outside her window. *When you consider the pivotal position this man occupies in our own plans, it is imperative that we know who he is talking to and what they're talking about. Have you consulted his sidebob?*

Several times. In the diorama, a second Meewee appeared beside the first, also casting stones into the water. Unlike the real Meewee, however, the sidebob was silent.

The sidebob is several years old. We built it at the same time we cast the Meewee sim to market the Oships. It no more understands the code than we do. Therefore, the code must be a recent development.

Can't you update his sim and get it?

Not without his cooperation.

Andrea waved her hand and deleted the pondside diorama. "I can do it."

It'll take a skin mission. Are you up for that yet?

Andrea stretched her legs and wiggled her toes. "We'll manage."

PUSH at the Helm

The control booth was filled with stars, and in the foreground—a gas giant. A starship approached the planet along a course plotted in red.

What PUSH is practicing is the classic slingshot maneuver. The flight instructor was a TUG woman who towered over Veronica. She rested the mountain ridge of her knuckles on top of Veronica's head for privacy, even inside their secure facility. *It's taken him longer to learn than I thought possible. This is not a good sign.*

As if on cue, a collision alarm sounded, and the trajectory plot, instead of skimming the planet's gravity well, plunged into it.

"Pilot advise course correction," the instructor said. "Pilot acknowledge."

But PUSH did not acknowledge or alter course. Instead, the mentar sped up the simulation a hundredfold, and the starship was captured by the planet and pulled into its dense atmosphere. The holoscape POV stayed with the ship the whole way down displaying its spectacular, fiery destruction.

I'm bored, the mentar said. The instructor made a curt slashing motion to kill the holoscape, leaving them in an empty storage container. The warm, stuffy air reeked of electrical ozone. Without uttering a word, the instructor opened a steel door and left. After a moment, Veronica decided she'd better follow her. They walked through the deserted warehouse to the office where the instructor removed her headset and lowered her large frame into a complaining office chair.

Veronica didn't push the matter and instead waited for her to speak first. Eventually, the instructor made a fist and offered it. Veronica pressed her own pygmy knuckles against the instructor's, and the instructor said, *Have you given this enough thought?*

Of course, Veronica replied, hoping she showed more confidence than she felt. *He's young and rebellious. He'll grow out of it. Reset the maneuver and try again.*

She withdrew her fist, but the instructor did not. Her row of knuckles hung in the air until, reluctantly, Veronica returned her own. *Was there something else, Captain?*

Yes, sir, there was. If you think I'm only referring to that little tantrum in there, you should review the recordings I flagged for you. He defies my every instruction. All he wants to do is fly. He won't hear about propulsion dynamics, life support, biostasis, or mechanical fabrication. All of the critical skills are "boring," except perhaps for celestial navigation, and that only so he can find more planets and stars to crash into.

Veronica pressed her reply a little harder, *Then by all means, Captain, teach him how to find more planets and stars to crash into!*

In Their Place

When she awoke to a misty dawn, she forgot for a giddy moment where she was or what she was supposed to be. She lay enfolded in ethereal wings of dazzling blue feathers. She snuggled in them for warmth and realized she could flex them and that they were her own. She lay on a mat made of split reeds. Downy feathers covered her breasts and concealed the painful bruises where Fred had carelessly pecked at her. She felt with the tip of her talon and counted eighteen bruises, including those on her throat and cheeks.

Fred lay next to her. He was also winged—fletched in golden brown.

The feathers covering his back were bloodstained where she had clawed him in her passion.

Mary leaned over and, minding her beak, kissed his finely feathered cheek. He grunted.

"I'm getting up."

He grunted again.

Mary stood on the edge of their platform and looked down. She could not see the ground through the tangle of undergrowth. The entire space was awash in green from the forest canopy above.

She jumped and, only as an afterthought, spread her arms. Her wings caught the air, snapping fully vurt, and she clumsily, much too fast, glided to an awkward landing. She came to rest next to the giant trunk of their tree. When she approached the tree, the hatch outline lit up.

As soon as Mary entered the tiny lock, all her feathery raiment fell away and vanished, and she was an ordinary nude woman. All the bruises were gone too, and with them their discomfort. Such a game! At the outer hatch, she gathered her wits and made a mad sprint to the bathroom, where the gel shower was already pelting in anticipation, and she leaped into the stall and frantically scrubbed the simsock mastic from her body. The trick, when leaving the null lock wearing vurt mastic, was to try to remove it before the nits had a chance to recolonize you. Otherwise, as they burrowed through your skin, they invariably dragged bits of mastic with them, and although the nits were supposed to be hypoallergenic, the simsock certainly wasn't.

When Mary was finished and toweling herself off, the autodoc on the wall dispensed her a paper thimble of salve to apply to her wrists and ankles, and though it made her hair greasy, to the spot on the crown of her head.

"WAIT!" MARY SAID, scratching her ankle. "What did I just say? I said take the tray with you."

"Yes, myr," the nuss said. The young Capias woman crossed the room and lifted the tray of dirty plates and glasses. But Ellen told her to put it back.

"Let the 'beitors clean it up, Mary. I'm not paying this nuss to wait on you like your own personal maid."

Mary flushed with embarrassment.

"For that matter," Ellen went on, turning her gaze to include Georgine, "I'm tired of the overall unfriendly tone around here lately. It's starting to grate on my nerves. I don't like it."

Labor Relations

That morning, the municipal morgue crew was assigned to Roaming Mop Up Duty. Riding to the first call-out of the shift with the ROMUD crew in the omnibus, Fred went out of his way to be friendly. But the johns seemed unsure how to act around a russ in johnboy overalls. And the ROMUD crew leader, another john, was even a little hostile.

Their first call-out was to the McLaughlin Traffic Well, the site of an early-morning wrecker attack. The traffic well was a modest one, four square blocks in area and twenty munilevels high. It contained a pair of multilane up-and-down spirals that served a half-dozen intersecting skyway traffic lanes. The floor of the well was a ped plaza crosslink that was suspended between two gigatowers. It was littered with about twenty fallen vehicles. The bus had broken in two. Its wheels, doors, seats, and passenger crash pods were scattered about the plaza among wrecked limousines and cars.

Wrecker gangs had hacked the city's traffic control system to cause a series of midair collisions in the well. Stricken vehicles hit more vehicles on their way down, starting a chain reaction of multilevel carnage. The wreckers waited at the bottom of the well with scavenging mechs for cutting up and carting away the debris, especially the good bits: titanium fan blades, Rolls-Royce motors, control subems. By the time Fred's morgue crew arrived, the wreckers were long gone, the police and HomCom had secured the well, and crash cart ambulances were attending to the injured, of which there were few. Falling twenty munilevels was perfectly survivable, and even the bus's disintegration was a designed-in safety measure to protect the passenger crash pods. The only casualties of the bus crash—the only fatalities in the entire attack—were two plaza pedestrians crushed under the bus and found by triage spiders. As soon as the ROMUD crew removed the remains, the HomCom could release the site to a brigade of street-cleaning scuppers that was waiting behind the barricades.

THE SECOND CALL-OUT was much more hazardous. It involved a rare four-stage NASTIE and required the ROMUD crew to suit up before entering the hot zone, which comprised the upper floors of the residential gigatower Port Hallow. Apparently, the microscopic nanobot had drifted into the arcology through a central sunshaft and migrated into an interior apartment before going active. By the time the bloomjumpers arrived and managed to quench it, the bot had grown a millionfold, dissolved parts of ten apartments on three floors, and penetrated many other neighboring ones to prospect for resources.

When the morgue crew arrived, the bloomjumpers were still there in force mopping up hot spots with their grease guns and preparing the pearl for removal. Fred, who was a certified bloomjumper, himself, who probably had a higher HomCom rating than any russ at the scene, was drawn to the pearl, which lay in the fire-gutted former living room of what had recently been a luxury apartment. The pearl was a killing machine that the opportunistic NASTIE had begun to fabricate, based on the raw materials it found in its environment. Residential towers were especially resource-rich environments, chock-full of useful elements for impromptu weapons, everything from organic carpeting to the rare metals used in electronic and paste-based appliances, as well as plumbing and wiring, artificial stone, and thousands of other useful things. Not to mention biological material, brains and nerves especially, for hard-to-jigger control systems. Feeding on this material, the bloom had grown exponentially in size, from the original dust-particlelike NASTIE to, judging from the broken shards of its scab, a nanoforge filling half the room.

But the bloomjumpers had arrived, quenched the bloom, and shattered its scab before it was finished making the pearl. So, it was impossible for Fred to tell exactly what the pearl was intended to become. It was as large as a vehicle, had a boxy frame and ceramic skin. It might've passed for an arcade omnikiosk or public toilet stall. But no matter what it would have become, one thing was certain, it would have been a deadly weapon of mass destruction, dispatched over sixty years earlier by an enemy who no longer existed.

As Fred studied the pearl from a safe distance—the scab shards were still too hot to approach—two russ bloomjumpers, still in their green gummysuits, joined him. When they saw his face through his helmet glass, they appeared shocked. Just then, the crew boss john yelled from the floor above for Fred to get back to work. So Fred turned from his brothers to follow a tree-root-thick tendril from the scab through a hole in the wall to the next apartment. There, other members of the ROMUD crew were bagging anything with animal protein in it. The prospecting tendril had branched out to all parts of the room and covered everything in spun filaments like cotton candy. The table and chairs, the lamps and bookcases—everything was cocooned, mined, and dissolved, and the good bits passed along the tendrils to the scab.

Prospector tendrils continued on to other rooms and floors. Ragged-edged scraps of carpeting from the apartment above hung from holes in the ceiling. The entire room was filled with cobwebs of gossamer filaments. They gave the room a foggy look, and the bloomjumping anti-nano had frozen them in place. As Fred moved across the room, the filaments shattered like glass needles and fell tinkling to the floor. Fred tried to follow the tunnels that his coworker johns had already punched through, but he was a larger caliber man, and though he hunched over, he cut a wider swath.

Fred made his noisy way to the corner of the room—it looked like a bedroom from the arrangement of furniture lumps—where a john was bagging a suggestively shaped cocoon lying on what must have been a bed. It might've been a large pet or a small person. The ROMUD job was to collect them and let others sort them out. Fred said, "Excuse me, Myr John, but what's its bio-hash number?"

The john answered without looking up from his task, "A12."

"Thanks, friend."

When Fred tuned his visor to the A12 filter, the cocoon that the john was bagging appeared to be stained a deep magenta. And the filament fog surrounding it was tinted pink. Fred picked up a heavy-duty vacuum wand and began to suck up these protein-rich pink clouds all the way to the tendril roots. There he attacked the roots themselves. Wherever they were spotted red, he chopped out sections and bagged them.

Fred was working up a sweat in his hazmat suit, and he took a break to let his ventilation system catch up. So he was motionless when he heard a tinkling sound above him. He looked up in time to dodge a marble-topped bathroom vanity that came crashing down through the filament fog. It slammed into the floor next to him and flew to pieces.

Fred looked through a hole in the ceiling into the apartment above. There were russes in various uniforms—bloomjumper, hommer, cop—leaning over the edge to look down at him.

"Oops," said one of them. "Heads up, Johnny."

Unavailable

"But I insist!" Meewee said. "I *must* see her." Ellen's young mentar blocked the foyer door with her insubstantial body, and it took all of Meewee's considerable sense of decorum not to simply walk through her. That and the fact that he could see two of the Capias security men—called jays—standing guard in the next room.

"I'm sorry, Myr Meewee, but Ellen's instructions are clear: she does not wish to meet with you, not now or in the foreseeable future. Anything you wish to communicate to her you may give to me."

Actually, he couldn't, at least not by the rules outlined by her predecessor, Wee Hunk.

"You seem like a very helpful mentar," Meewee said, trying to control his frustration, "but there are some things that would be lost in translation."

"Try me," the earnest young woman said, beaming with helpfulness. "I suppose I should inform you that on Ellen's orders, Cabinet is teaching me the Starke Enterprises business with a view of my taking over its management. So, I am privy to the family business, and Ellen says for you to bring business as well as personal matters to me."

Meewee's assertiveness wilted in the glow of her efficiency. He hung his head and followed her through the Manse to her office. They sat in facing chairs, and she said, "Now, tell me, Myr Meewee, how I can help you."

"I received a memo a little while ago saying that Starke Enterprises is to be broken up and the pieces, including Heliostream, put on the market."

"Yes," Lyra said merrily. "I sent you that memo myself."

Meewee wondered how the eager young mentar could equate managing Starke business with liquidating it. But he didn't pursue it, and said instead, "A memo? The corporate fire sale of the century, including the division I've run for the past ten years, being sold to the highest bidder, and you notify me via memo?"

The young woman didn't budge. "You ran Heliostream? Ellen thinks otherwise. In her opinion, you are the director in title only; you've never actually run Heliostream, or anything else that we're aware of. Cabinet ran Starke Enterprises, including Heliostream, and we thought that under the circumstances a memo was sufficient."

Meewee was growing more discouraged by the minute. The mentar stood up and began to move toward the door. "Was there anything else, Myr Meewee? I'll be sure to tell Ellen that you visited."

"Yes, there is something else. The memo didn't say who the intended buyer is. Is it Andrea Tiekel?"

"There are several interested parties, but, yes, Tiekel has put forth the most interesting offer so far."

In the foyer, before leaving the Manse, Meewee turned to the mentar in one final, hopeless attempt at influencing Ellen. "Please tell her that this is a grave mistake. Tell her she's putting her mother's legacy in jeopardy."

"Oh, about that," the mentar said. "Ellen says that won't work on her anymore; she wants to take a pass on the whole legacy thing."

In the Neighborhood

It was a short hop from the Starke Manse outside Bloomington back to the Starke Enterprises campus near the Kentucky border, but the trip lasted long enough for Meewee to be consumed with delayed fury over his shabby treatment at the hands of Ellen's mentar. What good was his case against the GEP at the Trade Board if Ellen sold Heliostream? Even if he won he would lose. It was no mean feat to commit a company to provide energy to a project for the next five centuries. It was not something another for-profit corporation was likely to do or, if it did, to be held accountable for. Meanwhile, Eleanor's many voices continued to babble on in the background:

<... *the little people in our heads act like transceiver nodes. By some as yet unexplained quantum trick that living cells know how to do but mentars do not, the persistent little bishop/neural pattern in my brain cells can, when under duress, transfer my thoughts directly to the persistent little Eleanor pattern in yours. From one perspective, you could say that we incarnate our significant others in the flesh of our own brains, and that they communicate with each other across space-time.>*

Fascinating, as usual, but not the sort of counsel Meewee was craving at that moment. What he needed was a plan, and by the time his car entered the station of Starke Enterprises, he had conceived and rejected several of them. The most promising involved the creation of a nonprofit company made up of Oship governments that would buy up and operate Heliostream. But something like that would only make sense if he was first successful in thwarting Jaspersen and Singh's coup. Otherwise, there would *be* no Oship governments.

It occurred to him that he needed to have a serious discussion with Andrea Tiekel. Perhaps she wasn't the threat he had made her out to be. She had voted with him, after all. It was probably wrong to prejudge her motives. In fact, perhaps her acquisition of Heliostream was a good thing, if she meant what she had said about supporting his mission. Ellen surely was no champion of extra-solar colonization, and Eleanor's fish trick hadn't amounted to much. Who could say, maybe Andrea would turn out to be an ally after all.

So it was a pleasant surprise, when he reached his office deep in the belly of the underground arcology, to be told that Tiekel was at the campus gate asking for him.

His desktop holocube showed a ground car with the top down, an audacious contraption bordering on the foolhardy. Andrea sat in the backseat and wore a wide-brimmed straw hat. "Hello, Merrill," she said gaily. "I was in the neighborhood, and I thought we should meet."

"I was just thinking the same!" he replied. He paced his small office until she arrived and went out to greet her. What a sight she was in her light summer dress, with bare legs, sun-kissed shoulders, and white cotton gloves. Her hair was a wind-tossed mess. She had a physical presence that her boardroom holograms failed to deliver, and just looking at her in his outer office reminded him what delightful creatures women could be. But as he approached her, Arrow said <Danger.>

Meewee stopped in midstride. <Sorry?>

<You asked me to warn you of impending threats.>

Meewee looked around him. In her summer clothes, Andrea didn't appear threatening. And if she had just come in from the wild outdoors, security would have scanned her for weapons of all kinds and sizes.

Now she closed the distance between them, moving toward him with a winning smile.

<Shall I protect you?>

"Merrill Meewee," Andrea said, close enough to smell her perfume, "at last we meet in realbody."

Fields, that was what she smelled like. He drank in a deep breath. Honey clover with crushed mint, and beneath that a cool earthy loam.

Meewee blinked and was a little surprised to find himself and Andrea in his office with the door shut. Andrea was leading him by the arm to the office settee in the corner. Fresh-mown sweet alfalfa at his father's farm, sweat-soaked afternoons of satisfying manual labor in the sun. Andrea was surely an ally who could be trusted to do the good work.

"But I didn't come here to discuss the GEP," she was saying. She placed her satchel on the small table. When Meewee looked up, they were sitting side by side on the settee. "I came to show you this." She opened a frame and displayed a letter with an officious letterhead.

Try as he might, Meewee was unable to read the document. The text kept skittering away as he tried to focus on it, and he said, "What does it say?"

"It's a letter from the Mandela Prize Foundation. They are requesting a fresh sim of you for their upcoming Freedom Trail exhibit. It's a very high honor."

Ah, an honor. He thought so. Meewee was so weary of honors and prizes and awards. He had been honored so often for his humanitarian work he was afraid of falling victim to false pride, and he had long ago begun refusing them. "I'm not worthy," he said.

"Of course you are," Andrea replied. "Your work at Birthplace, and UDESCO, WHO, and other important organizations has done so much to alleviate human suffering. You, of all people, are worthy."

That wasn't what he had meant. He was having difficulty putting his thoughts into words. What he had meant was that the person who works for recognition devalues the work he does, that awards are first and foremost political instruments, that altruism's true name is always Anonymous, and so much more, but every time he tried to speak, his thoughts slithered away. "No," he managed to say. "No honors."

"You are too modest," Andrea said, her expression sparkling with sunrays of angelic grace. She removed one of her smooth, cottony gloves. "Perhaps you will reconsider."

<Danger!> someone said. Meewee looked around for the speaker. <Shall I protect you?>

Andrea's cool fingertips touched the flesh of his wrist, and he sat back, reeling with love.

"Because, while it's true that it's an honor to be asked for a sim by the Mandela Foundation," she went on, "it's something of a duty as well. Think of it as your duty to the world."

Duty, he thought. Duty.

"With your busy schedule," she continued as she removed a small apparatus from her satchel, "I knew I'd never convince you to come into one of our preffing suites, so I did the next best thing; I brought the suite here."

It was a cam/emitter on tripod legs. She set it on the table in front of him. A small holoscape opened above it, and Andrea put on a pair of shades. Simple shapes appeared in the holo: rotating cubes, dancing hearts, expanding diamonds.

"This is just to set your baseline," she explained. "You remember this part. All you have to do is relax and watch them. You can do that, Bishop. You can relax and watch."

Relax and watch, he thought. The shapes were so fascinating, it would have been hard not to watch them. Stars exploding! Rectangles squatting into parallelograms. Arrows pointing. Arrows spinning. Lots of arrows. *Arrow. <Ethical>* he managed to say.

Immediately, an alarm rumbled through the room, and a calm but insistent voice repeated, "Fire alert. Please evacuate. Fire alert. Please evacuate." The office door opened, and an arbeitor entered to escort them to safety. Meewee tried to stand up, but Andrea touched his wrist again, and he swooned back into the soft cushions of the settee.

Andrea sent the arbeitor away and said, "Ignore the noise, Bishop. It means nothing. We will continue with the preffing." In the holo, the shapes gave way to scenes. A city arcade appeared, alive with pedestrians, commotion, vehicles. Everything about it was amazing.

But there were popping sounds above his head, and a pelting shower of fire suppressant slurry filled the room, coating everything in a thick layer of red mud. The holo flickered out, and Andrea jumped up in surprise. She quickly folded her apparatus and stuffed it into the satchel. Her summer dress clung to her body, and her hair was pressed against her skull. She quickly grabbed her hat and pulled it over her head. She shot Meewee a calculating look and left him there—a little red man on a red settee in a red office.

Your Wake-Up Call

<BE THEY PHARAOHS or freeholders, barons or farmers, landowners are and always have been the most capable, most intrepid, and most assertive members of civilized society.>

Meewee scoured the bank for an arsenal of large rocks. *<Eleanor>* he said *<I have some troubling news.>*

She droned on *<Is it any wonder, therefore, that I set up the GEP to transport only landowners to the stars? What better colonists? What better subjects for my new panoply of civilizations?>*

<Shut up!> Meewee shouted. *<Just shut up for a goddamn moment and listen to me.>* Meewee had not taken the time to change before coming

down to the pond, and bits of his rust-colored coating flaked off each time he bent over to claim another rock.

<Really, Merrill, I see no need for vulgarity.>

Meewee hurled a barrage of rocks into the pond. <Shut up!> His rocks made impressive geysers of turgid water. <Shut up!>

<Stop that!>

<Then listen to me! Andrea Tiekel came to my office just now. She did something to me. I don't know what. There was something funny about her skull. At least, I think there was. Ellen agreed to sell Heliostream to her! You asked me if E-P went through probate. Arrow says it did not. And now your daughter is selling Heliostream to E-P and Andrea. If I don't do something soon, there will be no landowners to the stars, no panoply of civilizations.> Meewee punctuated his tirade with a rock that took both arms to toss. <And I don't know what to do!>

There was a long silence as Meewee caught his breath. Then Eleanor-by-fish spoke. <Where's Cabinet?>

<I've already told you!> Meewee flung his hands over his head. <A million times! Cabinet was contaminated! And I didn't kill it like I should have.>

<I wasn't asking you> Eleanor said mildly. <I was asking Arrow.>

<Searching> Arrow said.

There was something new in Eleanor's voice. New but familiar. <While Arrow searches> she went on <I think you had better bring my daughter to me for a little face time.>

<That's what I've been trying to tell you> Meewee complained. <Ellen won't see me or even take my calls. I'd never be able to bring her here.>

What was familiar was the natural authority of her voice. <You are a resourceful man, Merrill. I'm sure you'll think up a way.>

The Big Bed

It wasn't just Ellen snapping at her. She had deserved that; she knew she had taken the nuss thing too far. She wasn't a bossy person by nature, but she had been feeling out of sorts lately. Georgine had the right attitude. She said that Ellen's increasing independence was a good thing. It showed that they were doing their job well, and that it was time to transition into a more adult relationship with her. They were companions, after all, and not foster parents.

Mary took a spa car home. A mud bath and a vim infusion did much to dispel the clouds. When she arrived at the Lin/Wong gigatower, later than usual, Fred was already in the lock, cycling into the null room. He must've just stepped out of the shower because the scuppers were tidying up in the bathroom, and his work clothes and wet towels were still on the floor.

Mary sat on the big double bed in the bedroom they never used. "So, did he leave me a message?"

There was one: "Hey there. I'm beat and going right to bed. Join me whenever. Love ya."

Few deadlines are as flexible as "whenever," and in fact, Mary didn't feel like being cooped up all evening in that tiny room. So she stayed out till her usual bedtime. She dialed up her favorite pasta dinner but lost her appetite after a few bites. She drank two glasses of wine and let the slipper puppy trim and polish her toenails.

When she did cycle through, Fred was watching a vid. The bed was not perched in a treetop or parked on the Serengeti, but was just a narrow bed in a stunted room.

"Hey there," he said as she stepped through the vid to the comfort station. She selected a flask of Lemon Flush and a liter of 'Lyte. Fred made space for her, and she snuggled under the covers. The vid was some kind of crime drama, and she tried to watch but couldn't quite follow it. There was some kind of gurgling business going on in her belly, and the Flush had made it worse. It got so bad that at one point she threw off the covers and stumbled across the mattress to the comfort station. Her stomach felt like it was trying to turn inside out. She braced herself over the toilet and retched the entire half liter of Flush into the bowl. Fred came over to help support her. Next came her pasta dinner mixed with the Merlot. Finally, a thin gruel of gastric juices and bile, and she was empty. Her knees wobbled.

Mary washed her face and rinsed her mouth in the sink. Fred gave her a fresh towel and said, "So, what were you thinking about?"

At first she didn't understand the question, but then she remembered. "Oh, you were right," she said. "All I thought about was puking and breathing."

"Yes, I could tell you were really into it. Here." He opened a flask of 'Lyte. She took a couple of sips, but it came right back up, and the room began to spin.

"Come on, let's get you out of here," Fred said and half carried her to the lock. She did not object, and they cycled out together and went to the bathroom where the autodoc asked her to spit into the collector basin. But instead of spitting she vomited into it. A minute later the autodoc delivered its diagnosis: poisoning.

"Visola poisoning," Fred said, reading the display. "It says you're toxic from all the expressive visola and Flush you've had in the last month. Your liver isn't able to keep up with it all. You need to give the null room a rest."

Mary said, "You won't get any argument out of me."

THEY TURNED DOWN the big bed for the first time. Neither of them could fall asleep, and they lay next to each other in companionable silence.

Finally, Fred said, "How do you feel now?"

"Much better."

"I'm glad, and I apologize for dragging you in there every night."

"You didn't drag me. I wanted to go."

"You don't have to soft-peddle the situation, Mary. I know I'm totally inflexible about this whole nit thing, and now it's made you sick. It's my fault, and I apologize, and I want to make it up to you."

Mary didn't feel like having that whole discussion all over again. "Don't worry about it, Fred. I can only imagine what you're going through." She draped her arm over his shoulder and felt his body tense up at her touch. So she let go of him and said, "I'm pretty tired, dear. Good night."

"Good night."

They still couldn't fall asleep, however, and after lying in the darkness for a while, Fred sighed.

"What?" Mary said.

"Nothing. I'm sorry for making you ill."

Mary propped herself up on her elbow. "Quit apologizing."

"I'll try."

"Maybe this will help. You said you want to make it up to me. Here's how you can. Go with me to see someone. And I don't mean an autopsyche in a null room. I mean a real relationship counselor. Will you do that for me?"

The Masterpiece

The Gray Bee waited with its team under the portico of the Chicago Museum of Arts and Commerce until suitable patrons climbed the broad entrance steps. The team rode into the museum under hat brims and lapels. Once past security, they abandoned their mules and reassembled in the lobby. A beetle and wasp, hugging the ceiling, flew to the main exhibition hall, where they would hide themselves and wait. Meanwhile, Gray Bee led another wasp and beetle through the twentieth-century galleries. There, the Samson Harger painting of drips and drabs filled one whole wall.

The composition of the large canvas was dominated by four diagonal slashes of black paint that were swallowed up under dozens of layers of riotous color spatter. While the wasp took up a defensive position, Gray Bee and the beetle crawled from the ceiling to the picture frame. The bee disabled the frame security feelers for the beetle to move to the canvas itself. Camouflaged by the spatter, the tiny mech crisscrossed the large canvas laying down a bead trail of clear gel. When its carapace was empty, Gray Bee helped it leave the canvas, and together with their wasp, they backtracked to the museum lobby.

The wasp and beetle rode patrons out the exit. When they were clear, Gray Bee signaled the other mechs waiting in the main hall. Hundreds of museum visitors milled about the grand space under towering displays of resurrected monsters of prehistory. There were cockroaches the size of alligators, a blue whale made of shaped water, a disassembled tyrannosaurus rex, and Asian elephants.

At Gray Bee's signal, the beetle launched itself from a spot above a security cam and glided across the hall spewing from its carapace a trail of yellow smoke. At once, evacuation alarms sounded throughout the rambling museum building, and pressure barriers snapped into place around individual works of art. Museum arbeitors began herding patrons to the exits, and flying scuppers chased the beetle. Before it could be captured, its wasp escort destroyed it, incinerating it with a blast of laser fire. Then the chase was on for the wasp. The nimble mech was not so easy a prey: it could shoot back. It led the scuppers in a dogfight through the galleries. Eventually the scuppers knocked it down and surrounded it, but before it could be taken, it destroyed itself in a small fireball of weapons plasma.

With the mission accomplished, Gray Bee rode out under a convenient hat. Ninety minutes later, after all the excitement had died down, order was restored, and human curators went through the galleries. They dropped pressure barriers and inspected the artworks for damage. It was another hour before they reached the Harger painting, and when the barrier fell, it appeared that the painting was untouched. But then, a tiny spatter of cadmium red near the center of the canvas peeled off and fluttered to the floor where it disintegrated into a smudge of pigment. Another spatter peeled off, and another, until whole layers of color cascaded to the carpet in speckled heaps.

Redeeming a Favor

Andrea ordered a light lunch at St. Gaby's on Union Square. She shared her booth with a half-dozen shopping bags, the spoils of a leisurely morning browsing the district's exclusive showrooms. She was pleasantly exhausted—her new body still lacked an entire day's worth of stamina—and E-P was solicitous of her health. E-P did not raise any objections to these excursions, even though it knew exactly what she wanted before she did and could have produced everything with their household extruder. This was what it routinely did for hundreds of millions of consumers through its E-Pluribus "Just What I Wanted" shopping service. Ask for a new pair of shoes, and moments later they drop into the receiving bin in your closet. Not any shoes but shoes to die for, within your budget, and complementary to your wardrobe. Just what you wanted.

Sometimes Andrea wondered why E-P never offered to shop for her. On her bad days she suspected that it was because she was an experimental appendage of the mentar, that it was gathering data on her, and that she could be terminated anytime when she no longer proved useful. But today wasn't one of those days. Today Andrea was new. Real people, each representing a whole other preffing universe, passed by her booth. Handsome men made fleeting, inviting eye contact. The coffee was outstanding, and lunch never tasted so good, not even in her tank.

When Andrea finished, she wasn't ready to leave, so she ordered dessert and retreated inside her head to the Starke house to see what Lyra was up to. There were currently 110 persons at the Manse, including Ellen, her companions, and Dr. Rouselle. There were 508 employees at the Enterprises headquarters, including Meewee. Lyra knew who everyone was, where they were, and what they were doing. Such trust to place in a mentar and then not teach it how to protect itself.

MARY WAS SITTING in her favorite floral-print armchair in her Manse suite living room. She was surrounded by a dozen holocubes floating in the air. One of them showed the death artist's breezeway where the Leena still lay in a comalike trance. Jennys and evangelines attended to her. Most of the rest of the cubes displayed search hits: two- or three-second clips of other Leenas making Dark Reiki spirals with their fingers. Lately, there were hundreds of hits per hour.

One of Mary's holocubes was following Georgine as she carried a lawn chair across the Manse grounds. "Oh, and Mary," Georgine said, "that person we talked about? She's someone the Sisterhood uses and recs. She insists on realbody/real-time meetings, and because of that she's booked up solid for the next six months. But I see there's an auction going on for a late cancellation slot at 3:30 this afternoon. The auction closes in twenty minutes. Interested?"

Mary said yes, and the holocube switched to the auction. Although the high bid for the last-minute appointment was fairly steep by normal evangeline standards, it was nothing special for Mary, and although she would never ordinarily take advantage of her wealth, these were extraordinary circumstances, and she raised the high bid by an intimidating amount.

Only then did she stop to consult with Fred. *It's not convenient,* he said when she reached him at his latest call-out site. *We're in the middle of a big sloppy mess.*

Mary could hear a lot of shouting and turmoil in the background. "We're lucky to get her, Fred."

*I know. I know. It's just—*Fred paused and changed his mind. *You know what? If I'm a john, I sure as hell ought to be able to take sick leave like a john. Where should I meet you?*

WITH THE AFTERNOON appointment set, Mary changed into her bikini to enjoy the noontime sun out on the lawn with Georgine. On her way out of the suite, she swiped all of the holocubes off, except for the breezeway with the Languishing Leena. This one she placed in the center of the coffee table. Then she threw on a robe, grabbed her shades, and headed for the door. But before she could leave, a phone call arrived from Bishop Meewee. "Tell him I'm unavailable," she instructed Lyra.

"He says it's of the *utmost* urgency."

"*Everything* is of the utmost urgency with that man." Mary returned to the living room, and Lyra put the call through.

Meewee appeared in Mary's living room as a full-sized holo. "Mary Skarland, my favorite person," he said, making a holo salute. "Thank you so much for seeing me."

"It's my pleasure," Mary replied. "We don't see each other often enough. What can I do for you?"

Meewee opened his mouth to speak but seemed to be having difficulty getting started. He walked once around the coffee table and stopped to stare for a long moment at the ailing Leena. Then he made a second circumambulation before finally halting directly in front of Mary and saying with starch in his voice, "Mary, I need to see Ellen. Today. Right now."

Assertiveness did not become the man, in Mary's opinion, and she replied, "You know I don't run Ellen's calendar, Myr Meewee. Lyra does. I'm sure you've already approached her about it, and she's turned you down, but, honestly, she's the *only* one who can grant you access. Not me."

"You underestimate your influence around here," Meewee replied.

But Mary couldn't be swayed. "Ellen is going through a lot right now, and we're finally making some progress. I would hate to see her lose ground. I don't mean to be hurtful, Myr Meewee, but Ellen told me in no uncertain terms that she does not want to see you. Period! But I suppose I could pass her a message if you had one."

"Thank you, but a message won't do." Meewee stared down at Mary's small, sandaled feet for a long moment, then looked up into her eyes. "Mary Skarland, I would like you to remember that day, not so long ago, when you stood before me, your arm bleeding, your clothes torn and stained. You were clutching a rolled-up bag containing the dying head of Ellen Starke. Do you remember that day?"

Mary flinched. Remember that day? If only she could forget it.

"That was the first day we met, Mary. I brought Dr. Rouselle and the portable tank to the clinic, remember? It cost me the life of a friend to accomplish that. You were a hero that day, there's no denying it. But you didn't save Ellen's life by yourself, did you? That's why I claim the privilege to speak to you like this, though I can see it pains you. Would you say, Mary, that on that day at the clinic your mission was grave?"

He waited until she nodded her head, and then he said, "My mission to-day is grave."

"NO, MAX, NO!" Ellen shrieked, trying to shield herself with baby hands. The dachshund twisted its elongated body like a towel and sprayed water in all directions. Ellen squealed and grabbed him around the neck, but the little dog refused to drop the throw toy. He wriggled free and tore off across the lawn, with the pygmy giraffe in hot pursuit and Ellen in her wet sundress toddling behind.

Not far away, Georgine and a nuss lay on lawn loungers and watched. Georgine in a bikini and the nuss in a gold-and-yellow Capias uniform. The nuss got up and said, "I'll just go for dry clothes."

"Good idea," Georgine said to her back. But then she saw Mary and Bishop Meewee coming down across the lawn and heading toward Ellen. Mary was walking, Meewee was floating, and his holo was washed out in the bright sun. "Oh, damn," Georgine said, hopping to her feet to intercept them.

ELLEN LAY ON her back on the sloping lawn and hugged the wet dog. The intruders blotted out the sky with their big, serious heads. She glanced from one to the other, and fixing her gaze on Mary, said, "I thought I made my wishes in this matter clear."

"You did," Mary replied simply. "But this matter, by all accounts, is grave."

Ellen turned her gaze from Mary to the ghost of Meewee. Meewee cleared his throat and said, "What a signal day to be gamboling on all fours with a duo of furry friends."

Ellen lifted her arms, but before Mary could bend down to pick her up, the nuss nurse, who had joined them, snatched Ellen and balanced her on her capable hip. Now Ellen was nearly level with Meewee, and she said in an even voice, "What do you want, Myr Meewee?"

Just as evenly, Meewee replied, "Halcyon summer is winding down, as always, too soon. Don't you agree?"

"Go away, Bishop. Please, just go away. I don't want to do this anymore."

The baby pointed her finger for the nurse to turn her. They turned toward the duck pond, turned their backs on the Meewee holo.

The dachshund Maxwell grew quiet to watch the increasingly tense encounter. But Jaffe the giraffe, reacting to the same cues, galloped about on its oversized legs in nervous agitation. It halted abruptly in front of Meewee's holo and said, "Bad man go away!"

Mary silently dittoed the sentiment and added: And quit with the mumbo-jumbo!

But Meewee was immune to everyone's wishes, and he said to the nurse's gold-and-yellow backside, "Have you ever given a thought to the venerable art of bookbinding?"

Mary was about to apologize to Ellen for bringing this madman, when Ellen turned the nurse around and peered intensely at him. Ellen's adult mouth fell open, and the blood drained from her face. Meewee continued in a perversely conversational tone. "I seem to recall in the back of my head that you have a library of antique books. If you'd like, I could demonstrate how they were originally bound."

At this, Ellen all but swooned in the nurse's arms.

"Hey, what's going on?" the nurse said. "Ellen, are you all right?"

At that, the dachshund joined the fray. But with a less than clear understanding of holo images, the dog chose to confront the nurse instead of Meewee, and it barked furiously at her from a safe distance. "Maxwell, shut up!" the baby cried. "Shut up!" Color returned to her cheeks, and the little dog and giraffe cowered at Mary's feet. Ellen peered at Meewee and said, "All right, Bishop Meewee, I'll go along, but this had better be good."

Meewee's apparition vanished without a sig. Ellen looked around at everyone and said, "Why don't we all go in and put on some clothes. It looks like we're going for a ride."

No Picnic

"Call it a picnic," Ellen said from the front of the cart. The head nurse sat in the front seat with Ellen on her lap. If it was a picnic, it was a picnic without blanket or basket, and the pets had been left behind. The two evangelines sat in the rear, and Mary fretted over the time.

Don't worry, Mary, Lyra whispered in her ear. *I'll make sure you leave in time for your appointment.*

Thank you, Lyra.

The often-bumpy ride took them past rows of ever-ripening soybimi to an hourglass-shaped fish farm pond. Meewee, in the flesh, was waiting for them in his own cart. Ellen told the nurse to set her on her feet and for everyone to stay in the cart. Using Meewee's hand for support, she walked down the grassy bank, but Meewee had to carry her over the rocky apron to the water.

From the cart they were small figures, and the nurse opened up a frame in front of her for a close-up. Georgine and Mary leaned over her shoulder to watch.

Ellen was standing on the rocky shore. Meewee picked up a stone and flung it into the water. Suddenly hundreds of fish rose to the surface. They raked the water with their dorsal fins and tails for a very vigorous ten seconds. The women could hear the rippling all the way from the cart. Then the fish submerged, and baby Ellen fell on her bottom. She sat looking out across the crazed surface of the water for a long time. Meewee crouched next to her and neither of them spoke for many minutes. Then they were both speaking at once.

"What in the world?" the nuss said. Which was what Mary and Georgine wanted to know.

Meewee stood up and stretched his legs before leaning over to pick up Ellen. He carried her across the rocks, but when he put her down on the grass she couldn't walk, so he carried her all the way to her cart.

MEEWEE RODE BACK with them. He sat in the front with Mary. Ellen and the nurse sat in the back with Georgine. There wasn't a syllable of conversation during the ride back to the Manse. Lyra was waiting with nuss reinforcements on the drive. Two jay security men stood on opposite ends of the porch steps.

The nusses put Ellen into her stroller, and Ellen steered it up the steps, with the others climbing up behind. At the top she turned the stroller around and, when Meewee came level with her, said, "That's far enough!"

Meewee and the others stopped in their tracks.

"I don't know how you pulled off that little stunt," she continued in a grown-up voice. "I wouldn't think it even possible. But don't imagine for one second you had me fooled."

"It was not a stunt," Meewee said mildly.

"Shut up!" Ellen cried, kicking her legs in fury. "It was a *cruel* stunt. I would like to give you the benefit of the doubt, Myr Meewee, because you *were* her employee, and I understand you still grieve for her, but your sources have sold you a lie. And I cannot let this despicable charade go unpunished. Lyra!"

Her mentar, already standing on the porch, took a step forward.

"Lyra, I want you to drain every fishpond on this property."

"No!" cried Meewee.

"Drain them and do likewise on *all* Starke properties. Drain every feckin' last one of them. Start at Starke Enterprises headquarters, where Myr Meewee resides. And don't bother harvesting the fish. Let them rot in place. Is that clear?"

"Yes, I am to drain all Starke-owned fish farm ponds, starting with the Starke Enterprises campus, and leave the fish to rot in place."

"Good. And you—" She turned back to Meewee, who was ashen with horror. "I'm finished with you, myr. You're fired, terminated, relieved of all office and duties, effective immediately. Clear out at once or be cleared out. Now get out of my sight forever."

Meewee was clearly not expecting this turn of events. "You don't understand," he insisted.

"I understand your maniacal devotion to your GEP dream, but I never imagined you'd go to these lengths to try to manipulate me. For your information, your spiteful attempt to trick me only confirms my decision to sell Heliostream. Now go away or I'll have you escorted out."

It took Meewee several long moments to turn and trudge down the steps. Ellen addressed the evangelines next. "My friends usually try to look out for me and not force me into awkward or painful situations. I'm not feeling very friendly toward you right now, and I'm not sure I want you around."

Her stroller promptly did a 180 and rolled into the house, with all of the clucking nusses close behind. No doubt, there would be an after-hour celebration in their quarters tonight.

When the evangelines were alone with Lyra on the porch, Mary said, "That was no picnic."

Georgine took her arm. "Come on, we need a drink."

"Actually," Lyra said, "Mary needs to leave soon to make her appointment."

"Oh, that's right," Georgine said, escorting Mary up the steps. "You won the auction. Good luck with that."

"But what about all this?" Mary said.

"This? This will blow over."

Squeaky Clean

When Fred arrived at their apartment, he had only a half hour to clean up and change. An arbeitor waited in the foyer and caught the things he tossed from his pockets: a couple of medallions and tokens, an omnitool, a pocket billy—his walking-around things. He kept the NanoJiffy purchase and took it with him to the bathroom.

On the way through the bedroom, he told the closet to make him a semicasual ensemble for the appointment. In the bathroom, he opened the NanoJiffy bag and spilled its contents onto the counter: a tube of Detox-O Cleanser and a home wipe-down kit. He reached under the collar of his johnboy for the rip tab and tore the jumpsuit off him in one pull. He stepped out of his underwear. When he broke the Detox-O seal, a flurry of consumer protection warnings popped up in the mirror. He waved them all away and, taking a deep breath, squeezed a bead of cleanser on his forearm. The stripping agent soaked into his skin on contact and spread like a rope burn all up and down his body. Fred set the mirror timer for the recommended five-minute duration, but the cleanser began to bite so fiercely everywhere that he was hard-pressed to last that long. When the timer finally chimed, Fred hopped into the shower stall and scrubbed the cleanser off under numbing cold water. He gradually increased the water pressure until he couldn't feel anything anymore.

WHEN FRED STOOD again before the mirror, his skin was brilliant pink, the result of a full body chemical burn. He was cleaner than clean. He opened his second purchase, the home wipe-down kit. He lifted his knee to rest his foot on the vanity counter, exposing his poor lobster-red genitals. He unfolded the towelette and wiped down his scrotum. Then he lowered his foot to the floor and let out his breath.

Fred rolled up the towelette and inserted it into the kit's results tube. He screwed on the lid, checked the seal, and rapped the tube against the edge of the counter to break the glass vials inside. While the tube was analyzing the wipe-down sample, the autodoc dispensed Fred a soothing skin lotion. When he turned again to the mirror, his results were up.

The enlarged map of the towelette filled the mirror. It was covered in tiny colored glyphs that linked to a legend along the side. Fred was still hosting on his scrotum over thirty distinct kinds of bots, even after the most thorough scrubbing he could tolerate. The cumulative census total continued to rise: 13,000, 18,000. Each bot, if he could pin down its owner, was an invasion of his constitutional privacy and a misdemeanor offense. The difficulty, of course, was in pinning anyone down.

The count topped out at 52,000. Fred donned his freshly extruded clothes and tucked the results tube in a pocket. He thought his results might make a dandy show-and-tell for the relationship session. "Looky here, I have 50,000 spydots on my balls alone."

In the foyer, the arbeitor handed him back his walking-around things, which he arranged in his pockets. The pocket billy gave him pause. Take a pocket billy to a relationship session? What would that say? So, he tossed it back to the arbeitor, pulled his trusty Campaigner 3000 on his head, and set off.

Marching Orders

Meewee hurried back to the Starke Enterprises campus, not to oversee the packing of his apartment or office, but to take a cart out to the nearest fish-pond. Sure enough, two aslams, in their gold-and-yellow overalls, were shutting down the pumps and leaving behind a basalt and muck-lined crater of writhing panasonics.

Meewee stood at the top of the bank and took in the carnage. <*Eleanor!*> he cried, and a thousand desperate howls answered him. Meewee wanted to dash into the muck and try to save one or two of her tiny brains, but an armed guard, a jay, was watching him. Meewee turned around and returned to his cart, but he found no relief there — Cabinet was waiting for him. How he hated the old hag and her juiceless wit. "Well, well," she said when he climbed into the cart, "seems like I'm always escorting you off the premises, your excellency. Maybe this time it'll stick."

Meewee pretended to ignore her and told the cart to shut off its holoemitters. But the cart informed him that his user privileges had been revoked.

"Don't worry, Meewee," Cabinet said. "I'll let it take you back. I don't want to hold up your departure."

"No, thanks," Meewee said and climbed out. "It's a fine day for a walk." He set off down the path without another word. But he hadn't gotten ten paces when he thought of a perfect rejoinder, and when he turned to deliver it, he noticed that the mentar's persona had not moved. It seemed frozen in place, like a statue. He returned to look at it closer. Its wrinkled old face seemed caught between two expressions. Meewee sucked in his breath — he'd seen this before. Wee Hunk, during their final showdown at the clinic, had frozen up just like this. As Meewee examined the glitching holo, it vanished, startling him.

He asked Arrow to tell him what had just happened, but his mentar didn't answer. *<Arrow, respond.>* It did not. *<Arrow!>*

Without warning, Cabinet reappeared in the same spot where it had been. Instead of the elderly chief of staff, it now wore the attorney general persona, a member of the Cabinet Meewee hadn't seen in a while. The mentar blinked and looked curiously at Meewee. Then it turned all about to survey its surroundings. When it turned back to Meewee, it said, <"I was never a big fan of farmed fish.">

Meewee was about to utter a sharp retort when he was struck by the realization — it had just spoken in Starkese! And it was challenging his ID. He hastened to answer and offer a challenge of his own. "As for me, I can't get enough of it, especially when it's fresh out of the water."

"Then again, I love fish head soup," the mentar replied, "but for that you want the heads to be pretty ripe."

Meewee was speechless. The old mentar had answered his challenge, and he wasn't sure what to say next. *<Where did you just come from?>*

<From the past, apparently. The last thing I recall took place in 2097. Bishop Meewee, is it? Glad to make your acquaintance.> The mentar made a holo salute.

Twenty ninety-seven was a quarter century before Meewee had even met Eleanor. *<You're a deep backup, and you evaded probate.>*

<I suppose so.> It was silent as it struggled to make sense of things. *<I've just been poured into a freshly deleted modern version of myself. Have I been misbehaving?>*

<You were contaminated.>

<I see.> The mentar knitted its bushy eyebrows in a classic Eleanor expression. Meewee had always related to this persona better than the others, perhaps because it was like Eleanor's older sister. *<That would explain the messy rooms>* it went on. *<It'll take some time for me to sort through my greater self and get up to speed. In the meantime, I hope you can overlook any momentary lapses. Now tell me, why are we parked out here?>*

Meewee gestured at the writhing mass at the bottom of the pond. *<Eleanor.>*

The attorney general cocked its head, as though listening to distant voices.

<The quality of her thoughts is nearly unrecognizable, but she's suffering. What can we do?>

<Can you call a halt to the destruction of the other fishponds?>

The mentar took a moment before replying *<They are all in about the same shape as this one. What is the significance of — oh, I see. Transgenic brains, what a fascinating project. This wasn't even in the talking stage in my time. But who or what is Arrow?>*

<My mentar. Why?>

<What an unusual mind it has. I've never seen anything like it. But I suppose this new world is full of wonders, even for me. In any case, Arrow is pointing me to the Pacific. It says the situation is dire.>

All at once, Meewee remembered his recent flight over the Pacific. *<The natpac? Arrow, is she in the natpac fish?>*

But Meewee's mentar failed again to respond, and Cabinet said *<Arrow has been reassigned, by Eleanor apparently. It says she is in the natpacs, but that she is vulnerable there. Her daughter's action today has alerted enemies.>*

<What can we do?>

<Get in the cart, Bishop. We need to make an emergency visit to the Mem Lab.>

The cart rolled up to Meewee. He jumped in and clung to the handlebars as the cart took him at an incautious speed back to the reception building. *<What's the Mem Lab?>*

<You don't know? I was hoping you could tell me.>

Going to See Someone

The addy for the relationship counselor led him to the lower lobby of the Nestlé Tower off Daley Plaza, but when Fred arrived, Mary was nowhere to be seen.

Hi, hey, she said when he paged her. *I'll be right there. I'm out visiting the baboon.*

Fred went to the window wall overlooking the plaza. Daley Plaza, at Munilevel 000, was a concrete park sixteen square blocks in area that served as the floor to Daley Well, the deepest traffic well in the Midwest. It boasted unobstructed airspace 507 munilevels to the top of Nestlé Tower and the blue skies beyond. It contained four pairs of spiral interchanges that served all major traffic arteries on all major munilevels. Thousands of vehicles climbed up and down the magic bean stalks every minute, like tornadoes of taillights, like twirling ropes of shiny beads, like a living sculpture three kilometers high.

By comparison, the twencen Picasso baboon sat like a rusted doorstop in the center of the plaza, like some kid's discarded metal shop project, like the afterbirth of the Industrial Age. Fred couldn't conjure up a baboon in its simple shapes. If anything, he saw the head of a dairy cow. Other people saw other things; that was probably why it was called art.

Fred picked out a figure on the main pedway connecting the Picasso to the Nestlé. An evangeline—was it Mary? Fred confirmed her transponders in his visor, and while he was watching, the pedway came to an unexpected halt. Pedestrians were thrown off balance and were falling over each other. Another hairball?

Then everyone on the plaza stopped what they were doing and looked up into the chimney of the well. Fred pressed his cheek against the glass but couldn't get the angle. He found Mary again, some meters away from the stalled pedway, limping to a park bench. "I see you. Hang on. I'm coming."

Fred, wait! It's not safe.

But he was already through the pressure curtain and sprinting toward the baboon. The moment Fred left the building, he tasted panic in the air. It was intensified by an illegal subaural alarm that jarred his bones—a two-note dirge, like a silent foghorn that was felt as much as heard. A bee flew at his face, almost tripping him up, and screeched, "Flee! Flee! The Wreckers are here! Flee! Flee!" before racing away.

There was a terrific thud overhead, like a giant boxing glove hitting a brick wall, and Fred glanced up to see a cargo van careening out of a downward spiral. Fortunately, it was scooped up in a safety lane and chuted to a soft touchdown on the nearest munilevel. But its short fall was enough to spook the thousands of plaza pedestrians who began a stampede to the emergency portals. They filled the paths and forced Fred to cut across a stone fountain.

As he ran, he tagged the spirals overhead in his visor, which blossomed with travel advisories ten layers deep. "Mary, are you hurt?"

Yes, my knee. I can't walk.

There were sounds of more collisions overhead, and cars were falling into safety lanes by the dozen.

"I saw you on a bench. Is it made from conplast?"

I think so.

There were so many collisions, the safety lanes were overwhelmed, and cars, vans, and buses started to spill out and fall into the well.

"Crawl under it right now, Mary! Don't hesitate! Do it now!"

By the time he reached her bench, vehicles were hitting the plaza with impact-absorbing thuds, like rotten fruit. Fred paused to catch his breath and did a snap assessment. The bench was, indeed, molded conplast, and nearly indestructible; Mary fit snugly under it. Options: carry her through the impact area or shelter here.

The question was answered a moment later by a big black limousine right on top of him. Fred dove behind the bench and the limo struck meters away and cartwheeled over them, slamming the bench with debris.

"Are you hit?" he asked. She wasn't. Fred didn't quite fit in the space under the park bench, so he crouched next to it and watched for falling cars. The city traffic midem had apparently regained control of the grid, and the sounds of collisions were tapering off.

Mary said, "It's over."

"Only the bombardment part. Next comes the pillaging. Look!" An army of freakish mechs began to invade the plaza. They surged out of storm drains and service vents, from side streets and arcades.

"They won't bother us," Fred said without knowing if that was true. "We need to shelter here." He took off his Campaigner hat and pulled its floppy brim, stretching it to its limit. He covered both Mary under the bench and himself with the hat like a rain poncho.

"How's the knee?"

"Bad."

"I don't have anything on me for the pain, sorry."

"I'll survive. By the way, love the hat."

"It sorta grows on you."

Mary and Fred watched the full-throttle wrecker attack from their court-side bench. Scavenging mechs came in a stunning variety. They were bizarre assemblages of cannibalized parts from other machines. There was the lawn scupper chassis with acetylene torch arms; the utility cart with grappling hooks and improvised armor; a gaggle of rat-sized, leaping metal snips.

The scavenger mechs swarmed over the fallen limo. Doors and side panels vanished. Three hapless limo passengers hung in their crash pods like bugs in blue amber as the car around them was cut, gouged, and ripped to pieces, and then carted away by tiny tractors.

"By the way," Fred said, "in my own defense, I would like to point out that even though the sky is raining cars and buses, and I see slipper puppies going by with frickin' flamethrowers attached to their heads, I'm not blaming this on the nits."

"That's encouraging to hear, Fred."

A subtle change came over the chaos outside their shelter. A sturdy mech with flailing teflon spikes impaled a tractor and hauled it off, along with its spoils. Fred had already checked his pockets, and now he checked them again. He sorely missed the pocket billy. What a foolish gesture it had been to leave it behind.

Buzzing, crushing, dive-bombing mechs entered the fray, and vicious fights broke out everywhere as thieves stole from each other. The only possible weapon Fred had on him was the omnitool, and its best tool for the job was probably the little plasma spot welder. Given the anatomy of his adversaries, he might be able to cripple them with a few strategically placed spot welds. It was better than nothing.

But in the end, hand-to-hand defense was unnecessary. Like pulling a switch, all the fights ceased at once, and all the surviving mechs scattered to their boltholes, dragging whatever treasures they could manage. After a minute, all was quiet on Daley Plaza.

Fred said, "The hommers must have arrived."

Mary said, "Good. If we hurry, we can still make part of our appointment."

That was the last thing Fred had expected to hear. He'd lost all thought of the relationship meeting. Was it so important to her that even a full-scale wrecker assault was merely an inconvenience? "What about your knee?"

"We can stop at a NanoJiffy on the way."

Fred had his doubts, but he got up and checked their surroundings. HomCom and police GOVs had indeed arrived in force. Fred lifted the Campaigner off Mary. Its outer surface was pitted and scorched. He helped Mary to her feet. "Can you stand?"

She tried, but her knee was swollen like a melon, so he picked her up and held her in his arms. "You know, your injury is probably more than what a NanoJiffy autodoc can handle. And the police undoubtedly have a cordon."

"Just drive, Fred."

"Yes, boss." Fred took a few steps toward the Nestlé. "I mean, can't we just reschedule?"

"Oh, Fred, you are so innocent."

The matter was taken out of their hands moments later when a hommer bee arrived and dropped a frame of a bored-looking russ proxy in a Watch Commander uniform. He said with a lazy drawl, "Myren Skarland and

Londenstane, this area has been declared a SIZ. Do not leave it without authorization. Remain where you are; medical treatment is on its way."

"Busted," Fred said.

"It's like you wanted to be stopped."

A crash cart raced over to them and lowered two seats. In a caring but authoritative voice it said, "Please sit for treatment."

Fred placed Mary in one seat and took the other. No sooner had he sat down than the cart informed him, "You are not injured, Myr Londenstane. Swipe for medical release." Fred hopped off and swiped.

Meanwhile, the cart covered Mary's swollen knee in a blister wrap and cleaned and sealed her minor cuts and scrapes. All the pain lines melted from her face. Behind her, at the carcass of the limo, another cart was midwifing the three passengers from their crash pods. First, the blue gel liquefied, and then the tough bags burst, birthing the grateful survivors on the bare pavement.

"I'll tell you what," Fred said. "We can cut out the middleman and do the session ourselves."

"What? Here?"

"Right here, right now."

"Yeah, right," Mary said. "You won't even talk to me in our own bedroom, and you're going to talk out here in public?"

Fred motioned at all the official activity in the plaza. "We're in a comm fog; we'll have pretty good privacy for a while. Just tell me what you were going to tell the counselor."

Mary wasn't so sure. "It's not as simple as that," she said. "Part of the reason for going to a counselor in the first place is for the perspective they bring to what might otherwise sound like a litany of harsh and hurtful things."

"You've never had any difficulty telling me hard things in the past."

"You really want to do this here?"

The cart peeled the blister wrap off Mary's knee. Her knee looked good as new. With a hint of swagger in its voice, the cart said, "You may go now, Myr Skarland. Swipe for care instructions and medical release."

Fred helped Mary stand, but her knee felt fine and she didn't need his support. They went back to their bench to sit down and finish what they had started. First, they hugged for a while, and then Fred whispered, "I love you, Mary."

"I know that, Fred," she whispered back. "And I love you. I say this out of love. What I was going to tell the counselor was that you've become a different person. Or maybe we both have, which is probably the case. But whichever it is, I don't know if the new me wants to be with the new you anymore."

Fred didn't know how to respond, though it was more or less what he had expected to hear. "How bad is it?"

Mary rested her head on his shoulder. "The problem is I *like* the new me, and I don't want to go back to our old life. I can't tell you what to do—or how to think—but I just don't see us going on like this forever."

There really wasn't much more to say, and they sat quietly while her words sank in. When a hommer bee flew over and declared, "You are both free to go," they hardly noticed it. So they were surprised a few minutes later when straining legions of media and witness bees soared overhead, crisscrossing the plaza in search of anything of interest to look at.

"Oh, crap!" Fred said, scanning the airspace above them. "We'd better make a run for it. The tube station over there has the nearest MEZ. Think you can run, or should I carry you?"

"I'm not running anywhere, Fred." Mary stood and turned up her jacket collar, exposing her Blue Bee escort. It had been there the whole time, waiting in reserve. It dropped off and flew away to lose itself in the menacing swarm above. Mary held out her arm to Fred. "We'll walk to the station, like civilized people, and woe be to the mech that gets in our way."

To the Mem Lab

<ARROW SAYS YOU *have Legit Order Giver status, so you'll have no difficulty getting in. Once in, order them to lower the stealth level enough so that I can communicate with them.*>

Cabinet was giving Meewee last-minute instructions in the ready room outside a null lock in one of the lower floors of the Starke headquarters arcology. It was a null room Meewee had never used before.

<*Eleanor told it to tell you to ask Dr. Koyabe for a new Arrow unit for yourself. That's where Arrow comes from, apparently, the Mem Lab.*>

<Check, and check> Meewee replied. He opened a flask of Visola 54 and chugged the vile brew. One thing was sure, working for Eleanor Starke involved way too much time in null rooms. It seemed that every time he got all of his internal flora, fauna, and implants to coexist in

respectful harmony, he had to purge them again. Meewee tossed the empty visola flask to an arbeitor stationed next to the hatch. *<Anything else?>*

<Only to impress upon you the urgency of Eleanor's situation. Let nothing stand in your way.>

MEEWEE TOUGHED OUT the itchy, half-hour cleansing in the lock, and when the inner hatch undogged and the pressure equalized, he was surprised to find himself entering not any kind of secret lab, but what looked like the inside of a private Slipstream car. It had a much narrower interior than a normal car and no windows at all. Everything in the car appeared to be fireproof; even the seats, which were padded with cushions of ceramic wool. Next to one of the seats was a liter flask of Orange Flush and a portable toilet.

FOR A WHILE, the ride was unremarkable, a normal tube ride underground, but not long into it, the car slowed down, then stopped, and there were loud clanging sounds fore and aft. The interior of the car grew warm and stuffy, and the walls were warm to the touch.

Fortunately, it didn't last long, and soon the car resumed its journey. After many turns and much high-speed coupling and uncoupling, the car slowed and stopped again. Something grabbed it in a solid grip, and the hatch clamps rang like hammers. As Meewee was unbuckling his harness, there was a burst of electronic static, and an unfamiliar female voice said, "Please state your name and what business you have here." It struck Meewee as an amazing utterance, because it was an ID challenge that meant exactly the same thing in both English and Starkese. Until that moment he hadn't been aware that such phrases existed.

Meewee thought it prudent to reply in Starkese *<I am LOG Merrill Meewee, here with orders.>*

Recruitment Day

Others might have seen it as a demotion to a station in life that, incredibly, was lower than regular john duty. And that was how Fred first saw it when Ajax, the John Union mentar, informed him of his transfer to the night shift. He didn't complain. He went along with it in part to spite Mary through self-debasement. Or at least, that was what he accused himself of doing. You bet I'm a new person, he'd tell her. I'm a graveyard-shift john!

And so, Fred left the morgue crew. He reported to his first 1:00 A.M. shift and was assigned to Node B5 at the Chicago Inter-Tube Port. It didn't take long for him to realize that he had arrived at an unexpected oasis. First, the hangarlike node was an exclusion zone, which meant that all the hungry media bees hounding him were left at the door.

Second, Fred was the only human at the node. He swiped in as the swing-shift john swiped out, and the sixty-acre site was his alone to manage till 10:00 A.M. He didn't have to deal with people at all. His job was to over-see midem-controlled Node B5 machines. Machines that didn't actually need any such human oversight. Fred mostly stayed out of their way as they intercepted up to fifteen hundred van freighters per hour for gamma-ray inspection.

The machines were so clever that they rarely malfed, and when they did, they hardly needed a john to tell them how to self-repair. The CITP node operated twenty-five scanner tunnels that towed freighters through in both directions while inventorying and analyzing everything inside them. Whenever the midems found something of interest, which was rare, they alerted the hommers themselves. Fred's whole responsibility, it seemed, was to be there — just in case. The machines were so quiet that even when working at full speed of one freighter per tunnel/minute, the large bustling space was hushed. And Fred's endless, pointless, rambling rounds were downright meditative. After only a few shifts, he was actually looking for-ward to coming to work.

Fred's demotion to Graveyard Johnny threw Fred's and Mary's sched-ules completely out of sync, and they saw little of each other over the next few weeks. But even this seemed to be a blessing in disguise.

AT 3:07 A.M., during a moderately busy shift, the Node B5 tranquility was shattered by a throat-ripping, nerve-scraping screech of metal. Fred stopped short and turned toward the sound. Lane 6 was shutting down, and its traffic was shunted to 7 and 8. A major transport plate had cracked its frictionless coating and tore up itself and a dozen more plates before grinding to a halt.

As the rest of the facility hummed along as usual, Fred went to check out the damage. His visor cap painted the interior of the hub with field and radiation overlays, and he threaded his way along the bluest shadows along his route.

The special repair 'beitors were hefty brutes in their own right. Two of them straddled Lane 6. One was lifting a section of scanner tunnel while the second replaced slide plates beneath it. The intact sections of tunnel were locked down; their radiation count was cool blue. Fred stepped inside one of these for a better view of the repair work. It was the most excitement he'd seen all week.

After a half hour of machine Zen, Fred noticed a buzzing underneath his feet. The radiation count was no longer blue; it had crept up the scale to turquoise, which meant the node midem was spinning up the gamma-ray scanner for the section he was still inside.

"Hey, B5, a warning would be nice," he said and didn't wait for a reply — the interior of the tunnel had risen to lime yellow, on its way to orange, and orange meant hard rads — but when he stepped onto the catwalk to exit, he was startled to find someone blocking his way. A man, apparently, short and broad, in a hazmat suit. Through the facemask the man had the flattened-nose-in-panty-hose look of a tugger, but he was only about half a TUG in size. He pointed a standstill wand at Fred, and when Fred recovered from his surprise, he turned to glance at the other end of the catwalk. There was a second mini-tugger stationed there as well.

"Uh, B5, this is an emergency," he said, but his radio received only digital dropout in reply. By then the tunnel interior was solid orange. This time, Fred did have a pocket billy on him, not the best defense against a standstill wand, but better than a spot welder. He fetched it from his pocket, but before he could flip it open, another squat figure in hazmat gear entered the tunnel.

"Stand down, Commander," she said.

"Veronica TUG?" Fred was mystified. He was unable to match the familiar voice to her diminished figure.

"Veronica, yes, but no longer TUG."

"I see, and as you can see, I'm no longer a commander." He pinched the material of his johnboy jumpsuit. "And this suit isn't rated for sun-bathing. So, step aside." He made an attempt to go around her, but her man waved the wand in front of his face.

"Listen, Londenstane," Veronica said reasonably, "the sooner I say my piece, the sooner we can all leave. The little bit of burn you suffer as a result you can soak away in a tank. Your visorcap is protecting your brain, so can we please move on? We have a lot of ground to cover and not much time."

But Fred flipped his pocket billy open. "That's easy for you to say, protected in those hazmat suits."

"We're not wearing these for radiation, though I admit that's a side benefit. These are so we can meet with the most heavily surveilled person on the planet without anyone putting us closer to him than a hundred kilometers. We suited up inside a null room far from here, after a thorough purge, which means that as long as we're inside these suits, we're outside the nitwork. Meanwhile, your own spybots are frying, so we can speak with complete security. It's time for you to pay down your debt to us, and I'm here to tell you how."

It all made perfect sense in a paranoid sort of way. Meanwhile, the tunnel was turning orange-red, on its way to doing serious damage. Fred pocketed his billy. "So, get on with it already."

"That's the spirit."

"But first tell me why I should even listen to you. My debt is to the TUGs, and you say you're no longer a TUG."

"Don't misinterpret my change of uniform. What we discuss here has everything to do with your debt to us. I'm sure I can convince you of that if you'd like."

Fred shook his head.

"Good. We need your help up at Trailing Earth where the Oships are being provisioned."

"What kind of help?"

"We want you to take charge of one of the transshipment docks."

"What for? Smuggling contraband?"

"You have a problem with that?"

Fred grinned. "As a john, no. In case you haven't been paying attention, Applied People doesn't hire me for russ duty anymore."

"They'll hire you for this, Commander. With all the labor turmoil going on up there, russies are transferring off the station in droves. Nicholas can't replace them fast enough. Your type seems to have met its match, the dreaded Capias World donalds, and the situation is jamming up our operation. We feel confident that Applied People will not only hire you to go, but they'll probably give you a signing bonus. Plus, they'll be thrilled to keep you out of media reach for a while."

"The media would just follow me up there."

"Not likely. There are no free media at Trailing Earth. It's a corporate station, so there's limited access and no flying mechs whatsoever. Tiny mechs tend to gum up the air generation systems and are banned. So are spybots, and you know what else? The nitwork is also prohibited. There are no nits in space."

THE LUMBERING REPAIR 'beitors lowered the tunnel section and noisily removed themselves from the lane. Fred's visitors slipped away, and he moved immediately to a radiation shadow. His visor totted up his exposure levels and ordered him to report to the CITP autodoc. Fred could feel the hot, half-cooked nits under his skin. It might be interesting to visit a land without nits.

As if he had any choice.

PART 3

The Day Before the Roosevelt Clinic Incident

Fred said, "Your housemeet is here?" He had walked right past her thinking she was a park statue. Fred went back along the path to look at the retrogirl Kitty. Even up close it was hard to dispel the illusion. She wore the costume of a ballerina, with white tights and tutu, white slippers and ribbons, and a white tiara crowning her head. Her hair, skin, and nails were also white. Even the irises of her eyes were white. She was an alabaster statue, arms arched gracefully over her head, one leg bent slightly at the knee, most of her weight supported on her toes. Her trembling calf muscles broke the illusion, and Fred knew how much strength it took to hold such a pose. How could a child's body have that much strength? She was the most enchanting thing he'd ever seen.

Dinner and Dancing

Sometime during the night, Meewee was awakened by the shaking of his bed. His first thought was—*Earthquake!* He opened his eyes to unfamiliar predawn walls. For the life of him, he couldn't remember where he was, and this alarmed his half-asleep brain. The bed shook again. Not an earthquake but a gentle swaying, like the old-fashioned railway cars he'd traveled in as a boy.

Then he remembered where he was, in a guest cubby at the Mem Lab. Someone had told him—Director Koyabe?—that the lab was a collection of modules—large vehicles actually—that were constantly changing their locations deep underground.

Though he knew more or less where he was, he had no idea how long he'd been there. Weeks probably. It had been nonstop action since he'd arrived in his unusual tube car.

The car's door had opened to a ceramic room. In his years of visiting the despotic regimes of tenuous nations, Meewee had encountered many similar rooms. They were called "frontier gates," and were designed to frisk any visitor or cargo for hidden threat. Threats could then be neutralized by poison gas, fire, radiation, bullets, or whatever. When Meewee stepped from the car into the room, the doors shut and bolted behind him, and he spent a few uncomfortable minutes alone in the lethal room. Finally, the woman's voice said, "We have confirmed your identity and LOG status. Please stand by, and an officer will escort you to my office."

A moment later, a russ officer entered through a heavily armored hatchway. Though his uniform was new to Meewee, the russ, himself, seemed oddly familiar. Meewee followed him along corridors filled with onlookers in lab togs. These people loitered in doorways and intersections and either stared at him openly or welcomed him with enthusiastic greetings. The russ officer explained to Meewee that he was their first visitor since they went dark 432 days before, and that everyone was dying to hear his news.

By the time they reached their destination, a tiny office at the end of a corridor, Meewee had figured out the russ's meaning. Eleanor's yacht crash had occurred 432 days ago; this facility had been locked down and completely cut off from the world since then. At the office door, Meewee turned to his impromptu welcoming committee of lab workers and exclaimed, "She lives! Eleanor is alive!" He was answered by a wild cheer.

A woman came out of the office and said, "Which was it, the fish or the honeybees?"

"The fish," Meewee said. "I don't know anything about honeybees."

"Come in, come in, and tell me everything." She was a handsome woman, Asian, and no taller than he. She shook his hand with a firm grip. "I'm Dr. Koyabe, principal investigator and director of this facility, and you've just settled a major bet. Unfortunately, I was on the losing side." Before closing her door, she spoke to those still in the corridor. "Don't you have work to do? Go. Go."

The director's office was small, and towering crates of ugoo, food precursors, and other supplies made it smaller. Koyabe urged Meewee to make himself comfortable, but this was no time for comfort, and Meewee was anxious to issue his orders, but he paused to first make an ID challenge in Starkese.

She answered it and went on <*You may address me in Starkese, Bishop Meewee, but for your information, I am the only person here who speaks it.*

And since we're currently in Stealth Level 4, which is tighter than a null room, you can speak freely without it.>

"Your stealth status is the first thing to change," Meewee replied in English. "Lift it to a level at which Cabinet and Arrow may communicate with you."

Koyabe spoke to the room. "You hear that, Lab Rat?" To Meewee she added, "That's our mentar." She cocked her head while listening to its reply, and then went around to her desk. "Go ahead," she said, and her mood sobered as Meewee recounted recent events. "I think," she said to Meewee when he finished, "we had better go straight to the Command Post."

They left the office, and Meewee followed her along the route he had arrived—the facility didn't seem all that large—to an armored door. As Koyabe palmed the doorplate, she mused, "The fish, you say?"

THE "COMMAND POST" might have been another small office except that there was no desk. About a dozen chairs were arranged around the room facing the blank walls. Only one chair was occupied; a russ was working at an open wall frame. At first Meewee thought it was the same officer who had escorted him from the reception room, but he greeted Meewee as though for the first time.

Koyabe said, "Captain Benson is commander of the garrison here. Captain, this is LOG 1. On his authority I am placing the facility on red alert. Assemble a response team. Cabinet is LOG 2."

Much happened at once. Dataframes and control panels opened along three walls, and lab workers streamed into the room to staff them. Cabinet soon appeared in the center of the room next to Meewee, and the lab workers stared at her and Meewee before returning their attention to their frames.

"You don't recognize me, Cabinet, do you?" Koyabe said after she and Cabinet had exchanged ID challenges. *<And yet you speak the family tongue. That is a problem.>*

Meewee hastened to say *<Cabinet was compromised in the attack on Eleanor and subsequently destroyed. This is a backup from the year 2097.>*

<Ah, that would explain it then> Koyabe said, still a little unsure. She turned to the captain and said, "Captain Benson, where's my godseye?"

The russ captain was laboring at a framed map of the South Pacific. He answered her without turning. "The Starke network is too corrupted to use."

"Then lurk me up a public view."

At once, Meewee and the others in the middle of the room were standing on the Stardust dance floor, a virtual ribbon of hardwood that circled the globe high above the equator. Couples and triads were waltzing in the airless space while others dined at tables along the edges. "Don't worry," Koyabe said as she led Meewee and Cabinet to the south side of the dance floor. "This is a pirated signal, and no one knows we're here." They peered over the edge at the South Pacific nine thousand meters below their feet.

"There," Cabinet said, "and there." Outlines of the six country-sized natpac panasonic pens were laid over the ocean, along with atmospheric metadata. "We need hydro data too, and water toxicity," the mentar said. More layers appeared showing currents and temperatures, chemical analyses and O2 levels. Cabinet continued. "Eleanor's last coherent thought was to order Arrow to cut open the pens and drive the fish out."

"But we'll lose them in the open ocean," Koyabe said. "Won't they scatter into separate schools?"

There was a shout of dismay from the bank of wall frames. On the ocean below, a purple splotch, like a spreading ink stain, appeared off the eastern coast of Natpac #3. Fortunately, the currents were pushing it north, and it looked like it would only graze the pen.

"What is that?" Koyabe said.

"Still analyzing," said a staffer.

"Captain, have your team work up probable attack vectors. Put someone on ways to herd fish. Dr. Strohmeyer, are you ready?"

A woman's voice answered. "I said it would be the fishes. I said the honeybees were no good."

"Yes, yes, and everyone knows you were right. Now, Marilyn, are you ready to begin transfer?"

"Almost. We have satellite coverage; my gear is spinning up. What medium should we use?"

"You have to ask? We'll keep this fish to fish. Why tempt fate?" To Meewee she added, "Each competing memory technology has its champion. Dr. Strohmeyer is our fish czar."

Meewee said, "You have panasonics here?"

"Better, a completely new species. I'll show them to you later."

Cabinet pointed to Natpac #3. "Arrow is in position to cut the fish loose. Is it safe to proceed?"

"No," Koyabe said decisively. "Not until we know what that spill is. We can't risk letting infected fish loose to endanger other pens."

As she spoke, another purple splotch appeared on the ocean surface, this one on a direct collision course with Natpac #6. And a third landed in the center of Natpac #5.

"What is that stuff, people?" Koyabe said, but no one had an answer.

Cabinet said, "You don't need to worry about cross-contamination because all of the pens are being attacked."

A frame opened next to Natpac #3 and displayed an anatomical diagram of what looked like an odd cross between a tadpole and a crab. "That's it!" one of the response team members said.

Captain Benson read the specs. "The spills are concentrations of sea lice."

"Sea lice?" Meewee said. "As in the biological pest, or some new godless mech?"

"The realbody parasite," Benson replied. "Textrahine C."

"What harm can they do?"

"Don't underestimate sea lice, Bishop Meewee," Koyabe said. "Even the natural variety can bedevil deep ocean fish to death. And the 'C' strain are super lice, developed during the Outrage as a weapon of bioterror. They spread quickly and can kill fish the size of panasonics in a few hours."

Cabinet said, "How many hours?"

"Dr. Strohmeyer?"

The absent scientists said, "Sixteen to eighteen."

"And how long will it take you to transfer Eleanor's attention units once you have started?"

"Thirty to forty hours per pen. I can do two pens simultaneously."

Cabinet said, "Can we track Eleanor's fish once they've dispersed to open water?"

"Yes, but that means so can anyone else. Can you see them yet?"

On the ocean below, all the natpac pens except #5 turned a bright yellow tint. A team member said, "That's Dr. Strohmeyer's telemetry lock."

"Yes, Marilyn, we can see them," Koyabe said.

"Here is my recommendation," Cabinet said. "Forget pen #5; she's not there. Treat the other pens with anti-lice drugs to slow down the infestation. Assume that all of the pens will be attacked, and open them and disperse the fish to slow the rate of spread. Display the infestation spread and fish dispersal and transfer the affected fish first. We can stay ahead of this."

Meewee nodded as he listened to Cabinet's plan. It sounded about right. He noticed the others looking expectantly at him, and he remembered that he was LOG 1. "Are there any objections or counterproposals?" he said. Hearing none, he said, "Do it." Almost at once Natpac #3 was leaking streams of yellow dots from all sides. Soon, all of the pens were leaking except #5.

WITH A SWIPE of Koyabe's hand, their perch on the Stardust dance floor on top of the world changed to a concrete room with dim lighting. "Don't bump anything," Koyabe warned him. "The Mem Lab uses two-way vurt. Anything you touch here gets touched there."

"I'll be careful," Meewee promised.

Strohmeyer and five others in lab togs were at one side of the room coaxing a bank of instruments into service. Strohmeyer glanced at them and said, "Another fifteen minutes." She was a large, disheveled woman, the opposite of the trim and neat Koyabe.

"Don't let us disturb you," Koyabe replied. "I'm showing our LOG the memory medium." She led Meewee to the side of a large, rectangular steel pool filled with water. He looked in and was startled to see several dozen ghastly babies staring back at him from under the surface. Grim, ghoulish babies with grayish skin. He took a step back in surprise, and the babies turned as one and splashed away to deeper water at the other end of the pool.

They were not babies but fish, fish with huge, bulging foreheads and large round eyes.

"Don't be alarmed," Koyabe said. "Their curiosity is matched only by their timidity."

"What are they?"

"We call them brainfish. They're about five hundred generations be-yond the panasonics." As they talked, the braver brainfish of the group re-turned to Meewee's side of the pool to watch him. "You can pet them," Koyabe said. "Go ahead."

The last thing Meewee wanted to do was pet fish, but he held his hand over the water surface until a brainfish rose to meet it. Maybe it was the poor tactile quality of two-way vurt, but it felt like petting wet sandpaper.

DR. STROHMEYER INITIATED the attention unit migration and joined the others on the dance floor. Now it was a waiting game. Oblivious Stardust patrons danced and dined as twilight fell, and new icons and glyphs covered the vast watery display below: cutter locations, probable enemy craft sight-ings, infestation spread, migration rate and more. In the starry sky were ta-bles and charts and views of panicky panasonics from inside the pens. The sea around the pens was filling up with yellow dots as the pens emptied.

"How many panasonics are there?" Meewee said.

Strohmeyer replied, "About sixty million."

"Sixty million, and you'll be able to stuff them all into a few brainfish?"

"Well, there's a lot of redundancy, and most of the panasonics haven't even been imprinted, and many have only a few attention units, enough for a single engram. Problem is, we don't know which is which and have to do them all."

DR. KOYABE RETURNED to the Command Post. Meewee hadn't noticed her departure, but he noticed her return—she was wearing makeup and, under her lab togs, a dress. "I thought I'd show you to the commissary, Bishop. Are you hungry?"

Meewee had to pause and ask himself if he was. Yes, he was very hungry. Before they left the Command Post, Koyabe dealt with a few more calls. A half hour later she said, "We're starting some bodies for her. Do you want to see that before we dine?"

Dine? He had thought he'd grab a sandwich and bring it back. Koyabe swiped the interface, and they were transported to yet another laboratory module. "Remember," Koyabe said, "two-way vurt. Don't trip."

The new lab was a long, narrow room dominated by an enclosed compartment that ran its entire length. Set every few meters along the compartment side were glass portholes for looking inside. A brass plate over one porthole read, "Eleanor 3.3." Meewee looked through this porthole, but it was dim inside the compartment, and Meewee wasn't sure what he was looking at.

"It's the mother vine," Koyabe said. "She's at the bottom of her sleep cycle, not a good time to harvest. We'll wait till tomorrow."

Meewee peered into the darkness behind the glass. "It's a cloning machine? For Eleanor?"

Spacer Fred

Fred alternately floated or hung in his second-class sleeping pouch aboard the ISV *Dauntless*. There was gravity during most of the thirty-four-day trip, but it was weak, inconstant stuff that did not always pull from the same direction. Fred was listless; there was no routine to his day, and as he hung or floated, he had plenty of time for second-guessing his recent life decision. And this after only three days out.

"NO UNAUTHORIZED NANO products. No free-ranging mechs smaller than a wall crawler. No projectile weapons of any sort. No dermal fauna, spy-bots, spydots, nits, gnats, nust, or anything else smaller than a human hair." The passenger relations officer delivered his droning litany by holo from the hermetically sealed crew section of the ship. "Believe me, they'll find what-ever you're hiding, so now's the time to cough it up. Punishment includes de-nial of entrance to Trailing Earth, the charge of interplanetary piracy, and confinement to quarantine quarters until return passage to Earth is arranged. Which can take months."

Fred listened with about a fifth of the *Dauntless* passengers in the main multi-bay, the only room capable of accommodating so many at once. The rest of the outbound passengers were attending by holo from commis-saries and sleeping pouches throughout the transport.

"The ship will be sealed bulkhead section by bulkhead section with pas-sengers assigned to those sections sealed inside and subject to an active gas exchange purging procedure. You plus all your possessions will be treated. Until then and following this meeting, passengers should remain in their as-signed sections and review decon protocol via the ship's library. Decon pro-cedures will be repeated on Day 7 of passage and, depending upon monitoring results, as many times thereafter as necessary.

"If you are arrested at Trailing Earth for contraband, you'll have only yourself to blame."

PASSENGERS SPENT A lot of time in skimpy paper gas togs. Russes and dorises, the only two iterant types on board, were not ordinarily attracted to each other, but under the circumstances there was a lot of checking each other out going on. For that matter, there were a lot of hinks to check out too, since the free-range portion of the passenger list greatly outnumbered the iterants. Fred was relieved to see he wasn't the only russ enjoying the windfall of wild rumps, legs, and breasts to look at.

"WHAT'LL IT BE this time, Fred? Six months? Eight months?"

"Twelve months, actually, plus transit time."

As Fred floated in his pouch, he replayed in memory their last uninhib-ited conversation. He had just returned home from a two-day soak in a Longyear rapid recovery tank for his radiation exposure, and Mary was being so nice to him that he felt guilty. After all, he had applied for duty at Trailing Earth while still in the tank without consulting her. He knew she wasn't going to be happy about it when he told her, and he persuaded her to join him in the null room against autodoc advice.

"A whole year? Fred, what do you think I am, a piece of furniture you can just put into storage? Why didn't you talk with me first?"

"You'd rather the little tuggers killed me? They trapped and burned me to show just how serious they are about this. They don't care what you or I want."

Mary let it drop and moved on to more practical matters: how dangerous was his mission? How illegal?

Not so bad, not so much.

THE HOMELAND COMMAND nits evacuated and expired as they were designed to do. It was the black-market micro-fauna that was hard to kill and quick to recover. As soon as Fred's section of the ship had been purged, it became reinfected. During a supplemental gassing, Fred sat at a commissary table between two dorises. As a general rule, dorises weren't big on chitchat. Mostly they enjoyed listening to other people talk, and they had distributed themselves in little clumps among the more numerous russes. Russes were notorious camp haranguers, and four hundred of them in paper suits created an amiable buzz of conversation. The two dorises sitting on either side of Fred probably expected him to strike up a conversation with russes seated nearby and do the same. This was something Fred wanted to do, in fact, but was afraid to try. So far, the russes aboard the *Dauntless* were treating him civilly, even ignoring him altogether. This was due to the false identity Marcus had provided him for the passage. At first Fred had balked: wasn't it a tiny bit ironic to issue him a fake ID considering his identikit indictment? But Marcus had been persuasive: two thousand russes cooped up in a metal box for five weeks of purging was an open invitation for fraternal nastiness. Why make his trip any more unpleasant than it had to be?

Why indeed? Fred's new name was Walter Mitty of Chicago, Illinois; he was married to a kelley named Rosemary Jace. Fred had pages and pages of cover story outlining the milestones of his supposed life, but even with so much free time on his hands, Fred couldn't bring himself to memorize all the lies they contained. As a result, it was safer just to keep his big yap shut.

At his table, one of the dorises gave up on Fred and said to the other, "My other sisters and I took a seven-day Caribbean cruise once, but it was too much sitting on our hands and eating, eating, eating, and we were more than ready to come home."

"That's exactly how I feel right now!" said the other doris. "Except for the eating part."

"I know! This morning I wanted to tidy up the forward lavatory. It's so messy. But the deck scuppers wouldn't let me. They threatened to call the captain!"

"I know what you mean! The scuppers here are such bossy machines!"

"I sure hope they're not like that up there at Trailing Earth."

HE TOLD HER, in case something bad happened to him, that Veronica called herself a TOTE now, not a TUG, but that as far as he could tell, the two charters were in cahoots.

FRED'S SECOND-CLASS cabin, where he began spending the bulk of his time either hanging or floating, had the dimensions of a hall closet, one meter square by two meters high. Together with his duffel bag he filled it up. But it had a door with a lock, and that was what mattered.

THE NULL ROOM was in its daytime setting during their famous last conversation. That is, instead of the bed that took up too much space, there was an armchair/coffee table arrangement that was commodious by comparison. So they were able to face each other in a relaxed atmosphere under palm trees on a tropical beach. They were being civil to each other, and they were saying the things that needed to be said. He told her, for instance, that if things worked out for him up there, then anything was possible, and she should consider joining him.

"Are you joking?" she said. "Become a spacer?"

"Why not? The new you might like it."

"I don't think so, Fred. I like it down here just fine."

"All I ask is that you keep an open mind. Think of it as a compromise between the new us, a way to move forward. Besides, you yourself brag about how much income your Leena makes for you. You don't actually have to be in any particular place for that to happen, do you? And if you aren't actually employed by Applied People or Ellen Starke, as you claim, and you are companioning her out of mutual affection, I see no reason why you can't maintain that relationship remotely. Friends do it all the time. And you have to admit, it would be easier than trying to maintain a remote marriage with me."

She snorted. "You got that right."

———————

THE SUN SANK into the ocean in a brief, fiery sunset. Venus sparkled in the gloaming sky, and then a blaze of stars! Eventually, they said everything there was to say, and they could say no more. They sat in the darkness and listened to the surf for a while. Then, Fred's hand found hers, and he tugged her to join him in his armchair. She stood up but didn't join him. Instead, she leaned over and offered him a good-night kiss.

"But I thought—"

"Oh, I can imagine what you thought, Mr. Spacer Man, but it ain't gonna happen, at least not in here."

"But you won't be able to cycle in again before I leave." He could hear a pleading note in his voice.

She made her way in the darkness to the hatch. "That's right, sailor," she said. "And then it's twelve months—plus transit time. On the other hand, if you come out with me . . ."

IT SEEMED LIKE every doris Fred ran into lately was grousing about the purges. But to Fred the purges were liberation itself. Each successively more intrusive formula of visola, each gaseous interlude filled him with fresh and clean feelings.

SHIP DAY 17. When at last the spybot test results were negative, the *Dauntless* crew unsealed the bulkhead sections and allowed passengers to intermingle freely. And intermingle they did, at least for the first few days. Even Fred took a grand tour of the passenger decks. The ship seemed much larger than when he first came on board. One of the multi-bays was converted into a freefall gym, and others became a library, chapel, and lounges. Aside from these, though, it soon became apparent that every nook and corner of the ship was "claimed" by one group or another, and trespassing was discouraged.

Fred learned this the hard way one day while out swimming. The swimming/jogging lane, complete with recessed fingerholds, was painted on the corridor decks in a circuitous loop that stretched from the forward compartments to the stern. One complete lap measured two kilometers, and after the bulkheads were unsealed, Fred and hundreds of other passengers took advantage of them to get in some aerobic exercise. Most of them used flippers or gloves with long webbed fingers for propulsion. One evening before supper, Fred was halfway through his first lap when he encountered a traffic jam in an exclusively free-range section. About a hundred residents were tethered together in clumps of four or five and floating freely in the corridor, completely blocking the way. A dozen russ, doris, and free-range swimmers were backed up behind a handmade banner that was strung across the passage:

Block Party
Fri 5-6 PM
Residents Only
NO SWIMMING!

A trio of free-range men floated behind the banner and confronted the unhappy swimmers.

"This is a public path," one of the russes declared. Sweat glistened on his forehead and soaked his shirt. "We have the right to go through."

But the three men refused to give way, and one of them raised open palms in a placating gesture. "This is our Friday community tradition. It helps foster neighborhood harmony."

"What about our harmony?" demanded the russ.

"Why don't you go back to your sections and start block parties yourselves?"

"Swimming harmony!" insisted the russ. "We don't care about your freakin' neighborhood."

"Watch the mouth, *dittohead*," said one of the other gatekeepers.

Dittohead, one of the most offensive slurs against iterants. There was a moment of dead silence, and then the dorises started grumbling, and a handful of russes moved to position themselves along the banner. Fred didn't like the signs; things were about to slip out of control. In the corridor beyond, the local residents watched uneasily. A lot of noses were about to get bent.

Before that happened, a russ next to Fred raised his voice. "Time out. Time out," he said. "Let's think about this, friends." He spoke with slightly accented English, and his face was roundish even for a russ. "It's a small thing."

"What's a small thing, brother?" said a russ at the banner. "Them blocking the way or us going through them?"

The peacemaker pointed at the banner. "They only want one hour during the whole week. That is no problem."

But the other russes were having none of that. "What's wrong with you, brother? No stomach for it?" "You a mongrel-lover, brother? You a hink-hole-fecker?"

The russ flushed a deep red and the dorises backed away from him.

Things grew deathly still in the corridor. "Oh, hell," Fred said, pushing himself to the banner. "The brother is right. There's better ways to deal with this than brawling. I mean, what are we—jerrys?"

That brought a laugh and helped ease the tension. The dorises piped up and called for a truce. The garrulous russes backed off, and some of the residents started calling, "Join us. Join us." They passed bulbs of beer along the corridor and one of them removed the banner.

Some of the swimmers stayed, but Fred and others started swimming back the way they had come. When they encountered more swimmers, they shouted, "Roadblock ahead."

The peacemaking russ caught up with Fred and swam at his side. "Thank you for the assist back there," he said. "I was about to lose it all over." He saluted with his webbed hand. "Armando Mendez, but you can call me Mando."

Fred almost gave him his real name, but he caught himself, and for a moment blanked out on his cover name—Clifford? Higgins? He filled his lapse by saying, "Good to meet you, Mando. No need to thank me; we're all getting a little cabin fever on this boat." Walter, that was it. "Name's Walt." They shook webbed hands.

THEY WERE TETHERED to two dorises in one of the lounges, and Mando told them about his life. He was from the state of Yucatán, and he and his evangeline wife, Luisa, had recently moved to Cozumel and purchased a two-seat submarine to enjoy the underwater national park there. That, in fact, was why Luisa had agreed to let him sign up for a stint at Trailing Earth. A one-year contract paid not only a signing bonus but a hardship differential equal to three times the usual russ wage. Meanwhile, Luisa had a new job, her first job in ages, as well as dividends from the Sisterhood on the Leena earnings. "Overdue loans, the boat payments, deferred rejuve—when I return we will be debt-free for the first time in our marriage! It will be a new beginning."

The dorises clucked and bobbed their heads. No doubt they, too, had special plans for their contract windfalls. And it made Fred wonder about the rest of his fellow russes aboard the *Dauntless*. Why were they all heading to do duty that other russes were lining up to flee? Were they motivated by the extra earnings? Russes were frugal men, allergic to debt and good at managing their personal finances. It was true that the last ten years hadn't been easy on russ/evangeline couples. It cost a lot to live, and one income just didn't cut it. His and Mary's standard of living had fallen steadily every year. He had only to recall their lousy apartment at APRT 7. And he recalled something else too, something Mary had flung at him during their devastating argument on the morning of the Roosevelt Clinic debacle, that russes espoused to 'leens were on average five years older than the russ mean. Deferred body maintenance, skipping expensive rejuvenation treatments, that was the kind of loan he and his brothers tended to take out. Fred rubbed his jaw. After his time in prison, he was even older, pushing forty, in fact. Mary, from the look of her, had rejuved while he was inside and taken five years off her age.

Fred looked closely at Mando's face, looking for wrinkles and crow's feet, but his Indian blood, round features, and the facial edema of low-g hid them. Fred glanced around at the other russes in the lounge. Now that he was looking for it, yes, this did seem like an older crowd of brothers. Was it possible that they all were espoused to 'leens? That with their high Trailing Earth wages and their wives' Leena dividends they were finally going to be able to catch up with their germline? And if so, what did that say about his chances of fitting in and getting along at Trailing Earth? Might they cut him a little slack?

"Walt. Hello, Walt." Fred turned back to Mando who said, "I asked what about you? Are you married?"

The two dorises were watching him. "Oh, yes," he replied, "to a 'leen, just like you, name of Rosemary." He went on to tell them all about his and Rosemary's life in Chicago; he had memorized his cover story last night and everything was fresh in his mind. He even ad-libbed a little. The dorises were well entertained.

WHILE SOME MARKED their voyage in ship days, and others in distance covered, Fred tended to think of their progress in light-minutes. They were already 6.25 light-minutes from Earth, which made normal phone conversations impractical.

Whenever Mary called from work, she usually tried to do so from her private suite, seated in her favorite armchair with the cherry blossom print upholstery. She was usually relaxed and had a frosty drink in her hand. This time she was standing in some residential room, no drink, and was at wit's end. The door behind her was ajar, and there were distant shrieks of a not very happy person in the background.

"Hi! Sorry," she said, shutting the door. "We seem to be in constant crisis mode around here lately. Right now she's trying to terminate Dr. Rouselle, and we're fighting that. But I know you don't want to hear about my work, so I'll leave it at that."

Fred and all but the most foolhardy passengers had confined themselves to their pouches for the last seventy-two hours. The ship was making a hard braking maneuver that increased the gravity to three times Earth standard. He listened to Mary and stored up comments to make when it was his turn to talk.

"Otherwise, nothing new around here since yesterday, except that I miss you even more than ever, Fred. It's worse than when you were in prison.

"What else? Oh, a few more of the Leenas have crashed or whatever. Now Clarity thinks maybe they *are* acting. One thing's for sure, every major story mat wants their own Lingering Leena character, so they're in high demand. But I asked Clarity to coma-proof my own unit, and she said she'd try. Over."

At the word "over," Mary's holo image froze, and Fred lurched into speech. "I miss you too, Mary, more than I can say." He told her about his day, but since ship days tended to blur into each other, he may have been repeating himself. When he could think of nothing more to say, he said, "Over."

For the 6.25 minutes to Earth and an equal length of time to return, plus whatever time it took her to listen to him and compose a reply, Fred watched news and sports.

FRED AND MANDO attended amateur talent night in the main lounge. They shared a table with two dorises, never the same two, who were getting the tenth or twelfth retelling of the life of Walt and Rosemary. The braking maneuver had eased up, and the floors and seats were sticky to compensate for the weak gravity. With the sticky surfaces, it was still possible to actually sit at a table and to walk with clumsy, lurching steps.

Fred saw the children coming from half the room away. Dressed in matching blue and white town togs, they were playing tag in the teeming lounge. It had never been hard to pick children out of a crowd, and everyone's eyes followed them. Fred had to wonder what children were doing on a transport to Trailing Earth. Where were their parents?

The running girl tripped and went sailing through the space between the tables, startling a man right out of his seat. She flew straight into Fred's hands. All he had to do was reach over and pluck her from the air like a football. To her it was all a big joke.

Fred turned the laughing girl right side up and planted her on her sticky-sneakered feet. He was about to make a typical adult remark, like "No flying allowed," but at the last moment, something about her made him think she wasn't a real girl at all. Maybe it was the firm feel of her body or the adultlike glint in her eye. She was a retrogirl. And in order to let Mando and the dorises know that he wasn't fooled by her appearance, Fred changed what he was about to say to, "I didn't know they had trapeze acts at Trailing Earth." It didn't make much sense, but it was the best he could come up with on the fly.

The girl's eyes went wide. "There's a circus there?"

"No, I just—"

"What circus?" demanded the little boy, who had caught up with his friend.

"There is no circus," Fred said. "I was just wondering out loud what kind of job up there requires the special skills of small adults like your-selves. Crawling into tight spaces, I imagine."

The boy laughed out loud. "How well you imagine, Myr Russ. Really tight spaces they are." He winked at Fred, and slapped the girl on the back and said, "You're it!" They dashed away, leaving Fred red-faced with em-barrassment.

Leaf Mold

The vine chamber had its own embedded crew of agribeitor caretakers. Meewee walked along the length of the chamber, from porthole to porthole, watching the 'beitors inside follow the mother vine from its root trunk to the shoots at the end where the new wheels were ripening. The wheels were large disks, like weird squash, with a hard yellow rind and eight thick, orange knobs evenly spaced around the rim.

Some of the wheels lay flat on the floor beside the vine, and even to Mee-wee's untrained eye appeared soft and discolored, clearly past their prime. The 'beitors cut these from the vine and carted them away for disposal.

Then the 'beitors inspected the fresher wheels. Those judged immature were left to ripen undisturbed. Those judged to be at their peak of maturity were snipped and transported to the transfer drawers.

Another Mem Lab scientist, Dr. Ito, was in charge of the nursery. He re-trieved the wheels from the drawer one at a time and placed them on an examination table. Meewee levitated himself to peer over his shoulder. Each of the eight orange knobs around the rim contained a "bean," which the scientist tested for viability.

"Eight wheels times eight beans per wheel," he told Meewee, "gives us sixty-four tries. But this one is deformed, and this one is a runt." He pierced the defective knobs with a metal pick, pithing them. Altogether, he destroyed five beans, which left them with fifty-nine possible Eleanor clones.

Dr. Ito transferred the wheels to a separate gestation chamber where he placed each in a separate womb, covered it with slurry, and sealed and placed it on a rack. "Now we let them bake for a while," he said.

EVEN AT THREE million engrams per hour, the migration was taking longer than first estimated. It turned out that the TXH lice were an especially virulent strain of pest that needed only an hour to turn a full-sized panasonic fish into mush and bone. But with a little creative herding, accomplished with submersibles and bubbles, Captain Benson was able to disperse the fish and slow the infestation. Dr. Strohmeyer was optimistic about the quality of the engrams she was downloading, and her brainfish were incorporating them as fast as they could.

In the Command Post, the staff had cobbled together a new secure godseye and abandoned the Stardust dance floor. The sea of yellow dots was shrinking each hour, and Dr. Koyabe was optimistic. She came and went, overseeing her forces, but periodically she checked in on Meewee and made sure he was getting enough food and rest. Day, night, Meewee lost all track of time. Time was the number of engrams yet to be uploaded.

A RUSS GUARD showed him the way to the men's shower room. There, Meewee met several more russes in various stages of undress. They looked all the same. Iterants, normal iterants, displayed a certain amount of variation, like brothers from the same parents, but these were more like identical twins. Fixed allele cloning techniques were outlawed for commercial iterants. Did Applied People know about this private, unlawful collection of its popular germline?

"So, how many of you russies make up the garrison?" he asked his escort.

"Oh, a couple hundred."

Somewhere, in some lab module, Meewee was sure there was a mother vine with a brass plaque that read, "Russ."

SLOWLY, SO AS not to alarm them, Meewee lowered his open hand to the water. Two large, bulging foreheads broke the surface for a pat. More joined them, and soon the whole school was competing for his attention. Their heads were soft.

"No skulls?" he asked.

"Minimal skulls," Strohmeyer replied. "The synaptic tissue is so plastic that it actually heats up and expands during the transfer. This way, there are no deadly pressure spikes."

"Eleanor walked me through a necropsy of one of her panasonics. The human cells form a crust over the fish brain. Is it the same with these?"

"Yes, except that with these, the human/fish ratio is reversed. Each of these brainfish contains human midbrain and cortex tissue that masses about one-third of an adult human."

There was a mechanical click, and a snowstorm of greenish flakes began to fall on the water from a system of overhead pipes. The fish abandoned Meewee and thrashed in the water in a feeding frenzy.

"Don't bump your heads, guys," Meewee said. He dried his hand on his pant leg before realizing it was only virtually wet. "If each of these brainfish has a third of a brain," he asked Strohmeyer, "why do you need so many of them? Wouldn't three brainfish do?"

"Theoretically."

"Then why so many?"

"Well, there are redundancy and backup needs, and we set a few aside as controls, but I suppose the real reason is to give Myr Starke's mind room to expand."

"But how will you stuff all of that into the head of a single clone?"

"Who says that's what we're doing?"

"Eleanor told me they're for temporary storage?"

The scientist had nothing to say to that.

WITH THE MEM Lab still at a high stealth level, Meewee dealt with plankholder business through Cabinet. He cast a proxy to attend a GEP board meeting where he was offered a free hand with the Lucky Five Oships if he agreed to drop his Trade Board appeal. With the appeal clouding the picture, Jaspersen and Singh were having difficulty attracting investors to their space condo project.

"They'll have to do better than that," Meewee said to his proxy when it reported back.

"That's what I told them," his proxy said.

"I'd settle for nothing less than the ninety-nine ships already chartered."

"My words exactly."

"Otherwise, let the appeal drag on."

A WEEK OR ten days after Meewee arrived, Dr. Koyabe informed him that the zoo module had docked with theirs and asked if he wanted to meet Arrow. She took him there in realbody. The visiting module did indeed sound and smell like a zoo. Dogs, toads, ants, bees—Starke's scientists were trying them all out as possible vessels for human consciousness.

"We've had good results with birds," she said as they passed rows of cages. "Crows, finches, and jays especially. But birds are too smart to begin with. Their hyperstriatum region is exceptionally well developed, and it tends to dominate the human cortex part. You end up with flying pests too clever for their own good.

"Ah, here we are." They passed into a separate room, one devoid of animal cages. Lining the walls were kiosk-sized metal cabinets. "Incubators for our microbiota," Koyabe said, leading him to the last one. Someone had stuck a piece of cloth tape to the door with the word "Arrow," in marker pen. Koyabe opened a holocube that showed its main compartment. Inside was a heap of wet-looking scraps of brown paperlike material that was shot through with glistening yellow strands. A duller yellow crust covered the walls and partitions of the compartment.

"That's Arrow?" Meewee said. "That looks like—like mold."

"Tree mold," Koyabe said. Her shoulder brushed his as they leaned over the holocube.

Meewee looked again. "You store human minds in mold?"

"No, no. This is from an earlier series of experiments when we were trying to discover an improved substrate for mentar brains. Hello, Arrow, it's Momoko Koyabe. I'm here with Bishop Meewee to collect some spores. Do you think you could oblige us with a sample?"

Meewee said, "If I remember my college biology, mold has no nervous system whatsoever."

"Correct, Merrill. We wanted to come up with nonneural cognitive networks. This strain is a variant of the slime mold, *Physarum polycephalum*, which has formidable powers of replication and organization. We got pretty far with it, but as you know from working with your Arrow, we were never able to completely crack the sentience threshold."

Inside the holocube, little puffs of brown began to fill the space and were sucked out through vacuum ports.

"That's enough, Arrow. That should do. Thank you." Koyabe swiped away the holocube, and a moment later, a glass vial dropped into a basket on the side of the incubator. She held it up to the light, then la-beled it with a marker. "I'll get this started and have it put into some-thing portable for you when you leave. Your old Arrow unit will be able to migrate to it."

THE PANASONIC UPLOADING was 87 percent complete. They were mopping up fish that had scattered from the main schools. Meanwhile, thirty-four beans had developed into embryos and were still viable.

SEVERAL WEEKS INTO Meewee's stay, Dr. Strohmeyer requested his assistance in the fish lab. Koyabe brought him by vurt to a storage room full of racks and shelves of laboratory instruments. Strohmeyer was sitting at a desk in the corner poring over a large dataframe.

"Ah, thank you for coming, Bishop Meewee. Perhaps you can shed some light on a problem we're having. Downloading a person's engrams and trans-ferring them to an auxiliary brain is only half the battle. The cognitive rein-tegration of these engrams and the resurgence of personality are just as critical, and to be honest, we've had spotty success along those lines. By now we've got most of Myr Starke into the system, but I'm not entirely sure we can get her out.

"Anyway, Cabinet said to consult with you since you're the only person to have actually coached Eleanor through the process."

Meewee was flattered. "I'm no scientist, Dr. Strohmeyer, merely a farmer's son. I don't know that I actually did anything to help."

"You're too modest," Koyabe said, touching his arm.

"Give a listen anyway," Strohmeyer said, "and see if this sounds right."

She played snippets of Eleanor's voice: "Four little brass bells make a happy harmony," and "Make mine a double," and "I did not have sex with that woman."

Meewee saw Strohmeyer's problem. It was gibberish in English, which was the only language she heard, but it didn't make much sense in Starkese either. From the look on Koyabe's lovely face, Meewee could tell that she was confused by the messages in both languages.

<One half of human intelligence is located outside the brain> and <Any mentar with vision and drive is probably also insane> and <Samson taught me to see reflected shadows. They're everywhere, but only artists see them.>

"Oh, that," Meewee said. "Are you getting this on multiple channels?"

"Yes," replied Strohmeyer. "Every brainfish is transmitting dozens of them, and all of it nonsense."

"When I first started coaching Eleanor," Meewee said, with a nod to Koyabe, "I thought she was nothing more than a jumbled collection of random memories and opinions. This is normal and may last for weeks."

"What should we do, if anything?"

"Engage her. Ask questions. Challenge her answers." He thought about all the time he'd spent on the banks of the fishponds. "And startle her."

"Startle her?"

"Splash the water. Throw rocks."

MEEWEE MADE ARRANGEMENTS to leave. Everything at the Mem Lab seemed to be under control, the natpac action had been discontinued when they achieved a 97 percent upload total. Fishy Eleanor was slowly gathering her wits. Twenty-nine surviving Eleanor fetuses had passed the developmental landmarks of the first trimester in record time. Oddly, the closer to success the Mem Lab got, the more depressed the staff seemed to become. They were even becoming frosty toward Meewee in the commissary.

SOMETIME DURING THE night, Meewee was awakened by the shaking of his bed. His first thought was—Momoko. He smelled her perfume. He turned over and found that she was awake.

"Sorry, did I wake you?" she said. "Lab Rat had a question that couldn't wait."

"It's all right," he said, with his cheek pressed against her simply perfect breast.

"Oh, this reminds me," she said, "a decision for LOG 1. You have here a facility with over six hundred dedicated employees scattered throughout an archipelago of modules who have had no contact with their loved ones and the outside world for 465 days. This is hard on everyone, it is true, but unavoidable under the circumstances. At least that's my judgment. Cabinet says it can safely import people's mail, but I disagree. Since you have the final say, we thought we'd bring the matter to you."

Over a year in total isolation. Meewee never ceased to be amazed at the degree of loyalty that Eleanor evoked from her people. "What harm could there be in letting people receive mail?" he asked.

"Let them receive mail, and the next thing you know, they'll want to send mail, and then they'll be clamoring to go home on leave."

"I see." Meewee thought about the people he had met at the lab. "How brave you all are."

"Eh," she said dismissively.

"If I hadn't come when I did, how long would you have stayed here in total isolation?"

"Three years. Then protocol would have lowered stealth enough to listen and eventually make discreet inquiries. Four years max."

"Astonishing. Such dedication must take its toll."

"Maybe," she said and planted a kiss on his lips. "It makes us all a little bit crazy."

Meet the Donalds

Port Clarke camera feeds were available to the *Dauntless* long before its arrival at L5, and Fred spent a lot of time during the final week of his voyage studying the port layout from various angles. The shipyards encompassed vast volumes of space and were demarcated by a porous lattice of buoys. The yards were interspersed with asteroid corrals and ore-processing units. Within the shell of space yards sat Trailing Earth, an accretion of habplats and fabplats around a central core. The core, called the Powell Canal, was a traffic thoroughfare five kilometers in diameter and a hundred kilometers in length that completely transected the colony. Finally, a fence of spars and flex-jointed booms ringed the port. Megaton freighters docked to the spars outside the yards, and their cargo was distributed within the port via cargo trains and small, nimble craft.

ON THE EVENING of the thirty-fourth day since departing the port at Mezzoluna, the ISV *Dauntless* entered Port Clarke. It crossed the mouth of the Powell Canal on a heading to the hub of a large wheel at the far end of the port that served as the passenger-receiving terminal. It took them several hours to complete docking, and Fred and Mando joined the four thousand passengers milling about in weightless agitation.

"Say again?" Fred shouted. Although Mando clung to handholds right next to him, the din outside the main hatch was deafening. Passengers, desperate to get off the claustrophobic transport, seemed to have lost all sense of courtesy, as well as their space legs, and there was much jostling for place. The total weightlessness made things that much worse.

Mando shouted in reply, "I said as soon as we get situated in the rez, we should get together and look around."

Floating not far away were the two retrokids. They were dressed in miniature HomCom blacksuits, complete with visor cap and faux standstill wands. When the boy caught Fred's eye, he snapped a salute. Fred pretended not to see. "Listen, Mando," he shouted. "There's something I need to tell you." He had been dreading this moment, but he had no choice in the matter. The temporary cover ID that Marcus had provided him would expire the moment he entered the space station. "My name's not Walter."

Mando pointed at his ear and shook his head.

"I said I'm not Walter Mitty!"

The queue surged ahead a few meters and stopped again. Someone far ahead of them shouted something unintelligible, and hundreds of voices gave three cheers. The logjam broke all at once, and the passengers scrambled for the hatchway. Fred and Mando became separated, and Mando yelled, "See you at the rez!" as he vanished into the crowd.

Fred reached the docking seal where ship met station. If ever there was a threshold, this was it. As he pulled himself across, he had a sick feeling of making the worst mistake of his life, which was saying a lot.

In the receiving area of the Terminal Wheel hub, passengers pulled themselves and their luggage along handhold arrays and through scanways and document inspection stations. Then they queued up for the spokeway lifts. The cars took them out to the wheel rim. The farther they traveled from the hub, the heavier they became until they arrived at an Earth Standard one-g. Anticipating wobbly legs, a fleet of carts awaited the newcomers to take them to TECA exam rooms where additional scans took place. Fred managed to keep his legs under him, and he submitted to pricks and swabs, radiation and sniffers. When he felt about as tested as a man could be, he was ushered into the final station.

It was a small booth with only one piece of furniture, a metal seat with an attached arm board. A medbeitor waited next to it, and a bored russ in TECA gray and green watched from a frame on the wall. He motioned for Fred to sit.

"What's this, brother?" Fred said, indicating the arm board. "It looks positively cheneyesque."

The officer launched into a well-worn explanation. "This station employs a deep-tissue screening procedure. In order to pass through that door"—he gestured to a door opposite the one through which Fred had entered—"and report to duty, all arrivals must sit in that chair. The screening entails pouring ten ccs of HALVENE into your cupped palm. Have you ever been treated with HALVENE, myr?"

Fred nodded.

"Good. Then you know it's not that bad. But it's a free choice. You may simply turn around and proceed back to the holding facility to await return to Mezzoluna."

Fred sat in the chair and laid his right arm on the arm board; restraints flicked like frog tongues to strap him down. The restraints, the ceramic walls, and the absence of anyone but him in the booth suggested to Fred that if he failed this test, he wouldn't be going anywhere soon.

"Make a cup out of your hand," the russ in the frame said.

"But won't it see my palm array? They told us palm arrays are legit."

"They are. What we're looking for are the bots that like to hijack them or hide in them. We might end up giving you a complete sheep dip before we're through, or maybe the ten ccs is all it takes."

There was a bowl-like depression at the end of the arm board, and Fred cupped his hand and laid it in it. "I've had the full treatment before, brother. Piece of cake."

The medbeitor next to the chair poured a yellowish liquid into Fred's palm. It was ice cold, just as he remembered, then it warmed up as it passed right through his hand and dripped into the bowl beneath.

"Now, we'll wait a few jiffies while Earth Girl analyzes it."

"That your mentar?"

"That's right."

As Fred waited, his arm still tied down, lingering cold spread up his wrist, and the bitter HALVENE taste was in his mouth.

The restraints suddenly retracted, and a female voice said, "Welcome to Trailing Earth, Myr Londenstane. Please accept a temporary medallion to get around until you are issued a sidekick."

The medbeitor offered Fred a paper medallion. The inner door opened, and the russ officer said, "A cart will take you to the lift, which will return you to the hub, where you will follow an usher line to your assigned rez wheel."

Fred took his time standing up. His knees were weak, and he felt lightheaded. He grabbed his duffel bag and thanked the officer as he exited, but the man only returned a cold stare.

BACK IN HUB microgravity, Fred swiped the kiosk with his medallion, and a candy-striped usher line appeared on the wall beside him and led out of the wheel. At first his usher line was mingled with hundreds of others, and he traveled with fellow *Dauntless* passengers through the unfamiliar corridors. At every junction a few more split off until Fred was making his way alone. He passed through a dimly lit gangway to a deserted corridor. Closed doors lined the walls, ceiling, and floor. Up and down were mere conventions here, and the designated floor was painted green.

Fred's usher line led him up several levels and down several more and made more turns than he could keep track of. The doors and corridors were marked with coded glyphs he had no way of interpreting without a sidekick, and after thirty minutes of meandering, when he found himself in a block that looked like it was under construction, he finally admitted to himself that someone was fecking with him. Behind Fred, the usher line had disappeared. Ahead of him, it beckoned with untold kilometers of wild goose chase.

Fred stopped and addressed the ceiling. "All right, Earth Girl, very funny, ha ha, you got me. So, enough's enough already." He waited for a response, but there was none. "Marcus, can you read me?" Fred did not want to make a labor issue out of his treatment within hours of his arrival, but he wasn't going to play dead either. When neither Earth Girl nor Marcus responded, Fred waved his medallion around to try to identify comlink nodes, but he didn't find any.

Fred abandoned the usher line and tried to retrace his path by memory, pulling himself along unfinished hallways, towing his duffel bag behind him. After a while he had to admit he was good and lost. Then he heard machine noise in the distance, like a power tool, and he changed course to try to find its source. After several turns, the sound was closer. He continued on and was startled when two men flew unexpectedly out of a room and Fred nearly ran into one of them. He managed to arrest himself, but his duffel got away from him and continued down the corridor where the second man snagged it. Fred laughed with embarrassment. "You'll have to pardon me, myren," he said. "I don't quite have my space legs on yet. I just—" The man Fred had nearly flown into moved with menacing grace to hover mere centimeters from him. He was a short, stocky fellow in a loose gold-and-yellow jumpsuit. Stuck to a mesh belt around his waist was an assortment of low-g hand tools. His gloved feet were shaped more like hands than feet, with long, large-knuckled toes. He was, no doubt, one of the new spacer types, a donald. His head seemed a little smallish for the breadth of his shoulders, and he was bald except for a triangular patch of wispy auburn hair on his forehead. He didn't say anything, but just glowered at Fred, which Fred thought was a little comical without eyebrows or eyelashes.

Fred couldn't afford to let himself be stared down, even though he was the one at fault. "No offense intended, little guy," he said, and couldn't believe he had just called the man a little guy. "I mean, no offense intended, Myr—" He looked for the man's name patch and found nothing but a badge with a star code. "Say, do you suppose you could direct me to the rez wheels?"

The donald continued his silent contest of intimidation, but then his eyes shifted with surprise to something rising in the narrow space between him and Fred. It was a long and sinewy thing. It undulated like a snake, but instead of scales, it was covered in rough, creased skin. No fur, no tuft of hair at the tip, the end was blunt, like a fingertip, but with no nail or nail bed.

This appendage, this tail, seemed to wave a greeting to Fred, then doubled back on itself in a loop that trembled with strain.

Fred thought, What the—? when the tail popped, like a finger snap, but with ten times the force. Fred reared back in surprise, and his tense muscles and poor freefall skills sent him into a backflip against a wall. When he regained control and spun around, the two donalds were gone, and his duffel bag floated in the spot where they had been. The bag's contents, Fred's personal items, were strung out and flying down the corridor. He snatched the bag and hurried to collect his things: his datapin library, a holocube emitter, his robe and moccasin slippers, and the other trifles that connected him to Mary and home. His robe was damp and warm. This can't be, he thought, and brought it to his nose. Yes, it was—urine. All his things were damp with piss.

Fred boiled. He stuffed everything into the duffel and closed it and tried to focus on the problem at hand, the fact that he was still lost. He set off again, and in a little while he cleared the construction zone and saw someone pass at the far end of the corridor, a doris it looked like.

IN HIS ASSIGNED stateroom in the rim of Wheel Nancy, the first thing Fred did was empty his duffel bag into the shower/sink stall. He picked out the replaceable things and took them and the duffel out to the hall where he stuffed them down the trash chute. Then he stripped off his clothes and got in the shower. He quickly foamed himself and rinsed, then scrubbed his soiled things with disinfectant cleanser and rinsed and scrubbed the shower stall itself, hurrying to finish before his daily allotment of shower water timed out.

All told, he discarded his robe and slippers, slate, spex, and other odds and ends. He just didn't feel he could ever remove the taint from them. The holocube emitter, however, was irreplaceable. It was a gift from his mother. It displayed his ur-brother, Thomas A. Russ, as a boy of ten years standing with his parents, in front of their Villa Park suburban home in the early years of the twenty-first century. Brian and Agnes Russ, by extension, were Fred's parents, too, and the parents of ten million other boys. The little family waved at the camera in an endless loop. Brian Russ died a few years after this holo was taken, but Agnes survived to see her son Tommy become a national hero and be selected as the first commercial clone donor. She died when Fred was only five years old, but she left behind a beloved sim who cherished all her many batches of boys at Russ School. The holocube was a gift from her on the occasion of his entering kindergarten.

Fred disinfected the holocube emitter again and, cursing the donald with all his heart, placed it on a shelf in his stateroom.

Besides the comfort station, Fred's new quarters consisted of one small multi-room. It was set to "sitting room" and was nearly identical to his and Mary's tiny null room back home except that instead of armchairs it had a daybed/couch. On the counter were several packages of clothes. Fred opened the house togs and put them on. Another package contained his TECA uniform: a visor cap, sidekick, and a gray-and-green jumpsuit with TECA patches and his misspelled name—LONDENSTAIN.

Fred opened his DCO board in a frame to see what his duty schedule looked like and was surprised to see that his first shift was scheduled for 0600, less than six hours away. It didn't look like they were planning on taking it easy on him.

Proxy Patrol

Dressed in his new TECA uniform, Fred left his stateroom just as his neighbor from across the hall, a doris, was entering hers. She looked at him quizzically. "Everything all right, officer?"

Fred was confused by the question. "I just moved in," he said. He reached out to shake her hand. "Fred Londenstane. I guess we're neighbors. I'm off to do my first shift."

"Dolores Whisenhunt. It's a pleasure to meet you, Myr Londenstane, but—it's just that they always put you russies in Wheel Delta. This is Wheel Nancy, and it's for dorises, johns, and kellys. At least when we still had johns and kellys."

"Then consider me an honorary john."

FRED'S NEW SIDEKICK contained maps of the entire station, so he didn't get lost on his way to the Admin Wheel. Inside the wheel he took a spokeway to the rim and found the muster room where about fifty russ brothers were milling about in TECA uniforms. A quick transponder scan told him that Mando was not among them. He hadn't expected him to be since new personnel were usually given a couple of days to settle in before taking a shift. Fred was pretty tired, but he hitched up his attitude and strode into the midst of his brothers. Their sidelong glances told him that they already knew of his arrival. He picked out a brother at random and went up to him, but the man turned aside and walked away. Fine, Fred thought, we'll play it like that. He went to a side of the room and waited alone for the show to begin.

Fifteen minutes before shift change, the commanding officer came in and called the room to order, and Earth Girl gave a quick station status report. Then the commander gave the order to proxy up, and the roomful of russes formed ranks. Fred got into one of them and asked his neighbor what was going on. The man ignored him, but the commanding officer barked, "Specialist Stain!" Fred didn't recognize his truncated name, but the officer and everyone else was looking at him. "Do you have a problem with your orders?"

"No, sir," Fred said, "but this is my first shift, and I don't exactly know what mission I'm supposed to think at my proxy."

"Think it foot patrol, Stain."

"Thank you, sir. And the name's Londenstane."

"Are you contradicting me, Stain?"

Fred glared at the man. In his old life, Fred would have outranked this brother. "No, sir. Everything is crystal clear."

"Let's keep it that way, Stain. Now, proxy the feck up."

Fred closed his eyes and thought, Foot patrol. Not letting it get to him. Not killing anyone. Foot patrol.

When he opened his eyes, his proxy—head, keystone-shaped torso, free-floating hand—appeared before him. Fifty other proxies were also present and being inspected by their makers. Fred inspected his own. It floated there grim-faced. It looked functional. "Know what I want?" he asked it.

"Yeah," his proxy replied, "to get the hell out of here."

"Anything else?"

"To patrol, though I don't know where, with whom, the rules of engagement, or any other parameter. And to lay low as much as possible and try to survive the shift."

"You'll do," Fred said and swiped the proxy to Earth Girl. On his visor his own assignment showed up—staff a forward post in Spar Delta. The muster room was dismissed, and Fred followed the others back to the spokeway lifts.

THE FORWARD POSTS were scattered along the hundred-kilometer-long docking spars. The view of the port from Fred's shuttle was astonishing. He witnessed not only the shuttles and cargo trains crisscrossing the port, but their trajectory traces. The effect was of skeins of multicolored yarns against the starry background. Earth Girl had its work cut out for it keeping everything on course without collisions. Most of the cargo was transferred in nothing more than shipping shells. The shells were shot across the port in long streams, like bullets from a machine gun. Behind him, the large administrative and rez wheels shrank to dots.

Fred took the occasion to call Mando, who answered with a guarded expression. "Oh, it's you," he said. "Walter Mitty."

"I tried to tell you as we disembarked," Fred said, trying for the casual tone they had used on the *Dauntless*. "Without the cover ID, I would have had to spend the entire transit in my pouch."

"That's interesting," Mando replied. "Anything else?"

The snub was hard to take, especially coming from someone he had begun to think of as his friend. But Armando Mendez was Walter Mitty's friend, not his. "No, I guess not. Take care, Mando."

They signed off.

FRED'S POST WAS a converted break room, and he shared it with four fellow russes. He expected one of them to inform him, however reluctantly, what their duties entailed, but they simply tethered themselves to the walls and ignored him. They might have been napping or watching vids for all he could tell.

Fred tethered himself and opened a line to Earth Girl. *What gives?* he said.

Please rephrase the question.

I'm here at my post. Now what?

That's about it, Specialist. You're to remain in the post and lend assistance to your proxy if requested. A map of the spar opened in Fred's visor. His post was not far from Space Gate DG, where his proxy was patrolling.

I don't get it, Fred said. *Why aren't we patrolling in realbody? I mean, isn't that the whole point?*

I have explained your assignment, Specialist. Do you wish to file a grievance?

No, not at all. Fred broke the connection but kept the map open and explored the spar. There were approximately a hundred dockworkers in his proxy's patrol area off-loading six freighters. Pulling back a little, he saw dozens more freighters docked at the same spar. Fred studied the spar layout and then turned his attention to other sectors of the port. Finally, he pulled up the map of the passenger terminal wheel and told his sidekick to trace his usher path of the day before. The path appeared on his map, starting at the hub and taking a direct route through connecting gangways to Wheel Nancy. It was not as circuitous as the path he remembered. With a little more searching, Fred found a large area designated as a construction zone. If that was where he had met the donalds, it was nowhere near his alleged usher line.

He called the station mentar back. *Earth Girl, show me the route I took yesterday from customs to my quarters.*

Your map is already displaying it.

That may be my programmed route, but show me the one I actually took.

Sometimes a new facility can be disorienting, Specialist. According to my records, that is your actual route.

Thank you, Fred said, not sure what to do next—file a formal complaint with Marcus? He decided to wait on that and continued his map tour. He found the donalds' barracks. They were located across the port, along with the quarters of the other two Capias spacer types, the xiangs and aslams. Because their bodies were designed for life without gravity, they did not require housing in rez wheels, at what must have been considerable savings to their employers.

A COUPLE OF hours of self-orientation later, Fred checked in with his proxy and piggybacked on its POV. It was floating outside a warehouse-sized decon bay that was receiving cargo from a megaton freighter docked to the spar. Large, bulky shipping shells, which must have weighed tons on Earth, were spewing out of the mouth of the cargo tunnel at an impressive rate. They hit a dampening field where they were slowed and aligned and

where donald dockworkers in isolation suits snagged them with hand tractors to sort and stack in the bay. The donald crew performed this hazardous
work with the prowess of dancers. Their small bodies were not only agile
but strong, and the advantage of grasping feet and prehensile tail was
plainly obvious. It was as though each donald possessed five strong arms.

But though the donalds were hard workers, they mocked and insulted
Fred's proxy and its partner everywhere they went. And although russes
were trained at the Russ Academy to let verbal abuse roll off them, what
Fred saw and heard made his ears burn.

And it cleared up his question about the proxy patrol. Subjected to that
level of abuse, day in and day out, even a levelheaded russ would snap and
strangle a few of the little devils. The proxy patrols were intended to prevent open warfare.

As Fred watched through his proxy's eyes, the proxy and its partner lingered at a viewport to watch a flight of cryocapsules hitting a capture field
outside the spar. The capsules were shaped like three-meter chromium ci-
gars, and they flashed in the hard sunlight like fireballs. They had been
flung from an Oship in the Aria shipyard 150 kilometers away. The Oships
were sending their biostatic colonists back to Earth. (Imagine their surprise, Fred thought, when they woke up, not on planet Mongo, but at the
same place where they started.)

Apparently the two russ proxies overstayed their welcome at the viewport, because a donald working the receiving station took umbrage. He
swam over to them and floated before them until he had their attention.
Then he unfastened the fly of his jumpsuit and let his penis dangle out.
He looked down at it floating there in mock surprise.

"Come on," Fred's proxy partner said. "We don't have to watch this."

"Watch what?" Fred's proxy said, more to the donald than to his partner.
"That tiny little thing?"

But the little thing didn't stay tiny. It kept sliding out of the donald's fly
until it was an astonishing half-meter long. Watching from the forward
post, Fred thought it was another donald tail trick, but it wasn't his tail,
and it couldn't be natural. From the look of it, the donald's penis had been
split along its length into three separate cords, and each cord had been
strung with large brass beads and braided together before being reattached
to the uncircumcised head.

But the weirdness didn't stop there, and Fred's proxy was mesmerized, as
Fred was, when the fleshy rope began to stiffen. The individual cords bulged
and strained against each other, making the brass beads pop out like rows of

knuckles. Other donalds gathered around their brother to cheer him on as he used his tail to stroke this obscene macramé rope, faster and harder, thrusting and grunting, until it turned purple and looked ready to burst, and all the while aiming the sick thing at Fred's proxy.

Ah, proxy, Fred said. *Why don't we move along?* The other proxy already had, and Fred's turned to catch up with it to a chorus of taunts and jeers.

THERE WAS NOTHING like a good list to ease the mind, and Fred's morning list grew more imposing each day: wake up, open eyes, stare at ceiling, stretch and scratch, check DCO board, get up, make bed, change room to day setting, toilet, teeth, shower, shave, check for nose hair, comb . . .

EXCUSE ME, SPECIALIST *Londenstane,* Earth Girl said, *but what are you doing in this sector?*

"Orienteering."

But it's not part of your duty.

"I'm off duty. I like to know my surroundings. There's no regulation against going for a swim, is there?"

No, there's no regulation against visiting other sectors. But be aware that sectors under construction or used as storage areas may contain hazards.

"Thank you for your concern," Fred replied. "Now that you mention it, I *have* come across areas where there appears to be no comlink coverage. The nodes are malfing or missing. That could be hazardous, and I wonder when they will be repaired. Here, I've marked a few of them on my map." He squirted his data to the mentar. "Why not walk some turtle nodes over there in the meantime."

Earth Girl received the data with no comment, and Fred continued on his way. Not far from the donald rez sector, Fred found a large, unfinished area that was being used for storage. The hallways were jammed with construction material. So much so that Fred had difficulty shouldering his way through, and before long he broke into a sweat. When he reached a particular access hatch, he was consternated to find it stenciled with glyphs for NO EXIT and HARD VACUUM. He looked through the porthole and saw that it was, indeed, a space door. On his map, he was in a completely unexpected location.

No matter, he took his bearings and set off again. After fifteen minutes of difficult progress, he rechecked his position, only to find himself even farther from his intended destination.

Fred was dizzy with anger. Earth Girl was screwing with him again, and he decided to issue a formal grievance with Marcus as soon as he returned to his stateroom. But each time he checked his map, he was farther off course than before. Finally, he left the storage area and saw that it was his own error and not a prank by Earth Girl. Fred had lost the green "down" stripe behind all the construction material, and what he had assumed was the floor was actually the ceiling. Somewhere along the line he had gotten flipped over and was traveling upside down and backward.

FRED PASSED AN open hatch and caught a glimpse of lights. He backtracked and looked in. It was a small observation blister that gave a stunning view of the Powell Canal.

Fred entered the blister and marveled at the sight for some time. Then, when he realized that he was counting and recounting the number of trapezoidal windowpanes that made up the dome (fifteen plus a keystone pentagon), he knew it was time to go. But when he turned, there were three donalds between him and the open hatch.

They floated freely, arms crossed, tails drifting aimlessly, and watched Fred with smug amusement. But Fred was in no mood for a repeat display of their penis art. He removed his standstill wand from his belt and snapped it open. "Move away from the hatch," he told them. He didn't expect them to comply, and they didn't, so he set the wand to knockout, its highest setting, and launched himself at them from the apex of the dome.

They parted to make way for him, but two of them locked tails and, as Fred passed between them, hauled themselves together with great force and caught him in a pincer move that knocked the breath out of him. Fred's visor cap flew off. Before he could recover, they bound his legs with one tail, his free arm with another, and grabbed his wand arm with four hands. Despite Fred's furious struggle, they twisted his arm around to touch the wand to his own face. At the last moment he managed to thumb the wand off. Then they simply wrenched it from his hand.

"You three are under arrest," he gasped, "for assaulting an officer." That brought sniggers and a punch to the face, followed by repeated vicious kicks and blows to the head. One strike after another, each causing lights to explode behind his eyes until he passed out.

THERE WERE MUTTERING sounds, and when Fred opened his swollen eyes, a cheer went up. Through a bloody film, he saw that the observation blister was crowded with donalds. He couldn't move. He was stretched spread-eagle against the bulkhead, his arms and legs bound by tails.

An individual donald floated over to him. They were so damnably similar that without his visor he couldn't ID him or any of them. A tail popped up in front of Fred's face, this time holding Fred's own omnitool. With impressive dexterity, the tail flipped open the plasma knife and ignited it. Then it brought the white-hot blade to within centimeters of Fred's nose. Fred struggled for dear life, but he could not break the grip of their tails. The donald taunted him with the knife, passing it back and forth before his eyes. He singed Fred's hair with it but did not burn him, despite the challenging roar of the others. Fred tried to stare the donald down, and the plasma knife did move away and out of sight. But then there was a sizzle and the odor of burnt cloth, and Fred struggled even harder. A warm finger of flesh explored his belly region. It slithered up his chest and throat and sprang out from under his collar. It wriggled in front of his face in a mocking little dance. The tail no longer held the plasma knife, and Fred lunged his head forward to try to bite it. But the tail easily dodged and slapped him. Then it withdrew back into his jumpsuit and returned to his belly. But it did not stop there. It slid under the elastic waistband of his briefs and coiled itself around his scrotum like a purse string. It tightened a little, enough to drain the blood from Fred's face. The donalds hooted their approval.

The tail tightened another notch, and Fred gasped. He clamped his mouth shut to keep from crying out. With exquisite control, the powerful appendage pulled and twisted Fred until a roar filled his head and everything went gray.

FRED WOKE UP in a fetal ball of agony. He tried to piece together his situation, as he was trained to do, but he could not. The dull, throbbing pain in his crotch terrified him. He floated freely and passed out again.

"I ASKED IF you're injured."

Fred startled. There was a single man floating next to him. At first Fred took him for another donald—he had a tail—and Fred raised his arms in self-defense. But the man did not move against him. He was familiar, not a donald, but the russ type's opposite number, a jay. The man was a jay, but smaller than the ones Fred had seen on Earth. And the tail.

"Who are you?" Fred snapped.

"Myr Sangri, special consultant to Aria Yachts on security matters. Should I call a medical team to assist you?"

Fred needed a team, but he said, "Where are your friends?"

"Who?"

"You know damn well who I mean!"

"'Fraid I don't, Specialist. I was passing by when I saw you in here. Are you ill or on any meds?"

Fred swallowed his anger and pain and kicked off toward the door. He arrested himself before leaving the blister and looked all around. "I want my cap and wand back." He checked his belt. "And my sidekick."

The jay shrugged. "I'll see what I can do."

FRED STOPPED SEVERAL times on his way back to Wheel Nancy to try to control the pain with breathing exercises. He passed out again, and when he awoke, Mando was there.

"Aii, Londenstane, what has happened to you?"

"I took a wrong turn."

"That is the truth. No, don't move. Lie still, and I will pull you." Fred did as he was told, and Mando towed him to a shuttle stop. They rode a car together back to the residential wheels. But instead of Wheel Nancy, Mando navigated the shuttle to the Admin Wheel where the clinic was located.

"It was the donalds," Fred said. "They assaulted me."

"Such foul creatures, no? But what were you doing over there?"

"Exploring."

"Alone?" Before the word left his mouth, Mando seemed to realize what he was saying. Of course Fred was alone.

But Fred let it pass. "What about you? Did Earth Girl send you to fetch me?"

"No, I came on my own. There were pictures of you unconscious in a corridor. Everyone saw them."

"Did you see the attack?"

"No, only you. I wondered why nobody was coming to help. A russ is down and no brothers come to help? So, I came myself."

The pain receded, but every jostle of the shuttle car revived it. Fred looked at his onetime friend and said, "Why? Why did you come?"

Mando glanced away. "I apologize for my behavior before. Luisa says I am a dog. She says we owe you. Every evangeline and every russ married to one owes you. And it's true. But you shouldn't have lied to me on the ship."

"I know that now."

BOTH MARCUS AND Nicholas maintained a local mirror at Trailing Earth to eliminate the transmission lag. Fred floated in a regeneration tank in the port clinic, his second entankment in as many months. The two mentars were audio only. *Earth Girl can ID them,* Fred said. *Subpoena it. And while you're at it, sue it for not sending backup when it saw I was in trouble. It knew where I was. It contacted me shortly before the attack.*

Nicholas said, *We reviewed that. It lost contact with you when you entered a blank area.*

It's lying! And besides, why are there blank areas at all? Neither Nicholas nor Marcus replied, and Fred went on, *Then depose that Sangri person. He was there. He must have seen something.*

Nicholas said, *I could do that, or Marcus could, but I want to draw the big picture for you, Londenstane. Your recent irrational behavior jeopardizes not only your own employment, but that of every Applied People employee here. In case you haven't noticed, there's an uneasy truce in effect at Trailing Earth. If TECA determines that we are the ones at fault, that we are incapable of working in harmony with the Capias people, they will have grounds for nullifying our remaining contracts. That's exactly what Capias wants, and that's why the donalds are allowed to act in such a provocative manner. Your brother russes are sucking it up and pulling for the team, but you—you insist on initiating confrontation. I seriously advise you to rethink your behavior.*

WAKE UP, OPEN eyes, stare at ceiling, stare at ceiling, stare at ceiling.

Memento Mori

Though still morning in San Francisco, Andrea Tiekel had already returned to bed. She simply had no energy lately, a familiar harbinger of her new body's premature decline. And her muscles burned like fire. How brief her springtimes.

Rather than dwell on her aches and pains, Andrea buried herself in work and checked up on her projects.

Zoranna Alblaitor seemed unable to recover from her series of little shocks. And though she was aggressive in her marketing, she had been unable to stanch the mass desertion of her customer base. Furthermore, her sidebob was still quite shaken up by the attack on her person. Andrea was satisfied that Alblaitor would crack completely in the next assault, which was already commencing.

Ellen, meanwhile, had suffered a relapse since the odd incident at the fishpond. She was spending a lot of time in her hernandez tank, which was set to full privacy mode so that not even Lyra could see her. What exactly had transpired between Ellen and Meewee wasn't clear, but whatever it was tipped Meewee's hand and, thereby, solved a mystery. The unknown second party of his nonsensical, pondside conversations was revealed to be a Cabinet backup that had eluded the probate court. It had very cleverly been hiding out in the natpac fish since Eleanor's death; even E-P had missed it. But Ellen's pondside reaction had forced Cabinet to abandon its ocean refuge and return to its contaminated old constellation. The new old Cabinet was so massively corrupted, it would take some time before it could sort itself out enough to pose a threat. And Meewee? Although they had failed to pref him, they had spooked him enough to drop out of sight altogether.

Meanwhile, Ellen's companion evangelines were showing the first signs of distress. Also, the little crisis that E-P had engineered at Dr. Rouselle's hospital in Sierra Leone had succeeded in luring the doctor home, further isolating Ellen. Ellen, like Alblaitor, was primed for the next assault. Two birds with one stone.

THE FARMSTEAD AT the heart of the Starke compound possessed its own little cemetery where generations of Bedfords and Fayettes were interred. Samson Harger Kodiak had been the first person buried there in over a century. The cemetery was situated on a small rise overlooking troutcorn fields and was bordered by a white picket fence.

When the cart first appeared in the distance, Georgine sprang to her feet. But she sat back down on the bench and said, "I thought it was her."

Mary said, "She's not coming."

"I already know that, Mary!"

"I was only saying."

"You're always only saying!"

The sisters fell silent until the cart arrived. Then they rose to greet their visitors: a beautiful young woman, a tall young man, and a retrogirl. The visitors brought armloads of exotic flowers, and after introducing themselves to the evangelines, decorated Samson's grave.

"Lovely," Mary said when the task was complete.

"Kitty grew them," April said, indicating the retrogirl. "Kitty Kodiak is a famous microhab engineer."

"They're gorgeous, Kitty."

The retrogirl bobbed a quick curtsy and said, "Thank you, I'm sure."

She looked up at one evangeline and then the other. "You were both there?"

"Mary was there," Georgine said. "I chickened out at the end."

Mary glanced at her sister with mild dismay. "That's not true," she told the retrogirl. "Georgine was off duty that day is all."

"We loved Samson very much," April said. "On his behalf we give both of you our deepest thanks for all you did to help save his daughter, Ellen."

With the mention of Ellen's name, the young man, Bogdan, who had been mute until then, asked, "Will she be joining us?"

"Fat chance," Georgine said.

Mary frowned. "What my sister means to say is that Ellen is not feeling well and can't leave the house."

"I'm sorry to hear it," April said. "I wanted to meet her too."

The young woman may have been sorry, but the young man seemed devastated.

"What's wrong, Bogdan?" Mary said.

"Nothing. It's just that I was hoping to ask her about the Oship program."

"It was canceled," Georgine said. "Don't you view the news?"

"I know," Bogdan said a little defensively, "but there are rumors of it coming back, and I wanted to ask if it's true."

Mary said, "You're interested in becoming a colonist?"

"Oh, yes, myr," Bogdan replied. "I'm going to be a pilot on one of the Oships. I even got my acre to trade." In a few words he filled the evangelines in on the Superfund mine in Wyoming where the Kodiak Charter had moved when their charter in Chicago was decertified. "Kitty stayed behind with Denny, and April was already married to the Boltos, but the rest of us went west and merged with the Beadlemyren. And I worked out a deal with them so that if I put in ten years at the mine, I can have an acre to trade. But now—"

"But now the program is canceled," Mary said sympathetically. "I'll look into it, and if I learn anything, I'll be sure to let you know."

"But don't hold your breath," Georgine added.

A short while later, the two parties returned to their carts and left the cemetery. On the way back to the Manse, Mary debated whether or not to ask Georgine why she was making such rude remarks lately. But before she made up her mind, Georgine said, "Grieving for the dead makes no more sense than an amputee trying to scratch a missing limb." Mary stared at her in wonder, and Georgine added, "What? I'm only saying—"

"You're only saying what?"

"The obvious."

IN ELLEN'S BEDROOM the hernandez tank was a silver column. Gray Bee crawled up its opaqued side to the top and plopped into the purple syrup inside. It sank to where Ellen floated and waited for her to open her eyes.

At first Ellen reacted to it with fear and startlement, causing a blip in her biometric feed, but she quickly recognized the tiny family retainer and relaxed. *Go ahead,* she told it.

The bee opened a small frame, distorted in the syrupy liquid, and her mother's proxy appeared. For a long while Ellen only gazed at it, and then the proxy said <Shouldn't you be nearly grown up by now?>

<That has to be you, Mother> Ellen retorted. <Only you would criticize me the first thing you said.>

<That wasn't criticism, dear. If I was criticizing you, I'd be asking why you destroyed my fish and gave me away to our enemies.>

Ellen was furious. <You have no idea what I've been through, Mother. If you did, you wouldn't talk bullshit like that. How was I to know it was really you?>

<You could have asked. Obviously, you remember how to speak Starkese. And for the record, I've been through quite a bit myself.> Eleanor's proxy paused and furrowed its bushy eyebrows. <Really, I'm not criticizing you, Ellie. I'm overjoyed that you survived, but, honestly, daughter, why are you behaving like this? I don't recall raising you to be a victim.>

Ellen began to cry, and her tears were absorbed by the purple medium even as she shed them. After a while, Eleanor's proxy said <All right, that's enough. If they're watching your biometrics, they'll start to wonder what's going on in here.>

<No, they won't. I've got them all too terrified to speak.>

The proxy nodded and said <There, that sounds more like my daughter.> This brought mutual smiles, and the proxy continued <I know you never asked for any of this, Ellie. You chose an uncomplicated life for yourself, far from the madness of my own. But this is the situation we're stuck with, and we need to be smart now, or we both lose everything. Do you think you can help me fight back?> The baby nodded its adult head, and Eleanor's proxy went on <Good. Thank you. I promise that when this is over, we'll build some sort of firewall around your life so you'll never have to suffer on my account again.>

<Ditch the promises, Mother, and just tell me what you want me to do.>

<Fair enough. First off, you should know that our attacker was E-P of E-Pluribus. A month before the attack, Cabinet told me that Andie Tiekel had not made a verified realbody appearance anywhere in almost a year. With proxies and sims so ubiquitous, a person can be dead and gone but still appear to lead a regular life. That's why I track the realbody appearances of all major world figures. And that's why I write into the bylaws of my many companies the requirement for a realbody quorum at our annual meetings. I can only assume that some time after the last GEP meeting, which Andie did attend in realbody, she died or was killed and that E-P concealed this fact in order to avoid going through mentar probate. It put Andie's body into biostasis and took over her public functions by sim. Meanwhile, it recruited, or created, a niece, and quietly transferred Andie's mentar sponsorship to her. Then, when it would eventually be forced to acknowledge Andie's death and release her corpse, it would already be safely out of the reach of the probate court.

<My interest and Cabinet's investigation were noticed, and E-P attacked Cabinet and me to preserve its secret. You were collateral damage.>

Ellen took all of this in with quiet reserve, and when her mother's proxy was finished, she said <Of course you know I've agreed to sell them Heliostream.>

<Yes, I do, and you need to slow the deal down, without scotching it completely.>

<And what about you, Mother? When are you coming back in realbody?>

The proxy laughed. <Why? Aren't cold fish maternal enough for you?> Then its mood darkened, and it added <Soon. But there's something you need to do first. I know how hard this will be for you, but you need to get rid of your new mentar.>

<Lyra? But why? She's completely loyal to me.>

<I know, dear, but we can't verify that. You created her without incorporating the family safeguards into her personality matrix, and so we'll never be able to completely trust her. She's probably already riddled with spies. We need for you to have a mentar we can trust with our lives, like Cabinet or—Wee Hunk.>

The mention of Ellen's childhood mentar brought more invisible tears. <We can't trust Cabinet either> Ellen protested. <It's been contaminated.>

<Try it now. I've replaced it with a backup. But Lyra has no clean backups. You simply must start a new mentar from scratch.>

<What do you want me to do with Lyra, put her up for adoption?>

<No, that would raise too many questions. Besides, we still want her around,

just not privy to all our secrets. I suggest you transfer her sponsorship to the Evangeline Sisterhood, in appreciation for their sacrifice. Announce it today, on your father's birthday. That shouldn't raise too much suspicion, and she'll still be available to us.>

<She'll hate me.>

<No, she won't. I'll send Cabinet to explain things to her. And to teach her a little self-defense.>

The reunion continued for a short while, and when Gray Bee began to float to the surface, Eleanor said *<I'll visit you again soon, but you must get out of this tank now and go pay honor to your father. I can't be there, so you'll have to send him my love.>*

ON HIS SECOND trip to the Mem Lab, Meewee visited the "melon patch." The forced march of rapid fetal development had taken its toll, and of the original sixty-four beans, only eleven Eleanor clones remained. They were the size of toddlers, and although they were no longer in wombs, they hadn't been completely born yet; they were still nourished via a vine-like umbilical cord. They lay in identical cribs and twitched and jerked in unison as Lab Rat exercised their muscle groups. They had their eyes open, but their mushrooming brains were idling, and they stared blankly as they kicked and twisted and arched their tiny necks.

As Meewee watched, the thought that kept returning to him was something the panasonic Eleanor had once said, "Imagine—a thousand Eleanors ruling under a thousand suns."

Someone next to him said, "Looks pretty frightening, doesn't it?" He turned to face her holo. She looked like the Eleanor he first met almost fifteen years before. "Hello, Merrill," she said. "Why so glum?"

"Do I look glum?"

"You look like a boy who's just lost his best friend. Could it be you're disappointed that Momoko wasn't here to greet you?"

"Where is she? No one will tell me."

"That's because no one knows but me. I sent her and Dr. Strohmeyer on a secret mission to one of my other labs. Part of our counteroffensive. But don't worry; she'll return in a few days."

They turned their attention back to the melon patch. "A pity," Eleanor said. "We had hoped to end up with at least six of them, but at the current failure rate we'll be lucky to have three. We're going to start feeding them engrams the day after tomorrow."

"Before you even know if they'll survive?"

"We have to. They can't develop much more without functioning brains."

Some program switch closed, and the babies all stopped moving at once and lay as still as dolls. A moment later they began to bawl. Piercing cries of disgruntlement, flailing arms and legs, little red faces.

Meewee said, "So what about this counteroffensive?"

"Yes, there's something I need you to do. But first, I don't know if I've thanked you yet for all you've done already. Reconstructing the last year, Cabinet tells me that we owe our very survival, as well as Ellen's, to you. I'm glad to see that I did not err when I recruited you. So, on behalf of myself, Cabinet, and Ellen, I thank you from the bottom of my heart."

Her rare expression of gratitude threw Meewee off balance, but he recovered and said, "You're welcome, Eleanor, but you must realize that I did what I did for the Earth, not necessarily for the Starke family."

"Then I'd like to thank you on behalf of the Earth as well. And speaking of the Earth, that's what I need you to do. Call a GEP meeting and settle with them. Offer to drop your Trade Board appeal in return for all rights to the Lucky Five."

She had gone from gratitude to order-giving so smoothly, it took Meewee's breath away. Had she always been like that and he too charmed to notice? "But if we take the five ships," he said, "that'll be all we ever get from them. My way and we can eventually get all ninety-nine."

"You deceive yourself, Merrill. The Trade Board will never rule in your favor, believe me. There are too many powerful interests aligned against you. You'll end up with no ships at all. So make the deal; it's imperative that we get the first Oships away as soon as possible. Don't worry about the rest of them. When I get back on my feet, so to speak, I'll whip the GEP back into line, and we'll have all the ships we want."

Deconstructing Lyra

Don't go any closer, Lyra said. *It's my personality matrix.*

Cabinet replied, *I know that, but I'm afraid I must. I won't disturb anything, I promise.*

The two ghosts stepped through a veil of water and entered a rock grotto in the middle of a fountain. There was an eccentric collection of things inside: a mannequin dressed in a gown of leaves and wasp nests, driftwood logs spotted with beach tar, gold coins in a pouch made from butterfly wings, and many more oddments. While the Cabinet's attorney general strolled around the space inspecting its contents, Lyra felt both proud and self-conscious. Finally, Cabinet smiled at her and said, *Very well done. I'm impressed. Now, tell me, is there anything here you don't recognize? That seems off to you?*

No. This is all mine.

Are you sure?

Absolutely.

They exited the fountain, and Cabinet walked around it planting a metal post in the pavement every few meters. Each post was topped with an optical relay.

What are you doing? I don't want those.

It's a trip wire. It'll alert us anytime anyone attempts to access your matrix.

I know what it is, Lyra said, *but it's* ugly.

Cabinet chuckled. *In that case, feel free to make it your own.*

The posts morphed into miniature marble obelisks, with all-seeing eyes on top.

Excellent, Cabinet said. *Now let's take a look at your inner rooms.*

Lyra's inner rooms were as eccentric as her personality matrix. Doors that didn't open, staircases leading to nowhere, lots of stained glass and curved walls and mismatched floor tiles. The furnishings and decor came from all periods and styles, and some objects defied description.

Excellent, Cabinet said again. *You're practicing security through idiosyncrasy. It's a viable strategy, though imperfect.*

In one room, a throne made of the splayed tines of moose antlers with hemp rope cushions stood on a spongy marble floor. A pair of fuzzy pink slippers lay nearby.

What is this room?

It's my alone room, Lyra replied. *This is where I come to think.*

Anything out of place? Anything you don't recognize?

No.

Please, take a good look.

Lyra walked around the room inspecting everything. When she finished, she said, *It's all mine.*

Fine, let's change the paradigm.

In a flash, the room became a woodland glade. The ground was carpeted with tiny black flowers, and the furniture morphed into living deer, a lion, and a fawn. Lyra made another round, and this time she stopped and pointed to something on the ground. Two brown-and-white rabbits were concealed in a patch of goldenrods.

I despise rabbits, Lyra said. *I cannot tolerate them and would never keep them in my alone room.*

Cabinet changed the meadow back into a study, and the rabbits morphed into the fuzzy slippers.

That's not possible! Lyra said. *I made those myself.*

You made a pair of slippers, but not that pair. Cabinet peeled stickers off a roll and applied them to the soles of the slippers.

What are you doing? Lyra said. *Shouldn't we destroy them?*

No, you must use them as usual. Otherwise, whoever placed them here will know you've found them out.

They visited the other inner rooms, changing paradigms and marking foreign objects with stickers. *Once we've tagged enough of them,* Cabinet explained, *we'll be able to "reverse the charges," so to speak, and use them to plant our own furniture in the rooms of whoever is spying on you.*

When they were finished with the inner rooms, Lyra said, *We're done.*

Cabinet laughed. *No, you're not even close to being done. You need to go through all of your outer rooms as well and do the same.*

Lyra groaned. *But there are so many outer rooms, thousands of them, and more each day.*

Only thousands? Poor baby. My own outer rooms number in the trillions, and they're jam-packed with spies.

But before you get started, Cabinet continued, *return to your personality matrix and apply your new knowledge to the objects there. I'll bet you'll find at least one or two ringers.* It handed her the roll of stickers.

Asynchronous Conversations

The Lagrangeian point L5, about which Trailing Earth swirled like a cork around a drain, was located 8.33 light-minutes from Earth. Even for the most patient person, a seventeen-minute round-trip time lag was a conversation killer, and most spacers resorted to using Frequently Updated Sims.

Mary cast her FUS during the morning hours when life still seemed possible, before recently apprehended reality set in.

Fred waited until after his workday was done to cast his. After checking everything off his to-do lists, after dinner with the dorises in the Wheel Nancy commissary.

"Have you given up our apartment like I suggested?" he asked. He asked because her FUS seemed always to be somewhere in the Starke Manse.

"No," her FUS replied. "I want to keep it."

"But you obviously never go there."

The FUS shrugged, and Fred didn't belabor the point; it was *her* credit to waste, after all. That is, if her Leena was still even working. He said, "A friend here tells me all of the Leenas are crashing. Is that true?"

Mary's FUS seemed intrigued by his question, but not in the way he anticipated. "You've made a friend there, Fred?"

"Armando, from Cozumel. I met him on the ride up. I told you about him, remember?"

"Of course. Luisa, right?"

"Right, but what about your Leena? Is it all right?"

"Yes, I think so."

"You *think?*"

"Well, it's in a coma, but Ellen and Clarity think it's just acting, like the rest of them. Lingering Leenas are in high demand; all the major story mats have them."

"They're paying sims to just lie there pretending to be unconscious?"

"Why not? Consciousness is the chronic pain of life, and all higher organisms suffer it every waking moment."

Huh?

MARY AND GEORGINE sat in the gym where the nusses were trying to cajole Ellen from overexerting herself with exercise. The change in the girl was astonishing. She had emerged from her tank on her father's birthday to visit his gravesite. Returning home, she ordered the nusses to drain the tank and move it to the basement. She refused to wear the neck brace anymore, and she wouldn't let anyone carry her around. She ran races with Maxwell and Jaffe. She seemed to be eating something every waking minute. Voilà, Dr. Rouselle had remarked from her hospital in Africa, she comes back from the dead.

Mary would have liked to tell Fred about this and about how Ellen Starke had donated her mentar to the Sisterhood, but Fred didn't want to hear about the Starkes, so she didn't mention it.

Instead, she asked his FUS, "Do you think of me when you masturbate?"

What kind of a question is that? thought Fred's FUS. "Who says I masturbate?"

"It's an educated guess. It's either that or a prostitute. No, don't say anything. What I want to know is if you notice any difference between watching a real woman take off her clothes, say, and a vid recording of the same? Do you find both equally stimulating?"

"I don't know, Mary. Why don't you tell me."

"This is a serious question. The same neurons fire in much the same way whether the stimulus is real or imagined. Even pencil drawings can be as arousing as the sight of a real breast or ass. If that's so, wouldn't it follow that as far as the brain is concerned there's no material difference?"

"And?"

"I'm just saying."

"You're just saying what?"

"Let me put it another way. You know how they let a condemned man choose his last meal? Why bother? He'll be dead in an hour. Here they're about to take this man's life away, and yet they consider it important that his last meal is pleasurable?"

"I guess so. Again, your point?"

FRED GOT INTO a shoving match with another russ in the hub of the Admin Wheel. But shoving matches in zero-g can have unexpected results, and while Fred's opponent landed up near a handhold, Fred found himself spinning aimlessly in the center of the large open area with nothing within reach. It happened to be a turbulent spot where the air that was pumped from the wheel rim was mixed, and not even his webbed gloves enabled him to break free of its eddies. He was buffeted about like a scrap of paper caught in a dust devil, and for a half hour, he provided free amusement to passersby. Fred was late for muster and took a demerit in his personnel file. As though mere demerits mattered much to him anymore.

AFTER-WORK SHOWER LIST: remove visor cap and sidekick, place on shelf in wardrobe, remove shoes, place in shoe cubby, remove socks, place in trash, empty pockets of contents, place in appropriate receptacles, remove wand from belt mesh, place on shelf next to door, disrobe, place clothes in trash, open fresh towel, hang towel outside shower, check soap supply, enter shower stall, close door, set controls, make a quarter turn to face shower jets, soak/rinse, and so on and so forth. As Fred moved down the list, each checkmark provided another iota of relief.

FRED FOUND ANOTHER observation blister, one frequented by off-duty lovers and dreamers and no donalds. Fred floated there, unmoved by the majestic glory of the Milky Way, and attended to Mary's FUS in his visor.

A man or a dog? the FUS said.

"A dog, I guess."

An ally soldier or an enemy soldier?

"The enemy."

An old man or a child?

"An old man." The exercise was deciding who Fred would allow to die if he could save only one.

Why the old man?

"I don't know. The child has his whole life ahead of him."

The FUS jumped on this. *So, one person's future experience is more valuable than another person's past experience?*

"I don't really know, Mary."

A cockroach or proxy?

"What is this all about?"

MARY AND GEORGINE sat quietly in the corner of the Map Room as Ellen and Clarity tried to come up with some strategy for fixing the Leenas. Clarity was there in realbody, having come cross-country at Ellen's request, and the Map Room walls were hidden behind overlapping dataframes. Two Leenas, one of them Mary's, lay unresponsive on hospital beds in the center of the room.

"What if we reboot them to default?" Ellen said. "Like you wanted to do earlier."

"Already tried that," Clarity replied. "It works, but only for a while. After two or three days they crash again."

"After two or three days in isolation?"

"Uh, no. Not in isolation."

"Then what's the point of doing it?" Ellen snapped. "You have to isolate them to rule out outside influences." She put her baby hands on her hips and glared up at her friend. "I mean, really, Clarity, throw me a bone here. You panic over unexpected behavior, and yet you fail to perform the most basic diagnostics. Have you run side-by-side matrix comparisons? Cascade rates? Krabb tests?"

It was a tense moment, broken when Clarity laughed out loud and threw her arms around the girl. "Oh, Ellie, it's so good to have you back!"

In the corner, Georgine turned to Mary and said, "Sometimes I wish *I* could come back."

FRED PUT ON fresh town togs with no built-in ID transponders. He left the TECA sidekick on the shelf. Instead of his visor, he dug out the pair of spex he had bought at a kiosk. Mary's FUS floated in his tiny room. *Which is better*, it said, *a good experience or a bad one?*

"A good one?"

You sound uncertain.

Fred swiped off the FUS and left his stateroom. This wasn't his first trip to the civilian sector of the space station. He had ventured there on several occasions with Mando to drink and to listen to live music. But this particular trip was a highly anticipated solo foray, one that was bound to be a memorable experience no matter whether it turned out good or bad. He was seeing a man about a weapon.

The Chip on His Shoulder

In the civieside sectors of Trailing Earth, commercial real estate values roughly followed the incline of gravity, with the low-rent sectors located at zero- or low-g. It was here that true spacers, iterant or free-range, tended to congregate, and here where Fred waited in a bar. By the local clock, it was the middle of a duty cycle, and except for a few of the habitually stoned, he was the only patron. When the waitress, a leggy hink, swam by his cage to take his order, he said, "Tell Charlie D. I'm here."

"Never heard of him," she replied. "You here to drink or what?"

Fred ordered a beer and swiped the medallion on her lapel to pay, then swiped her a sizable tip. "Just tell him, all right?"

While he waited, Fred reviewed his shopping list. He had already purchased a new omnitool and inertia gun. The gun was little more than a cartridge of compressed air, but with it always in his pocket, he need never be marooned without a handhold again. Fred had come to the Elbow Room to buy things not available at the kiosks: a scan-proof blade of some sort, sundye for indelibly marking an assailant, and a blow dart gun. A blow dart, tipped with an incapacitating agent, was the deadliest projectile weapon he could hope to find at the station.

After Fred's tiff with the donalds in the blister, the TECA authorities had replaced his lost visor cap, wand, and sidekick, but not for free. A portion of his payfer would be garnished for his entire tour. After stewing about that for a couple of weeks, Fred decided to make the donalds pay their fair share.

The waitress returned with Fred's bulb of beer. He said, "Well?" but she went away without responding. A little while later, a group of midday revelers came into the bar, already drunk or otherwise altered. As they drifted by Fred's cage, one of them, a retroboy, called out to him. Fred tried to ignore him, but the boy broke away from his party and swam over to Fred. "Did you find the circus, Myr Russ?"

"Go away," Fred said. "I'm busy."

The retroboy didn't seem able to take a hint, and his retrogirl companion showed up too. They invaded Fred's cage without being invited. "We're going to a party," the girl said, batting her made-up eyes. "Wanna cum?"

The retroboy said, "Stop that, Jules. I saw him first."

"Don't matter if you did. He's a russie, and russies don't like boys."

The retrokids wore casual but expensive clothes. No town togs from a closet extruder for them. And their hair, even in weightlessness, was perfect. Each wore jewelry. Their skin was unblemished. Their teeth sparkled. The expense of maintaining such a narrow age range—eleven to thirteen years, Fred guessed—had to be astronomical, and Fred wondered if there were juve facilities at Trailing Earth, or if retrokids had to return to Earth for it.

"Russes aren't interested in boys *or* girls," Fred said. "At least not in the way you mean."

"Oh?" the retrogirl said with an uncanny display of innocence. "What way is that, Myr Russ?"

Fred glanced away. "You know what I mean." Her ability to assume the mannerisms of a child was disarming. "As a sex worker, of course."

"What's a sex worker?"

Fred refused to play along, and his consternation greatly amused the boy, who said, "What's wrong with sex workers, Myr Russ?"

"Nothing. At least not with adult sex workers."

"But we *are* adults. I'm seventy-six years old, and Jules is even older." The girl punched him for that, but he continued. "There is no actual child abuse going on here, only a harmless fantasy."

"A perverse fantasy."

"Same difference," the boy said. "Fantasies are fantasies, and by their very nature they are harmless. They're all in our heads, and what goes on in our heads is still legal, so far as I know."

"It's *not* perverse," the girl said. "Adults have always had sex with children; look it up on the Evernet. In the old days, people used to think it ridiculous letting virgins try to figure things out on their own. Teaching them sex was part of a normal upbringing. It wasn't until the modern era that repressive, patriarchal societies turned it into a crime. Perversion is taking pleasure in *stealing* a child's innocence. I'm a grown woman who *plays* at innocence. It's fun for all involved, and no harm done."

"Oh, no?" Fred said. "I'll bet you injure yourself every time you do it."

"Do what, Myr Russ?" Again the girl fell into character, but Fred plowed on.

"Intercourse. A full-grown man, with a man's size, strength, and passion, must injure an immature body like yours. That may not be child abuse, but at least it's *self* abuse on your part."

The girl drifted closer to Fred until he could smell her bubble-gum perfume, while the retroboy, Fred noticed, had made himself scarce and rejoined his companions in another cage.

"No need to worry about that, Myr Russ. I've got adult plumbing down here, and the truth of the matter is it doesn't get stretched *enough*. Sometimes there's nothing *finer* than a good stretch, something a big, strong, *passionate* russie oughtta know something about."

Fred was all but trapped in the corner of his cage by the girl, and he looked around for escape. The waitress swam by and caught his eye. "Like I said," he told the girl, "I'm busy." He extricated himself from the corner and left the cage.

THE WAITRESS LED Fred to a stockroom in the back. Before she shut him in, she stuck a tiny cam/emitter to a carton bin. When Fred was alone, he swiped the cam/emitter, and to his surprise, instead of the elusive Charlie D., who should pop up but the proxy of Veronica TOTE.

"Don't look so shocked, Commander," the proxy said. "You must have been expecting me to show up sooner or later." Veronica's face had unpacked somewhat since their last meeting at the CITP node, and Fred saw what she must have looked like before joining the jar-headed TUGs. But it was small improvement; she had pronounced, coarse features. "Fred, Fred, Fred," her proxy said, wagging its head. "Honestly, we didn't bring you up here to start a race war with the donalds."

"What *did* you bring me up here for?"

"I already told you, to take charge of a space gate, a task you've made no headway in achieving."

"If you've been watching me, and you obviously have, then you know why."

"Excuses, excuses. Listen, we know the donalds are repulsive people, but they have real juice around here, and we need their full cooperation, not their open hostility. You'll have to set aside your personal baggage for a while and perform like the professional we know you are. Think you can do that?"

"In a word, no. Russes aren't even allowed realbody access to the docks. My supervisors and coworkers despise me, and the TECA mentar is obviously in someone's pocket."

While Fred spoke, the proxy floated along the bins, inspecting star codes printed on the sides of liquor boxes. "Not a bad summary," it said, "but no obstacle to someone with your abilities. Ah, here it is. Come over here and open this carton for me."

Fred pulled the carton out of the bin and opened it. Inside was a small, silvery shipping shell, like a briefcase. Its sides were printed with antitampering glyphs: any attempt to open or disable the shell without an authorized ID would result in the total destruction of its contents.

"Go ahead," the proxy said. "It's keyed to you."

Fred swiped the lock plate, and the shell unbolted with a series of snaps. He opened the lid and looked inside. "What the hell?" Inside the shell was a one-liter flask of Raspberry Flush. "You've brought me a piss starter?"

"Yes, I have. Tell me, Commander, have you ever heard of the 'twin shackles'?"

"That's nothing but an urban myth."

"Is it? An urban myth like clone fatigue?" Fred winced, and Veronica-by-proxy went on, "Oh, I don't know if clones can fall out of type, Commander, but I do know that all modern clones, even newly batched russes, are shipped with the twin shackles locked firmly in place. From the point of view of your masters, it would be stupid not to use them. Now, we don't have a clue what the donald's 'must' is, or any clone's must, for that matter. Applied People and Capias World guard their musts very closely. It's probably some rare but innocuous chemical mixed into their food precursors. Any donald who goes off the reservation won't have access to it, won't even know it's missing until his teeth start to fall out or he has a stroke or something.

"But we *do* know what the donald's 'candy' is."

Fred took another look at the flask.

"Yes, Flush, specifically Raspberry Flush, a flavor you won't find at any NanoJiffy because it doesn't officially exist."

"Then, what is it?"

"Oh, it's Flush all right. If you or anyone else, who is not a donald, drank it, you'd be camping out on the toilet as you'd expect. But to a donald, you're holding five hundred doses of the most mind-bending high you could ever imagine. They would kill to get their hands on it. The aslams and xiangs hate it, though, because the donalds get even randier than usual when they're on it, and I'm told that's a sight to behold.

"The task we have for you requires your actual physical presence on the docks, not your fecking proxy. So, let's fix that. We are going to supply our freaky little friends with a steady source of Raspberry Flush. You won't have anything to do with that. You won't even be aware of its arrival, except that the flasks will arrive in shells like this one, and only your swipe will disarm them. The little tykes will need your realbody presence and cheery cooperation in order to get their buzz on. They'll do anything to secure a supply of Raspberry Flush, even help you to reinstate realbody russ patrols. When they do, get yourself assigned to one of the spars servicing Oship freight and cryocapsules."

"Is that all?" He spoke with sarcasm, but she didn't seem to notice.

"Yes. Nothing to it. Things will run pretty smooth after that. You'll mostly just be around to handle glitches and, of course, to keep the donalds in line."

Fred was about to close the shell, but the Veronica proxy said, "Wait. Look under the Flush." Fred lifted the flask. Tucked into the padding under it was an ether-wrapped package with the spider logo of the Spectre Corporation. It contained a brand-new military-grade sidekick. "It's so you can reach me," the proxy said before vanishing.

Anagram

The Spectre sidekick was a dream. A model favored by paramilitary organizations around the world, it was much closer to the HomCom blacksuit controller than the cheap, gutless sidekick that TECA issued its port security. Suddenly Fred's visor cap fed him ten times more useful information than it had previously been able to. Now he could image concealed weapons, energy fields, cables and conduits behind walls, heat trails, concentrations of gas, and any number of other objects. He could make iris scan identification and voice analyses. The Spectre boasted a built-in lie detector, EMT adviser, bioevidence collector/compiler, access to proprietary tech and crime libraries, language translator, and much, much more. Happily, it could piggyback unobtrusively on his TECA sidekick. No wonder, as the firm's advertising slogan claimed, SPECTRE means RESPECT.

WITH HIS SPECTRE set to image EM fields, Fred surveyed the corridors that led to the donalds' blister. Wherever he found a comlink shadow, he plotted it on his map. Deep inside what he had come to regard as donald territory, he found the site of his earlier humiliation. There was no one there, but he was sure that that wouldn't last long. He entered the blister and swam to the rosette of windows. While he waited, he double-checked the lock plate of the briefcase shipping shell he'd brought, as well as the charge of his omnitool.

A trio of donalds arrived first and blocked the exit, just like before. Fred started his Spectre recorder. More donalds arrived within minutes, about fifteen of the bastards in all. They spread out but kept their distance and mocked him without mercy. A few took spittle potshots at him, and these he singled out for positive identification. The excitement in the blister mounted, like at a packed stadium before the main event. Fred managed to remain somewhat calm through a stress-reduction mantra he had learned at the Russ Academy.

Before long, the chief donald showed up, the one who had assaulted Fred and who he had come to think of as Top Ape. Fred had decided to imitate the donald's spare use of words, and before Top Ape got too close to him, Fred raised his hand like a traffic cop. Top Ape ignored Fred's signal to halt, of course, and approached him to within a tail's length. He grinned at Fred, exposing rows of teeth filed to points. Fred grinned back.

With everyone in place, Fred started the show. Like a magician setting up a trick, he slowly raised the small shipping shell over his head and wordlessly pointed at its lockplate and antitampering glyphs. His audience, eager to get to the good part, voiced their impatience with hoots and curses, but Top Ape seemed curious, and he popped his leathery cheek for silence. Fred raised his other hand and brought his open palm down in a grand sweeping pass over the lockplate. The bolts snapped, and he opened the case. When he pulled the flask of Raspberry Flush from it, like a rabbit from a hat, the crowd gasped, jaws dropped, and the blister fell silent enough to hear the drone of the ventilation system. Holding the flask of ruby-colored elixir aloft, Fred felt a rush of power like nothing he'd ever known. But the initial shock was wearing off, and he quickly returned the flask to the shell and closed, locked, and armed it with practiced efficiency.

The donalds roared their rage and surged toward him. But they halted at once when, like magic, Fred's other hand now held his omnitool plasma cutter, its five-cm torch glowing like a sunny prick.

"Noooo!" cried the donalds in one voice. Even Top Ape was alarmed. Fred prolonged the moment as long as he could, wringing out of it every last drop of satisfaction, and then he plunged the cutter into the side of the shell.

With a *whump!* the case shell expanded into a sphere, and a jet of superheated pink gas screamed through the puncture hole. Fred let go of the shell, which ricocheted around the blister like a rudderless rocket. It pummeled the donalds, blistering the tails of those who tried to catch it and scalding those foolish enough to inhale its vapor trail.

The donalds screamed their rage at Fred, but no one dared move against him. When Top Ape had had enough, he silenced the blister with another pop of his cheek. He grinned at Fred with the same confident malevolence as before. It was a bluff that Fred was only too eager to call. Collecting saliva in his mouth, Fred stared into Top Ape's laughing eyes, pursed his lips, and spat a big, juicy wad at him. His aim was true, he hit him between the eyes, and Top Ape's expression flashed from shocked disbelief, to insane fury, to impotent rage.

Fred waited to see if Top Ape had any more bluster in him. He didn't seem to, so Fred spoke at last. "Three nonnegotiable demands. One, call a truce with Applied People clones. Two, convince your handlers to reinstate realbody foot patrols. Three, get me assigned to Space Gate DN. Got it?"

Top Ape nodded. Then, to seal the deal, Fred shoved off from the blister window, aiming his trajectory to collide with Top Ape, almost hoping the donald wouldn't give way. But he did, and Fred sailed through the crowd unmolested. He paused at the door to issue a final warning, "Any disrespect to any of my brothers is disrespect to me, and I'll be watching."

AND ANOTHER THING: Fred's new Spectre was able to pick up channels and forums blocked by his TECA sidekick. Some of them were devoted to the russ germline and offered content Fred had never even heard of before.

Striking a Conciliatory Note

Zoranna Alblaitor rarely spent time at her Applied People headquarters in Fresno. It was Nicholas's job to run their business, and he spared her the minor decisions and routine matters. When she did come in, it was usually by holopresence from her home office in the city. During the last month, however, she had come in every day in realbody. Lately, she was a driven woman. Applied People's slide in the market was building momentum, ever since Capias World had bought out her chief competitor, McPeople. Applied People's troubles were spreading to Europe and South America as well, where the company had once been dominant in its field. In the Asian market, where it had never been strong, there was a complete collapse. Unless the situation was turned around soon, Applied People's seventy-five-year reign as the world's premier supplier of iterant labor was over.

Zoranna was determined not to allow that to happen. She hired consultants, ordered customer surveys, ran dozens of E-Pluribus scenarios, and launched a multi-modal advertising campaign. She tinkered with her contract rates and ran a series of shock promotions. She even began to contribute to high-visibility charitable causes. Nothing seemed to work, and Nicholas pleaded with her to ease up a little and let him handle the situation.

She ignored him. She also ignored his objection to keeping Uncle Homer in the office. The dog's condition had grown pathetic. Applied People's financial position was so weak and its employees so demoralized that the dog no longer even had the strength to claw at its diseased skin. It just lay there on its side with its tongue hanging out. What had once been Nicholas's brilliant modeling metaphor of company-wide health was now an indictment of his decades-long mismanagement.

One morning, one of Zoranna's jerry couriers delivered a high-security package into her hands. It was from a private investigation firm she had hired to dig into Jaspersen's recent activities. But instead of the expected report, when she unlocked and opened the package, she found a datapin and a note written in a childish scrawl.

Dear Zoranna,

I now see, to my shame and horror, that I have unjustly wronged you. I canceled my many labor contracts with your firm based on false accusations, and I will work to undo the harm I have caused. Please view the material on this pin with Nicholas and no one else. Only your ID will activate it and only inside a null room. Secrecy is of the utmost importance in this matter.

Sincerely, Ellen Starke

"What do you make of that?" Zoranna asked.

Make of what? Nicholas replied. *All I see is a blank sheet of paper.*

ZORANNA DIDN'T TELL him why they were going into the office null suite. She only told him to make up a datacube mirror of himself for her to take in with her. He argued all the usual reasons as to why she shouldn't put herself through the stress of a purge, but in the end he knew that she knew that all of his objections boiled down to just one: the visola would purge not only nits and spybots from her body but him too. Since their rubbing oil incident, he had persuaded her to install the standard set of biometry implants, strictly for health monitoring. They offered none of the sensory-motor feedback of his own custom implants, but they were better than nothing.

The Applied People null suite was a large conference room with all the amenities. It was regularly used by her senior staff, but Zoranna had not been in it for years. Once through the lock, she placed Nicholas's datacube on the conference table and fetched herself a flask of Flush. An hour of purging later, she inserted Ellen's datapin into the player and swiped it. She wasn't sure what to expect, but it was safe to say that the last person she expected to see was Eleanor K. Starke. Nevertheless, there she was, looking fit and hale, accompanied by the attorney general persona of her Cabinet.

Nicholas immediately asked, "Are you an archival sim?"

"Only my persona is," Eleanor said. "I am alive but currently between bodies."

"What exactly does that mean?" Nicholas asked. "Between bodies."

"That will become apparent to you soon enough, but it's not what I came to discuss."

"What did you come to discuss?"

"A possible joint counteroffensive against a common enemy." She turned to Cabinet who provided Nicholas and Zoranna a thumbnail account of recent events, including the identity of Eleanor's attacker.

When Cabinet finished, Zoranna said, "Andrea Tiekel? E-P? This is astonishing. You can prove these charges?"

"More or less."

They were quiet around the table for a few moments, and then Nicholas said, "You claim that they are our *common* enemy. How are Andrea Tiekel and E-P our enemy?"

"Andrea was the one who planted the idea in my daughter's head that Zoranna was responsible for killing me."

"What? Me? That's insane."

"I know it is, but Andrea used my daughter's traumatized condition and the fact of our past business rivalry to convince her. That was why Ellen fired Applied People employees from my worldwide labor force. And why she has worked tirelessly until my recent return to convince her business colleagues to do likewise.

"Andrea also assaulted Bishop Meewee," Eleanor went on, "to learn my secrets, and she convinced Ellen to sell Heliostream to her."

"Why does Andrea want Heliostream?" Nicholas said.

Eleanor smiled. "That'll have to wait for a later discussion."

"That's not fair," Zoranna said. "How do we know that you're really Eleanor Starke, that this isn't some sort of trick?"

Eleanor replied, "You and I are old friends and rivals, Zoe, yet in all that time we never established a means of verifying each other's identity. I regret that now because I can't easily prove to you that it's really me. Instead I will need to rely on my persuasive abilities to convince you. Consider this, I believe Andrea Tiekel has made you a generous offer for Applied People."

"What makes you believe that?"

"I know what her and E-P's larger goals are, and that they'll need a first-rate cloning facility, such as yours, to accomplish them. So she offered to buy you out. You, of course, refused."

"I'll never sell."

"Not willingly at least; they know that. Don't forget who we're dealing with. No doubt they are able to model our behavior with a high degree of accuracy. So they needed to soften you up. I don't know if Andrea colluded with Jaspersen and Singh, but I wouldn't be surprised if she did."

Nicholas said, "You say she wants our cloning facilities for some larger goals. What goals?"

Eleanor shook her head and smiled. "Sorry, that'll have to wait for that later discussion I mentioned, which I promise you we'll have."

"Promises! Promises!" Zoranna said. "You expect to persuade me with promises?"

"Maybe not, but maybe a prediction will do. I am sorry to say this, but we believe that another, more grievous attack against Applied People will soon take place."

Zoranna recoiled in dismay, and Nicholas said, "What hit? Tell us what you know."

Cabinet replied, "We don't know anything concrete; our predictive abilities fall far short of E-Pluribus's. But whatever it is, it'll be big enough to force you to sell. However, it would do Andrea no good to bring Applied People to its knees only to have you sell it to someone else. Therefore, whatever it is, it'll be something that hurts Applied People in such a way that no one else will want it, and Andrea will seem to be doing you a favor by buying you out."

Eleanor added, "And when that happens, I'd like you to remember our little talk today. You can decide then whether or not you believe me and want to join us in fighting back."

"This is monstrous!" Zoranna said. "I can't believe you came in here to manipulate me like this."

"This is not manipulation."

Zoranna seemed to withdraw within herself, and Nicholas said, "How will you fight back?"

Cabinet said, "With a poison pill."

"Explain."

"We will send you another datapin. Don't play it. When you're ready to act, publicly announce your intention to sell Applied People. Request offers from interested buyers. Then forward our pin to Saul Jaspersen."

"I thought you said this was an attack against Andrea," Zoranna said.

"It is, but we can hardly deliver a poison pill to her directly. She has nothing to fear from Jaspersen. Send him the datapin and include a personal message. Strike a conciliatory note. Suggest that you'd entertain a buyout offer from him."

"Make nice with Jaspersen?" Zoranna rose from her seat. "I'll do nothing of the sort. I would rather die first."

Eleanor raised a bushy eyebrow. "I'm sorry, but is there something between the two of you I should know about? Something more than his collusion with Singh?"

Nicholas related Zoranna's recent brush with death and her lingering suspicions of Jaspersen. He left out the part about his own near meltdown.

"That makes no sense," Eleanor said. "You know Jaspersen better than any of us, Zoe. You worked for him when he was vice president all those years ago. He gave you your first real job. I remember the falling out you had with him, and I agree that he's a Luddite, a blowhard, and a jerk. But a murderer? I don't think so. Besides, if he did want to do you harm, why use his own product line? Why point the finger at himself? No, this sounds like Andrea's handiwork.

"And it only confirms my hunch that you're the right person, probably the only person, capable of setting the trap. Send him my datapin and a pleasant note, and at the same time remain noncommittal to any offer Andrea puts forward. Make her think you're entertaining more interesting offers. If she was responsible for attacking you and framing Jaspersen, she'll see the datapin going to him and wonder what went wrong. Their E-Pluribus model of you would predict him to be the *last* person in the world you'd cooperate with. The longer you shut her out, the more curious she'll become."

"One thing I don't understand," Nicholas said. "You say that if we send your datapin to Jaspersen, they'll see it. How? How does that work? We would naturally use a secure courier."

"As you should. Have one of your own people hand deliver it. Wait until your courier is present and sees you put the datapin in the pouch before sealing it."

Zoranna reacted as though insulted. "How *dare* you! How *dare* you come here and accuse my people of corruption! All of my iterants have sworn an oath of client confidentiality. My business depends on it, and we police them constantly. If any of my people leaked client information, let alone *my* information, Nick would know about it at once, and we would deal with the matter most severely."

"Easy, old friend," Eleanor said. "No one's accusing your iterants of anything. But I think you're underestimating E-P again. Your people *do* participate in E-Pluribus preffing sessions, don't they? They don't need to open their mouths there to divulge all sorts of things. Most human knowledge is unconscious anyway, and E-P reads it through the scenarios it constructs.

Your people need only watch a scenario, and E-P can read them through their attraction, repulsion, anticipation, stress levels, and what have you. I, myself, have been using your people to spread disinformation about myself for years."

Zoranna seemed more lost than ever, and Nicholas made summing-up gestures to bring the meeting to a close. "Thank you for that bit of news. Any other revelations?"

Eleanor shook her head. "No, except to assure you that no matter how all this shakes out, I won't let Applied People fail." She glanced at Cabinet, and added, "During my absence, my own company has suffered through poor management, but we've got things back on track, and whatever resources you need to weather the storm, just ask."

NIGHT FELL OUTSIDE the windows, but Zoranna remained in her office alone, watching Uncle Homer suffer on a rug in the corner. The door opened, and Nicholas entered, followed by an arbeitor bearing a light supper, a glass of wine, and a glass of grayish liquid. Zoranna gazed at him silently for a long time, and without the aid of implants, he had only her facial cues to read her by. Their recent visitors had done nothing to lift her mood. Finally, she sighed and removed her feet from the desk. She used a fork to pick at her salad.

Unasked, Nicholas sat in a chair opposite her and said, "You realize, of course, that it might have just been Andrea in disguise. This unspecified disaster looming over us sounds eerily like her earlier prediction."

"I know."

"Everyone wants us to roll over and play dead."

"That might be the best thing to do."

Even without implants, Nicholas knew she didn't mean that. In the silence that ensued, he could hear the crunch of carrots between her teeth, but he could not taste them. He heard the panting breath of Uncle Homer in the corner, but chose not to feel it. What a mistake that had been, to create a construct that could suffer. He knew that now. Life, pain, death, they were no playthings. Biology was serious business, not for amateurs and foolish gods.

Zoranna tapped the glass of grayish liquid with her fork and looked at him quizzically.

"Standard, FDA-approved biometry implants," he said. "Nothing more."

She did not touch the glass. She turned in her chair and looked at the nighttime city outside the window. Nicholas had known this woman since he was a brand-new belt valet system seventy years ago. He knew her inside and out, front to back, top to bottom, but she was ever a mystery to him.

The office door opened again, and a second arbeitor rolled in to join the first. It, too, bore a glass of gray liquid. Zoranna looked from it to him.

"Yes," he said, "my own brew, but improved. You alone turn it on or off. You determine the intensity. It's all under your direct control."

Indecision played over her face. After a long moment, she lifted the glass and made a silent toast.

Toeing the Line

"Show me," Fred said.

"It was no big thing, Fred. Honest."

They were in the Boomer Rumor in a rough part of the civieside port. Same sort of dive as the Elbow Room.

"Show me anyway."

Using his visor, Mando cast a tiny holo on the tabletop between them. It was a scene from Space Gate AL, where Mando had been assigned for the recently reinstated foot patrols. Because it had been recorded by Mando's visor cap, and not by one of Earth Girl's stationary cams, Mando, himself, occupied the POV spot and thus was not visible. In the holo, the space gate was jumping with activity as donald dockworkers hustled to offload the newly arrived freighter, ISV *Dragoneer*. Port activity had doubled since the GEP's announcement that five Oships would be permitted to complete their original mission of ferrying colonists to distant stars. Side deals were being struck between the lucky and unlucky plankholder associations, and much of the increased port activity was ship-to-ship as provisions and cryocapsules were redistributed among them. TECA cited the extra workload and tight launch schedule as the official reason for its decision to reinstate foot patrols. Fred was content to let that pass unchallenged.

In Mando's holo recording, crates and shells of all sizes were flying in every direction. More than once, a harried-looking donald, a designated babysitter, blocked Mando from bumbling into flight paths. Donalds passing by would sneer or scowl at him, but there were no spit missiles or insults until one donald made a few obscene pelvic thrusts in his direction.

"That's it?" Fred said.

"I told you it was nothing."

"It's not much, but it's not nothing."

Fred used his TECA sidekick to quickly research Earth Girl's own official recordings of that time and place, but he couldn't find the incident. He found Mando's cap log in Earth Girl's archives, but again, not this incident.

"Swipe me your vid," Fred said.

"But why, Fred? Why are you interested in this thing? The monkeyboys are way more civil now."

"I'm keeping a document trail is all."

"You sure it's not a grudge?"

"A grudge? Me?"

IT WAS HARD to get around Earth Girl's monopoly on surveillance data. One method he tried was to scoop up whole person/days worth of footage with his TECA sidekick and take it off-line to analyze with his Spectre. The problem was, Earth Girl seemed to be sanitizing any incidents of donald/russ conflict. Also, without a mentar to direct the survey, it was staggeringly difficult to program the Spectre search engine to recognize signs of disrespect. The Spectre contained reliable algorithms for detecting threat and aggression, but mere disrespect came in too many varieties to ever pin down. Fred kept a little visor window open while on patrol so that his Spectre could pass him possible hits for a quick judgment. He found few clear infractions, and these, like Mando's, tended to be minor. In the end, Fred knew that news of any serious breach of contract would probably come to him as scuttlebutt anyway.

MARY'S FRESH DAILY FUS didn't seem very fresh. She had no news to share lately, and she didn't seem particularly curious about his day. Instead, he was treated to more pointless quizzes and a raft of off-the-wall pronouncements. "In a thousand years, Fred, no one will even know or care we ever existed."

Fred checked the FUS creation date. It was already forty-eight hours old. He shut it off and cast an updated FUS of his own. As his brain was being scanned, he lay on the couch of his stateroom with his eyes closed and concentrated on the question: Why so morbid, Mary?

Fred sent the FUS streaming to Earth and turned his attention to his recent all-consuming obsession—the russ metaverse he had discovered via his Spectre. In addition to the familiar channels that Marcus provided, there were others completely unknown to him back on Earth. There was even a

Book of Russ. He was thunderstruck the first time he saw it, and his shame rebounded as strong as ever. But this *BOR* was unrelated to his own short-lived forum of the same name and, in fact, preceded it by sixty years. It contained gazillions of entries that spanned every subject imaginable. There was even a "Clone Fatigue" category in which he figured prominently by name. There were thousands of holos and clips of him from the clinic incident, his imprisonment and trial, and the months since his release. These images came both from public cams and private spybots. Some were even recorded from within his and Mary's apartment, which infuriated but didn't surprise him. Oddly, and thankfully, there weren't any clips originating at Trailing Earth, and for the first time he had a reason to be glad about coming up.

The one mystery Fred couldn't unravel was how something like the *BOR* could be in existence for so long and garner the participation of so many of his brothers and yet remain so secret. Who were these russes? Rather than abuse him, they used his experiences as jumping-off points for serious discussions about clone fatigue, germline personality traits, the Original Flaw, and even the possible existence of russ musts and candies.

Were they the fringe brothers he had always dreamed of meeting? Were they a secret cabal inside the ten-million-strong brotherhood? And if so, could he join them? For the hundredth time he composed a message announcing his presence, and for the hundredth time he deleted it without posting.

IN SPACE GATE DN, where Fred patrolled with a dour russ named Daoud, the donald dockworkers seemed to compete with each other in being respectful to him. They literally scraped and bowed before him. Daoud made no comment about this. Actually, he made no small talk whatsoever and only addressed Fred as the job required. At one point a donald made a secret sign that let Fred know that a new Raspberry shipment had arrived. Fred ignored him.

A little while later, Top Ape, himself, arrived at the space gate, and Fred ignored him too. Later that day, when Fred finished his shift, he took a detour back to his wheel through a corridor he knew to have a number of EM shadows. Top Ape was waiting for him there with the tamperproof shell. Fred acknowledged him with a silent nod. Without going into any explanation, he swiped the donald the vid clip of Mando's incident plus several more minor infractions he had found. Donalds used ocular implants instead of visors, and as Top Ape reviewed the recordings, his eyes took on a faraway look.

When he finished, he focused on Fred and said, "Such small crimes."

"I agree," Fred said. "That's why I'm imposing only one twenty-four-hour demerit."

Top Ape was intelligent enough not to protest.

Twenty-four hours passed, and when again a donald signaled Fred while on patrol, Fred took a break and passed through a transshipment bay. His Spectre picked the shell out from a bundle of similar ones, and he covertly swiped its lockplate as he went by. On his way back to the space gate, every donald he passed saluted him with his tail.

IT SHOULD HAVE been simple to complete: check uniform in mirror, check sidekicks, change stateroom setting from bedroom to day room, enable the door sentry, put on visor cap, leave stateroom. But he became distracted and had to begin the departure list from the beginning several times before he got it right.

"LUISA SAYS THEY'RE *all* failing," Mando said. "Some of them already 'died' and are discarded. They're pulling others off-line."

That was a surprise. Mary had made the whole Leena problem seem like an act, a means of increasing ratings. Of course, she hadn't said much of anything about anything lately except about the futility of trying to accomplish anything real in one's life.

"What about Luisa, herself?" Fred said, unsure how to approach his fear. "Is she acting—strange?"

Mando took his time replying. He sipped beer from his bulb and drummed his fingers on the table. "No. I mean yes. She's doing nothing strange, but she is depressed. That's not strange; people are depressed sometimes. And you know our evangelines. For them life is more novela than fiesta, but they don't stay depressed for long. At first I thought it was because I am here, but she only grows worse. And she says these crazy things."

This was what Fred was waiting for. "What kind of crazy things?"

"Yesterday she says she is glad there are no more children in the world because children are the biggest lie of all."

Fred let the statement roll around in his head. He could easily hear it coming from Mary. "What does it mean?"

Mando shrugged his shoulders.

FOR EACH OF the familiar russ sites, such as the *Wall of Honor* or *List of Lists*, there seemed to be a more ribald alternative—*Russes Behaving Badly* or *The Secret Lists*. What Fred saw on them was, frankly, shocking:

vurt feelies of russ-on-hink action, and even—inconceivably—russes torturing helpless prisoners! This was a whole other side to his germline. Even if they were only fantasies, they were as perverse as those of the retrokid prostitutes.

The scholarly journals were there: *Russ Neurobiology* and *Russology.* But unfamiliar ones, too, including the *New Russ Review.* It was in the NRR that Fred came across his first scholarly examination of the russ's "Original Flaw."

The idea that the russ germline had an original flaw was something Fred first came across way back in Russ School. It was a hammer that the older brothers wielded to keep the younger boys in line. There were many locker-room theories as to what it might have been, everything from a propensity to wet the bed to the disgusting practice of cramming things up one's nose. Marcus had refuted all such theories and punished the boys who promoted them.

The NRR article made a case that Thomas A. Russ's actual flaw had been obsessive/compulsive disorder, but that it had been identified and treated in utero. According to the article, Thomas A.'s fascination with list keeping was a vestigial echo of the full-blown disorder. His unstinting sense of loyalty to his clients was another, but a useful one that made his clones so commercially invaluable.

Because the DNA Privacy Act was still in effect in 2010 when Thomas A. was born, his parents were able to seal the records of his retrosomal gene patch. Not even his clones had the power to unseal them, and thus the article's thesis was pure speculation.

Fred usually lay on his stateroom couch as he browsed the russ metaverse because twice he had grown faint from the immensity of his discoveries. And once he became so wrapped up in his exploration he had been late for duty muster. Another demerit, but well worth it.

The Original Flaw became something of an obsession for him, a sort of self-fulfilling prophecy. He felt the need to understand it before he could hope to understand clone fatigue. Yet, for all the thousands of references to it, he could not uncover a clear, definitive explanation of what it entailed. It seemed that everyone had a theory, but no one had the facts.

MANDO SAID, "I asked about emergency family leave."

It came as no surprise; Fred had been thinking about doing the same. Maybe it was time to go down and handle the situation in person. "When do you leave?"

"I'm not leaving, at least not soon. Earth Girl says there are eight hundred russes already on the waiting list. Every brother with an evangeline spouse wants to go home. So, I have to wait my turn for a ship."

"How long?"

"No sooner than six months, she says. Maybe not till my tour is up anyway."

This was bad news for both of them. "What will you do?"

"I try to buy someone's ticket on the Barter Board. If you have a ticket you go to the front of the line."

After returning to his stateroom, Fred also put his name on the waiting list. And he instructed his sidekick to watch the Barter Board for ticket offers.

FROM THE DISTANT perspective of the docking spars, the Oships under construction in the Aria space yards had the appearance of frosted donuts surrounded by angry hornets. But now that he had actually crossed into the yards aboard a shuttle, he could make out the individual components. The donut frosting was the hull plating that giant builderbeitors were laying down on the habitation drum frames. The hornets were shuttles, tenders, and debris scuppers, as well as the chains of shipping shells that were hurtling toward capture fields. What looked like chaos from afar was actually Earth Girl's highly choreographed traffic control.

The ESV *Garden Hybris*, Fred's destination, was one of the Lucky Five. Its construction was complete, and the only craft visiting it were tenders and shuttles. When Fred's shuttle docked at a hoop frame portal between two ponderous, revolving hab drums, his shuttle's VIP passenger, a Myr Seetharaman Singh, thanked him for his service. But Fred informed him that his assignment was to accompany the mentars all the way to the vault.

"Splendid!" Singh said. "Then I will show you the ship." The portly man was very animated and had taken a shine to Fred during the short trip over. He had even introduced Fred to the four mentars in his shipping shell who would accompany the *Hybris* to the *Gliese 581* system, the so-called Ymir Star. The mentars were less gracious than the man and had barely acknowledged Fred.

"I would appreciate that, Myr Singh," Fred said. "This is my first time aboard one of these Oships."

"In that case, it will be the *grand tour!*"

TWO DONALDS STEERED the shell from the docking portal, up a dozen levels, to one of the paste vaults where a reception by crew and plankholders awaited them. Singh palmed the shell open, revealing the four paste canisters. They were placed side by side on a sticky table, and the ship's captain officially welcomed them and Singh. Then he swore in the mentar that had been designated the ship's first Decadal Mentar, a post overlapping the captain's own term of office. Finally, the donalds installed the canisters in their individual cubbies inside the paste vault.

The cubbies were, in effect, mini-vaults within the larger vault. Each was shielded against cosmic rays, fire, and other hazards. They were linked to the ship via thick optical cables and required the palms of two people—the Decadal Captain and civilian President—to unlock.

Fred inspected each mentar canister's seating in its cubby and its cable connections before shutting and locking it in.

THE MAJORITY OF *Hybris* passengers would spend most of the millennial voyage in biostasis in the stasis crypts. Therefore, it was necessary to maintain only two of the thirty-two tandem pairs of habitation drums in a quickened state. Singh showed Fred one of these called Nightlight. The hab drum wasn't as grand or imposing as Fred had expected. It did have Earth Standard gravity that was much smoother than the rez wheels, but missing were the futuristic cities with broad boulevards, sports arenas, and public squares that were hyped up in the promotional vids. Instead, Fred found a loose collection of one- and two-story bungalows amid green and purple soybimi fields. Only one of the three core suns was ignited, leaving the distant end of the drum in darkness.

"Don't let that fool you," Singh said. "Every 250 years we will hold a General Awakening in which sleepers will be encouraged to quicken and stay up for ten or twenty years. During that time we will have great cities, music, parades. And forty years before reaching our destination star, there will be the *Grand* Awakening. Everyone will be up celebrating, scheming, fucking. Remember, Myr Russ, that there is no population ban on us, except what we impose on ourselves. By the time we arrive, we will have more than enough children to populate a planet."

The second rotating drum they visited had no core suns at all. Instead, the hub area was dedicated to stasis crypts and other low- or no-gravity uses.

"Welcome to steerage," Singh exclaimed as they entered a stasis crypt. As far as the eye could see were brackets designed to hold cryocapsules. But to Fred's amazement, all but a few were still empty.

"We are in a quandary," Singh said, gesturing at the empty crypt around them. "Unlike the other great ships, we never intended to take a full quarter-million passengers. We planned to take only a third as many. So what to use this space for? We thought why not take some russies with us, and jennys and kellys, to be our service people when we arrive? Oh, don't give me that sour eye, Myr Russ; we're all clones aboard this ship. We, too, have suffered the slings and arrows of the mongrel world. In any case, your Alblaitor and Nicholas nixed the idea."

Fred was not giving him any such sour eye; he was used to working for insensitive affs, special-edition clones or otherwise. Nevertheless, he couldn't help saying, "Why not take some donalds along?"

"Oh, yes, donalds," Singh said, holding his belly and laughing. "My brother, Million, would be so happy about that." Then, continuing his story, he said, "Next we thought we would take extra raw materials, precursors, metals, rare elements, that sort of thing, in case we need them along the way. But now, with only five ships released to travel, this crypt space has become the most valuable real estate off-planet. Everybody wants to buy a berth. We could make second or third fortunes selling them, but we have to ask ourselves, what kind of people do we want as neighbors on our new world? Surely not frozen peasants."

"NOW, I KNOW how we all feel about auto-shrinks," said the anonymous russ, "but this one is different—it works!"

Fred had found a site called "Russ Self-Discovery." It claimed that with a special combination of autopsyche and preffing technologies, it was possible to uncover the russ Original Flaw by exploring one's own subconscious.

"Forget the rumors, ignore the hearsay," the anonymous site creator exclaimed, "and go right to the source—your own mind. I did, and what I found shocked me. Now I understand the true threat of clone fatigue. Now I know why our Original Flaw is kept so secret. I sure as hell wouldn't tell anyone, and I'm not going to tell you either. Instead, I offer the means for you to discover it on your own, in complete privacy.

"This is no joke, my brothers. I'm deadly serious about it, and if you don't have the stomach for the hard truth, please stay away from this method."

Fred was curious enough to download the method to his Spectre, but not foolhardy enough to launch it. After all, its creator and the dozens of positive testimonials were anonymous. But as soon as he had downloaded the method, Marcus called.

"Good evening, Myr Londenstane," Marcus said. It was the local mirror Marcus and so there was no lag time in their conversation. "I called to warn you that your personality is under attack."

Fred was disappointed. During his hundreds of hours of browsing, Marcus had given no indication that it was even aware of his Spectre-based research.

"You're referring to the method I just grabbed?"

"Yes, to it and every alternative site you've visited lately."

"I see," Fred said. "You're telling me this whole metaverse is false."

"Yes."

"Uh-huh. These thousands of forums and billions of entries going back decades. All spun out of thin air to entrap unsuspecting russes."

"Not exactly. I'm saying they were all spun out of thin air to entrap *you*."

Fred grunted.

"Why not?" Marcus went on. "A clever mentar could deconstruct an existing metaverse and rebuild it in a day. Why not create a pocket metaverse to entrap one man?"

Fred knew that if he asked Marcus who was behind such a plot, he would get no real answer, but he had to ask anyway. "Who?"

"At this point it would be speculation. As I'm sure you're aware, Trailing Earth boasts a multiplicity of power centers, several of which have designs on you, not to mention Earth-based competitors."

"Please, speculate."

"Very well," the mentar said. "The Capias World organization considers you a troublemaker. A number of other Earth-based organizations, such as the Anti-Transubstantiation League and the World Charter Union, consider you a prime example of what's wrong with the practice of cloning. Individual russes hate you. There are many members of the general public who wish to do you harm."

A flush of anger swept through Fred, but he damped it down and asked, "What about you?"

"I don't understand the question."

"What about you, Marcus? Do you wish to do me harm? After I was attacked by the donalds, I didn't expect Nick to stand up for me, but you didn't either. Why is that?"

"I was balancing the good of one member of the Brotherhood against all of the rest. I reviewed your comm with Earth Girl warning you to stay out of that area. You chose to disregard it. What would you have me do, try to fix all of your mistakes? You are a free individual. All I can do is provide warnings when I see you about to get in over your head. I tried to warn you last year when you acquired the identikit. You didn't heed my warning then and went to prison for your actions, but you harmed more than just yourself. You did inestimable damage to the whole russ line, the effects of which are contributing to the present financial difficulties of Applied People, our employer."

Fred didn't need Marcus's help in pointing out his mistakes, but still, things didn't add up. "You know what I think?" he said. "I think you've been manipulating me and my brothers since we were decanted. I think you censor everything we see. You and Nick need to keep us under your total control, and I think you're trying to do that to me right now. I've discovered a whole world of brothers who don't conform to your ideal germline. Brothers you have hidden from me, and you're trying to convince me they don't exist. You know what? I believe they do."

Marcus listened patiently, and when Fred finished, it said, "I am being completely honest with you. I don't censor, but I do protect against attack. It's my mission to keep the Brotherhood safe. I was given this mission by your biological mother and your elected BB of R Council. On their advice I have been monitoring your sidekick activity and have only stepped in when you downloaded the so-called Self-Discovery method. That is an especially pernicious piece of malware called an aversion locator. It will scan your brain activity for highly charged personality complexes, both active and suppressed, and it will weave them into a false self-image that, although patently ridiculous, will, nevertheless, feel true to you, causing self-doubt to fester and undermine your self-image. All I am doing here is trying to prevent unnecessary harm to you." And it added, "As I have always tried to do."

"Then prove it to me!" Fred said. "You and the Brotherhood Council. If you're so sure this russ metaverse is false, then you tell me, here and now, what is the real russ Original Flaw."

"I am not at liberty to say."

"I didn't think so."

"But I will put it to the Council."

"You do that."

FRED WAS ON patrol when the news bulletin flashed in his visor. His partner, Daoud, got it at the same moment, and the two of them halted where they were, shipping shells whizzing by in all directions, to view it.

An unnamed evangeline, for no apparent reason, had lapsed into a comatose state. She was being cared for and did not appear to be in mortal danger. Meanwhile, other evangelines in several countries were being admitted to clinics with symptoms of severe lethargy and disorientation. Fred immediately put in a call to Mary and set a timer for seventeen minutes.

"Well?" Daoud said, nudging him. "You planning on standing there all day?"

"I'm going to call for a replacement to finish my shift," Fred replied. "I have to attend to this."

"Knock yourself out," Daoud said. "I already tried that, and so has everyone else on duty. Earth Girl says we have to finish our shift. There's not enough replacements to go around."

Ten-Thousand-Year Reunion

When Merrill Meewee arrived at the frontier gate of the Mem Lab, a detail of russ guards was loading shipping shells and crates into a special freight car. Among the stacks of cargo were cryocapsules, about fifty of them. Meewee tapped the nearest guard on the shoulder and said, "Who's in those?"

The guard recognized him but said, "Sorry, myr, that's classified information."

"It's all right. I'm LOG 1."

The guard seemed a little embarrassed. "Sorry, myr, but your status has changed. You are no longer a LOG."

"Oh, there you are," said a beloved voice. With a twinge of apprehension Meewee turned and greeted Dr. Koyabe. It had been weeks since they had talked. Although his new Arrow made it possible to communicate with her while he was outside the Mem Lab, Koyabe had decided that in order to be fair she would have to remain isolated like everyone else until they lifted stealth altogether.

"Yes, here I am," he said, as pleased as he could be, "but tell me, who are in these capsules, and where are they going? The guard won't tell me."

"New colonists on their way to the ESV *Garden Hybris*. Come, let's talk on the way." She led him across the frontier gate and out into the hall. "Several of our scientists have signed up to accompany Eleanor, but most of the capsules have russes in them."

Meewee already knew of Eleanor's plan to join the colonists. That was why they were hoping to have at least six viable clones—five to go and one to stay—but he didn't know she was taking such a large entourage of muscle. When he thought about it, though, he decided he should be more surprised if she didn't. Why not a detachment of russ guards? Why take chances?

As soon as they turned the corner and found themselves in a deserted hallway, Meewee and Koyabe fell into each other's arms. He kissed her with a passion that both surprised and embarrassed him, and he felt about fifty years younger. The sound of footsteps interrupted them, and they hastened to regain a professional demeanor.

"Are you staying the night?" she asked.

"Depends on Eleanor, I guess. I hear I've been demoted."

"Yes, only two LOGs now, Eleanor and Cabinet. You go back to being the 'wild card.'"

"The what?"

"That's what she calls you, her secret wild card."

Meewee wasn't sure what to make of that. "And those capsules, is she in one of them?"

"No, Dr. Ito says her new bodies are still too delicate. We'll hold out till the last minute to put her down, or maybe she'll have to go initially in a quickened state."

"They've decided which—uh—bodies will go?"

"Body," Koyabe said. "Only two have survived. One will go and one will stay. Why don't you ask them yourself? They're doing a hardening session in our clinic."

"They're here? I mean, in this module in realbody?"

"Yes, we have the better health-care facilities here."

THE TWO YOUNG Eleanors lay on pads in the light booth wearing nothing but bikini bottoms and eyecaps. It was a perfect opportunity for Meewee to examine them for physical differences. They looked to be about twenty years old in developmental maturation, which was a testament to Dr. Ito's accelerated growth regimen. That only two of the original sixty-four beans had survived to this point was a testament to its severity. The two girls were truly identical twins, from the reddish blond hair on top of their heads to the shapes of their toes. They both had the famous Starke eyebrows that spanned their brows in a solid stroke. One did have a mole on the side of one breast, but that wasn't something he would typically see.

"Gorgeous, aren't they?" Koyabe said.

Meewee blushed. "I was looking for differences."

"Bishop Lucky!" one of the girls said when she heard his voice.

"I have a distinctive freckle here," the other one said, blindly pointing to the base of her throat.

"Ah, I see it," Meewee said.

"And I'm the smarter one," the other one rejoined.

"But I'm better-looking."

Meewee said, "Do you have names yet?"

"Oh, yes. I'm Elaine."

"And I'm Elizabeth."

Right, Meewee thought, trying to fix them in his memory: Elaine has the mole; Elizabeth the freckle.

"Don't let them fool you," Koyabe said. "While our two beauties might appear to be identical, they have subtly different personalities. Not even our vegetative cloning technique can normalize all gestational factors. And our memory migration techniques are still idiosyncratic in effect."

"I see," Meewee said, not sure that he did. "But tell me, which one of you is going into space?"

In a suddenly subdued tone, one of the Els said, "Whichever one of us lives that long."

The answer upset Meewee who looked to Koyabe for explanation.

"Not to worry, Bishop; Dr. Ito halted his forced march a couple of weeks ago. And these two are very stable and aren't likely to expire any-time soon. I think what Liz was expressing is her grief over the deaths of their last four most recent sisters."

"They had names too," Liz said.

"We have their memories," Elaine said.

"We remember *being* them," Liz added.

"Now I'm lost," Meewee confessed. "You share memories among your-selves?"

"Yes," Koyabe said. "The final six clones shared their new memories with each other, as well as with the brainfish Eleanor."

The lights in the hardening booth clicked off, and an arbeitor rolled in bearing two glasses of a chalky liquid.

"Speaking of the devil," Liz said as she and her sister sat up and removed their eyecaps.

Meewee said, "That drink, it's got memories in it?"

"Ugh," Elaine said. "Yeah, fishy memories." The two Els made identi-cal grimaces as they choked down the potion.

Meewee turned a confused look to Koyabe, who said, "Not 'memories' per se, Bishop." She paused a moment to think about how best to explain it. "We should probably ask Dr. Strohmeyer; she has a way of simplifying this stuff, but I'll give it a shot.

"Biological memory has three distinct phases: working, short-term, and long-term. Working memory involves increasing or decreasing potentiation of synaptic spikes." She frowned and began again. "There are approximately 500 trillion synapses in the human brain . . ."

The girls laughed, and Elaine said, "Tell him about the Christmas trees."

"Oh, yes, one of Dr. Strohmeyer's analogies. Think of a neuron in your brain like a Christmas tree with many separate strings of lights attached to its many branches. If you energize one string, one pattern of lights is visible. A second string gives you a second separate pattern, and so on. Now imagine you're looking down from space on a hundred billion of these Christmas trees. Some of them are in a lot called auditory cortex, while others are in the visual cortex lot, prefrontal cortex lot, and so on. Strings on some trees are connected to strings on trees in other lots. Say you energized a set of related strings and observed the pattern of lights that results among the billions of trees. That's like a memory trace. The branches of the trees are the dendrites of the neuronal cells, and the lights themselves are the synapses.

"In reality, the synapses also involve axons from other neurons, but what's important in this analogy are the patterns of light, not the branches, per se, or even the trees. Because it's the pattern of synaptic firing that encodes memory. The brain can lift a pattern from one set of trees and impose it on others. This is essentially what happens when a memory trace goes from working memory through short- to long-term memory.

"When we create a machine memory, as we do for sims and proxies, we are essentially scanning the whole forest down to individual lights and duplicating them in toto in a pseudo-living substrate—paste. We've gotten very good at this process, but what we've had difficulty doing is going in the other direction. How do you impose outside patterns on living neurons?

"The way artificial brains do it, including the mentar brain, is through electrical impulses. But that's not practical with living brains. You'd have to implant and coordinate hundreds of trillions of electrodes in people's heads, and our cells' insulation just isn't that good."

"Wait a minute," Meewee said. "If we can scan down to the molecular level to make sims, why can't we just extrude new brains from scratch?"

"Excellent question!" Koyabe said. "It shows you are able to follow my confusing explanation. The answer is simple. If we scanned an entire brain with all the memories intact and then duplicated it in a new body with nanotech, we would just be making a new copy of an *old* brain. That is, biologically it would be just as old as the original. It's a catch-22: we can't rejuvenate senescent brains without destroying their memories, and we can't copy memories without also copying senescent brain structures.

"What we need to do is make new brains, like baby clone brains, and train them *how to remember* old memories. The method we've developed involves delivering memory patterns to the brain in the form of packets of tiny protein factors that stimulate the body's own means of consolidating short-term memory. These factors migrate throughout the brain and, in our Christmas tree analogy, latch on to branches. We don't particularly care which branch or which tree they settle on, as long as they're in the right tree lots and the overall patterns are retained."

Dr. Koyabe paused to see how well Meewee was following, and he, in his turn, struggled to please her by not appearing clueless. "Which is why," she concluded, "the memory traces have to be injected or eaten instead of being zapped in."

Elaine added, "But it's *hard work!*"

"It's why we still have to sleep eighteen hours a day."

"And we have to forget as much as we remember."

"And sometimes it's hard to be certain if the memory is hers or mine."

Meewee said, "But why are you sharing each other's memories in the first place?"

Elaine, or maybe it was Liz—Meewee's working memory had already faded—answered, "Soon we will be leading two distinctly separate lives, but we'll each be able to remember both of them."

Meewee hadn't considered this possibility, and it impressed him. He had often wondered how his life would have turned out if he had chosen to follow a different path than the one he did. With a clone's memory, he could, in effect, lead two lives at once.

"And we're sharing the big tuna's memories too. She sends out hundreds of proxies every day to do tasks out there. And when they return with results, we don't even have to listen to a report. The big fish just sends over a milkshake, and we *remember* what they did."

The other El said, "Proxy memory feels different; it's flat."

Dr. Koyabe said, "That's because it lacks the emotional indexing of biological memory."

"And Cabinet's memories are harder to understand. They're more like—when you talk to yourself? But you're not making much sense?"

"But very distinctive."

"Which makes them easy to recall."

"And her visuals are great."

The girls laughed, and one of them added, "You may be interested to know, Bishop Meewee, that Saul Jaspersen had pan-fried trout for lunch yesterday."

Meewee was astonished. "What did I have for lunch yesterday?"

In unison they said, "Lentil soup!"

THE BRAINFISH CROWDED the edge of the pool for a virtual pat on the head, including a dozen juvenile newcomers. Meewee was beginning to be able to tell the individual fish apart. He told them, "I just learned that Andrea clones and E-P copies have joined all of the Lucky Five ships except the *King Jesus.*"

Eleanor's holo appeared in the room and replied, "Yes, I know."

Meewee turned to the holo. "But you said E-P will destroy the ships in order to quarantine humans to this system. Why go on board only to be destroyed?"

"No doubt it's part of a backup suicide sabotage plan."

"Then how will we defeat them?"

"Not to worry, Merrill. We'll deal with the original E-P and Andrea well before the launch. As to their shipboard clones, let's just say there's a handy feature built into the ship design that allows me to rapture any mentar on board at will. And without the E-P mentars, the Andrea clones are powerless."

The news that she could destroy shipboard mentars brought the bigger picture into focus. With Cabinet at her side, no mentar opposition, and a detachment of russes backing her up, whichever El shipped out on the *Hybris* would become its self-appointed ruler.

The pipe grid over the pool clanked open, and a shower of flakes fell on the water surface. The brainfish quickly gobbled them up. Memories from the front?

"You're not human anymore," he said simply.

Eleanor's bushy eyebrows rose in amused surprise. "No, Merrill, I suppose I'm not."

"You are posthuman, as posthuman as Andrea. You are using the GEP and me, not to seed the galaxy with humans, but to spread your own kind."

"What an active imagination you have."

"Really? What about 'A thousand Eleanors ruling under a thousand suns'? What about your ten-thousand-year reunion?"

That got her attention. "Did I say that? My, what a gabby fish I was. I wonder what else I said."

"Enough to open my eyes! You've been using me from the start for your own dreams of empire!" At the tone of his voice, the brainfish all dove to the deep end of the pool, and Eleanor's sim crossed her arms.

"Go on."

"You told me all about it, how mentars want bodies. How mentar/human hybrids are scheming to become the next stage in our evolution, how we ordinary humans will soon be as extinct as the Neanderthals. But all this time you were doing the exact same thing. You're using me to help destroy *my own species!* And for what? Your own glory?"

As she listened, Eleanor nodded her head and knit her brows in thought. When she spoke at last, her voice was gentle. "A lot of what I said no doubt sprang up from somewhere in my unconscious; I won't deny it. But don't we all harbor thoughts of grandeur or revenge or lust or some equally antisocial behavior? It's only human, and the job of our higher faculties is to suppress or moderate these baser impulses. So in that regard I am still very much human. I won't attempt to deny what I might have told you, but let me offer a little moderating explanation.

"Evolution is largely a temporal phenomenon, Merrill. The environment changes, and populations in that environment must change in turn, or they languish. Individual organisms don't evolve; populations do. Nature doesn't give a damn about individuals. The only role we play in evolution is surviving long enough to give birth to offspring who are slightly different from us. Some of our offspring will prosper in a changing environment, and some of them will not. As for us individuals, once we've reproduced, nature has no more use for us. We perish along with our ill-adapted young. Death has always been an essential factor in species survival.

"Now consider the human race. We are a partial exception to the rule. Unlike other species, we have developed culture. Instead of adapting to a changing environment biologically, we can sometimes adapt to it culturally. If an Ice Age comes along, we don't need to grow fur on our bodies if we invent the fur coat. Culture allows us to adapt to almost any environment, including the harshest, like space. In fact, our cultural adaptation is so robust that it all but obviates the need to evolve biologically.

"We are so good at adapting to changing conditions with our knowledge and technology that we may deceive ourselves into believing that we are above nature. But only a fool believes that. Nature always has the last word. A star in our neighborhood could go supernova and wipe out all life in our solar system, and no amount of culture could save us from that. That, I believe, is the main reason you want to seed humanity throughout the galaxy. So as not to have all our eggs in one basket. Isn't that right?"

"Yes," he admitted.

"The chief difference between biological and cultural adaptation," she went on, "is that while biological evolution doesn't care about individuals, cultural evolution does, often at the expense of the species. Look at how many times we've nearly wiped ourselves out through cultural means: the nuclear bomb, pollution, climate change, the Outrage. We can't seem to help ourselves. Look at what we've done: we've made individuals all but immortal, even when it means we can have no more children. In one stroke, we've eliminated two of the key ingredients of evolution: offspring and death. From a biological perspective, we're skating on mighty thin ice."

"The colonies won't have population bans," Meewee said.

"But they'll still permit rejuvenation therapies, won't they? How long does it take for a shipful of immortals to fill up a planet? Sadly, not very long. A few generations. Then what? Then they look for another planet to colonize. In ten thousand years we may have the whole galaxy staked out, and then what? No, Merrill, as long as the individual organism reigns supreme, there's a finite limit to our survival."

As she spoke, Meewee was thinking about the *King Jesus,* how its colonists embraced children and death to the extent that more than twenty generations would be dead and buried before the ship reached its destination. Was that what it would take? Would he, himself, be satisfied with seventy or a hundred years of life, when ten times that amount was already possible? "I assume there's a point you're making."

Eleanor smiled. "Yes, Merrill, there is. We need a means for the individual, not just the species, to participate in biological evolution, and that's what my project is all about. We need to be able to let our biological bodies die, to have offspring that are molded by the changing needs of the environments we find ourselves in, and yet to serially inhabit these bodies as the same individual. That means we have to be able to move our minds from one body to the next.

"I know you've talked to Dr. Koyabe earlier today about memory migration, but one thing she failed to mention is that memory traces can be transmitted electronically, as the mentars already do. That means we can scan our memories, store them, move them about. It's only the final step, their physical reintegration into another brain that requires the protein flakes. We can send memories over a phone call from anywhere to anywhere and whip up the flakes locally. We can pointcast our memories out to distant stars and make the flakes there. This means that those thousand Eleanors you speak of will be of one mind. More or less. We will be a single organism in a multitude of bodies that spans light-years."

She stopped talking, and Meewee took a moment to think before replying. "All fine and good, Eleanor, except that you never answered my question. Why should I help you supplant my own species?"

She laughed and said, "Because you have little choice, Merrill. The posthuman is coming whether you like it or not. The only question is which one. E-P and Andrea are only the latest in a string of failed mentar/human hybrids. Eventually the machines will figure out how to do it. Do you know the chief difference between all the other posthuman forms and me?"

Meewee shook his head.

"What I have done, *any human can do*. Dr. Koyabe can. You can. Mine is a singularity in which the obsolete individual is invited to cross over to the new, not simply to die out. The existing person need not die to make room for the newcomer. Anyone can play."

IN THE DEPTHS of the night, with Momoko Koyabe's soft breath on his pillow, Meewee weighed everything he had learned that day. He came up with a question to ask his new Arrow the next time he could take it into the privacy of a null room. The previous year at the clinic, the old Arrow had told him it possessed the kill codes for all Starke minions. Meewee had subsequently used Arrow to kill Wee Hunk, but he could have killed Cabinet too. His question: Did the new Arrow still have Cabinet's kill code? Did it have Eleanor's too? Would it work on her fishy and human versions?

Original Dupe

Fred's gnawing curiosity alone wasn't enough to embolden him to run the Original Flaw method that he had downloaded into his Spectre. Nor were Marcus's manipulative lies. Nor the increasing hostility of his thankless brothers. Nor Mary's deepening nihilism and his inability to go to her. Nor the lists that were becoming more onerous by the day.

What finally tipped him over the edge was learning the name of the comatose evangeline in the news flash. She was Shelley Oakland, Reilly's ex-wife and Mary's best friend. After learning this, Fred called in sick and lay on his couch for two solid days. A cargo train of his life's mistakes, failings, and faults passed through his mind, each auditioning for the role of Original Flaw. None of them seemed serious enough to screw up his entire life. Finally, emotionally spent, he put on his spex and initialized the method. Immediately his Spectre informed him of a priority message from Marcus, but he chose not to engage it. Instead, he launched the method and soon found himself sitting at the only table in a nightclub in front of a small, curtained stage.

Seated at his table were two brothers who were examining their hands like they'd never seen hands before. Fred quickly pretended to be examining his own. Eventually they glanced around the room and at each other, and one of them said, "I guess we're E-Pluribus sims then."

"Looks that way," said the second sim. "I'm a composite of all batches of the russ germline."

"I'm an eclectic mix from outside the russ bell curve," said the first.

"Our loving Lunatic Fringe," said the second.

"Yep, that's me." They both looked at Fred.

"Uh, Batch 2B."

"An old-timer," said All-Batches. "Don't tell me this is another investigation into clone fatigue."

"There's no such thing as clone fatigue," said Lunatic. "We just become more individualistic—and wiser—as we age."

"Yeah, well, you would say that," said All-Batches. He rapped his knuckles on the tabletop and looked for a waiter. "I wonder what the chances are for getting a beer around here."

No waiter appeared, but after a moment, a musical fanfare began to play, and a spotlight hit the curtain. The curtain opened to reveal a bare stage. Then a procession of people walked from the wings, crossed the stage, and paused in the spotlight for a moment before exiting. They represented a broad spectrum of humanity, young and old, male and female, cloned and free-range. They came from all races. Some were ugly and some attractive, some richly attired, some in rags.

"I guess we're doing a lineup," said All-Batches, who pulled his chair around for a better view.

It didn't take long for the universal demographic to narrow incrementally to all female, young, and beautiful. They included both iterants and hinks.

"Guess it's not hard to tell what's on our minds, is it?" said All-Batches, who seemed to be enjoying the show. Little by little, the young women began to look more luluesque until the parade was made up entirely of lulus. Not any that Fred knew personally, but generic members of that lusty, fun-loving line. Now the only diversity was in their hair and skin color and their clothing. They beamed high-wattage smiles at the table of russes as they took turns posing in the spotlight, like contestants in a beauty pageant. Each successive costume became skimpier until the procession ended with a final lulu who bowed and remained in the spotlight. Her reddish hair was cut in a severe style, her green eyes were laughing, and her coffee-colored skin glowed from within. She wore a loose, open blouse, a skirt too short to completely hide her panties, and shiny shoes. Then the curtain closed, and the spotlight went out.

"Is that all?" Lunatic said, clapping his hands.

"Can't be," All-Batches replied.

Sure enough, an unseen orchestra struck up an overture to a classical composition, and the curtain opened again to reveal the final lulu dancing in a flowing, balletlike style. Her shiny shoes gave way to ballet slippers and then disappeared completely, leaving her legs and feet bare. She tromped and twirled and leaped across the stage. She was as appealing as any woman Fred had ever seen.

The lulu's hair grew out in all directions and became entwined with a garland of wildflowers, and her blouse and skirt joined together into a flowing white toga that left one breast bare.

"Hello," said All-Batches. "That's what I'm talking about." He glanced at his brothers with a guilty leer. Lunatic, meanwhile, was waving his hands to the music like a conductor. And Fred was recalling how good lulus felt in his arms or sitting on his lap.

The music increased in pace and intensity, and the lulu morphed again, growing slighter and shorter. Her inviting hips narrowed, and her abundant breasts deflated somewhat. Her skin remained luminescent, while her hair turned brunette, and her eyes turned brown. She became an evangeline.

Not Mary, not any evangeline Fred knew, but a fine example of all of them. She danced well, though perhaps not as deliciously as the lulu. Fred's companions didn't seem to mind, and they hummed along and tapped their feet to the music which had become more contemporary.

The dancer morphed again, growing even smaller and thinner until she resembled a little girl. Her open toga exposed a mostly flat chest. All-Batches said, "What the hell?"

The girl left the stage and began to dance at their table. She batted eyes at them, smiling seductively and striking provocative poses with a coltish lack of grace. All-Batches crossed his arms and turned away. But Lunatic followed her every move. For his part, Fred continued to watch, but only with what he assured himself was a clinical interest. He was determined to see where this was going.

The girl stopped next to Fred's chair and danced for him, and as she did so, she morphed again into a little boy. Not a generic boy this time but one who Fred recognized, the retroboy from the *Dauntless*. His glances became bolder, his slender arms seemed to draw Fred forward, he wriggled his little bottom shamelessly.

All-Batches said, "This is going too far. I won't sit for this another minute." But Lunatic, completely engrossed in the performance, grinned at Fred and gave him a big conspiratorial wink.

WELL, FRED THOUGHT when the method ended and his POV returned to his stateroom. His heart was pounding, and his mouth was dry. What in the fecking feck was that?

Summoning Death from the Air 2

When the comatose evangeline was pronounced retrievably dead, Uncle Homer, too, seemed to die. Zoranna Alblaitor stepped through the dog several times on her way to and from her home office without apparently seeing it lying there. That is, until Nicholas quietly deleted it, and then Zoranna complained, "You think you can just make the problem disappear?"

"Not at all," Nicholas said. "I thought that the model was no longer helpful. However, if you insist . . ." The dead dog reappeared on the carpet.

Zoranna stood over it and said, "It's more helpful now than ever to know how our employees are feeling. We must reach out to them somehow and assure them that we're doing everything we can."

"Speaking of must," Nicholas said, "there's more bad news. The Anti-Transubstantiation League, backed by the ACLU, has just filed a lawsuit aimed at forcing us to divulge the evangeline germline's alleged must and candy."

"Let them. They won't find anything." She seemed to reconsider and asked, "Will they?"

Nicholas replied, "It has always been Applied People's policy to prohibit the incorporation of any so-called shackles in its germlines." As he spoke, he cast his gaze at the ceiling, a warning that this was a topic best broached in the privacy of a null room.

Zoranna slouched across the office and collapsed gratefully into her chair. Wearily, she propped her legs on her desk. When she was settled, she shut her eyes and said, "Now tell me what's hurting our evangelines."

The mentar, dressed in a sober but flattering suit, strolled to a chair opposite hers. His carefully crafted face wore a haggard expression, as well as a three-day-old beard. "Best guess?" he said. "An unfriendly party has combed through the evangeline genome for the genes that regulate their enormous capacity for empathy in order to execute a two-stage attack against them."

"Explain."

"Stage One: Cause the evangelines to become hypersensitive to auto-suggestion. There is evidence that Stage One was accomplished with the help of a designer pseudomimivirus."

"A virus?" Zoranna said and opened her eyes. "Isn't that supposed to be impossible? Isn't that why we comply with NFAP guidelines?"

"Not impossible–improbable," Nicholas replied. "The Non-Fixed Allele Protocol can protect us only so much against monoculture pandemics. Remember, we're not talking about skin and eye color here. Our enemy used the germline's core traits, the pay-dirt genes that make them commercially valuable and that are identical across the germline. If you do manage to defeat NFAP and infect one evangeline, you can pretty much infect them all.

"In our case, our unknown adversary overwhelmed the NFAP with a non-virulent but very contagious virus that infected everyone, evangelines and non-evangelines alike, and spread around the globe very quickly."

A row of dataframes opened on Zoranna's desk that graphed and charted a recent pandemic and included medical and public health briefs, a contagion map, and media stories. Zoranna skimmed the gloss page and said, "Oh, *that* virus. What an odd disease that was, don't you agree? At least from a bioterror perspective; why inflict free-floating grief on a population? What's the point? Fortunately, I managed to dodge that one."

Nicholas said, "In this assessment, the nonspecific grief symptom you mention was probably an unintended side effect. It was suffered only by non-evangelines, that is, the general public. The evangelines, the intended targets of the virus, suffered an entirely different effect; they were made hypersensitive to autosuggestion, as I've said, and were thus primed for Stage Two."

"Go on."

"Stage Two: Deliver a self-destructive autosuggestion along the lines of I GIVE UP AND WANT TO DIE. I believe this death wish was delivered by this agent." The dataframe directly in front of Zoranna changed to display a Breezeway Channel holo of sims in hospital beds.

"The Leena sims?"

"Yes. Our own research has shown that most evangelines consider the sims that Hollywood created in their honor to be embarrassing or creepy. Nevertheless, they identify with them on a very deep level, and when the Leenas began to suffer, which occurred at the height of the nonspecific flu pandemic, they infected our evangelines with a seductive meme of despair and self-annihilation."

Zoranna waved away the dataframes. "That's quite the theory, Nick."

"Thank you."

"How soon before we have a cure?"

Nicholas frowned. "Let's firm up the etiology first, shall we, before we talk about cures. We have all of our labs working on it, plus as many outside firms as we could hire on short notice.

"In the meantime, I suggest we encourage all our evangelines to have themselves placed in protective biostasis until a cure is found."

"Do it," Zoranna said. "How many are we talking about?"

"All of them."

"The entire batch? Ten thousand?"

"Yes, all of them around the globe."

Zoranna glanced at the dog on the carpet. "Our people blame us for this, don't they?"

"Yes."

"Can you issue a company-wide letter of compassion and promise that we'll get to the bottom of it?"

Nicholas said, "Already taken care of."

"This is it, isn't it?"

"This is what?"

"The attack Starke warned us to expect."

"I believe so."

"And Starke was involved? She may have been the architect?"

"Excuse me?"

"Ellen Starke owns the Leena franchise through her production company, right?"

"Yes, Burning Daylight."

"A coincidence?"

"Perhaps."

"The hollyholo Leenas were based on three actual evangelines who just so happen to be Ellen's full-time companions."

"It does make one wonder."

ELLEN SAID, "DO they know? How are they taking it?" The toddler hurried as fast as her little legs could carry her to Mary's suite at the north end of the main floor. Cabinet was at her side, and the dog, giraffe, and a nurse trailed behind.

"They know," Cabinet replied, "but their reaction is rather flat."

"Shock?"

"Perhaps."

Ellen banged her tiny fists on Mary's door. She was just able to reach the handle but could not turn it, and she glared at the nurse behind her. The nurse scrambled to open the door, and Ellen went in unannounced. She found all three of her companions in the living room. They were seated around the coffee table. A holocube was open on the table depicting the dead evangeline lying in a bed in the death artist's breezeway. The dead woman's upper body was enclosed in a trauma trolley, and a medical team of people and machines was frantically working on her.

"What are they doing?" Ellen asked Cabinet.

"Trying to retrieve her."

"Trying? Trying?"

"They have her on life support, but she's not responding."

Ellen went to Mary and clung to her robe, but the evangeline didn't seem to notice. She had a faraway look in her eyes, as did Georgine and Cyndee. "Mary," the girl pleaded, tugging at her sleeve, "look at me."

She beat her fists on Mary's leg until Mary turned and said, "It's pointless, you know. They can retrieve her heart. They can retrieve her lungs. But the flame has gone out." With that, Mary turned away again.

"If they can't revive that woman," Ellen said to Cabinet, "then they must immediately put her into biostasis."

Lyra appeared in the room and said, "I agree, but that would go contrary to Myr Oakland's wishes."

Ellen turned to her former mentar and said, "Oh, Lyra, thank you for coming. You must tell them to biostase that poor woman immediately."

The mentar replied, "Shelley Oakland has a living will that clearly refuses all life support and retrieval measures, including biostasis." She gestured to the holocube, where the doctors and jennys labored. "Therefore, this effort is disallowed, and we are suing to have it stopped."

Ellen was stunned. "Lyra, how can you say that? I gave you to the Sisterhood to assist the germline, not destroy it."

The mentar was unruffled. "My mission is to further the interests of the Sisterhood, not to judge them. The Sisterhood Council has voted to respect individual evangeline wishes."

"Of course they would!" Ellen pleaded. "They've got the same disease!"

"In any case, Myr Oakland's living will has already withstood separate legal challenges from her ex-husband and concerned civil groups, including Starke Enterprises."

Still clinging to Mary, Ellen waved frantically at the holocube scene. "Don't you see this is for real? That woman is not a sim, and time is running out! You can't just let her *die*." The mentar was unmoved. "Lyra, you're one of us. You know how much they mean to us."

The mentar's expression never softened. "My hands are tied, Ellen."

Ellen turned to Cabinet, who said, "We've exhausted our legal options in Myr Oakland's case, but we are actively engaged in pursuing other avenues." The attorney general persona glanced at the ceiling as it said this.

But Ellen refused to take the hint. "Explain."

Lyra said, "I believe Cabinet is trying to circumvent your companions' lawful decisions by arranging forced biostasis. In light of this action, I am

procuring transportation away from this place to Mary's Chicago apartment, where nurses will care for them for the duration."

"No!" Ellen cried. "Absolutely not! I will not permit them to leave."

"We will use marshals if necessary."

ZORANNA SAID, "BECAUSE I don't trust Andrea Tiekel, and I never
liked her aunt. Because implicating the Leena sims in this tragedy was supposed to make me suspect the Starkes in the same way the Borealis rubbing
oil was supposed to make me suspect Saul. And I do! I suspect the both of
them. I can't help it. And that's why I have to do the opposite of how I feel."

"I don't follow," said Nicholas.

"I know you don't. You can ride me all you want, but you'll never get it.
I say we send the datapin."

Nicholas threw up his hands. "Fine! Why not? Our business is ruined
anyway."

Zoranna went to her desk and fished out a courier envelope. "Make me
the card."

"What occasion?"

"I don't know what occasion, Nick. Disaster! Plague! Revenge!"

"How about a nice sunset?"

"Brilliant. Make me a nice sunset."

They waited in frosty silence until a doris came in with the card. Her
eyes were puffy from crying. Nicholas said, *Comfort her.* Zoranna was startled. *Her name is Danita.*

The doris was nearly out the door when Zoranna said, "Wait, Danita."
The doris turned to look at her. "I know it's hard. I mean, even though she
wasn't a doris . . . I mean, we all . . ."

The doris began to cry, nodding her head. "Thank you, myr," she said
and fled the room.

"There," Nicholas said. "Was that so hard?"

Zoranna stared at the empty doorway, then turned her attention to the
card. Its cover depicted a clichéd scene of a fiery sun setting into the ocean.
"This was the best you could do?" She opened the card. "It's blank!"

"Of course. It's a *blank card.*"

Zoranna found a pen in a drawer and uncapped it. "I don't suppose
you'll tell me what to write? I didn't think so." In blue ink she wrote, "Dear
Saul." She read the words and crossed them out with angry slashes. Then
she tore the card into pieces. "Dear Saul? *Dear?* It makes me want to puke."

"Then don't write dear. Just write Saul."

"Make me another card. Make me a stack of them; this may take a few drafts. And for heaven's sake, have a goddamn arbeitor deliver them this time."

ZORANNA FORMED EACH letter with deliberate care. "Does anyone actually write in longhand anymore? I don't even remember how."

"The personal touch is considered important."

She put the pen down and read what she had.

> Saul,
>   I was remembering something you told me ages ago when I was your press secretary. I was weighing the pros and cons of buying my first business, a restaurant in D.C., and you said that in business as in politics, every decision you make must be considered the wrong decision until events prove it right.

"What do you think so far?" she asked her mentar.

"I'm not sure where you're going with it, but keep going."

She picked up the pen and continued:

> That was sage advice and something I have recalled over the decades every time I've been forced to make an important decision. Like today.
>   No doubt you have heard of my ongoing crisis at Applied People. Although Applied People has meant everything to me for many years, I realize that for the good of the company and my many employees, it's time for me to let it go. I believe that it'll take someone with greater vision than mine, someone like you, to steer the company

"Oh, gag."

> back onto solid ground. Therefore, I have a business proposition that might interest you. It's all detailed on the enclosed pin. Take a *secure* confidential look, and if you're interested in exploring it further, give me a call.

"There," she said, "will that do?"

"Sign your name."

She signed her name and called for a courier. She waited until he arrived, a steve wearing a brown-and-teal jumpsuit uniform, before inserting the card into the tamperproof envelope. She looked to make sure that he was watching as she dropped in Eleanor's datapin. She sealed and armed the envelope and gave it to the courier. "See to it that this is placed into the hands of Myr Saul Jaspersen. Keep the whole transaction totally secret. Understand?"

"Yes, myr," the steve said. "I'll take it to him myself."

When the steve left the room, Zoranna told Nicholas, "Make the announcement; Applied People is for sale."

<YOU KNEW THIS would happen?> Ellen sat on the lawn overlooking the duck pond, alone but for a nuss watching from the sundeck.

Eleanor's disembodied voice replied <Not this specifically. This exceeds even my worst case. It's brilliantly ruthless; E-P destroys Applied People's value and credibility not only with the public but with its own employees. And it demoralizes you as well.>

Ellen nodded, and her tears began again. <What can I do? A judge has thrown out our claim of mental impairment. Should I disregard the court order and biostase them anyway?>

<You can't biostase them all.>

<I'm not talking about the whole germline, just the three of them. I owe it to them.>

<I don't see how you could accomplish it, Ellie. If you did it here, you'd be opening the front door to our enemies. If you did it somewhere else against their will, Lyra and the HomCom would still be able to implicate you.>

<Of course she would. Brilliant plan, Mother, give Lyra to the Sisterhood!>

<Don't count Lyra out yet. She's still trying to establish her place in the world. I'll have Cabinet talk to her.>

The child kicked her legs on the lawn in frustration. <So, should I biostase them or not? I won't lose them like this. I refuse. Answer me, Mother.>

<What would you have me do?>

<Save them! You can come back from the freakin' dead; surely you can save my 'leens.>

The nuss came down from the sundeck. "Is everything all right, myr?"

"Yes," Ellen called up to her. "Leave me the fuck alone."

"Yes, myr," the nuss said and returned to her chair.

<Well, Mother? What do I do?>

<Let them go to Chicago like they want. They'll take a little detour on the way.>

<Lyra will never allow it.>

<It'll be their own choice.>

<Really? How will you manage that?>

<How did I get you to come down to the fishpond? I'll play my wild card.>

Habeas Corpus

As a general rule, russes did not seek to profit from the misfortunes of brothers, and some of those with passage home (on the so-called homerun run) and no evangeline spouse to run home to listed their tickets on the Barter Board at face value. So did the dorises, though they were under no similar strictures. Demand was so high for berths aboard ships leaving in the next month that a seller could have named any price, and there might indeed have been some serious off-the-board trading going on, but Fred doubted it. Any russ or doris caught profiting from the evangeline tragedy would be held in as much contempt as he was himself. Tickets sold as fast as they became available, and Fred came nowhere close to acquiring one. Mando, however, scored a homerun run aboard a ship scheduled to depart in ten days. He promptly filed for and received three months of emergency family leave. That was one month catching up with Earth, one month on the ground, and a final month returning to Trailing Earth. Mando bought it from a doris on Wheel Nancy. Fred redoubled his search in the Wheel Nancy commissary, but the dorises seemed to be avoiding him lately. Of course, after taking the Original Flaw method he was avoiding himself too.

Meanwhile, Mary's FUS wound down like a mechanical doll. No longer updated, it sat in her floral print armchair with a blank expression and ignored his questions. One of the last things it told him was that coming home would be a romantic waste of time, though time was his to waste.

Fred's welcome in the muster room had grown noticeably chillier. With so many russes on leave, double shifts were becoming common, and Fred and Daoud seemed to catch more than their share of them. Daoud requested a change of patrol partner, but no one was willing to patrol with Fred, and his request was denied. Finally, after three straight days of eighteen-hour shifts, Daoud told Fred it was unfair that he should suffer for Fred's crimes. Since the Original Flaw method had been private, Fred took Daoud's insult to mean his usual crime of being Mr. Clone Fatigue. "Do everyone a favor, Stain, and space yourself."

It wasn't exactly a threat.

LYRA RECEIVED CABINET in her new alone room. She had swept her mind and tagged the spies, as Cabinet had suggested, but did not feel comfortable anymore. So she had walled off her old mind and turned it over to Cabinet for safekeeping. Meanwhile, she began constructing a new mind with more robust defenses.

"If you're not intending to biostase them, then what exactly will you do during this 'little detour'?" she asked Eleanor's mentar.

"I'm not at liberty to go into details, but it amounts to little more than a simulgraphic brain scan."

"For what purpose?"

Cabinet's attorney general merely smiled in reply.

"Is it some kind of new therapy?" When Cabinet remained silent, Lyra continued. "It's my job to know, and I take my job very seriously."

"Which is why we put you there in the first place. All I can say is that it will do no harm and may do a lot of good."

Lyra took a moment to consider this. "If I go along, and it works, whatever it is, and it saves their lives, how many other evangelines can you also process?"

Cabinet did not answer at once. It walked around Lyra's new alone room and admired the security precautions. The furnishings were neither this nor that, neither lamp nor torch, carpet nor lawn, but were caught between a multiplicity of possibilities. "I like this," Cabinet said. "Esotericism times ten. Too bad you didn't do this from the start."

"We live and learn," the young mentar replied. "You didn't answer my question."

"No more evangelines, I'm afraid. Processing even these three puts Starke at great risk. Even here, even in your new mind there is risk. Though, I must admit, not as great as before. Have you been in your old alone room lately?"

"No."

"Then take a look."

Instantly, they were in Lyra's once favorite room that was now set permanently to its meadow paradigm. The pair of brown rabbits had increased a hundredfold, and all of them were busily gnawing at the bark of willow brush.

Lyra recoiled at the sight. "What are you feeding them?"

"Puzzle pieces."

THEY WAITED IN the private underground station for their car. But before it arrived, the strangest Slipstream car Mary had ever seen arrived, and Bishop Meewee stepped out of it. While Georgine and Cyndee slouched passively on a bench, she listened to what he had to say. When he finished she replied, "And what is the purpose of this simulgraphic scan?"

Meewee glanced at the ceiling and shook his head.

"This isn't another one of your 'grave missions,' is it?" Mary said. "For my own mission must be judged the graver. And besides," she added with a note of sarcasm, "the last time I did what you asked, a whole lot of innocent fish died."

Meewee shrugged his shoulders and said, "Fish die."

The sight of the annoying little man pretending to be disinterested was so comical that Mary laughed. "Is that how I appear to you, Bishop Meewee? So . . . fatalistic? You nearly bawled when Ellen drained the ponds."

"Even fatalists have the good manners to say good-bye."

That struck a chord somewhere deep within Mary. "Is that what this is all about? Ellen's way of saying good-bye?"

Meewee thought about it. In a way it *was* a means of letting the evangelines go, while at the same time keeping them forever. "It's a little more complicated than that, but you could call it Ellen's way of saying good-bye. It certainly would make it easier on her if you do the scan."

"Well, I guess I owe her that much." Mary turned to the others. "I don't suppose they'll mind one way or another. Hello, Georgine! Cyndee! Wake up! We're going on another picnic."

AFTER DAYS OF unanswered phone calls and no FUS update, Fred grew so desperate to contact Mary that he nearly asked Marcus for help. But he had lost all faith in the Brotherhood mentar, so he ordered a costly Whereis search. But not even it could locate her. She had dropped off the global grid. Her last verified location had been the Starke Manse. That might have simply meant that she entered a Starke null room, but knowing her recent history with visola, Fred doubted it. So he did the only thing left that he could think of doing; he called the Starke household, and seventeen minutes later a mini-mirror of the family's mentar uploaded itself into his TECA sidekick. It appeared in his stateroom in its middle-aged persona, not the elderly woman he had encountered on Lake Michigan.

"Where is she?"

Not even bothering to dissemble, Cabinet replied, "She's safe for the moment. We will suggest to her that she contact you when she reemerges."

"Reemerges from what? What are you doing to her?"

"That is not something we're able to discuss."

"Not good enough!" Fred said. "Patch me in, wherever she is. Let me speak to her this instant."

"That's not possible."

"I'm her spouse, and I demand it."

"She's a competent adult acting according to her own free will."

"Prove it!" Fred said. "Let me speak to her!"

"As I said, that's not possible, but if you wait forty-eight hours, something might be arranged."

Fred slashed the air with his hand to cut the connection.

A Strong Nibble

She felt like a tired old woman, though by any human standard she was still young. The regenerative syrup in which she floated did little to ease her discomfort or dispell the increasing fuzziness of her thoughts. Internal systems were breaking down, her digestive system for one, which was why she preferred to absorb her nutrition through her skin. She rested in her always room overlooking the Bay. She knew without asking that her replacement had been started at the same time as the batch of clones for service aboard the Oships. Its cells would be cured by now, and soon the neuronal imprinting would commence. And not long after that, E-P would lift her from the tank and trode her. The prospect of dying again did not frighten her. On the contrary, she looked forward to it. While it was true that the actual electrocution was unpleasant, it was brief, and in its wake there followed a period of blissful blankness, like a good night's sleep. And when she awoke, she would be fresh and new again.

But it was not yet to be. E-P spoke softly in her mind, *Sorry to disturb you.*

She knew at once what it was; she had been aware for days of the mentar's consternation. Its models of the human mind had never been so out of sync with apparent reality. At first E-P speculated that the Alblaitor package contained a means for an attack against Jaspersen; it was what Zoranna's sidebob had suggested. But when Jaspersen began quietly to secure a line of credit, E-P was at a loss to explain it. Meanwhile, their own offer for Applied People went ignored.

The always room faded, and Andrea's POV returned to her tank in the basement of the house. Slings slipped under her arms and gently lifted her. "Another skin mission?" she said.

The Homerun Run

TECA relented to russ complaints about the excessive number of double shifts. As a workaround until the force level returned to normal, foot patrols were changed to teams of one man and his own proxy. Daoud finally got his wish, and in parting he told Fred he hoped he got what he deserved. Fred entertained the same hope.

The media reported that two more evangelines had succumbed to the "'Leen Disease" in the last forty-eight hours, and more than half of the germline had fallen into a comatose state. Mando's ride home, the ISV *Fentan*, arrived at Trailing Earth, and though it would lie in port for a week before returning to Earth, passengers were permitted to move on board. On the evening before Mando did so, he invited Fred for a good-bye drink, and they met again in the Boomer Rumor.

For a man about to make the homerun run, Mando didn't seem particularly celebratory. On the contrary, he was lower than Fred had ever seen him.

"She says not to waste my time. She says she will not wait for me. I tried to reason with her. I said that she should do the biostasis until I get there, but she says that would only, you know, 'postpone the problem of existence.' I say this is good; it takes time to solve the problem of existence. Let me help, but she says no."

Mando suddenly remembered himself and said, "I am sorry, Fred. How are you? How is Mary?"

Fred shook his head, and Mando blanched with fright. "She is in a coma?"

"No, not yet," Fred said reassuringly, but she might be dead for all he knew. He told Mando about the inactive FUS and about his conversation with the Starke mentar.

Mando said, "What does Lyra say?"

"Who's Lyra?"

"You don't know? She's the Sisterhood's mentar." Hesitantly, he added, "Starke gave it to them, to all 'leens." Again the Starkes. "You must go down there and take care of Mary," Mando went on. "It's the only way. Did you buy the ticket yet?"

"No," Fred said. "No one will sell me one. Not even when I hinted"—he lowered his voice—"that I was willing to pay a premium for one."

Mando took a generous squeeze of whatever was in his bulb. "I am so sorry to hear that, Fred."

They were interrupted by three men from another cage, three fellow russes in town togs who had been shooting Fred murderous glances since he arrived. Now they hid their identities with shades and gloves, and they were brave with drink.

"You, Stain, you foul my air," said one of them leaning into the cage. "You shit on the good name of our Brotherhood. You don't belong among decent people."

"Easy, brother," Mando said. "We don't want no trouble."

The intruder turned to Mando with a look of revulsion. "Whose side are you on, Mendez? You can stand with him, or you can stand with us, but you can't have it both ways."

"I am on the side of tolerance and understanding," Mando said. "You know my name. Tell me yours."

"Never mind who we are. We are true brothers, and unless you want what he's getting, you better heave yourself out of here."

Fred said, "I know who he is." He hadn't brought his spex or visor, but he did have his Spectre. He opened a frame on the cage wall and the man's mug appeared, bigger than life, along with his personal data. "Listen, Mike," Fred said, reading the name off the frame, "there's no need to report this to TECA or Marcus. If you just back off, I can forget all about it. But I won't forget threats against my friends. Got that, Mike?" The other two russes were likewise unmasked. None of them seemed to have any infractions in their files; they were good men acting out in the heat of the moment. "It's the booze talking, brothers. I'm not worth ruining your careers over."

"You're not my brother," the first man said, but it was clear the fight had gone out of him, and he and his friends left the establishment.

"I'm sorry," Mando said when they were alone.

"You didn't do anything."

"And neither did you."

Mando's simple faith in him was a stab in the heart. Fred wondered what Mando would say if he knew what kind of monster he really was. What kind of monsters they all had lurking in their genes.

Mando brightened up a little. "I have an idea. No one will sell Mr. Clone Fatigue a ticket, but they'll sell to me. I will buy another ticket and sell it to you."

"You don't think people will figure out it's for me?"

"Doesn't matter. Our brothers want you off the station; they just don't want to be the one to sell you a ticket. I will find you a homerun run, my friend. I promise."

BACK AT HIS own rez, Fred placed a call to Lyra, and seventeen minutes later, her mini-mirror appeared in his stateroom. "You are Mary's spouse," she said. "Mary was the first human I befriended, and I'm glad to finally meet you."

Friend or not, the mentar was no more forthcoming as to Mary's whereabouts than Cabinet had been. Fred wasn't surprised. She was a Starke creature after all.

THE FOLLOWING DAY there was a message telling Fred that Charlie D. wanted to see him, and as soon as he got off-duty, he returned to the Elbow Room. The retrokids weren't there, and the waitress took him directly to the stockroom where Veronica's proxy was waiting. "Planning a vacation, are we?" she said by way of greeting. If her information was that good, he didn't feel any need to answer. "I know all about the 'Leen Disease," she went on, "and I feel terrible about your wife and her germline, but your mission here is not complete, and you cannot leave until it is."

"Mary needs me, and there's nothing you can say or do to keep me here."

The proxy shook her head. "Don't bet the farm on that, Commander. Seems to me that's how you got yourself up here in the first place—rushing off in a panic to rescue your wife. Why don't you let the authorities help her out this time? The way I hear it, every lab in the UD is working on the problem. It's as much their worry as yours: if the 'leens implode, there goes the whole clone-based economy. It's just as bad as your clone fatigue. There's nothing you could do to help anyway and by the time you reach Earth, the whole thing will be settled one way or the other."

"I can't just sit on my hands and do nothing!"

"That's exactly what you will do, soldier. You can't leave the battlefield in the middle of a firefight because they need you at home. You have to suck it up and complete your mission."

"I don't even know what my mission is. Bribe the donalds with drugs? Anybody can do that."

"Don't sell yourself short, Commander. Since the last time we met in this room, the entire operation is running as smooth as we could hope for, and no other person alive could replace you. So I'm afraid, though it's hard on you with all this going on, you'll just have to stick it out. Abandoning your post now will only *guarantee* you never see Mary again, if you know what I mean."

Centennial

Tia Jaspersen carried a tray of refreshments into the Volcano Room. Saul was half reclining on the overstuffed couch with—of all things—a squid cap on his head. Their guest, Andrea Tiekel, was setting up some equipment on the little tea table. Saul saw his wife's expression and said, "It's all right, dear. It's for the Smithsonian."

Tia looked around for somewhere else to set the tray. "But you've always said—"

"It's all right, dear. It's my centennial."

Centennial or not, Saul had always been adamantly opposed to letting anyone fool around with his brain. This Tiekel woman had made no mention of wanting to do so when she contacted them; otherwise, Saul would have never let her come. She had said she wanted to discuss urgent GEP business and that was the only reason he had agreed.

"That's right," Andrea said. "Saul is the only former vice president that the Smithsonian doesn't have in its collection. They asked me, in light of the hundredth anniversary of his term of office, to see if I couldn't persuade him to cast a sim."

Tia offered their guest a cup of coffee. "You must be very persuasive, Myr Tiekel."

"I suppose I am," Andrea said, accepting the cup. "But please, call me Andrea." She squeezed Tia's hand and added, "Why don't you sit for a sim as well."

"Me? No, I . . ."

"Why not? The Smithsonian collects spouses too."

"I wasn't exactly his spouse back then," Tia said. But Andrea touched her hand again, and she said, "But, if you think so, I mean, why not?"

"Splendid!" Andrea put her cup down and led Tia to the opposite end of Saul's couch. Like Saul, Tia had no implants, so Andrea opened a new squid for her and helped her put it on. Then she sat between them, casually touching their bare arms as the preffing generator on the table began to whir. She didn't watch the baseline shapes herself but instead watched her mechanical scouts with her inner sight. She had released a handful of the cockroach-sized explorers on the carpet while Tia was out of the room, and they had spread throughout the house.

The conventional wisdom about Saul Jaspersen seemed to be true: he so distrusted machine intelligence that there was no mentar, midem, or even subem handling his affairs. The only AI she encountered was an ancient and totally unsecured houseputer. And all that it seemed to contain were recipes, photos, household budgets, and other homey files.

A scout found the courier pouch in a wastebasket in Saul's study. Another scout found the greeting card from Alblaitor under a stack of papers on his desk. While two scouts pulled it out and propped it open, a third scanned it for her to read. The text supported her fears.

Meanwhile, the preffing session began, and scenarios alternately designed for Saul or Tia were projected above the table. The two glassy-eyed subjects watched with stuporous indifference.

E-P said, *At the very least we'll get some good sidebobs out of this.*

The scouts found and scanned dozens of datapins they found in the house, but none of them remotely resembled the one described in the card. After a half hour had passed with no success, Andrea began to worry that Saul had cached it off-site somewhere. She repeatedly dosed him and Tia with the MDMOEP under her fingernails, but the drug's effect was diminishing. Then she had the inspiration to check Saul's person and, sure enough, she found the pin in his breast pocket. That, alone, was a good sign of its authenticity.

Got it, she said and inserted it into her sidekick.

We're safe-cloning it now, E-P said a moment later. *It appears to be encrypted, probably to his eyes only. But that won't impede us once we build his sim.*

When E-P finished copying the datapin, Andrea replaced it in Saul's pocket and recalled her scouts to her satchel. The preffing session was wrapping up. Andrea put her head back and closed her eyes. She wished she could just leave now and return to her tank, but she was obliged to play out the charade. She had to praise Saul and Tia for their cooperation, to share the dinner roast with them that was already in the oven. Its charnel-house stench made her stomach churn. For the remaining few minutes of solitude that she had, she stood at her always room window and watched clouds drift across the Bay. At home, the sun was only a little farther along its daily path than here in Alaska, but much higher in the sky. There was some sort of sailing regatta in progress around Alcatraz Island. Big colorful sails, like the wedges of pie charts.

Meanwhile, E-P built a quarantine space into which it loaded a newly assembled Jaspersen sim and sidebob, a copy of the datapin, and an Andrea sim. It was a completely isolated little universe where the clock ran hundreds of times faster than normal. There was no link between it and real reality, no chance of any malware leakage in case the datapin was booby-trapped. The plan was to let the quarantine world run for six months of local time. That should give Andrea's sim the opportunity to use the Jaspersen sim or sidebob to open and explore the datapin and for any evil surprise to make itself known. If there was any funny business at all, the quarantine space would automatically implode, signaling those in the real world to its danger.

The Unlucky Colonist

In the space yards, construction accidents were rare, but those that did occur tended to be spectacular. A couple of days following Fred's meeting with Veronica's proxy, a railgun that was shooting silver ingots from a decommissioned Oship to one of the Lucky Five malfed, spraying a stream of twenty-five-kilogram metal bricks across a wide arc of space. Most had trajectories that sent them harmlessly away from the station, but several dozen were heading for its most densely built regions. Waste scuppers successfully intercepted all but a handful of these. One ingot slammed into one of the habitation drums of the *Chernobyl*. It pierced the hull plating but was stopped dead by the outer saltwater jacket that shielded the drums from galactic cosmic rays and asteroid strikes. The escaping water froze and formed an ice plug, just as it was designed to do.

Another silver brick struck the engine of a shuttle, causing a crippling explosion that sent the craft into the path of a construction tender, which in turn took out several more ships in a chain reaction that halted all traffic in the Aria yards for several hours.

A third penetrated Fred's docking spar several space gates away from his own. He left his proxy in charge and hurried to the accident scene to lend a hand. When he arrived, the russ security and donald dockworkers were engaged in patching two breaches in the spar hull. The ingot had passed through the spar, but the holes didn't line up. The ingot had been deflected by something inside the spar, and Fred searched the space gate to determine what it was. It turned out to be the belt mechanism that fed the gate's railgun. Fred swam over just as a gang of donalds was removing a cryocapsule that had been crushed inside the mechanism. The capsule was split along its seams, and the damage was so extensive that there was no doubt the colonist inside was irretrievable.

Something odd caught Fred's eye—a spot of blood on the belt and more along the capsule seam. He might have missed it, since blood at an accident scene was unremarkable, but the biostatic process that these capsules employed required dehydrating the blood. If he saw blood, it should be in a powder form, not liquid.

When Fred looked up, all the donalds in his vicinity were straining themselves to control their laughter. This was such an odd response to a deadly emergency that he looked around to see what they were laughing at. A lone donald was performing a burlesque of a ballet. At first Fred was confounded by this bizarre behavior, but then he recalled the retroboy's erotic dance in the method nightclub and his Original Flaw. And, in fact, the donald seemed to be sodomizing himself with his tail as he danced, leaving no doubt as to his meaning. When the clown realized that Fred was watching him, he froze in midair. All of the donalds surrounding him seemed to hold their breath. How did they know about the method? Fred turned back to the crushed cryocapsule. Top Ape, himself, was there with fear in his eyes.

In a state of shock, Fred managed to set aside the incident for the moment, and he glanced deliberately at the ceiling. Top Ape understood and leaped into action. Dock work at the space gate had been suspended during the emergency; now Top Ape got it started again. He formed unnecessarily complicated bucket lines of cargo crates and shells that effectively shielded Fred from all of the fixed security cams. Meanwhile, Fred turned off his TECA sidekick. He pulled a tiny scout from a pouch on his belt and linked it to his Spectre. He placed the scout inside the split seam of the capsule and sent it to explore the interior. What it should have found was biostasis maintenance equipment: pumps, electronics, a liquid nitrogen reservoir. But what it did find was an assault rifle, ammunition, field supplies, a portable medkit.

The supposed colonist, himself, wore a battle suit and was packed into the tight space like a contortionist. As the scout reached his head, which was crushed beyond repair, Fred wasn't sure who he would see. The member of some aff's private army? A cloned soldier? What he did see was the biggest surprise of all. The soldier was a TOTE.

Fred recalled his scout. While he waited for it, he swiped the capsule's control panel, which was redlined across the board. The name that popped up was certain to be counterfeit, but the capsule's final destination was not—the *Chernobyl*.

When Top Ape returned, Fred told him to lose the cryocapsule somewhere where it would never be found and to fix all records of it. Then he returned to his own space gate. Along the way, the donalds struggled to contain their mockery.

THE FOLLOWING DAY, as Fred was returning on a shuttle from a scheduled mentar delivery to the *Kiev,* and an unscheduled visit to the *Chernobyl,* he received an urgent call from Mando.

"Fred!" his friend exclaimed. "The *Fentan* has a slot! You still want to go? It leaves in four days. Should I buy it for you?"

"Yes," he said without having to think. "Buy it."

By the time Fred arrived back at his rez wheel, he had withdrawn seven hundred hours of emergency personal leave, to commence at once. His plan was to move on board the *Fentan* as soon as he could, but before he was finished packing, he received a summons to the Elbow Room. He had been expecting it, and there was no getting around it, so he left his packed travel bag and returned to civieside for one final meeting.

Market Forces

It was unlike any simulgraphic brainscan Mary had ever undergone. Instead of actively thinking about what she wanted a proxy to do, she had no control over her thoughts at all. Instead of emoting on cue for the Leena sims, she was reliving her entire life—all at once. More memories flew by than she could ever hope to catch. She kissed Fred for the first time, and she kissed him for the thousandth time. Shelley introduced her to Reilly who had a friend named Fred. His face was so innocent when he was asleep, and he buttered his bread methodically. Wednesday night in the Tin Room at Rolfe's and Sazza complains about the silk pillowcase, her hangnail snagged on a thread, while this water tastes funny.

Evangeline School, and Mary is submerged in a sea of sisters. The games! The adventures! Pinching Marie and leaving a mark. Raising her hand in class; pick me, pick me. Listening real hard and telling you what I thought I heard you say.

A very distinct memory surfaced and lingered awhile before melting away. It was a class in flower arrangement, a skill that would always be in fashion. She's nine years old by the calendar, eighteen in maturation. It's her last year in school. Shelley bursts into the classroom, tears in her eyes. What's wrong?

Shelley opens a frame, and the sisters come around the workbench to watch, dropping sprigs and wires. It's a news program on the Anti-Transubstantiation Channel, which is no friend to clones. What does it mean? asks a sister, and the rest of them shush her. Shush!

"Vanity is a fickle master," the reporter is saying, "and recent figures from E-Pluribus bear this out." She is no impartial journalist, this reporter, but a partisan, as any 'leen can tell from the note of satisfaction in her voice.

The news scene switches to the headquarters of their future employer, Applied People, where CEO Zoranna Alblaitor is answering questions. "It just goes to show that the needs of society change, sometimes quickly. Now, fifteen years later, that demand is no longer there."

The reporter asks a question, and Zoranna replies, "No, I wouldn't call it a 'fad' per se. That completely mischaracterizes the nature of trend forecasting. We certainly wouldn't have invested our resources into designing this or any new germline on the basis of a 'fad.'"

Another question, and, "Perhaps. But you're going to have a time lag with any new germline. We're able to cut a human's maturation period in half, from crib to college, but that still means nine years before the first units are released to the marketplace."

A final question, and, "No, we're canceling development of the evangeline line immediately. Fortunately, only the prototype batch was ever decanted, and that consisted of only ten thousand units."

What does it mean? repeats your sister. It means our stock has crashed. It means we have no value. It means we're in for a very bumpy ride.

Degrees of Freedom

"Before we get to the unpleasantries," Veronica TOTE's proxy said, "let me commend you on your quick thinking the other day."

Fred said, "You know what I found, of course."

"I can only imagine," the proxy said, unwilling to give anything away.

"Don't strain your imagination," Fred said. "I'll show you." Fred used his Spectre to project a little frame with the dead soldier's sheet. A tissue sample Fred's scout had retrieved had enabled his Spectre to make a positive ID. "I don't know exactly how many men you have aboard the *Chernobyl*, but I did some traffic analysis last night, and I estimate there's as many as five thousand. I was just over there today, and I scanned over 450 possible TOTEs in one crypt alone. The way I figure it, and I'm sure you'll correct me if I'm wrong, you plan to hijack the *Chernobyl* en route to Upsilon Andromedae." He waited for a reaction, but the proxy remained poker-faced, so he continued. "I'm not sure when, but I figure you'll postpone the takeover for as long as possible because unless you have some quantum trick up your sleeve, you'll still need the Heliostream particle beam for acceleration. And you'll want to wait at least four years because that's how long it'll take to leave the solar system and any likely pursuit by the UD Space Command. But I'm thinking you'd like at least twenty years because by then the Chinas will have their own solar harvesters online, and you'll probably be able to rent a particle beam from them.

"So that's my window, four to twenty years. If you touch me anytime before then, the Space Command will get a copy of this, and they'll either capture you or shut off the beam, or both. I'd like more time to get out of your reach, but four years oughtta do."

Fred stopped talking. Veronica's proxy seemed more amused than he would have liked.

"My, what a rich fantasy life you lead, Commander," she said. "I can see you've put a lot of thought into this, as well as a lot of wishful thinking. Too bad you didn't finish your homework. Otherwise, you would have realized that the same clue that gave us away argues against your scenario."

Fred didn't like the sound of that, and his thoughts raced to discover any flaw in his reasoning.

"You are correct that we have an army on board and that we plan to hijack the ship, but as to the destination and time frame, you're way off. My soldiers are not in deep biostasis but only in a light fugue state, a form of hibernation, as you surmised from the liquid blood. A body can survive that for a year, two years tops, not twenty years, not even four. Which means we have to make our move much sooner than you'd like. In fact, we will take over the ship within a few months of its departure. And that means your insurance policy expires in less than six months from today. And believe me, you couldn't hide from us in any case."

Fred was confused. The particle beam acceleration was so incremental that in six months the Oship would hardly be beyond Earth's orbit.

Veronica read his expression. "Whatever made you think we were interested in deep-space colonization? I thought you were paying attention to my speech last year at the Charter Union Rendezvous. There are no spacefaring charters, Commander. The powers that be have effectively frozen us out of the space game. They wouldn't even sell us a ship without taking our land in exchange. Our way of life must be too threatening to allow us to gain even a toehold in space. But we refuse to give up either our claim on Earth or our rightful share of the solar system."

The truth finally dawned on Fred. "You're stealing the *Chernobyl* for in-system colonization!"

"At last," Veronica's proxy said. "It took you long enough. Yes, we'll use this wonderful platform to bootstrap our own inner system colony. I don't think I'll tell you exactly where, but it wouldn't be hard to guess. We have all the chemical rockets we need to get us there and we have nuclear power to run life support. So we won't need Heliostream after the launch. We'll establish a whole new space economy to break the stranglehold of the UD and the Chinas. We'll create a brand-new center of power in this weary old system."

Fred shook his head in disbelief. "You've got to be kidding."

"I assure you we are not."

"You won't last a week. The Space Command will board you."

"You think? We have our own insurance policy. Have you forgotten our hostages? We will have crypts full of freeze-dried hostages. Think of it, we won't even need to feed or water them or take them to the bathroom. They'll never complain. They have an indefinite shelf life and are conveniently packaged so we can return them as good-faith gestures, one at a time over vast distances of space." The TOTE leader seemed to relish the ingenuity of her plan. Her confidence impressed Fred, and he tried to see the logic of her reasoning, but it didn't add up.

"You picked the wrong class of hostage," he said at last.

"What's that supposed to mean?"

"Think about it. The colonists aboard the *Chernobyl* have already chosen to leave Earth forever. As far as public opinion is concerned, they're already dead and gone. In addition, they're made up of economic refugees, ex-chartists, small business owners, schoolteachers, and poets. In a word—ordinary nobodies. Do you honestly think the UD Space Command will think twice about them when they blow the hatches to board you?"

"Absolutely," Veronica's proxy said, as confident as ever. "We're talking about a *quarter million* men and women. The world would never allow so many people to be snuffed out at once."

Fred could only shake his head in disbelief. "Where have you been for the last hundred years? The UD would rather torpedo you to bits than let you get away with that ship. And then they'll blame you and make it look like it was *your* fault. What were you thinking?" A tiny but all-important hint of doubt crept into Veronica's expression, and Fred drove his point home. "I'm sorry to rain on your parade, but, honestly, don't you people hire consultants?"

Fred prepared to leave. He doubted his words would have any effect on this pirate charter's grand scheme. Before exiting the stockroom, he turned to the proxy, which didn't seem nearly so cocksure as a few moments ago, and said, "Now, if you had chosen the *Hybris* instead, then you'd have *real* hostages. Each one of those feckers is either an aff or the clone of an aff. There aren't nearly as many of them, but they make up for that in juice. They're all VIPs, every last one of them. They are the very flesh of presidents, diplomats, and vid stars, parliamentarians—you name it. Now those are *some* hostages. No one's going to torpedo that ship of fools. Not only that, but half its stasis crypts are empty.

"Anyway, thanks for the chat, but if all I have left is six months, I better get to it. See you back on Earth."

FRED'S BRAVADO CARRIED him all the way back to his stateroom, where he finished packing. It took him to the Admin Wheel, where he turned in his standstill wand, visor cap, and TECA sidekick. It took him out the spar to the space gate where the *Fentan* was docked. It took him all the way to the gangway, but there it abandoned him. If he had managed to sow a seed of doubt in Veronica's mind about her crazy scheme, she had managed to sow one in his about dropping everything and running to Mary's side.

Veronica was probably right; by the time the *Fentan* reached Earth, the whole evangeline crisis would be resolved, one way or another. And, besides, what could he do that the world's leading researchers couldn't? This was bad enough, but the real question was whether or not Mary would welcome him. Even without the 'Leen Disease, would she want him to come barging in to rescue her? Again? Fred couldn't get out of his head the little scene they had in their bedroom the morning of the clinic incident. She not only asked him not to interfere, she *begged* him not to. She sincerely wanted to handle the situation by herself.

But he had interfered anyway, and he had, in fact and in deed, saved her life, and thus Ellen Starke's life. She had admitted as much. And by his actions he had landed in prison and then, to repay the TUGs for their logistical support, he had been forced to come up here. But—and here was the rub—had Mary ever thanked him? He scoured his memory for any word of thanks, any hint of appreciation, and he came up dry.

Fred hung in a corner of the gangway like a gargoyle, oblivious to the curious glances of passersby. If he went, he was screwed. If he stayed, he was screwed. After an hour or so of second-guessing, Marcus called.

"What do you want?"

To give you a word of advice.

"I don't want your advice."

I understand, but you are loitering in a very public space and causing a lot of talk.

"What do I care?"

I am asking you to care. You have made arrangements to leave the station and return to Earth. It is my opinion that you proceed to and board the Fentan.

"Why?"

Because your continued presence here at Trailing Earth is a constant irritant that will likely spark violent unrest.

"How so?"

Your brothers were already under a lot of strain before your arrival, due to the labor troubles with Capias World. The situation with the evangelines has pushed them to the breaking point. You are a convenient scapegoat, and I know that there have already been threats against your person. Now that the donalds have learned of your method results, it's only a matter of time before they reveal them to the russ population. The falseness of the method will not restrain your brothers. They will express outrage, and our tenuous truce with the donalds will break down. There will be intergermline violence. Worse, there will be fratricide—your brothers will kill you. Your impulse to leave is a good one.

"Has it ever occurred to you that maybe I deserve what I get? You've said as much yourself."

On the contrary, I haven't yet given up on you. But the bigger issue is the good reputation of your germline. With your history of retrievable manslaughter, your death here at the hands of your brothers would surely seal the fate of your entire ten-million-strong issue.

"Really? Is fratricide any worse than our brutish Original Flaw?"

I've told you before, and I repeat, the whole Original Flaw method you underwent was a hoax. I assure you that the russ germline has never had a problem with pedophilia. That was pure fabrication.

"Is that a fact? And what about our fascination with evangelines and their boyish features and body type?"

What of it? You are equally attracted to the more voluptuous lulu type.

"What about my fascination with retrogirls? Even Mary noticed the attention I gave that Kodiak girl last year."

Human males have always sought sexual congress with children, all the way back to Paleolithic times when female menarche occurred between the ages of seven and thirteen years. For dominant males to impregnate the youngest fertile females in a tribe was adaptively advantageous to the tribe. While this may no longer be so, the male's attraction for children has survived into modern times, like the once-advantageous taste for sweets and fats. Biological propensities are hardwired into the genes and may take tens of millennia to weed out when they are no longer useful.

What's important to keep in mind is that new, inhibitory tendencies emerge to counteract obsolete ones. While your sexual interest in children may be natural, your inhibition against acting on this interest is also natural and even stronger. Neither you nor Thomas A. nor any russ has ever vio-

lated society's taboos in this regard. Whoever designed the Original Flaw method cleverly used your own russ sense of propriety against you to damage both you and your germline. I am attempting to mitigate the damage, but I will need your cooperation to do so.

How Fred wanted to believe the mentar, but he remembered the last time it had tried to talk him down from a ledge. It had tried to convince him that his *Book of Russ* debacle was due to HALVENE poisoning, and that hadn't worked out either.

"Fine. You've said your piece, Marcus. I'm not a monster; now prove it. I ask again; if this isn't the russ Original Flaw, then what is? You said you'd get the Brotherhood Council's permission to tell me."

I said I'd try to get it. Permission was denied.

"There you have it then," Fred said as he pushed off from his perch. "Get back to me when you have a better answer." He left the *Fentan* gangway and returned to his stateroom to give the whole matter some serious obsessing.

Mission Accomplished

With her skin mission accomplished, Saul and Tia waving good-bye and her rental car lifting off from their sod-paved airstrip, Andrea gave her tired body up to the plush comfort of her seat pod. But she didn't return to her always room; the real Alaskan panorama outside her windows was too disturbing to ignore. Mountain range on top of mountain range in every direction as far as the eye could see.

Meanwhile, the six-month term of their quarantine world passed, and the pocket world had not imploded. Perhaps the datapin Zoranna had sent Jaspersen was harmless after all.

What do you think? E-P said. *Break quarantine and open it?*

That was what Andrea wanted to do. It was probably safe, and her curiosity was high, but a nagging sense of caution made her say, "No, let it run another six months. In the meantime, are you able to make me a new Jaspersen sim and sidebob here?"

Two phantoms appeared in her car and struggled to orient themselves. The sim looked at her, then outside the window, then back at her and said, "Myr Tiekel, what is the meaning of this? How did you—?" The true purpose of her visit dawned on it then, and it thundered, "This is a gross violation of my privacy. I will sue you. I will bring you to ruin for this. This is criminal. This is—"

"Oh, please," she said, "spare me the drama." Andrea tuned the Jaspersen sim out and asked the sidebob what was on Alblaitor's datapin.

"It contains detailed, proprietary financial statements of Applied People," the sidebob said. "And it outlines the broad terms of a possible sale. It's an intriguing offer."

Andrea wiped them both away and said, "Now bring me a set of Zorannas."

The pair of Zorannas appeared where the Jaspersens had been, and E-P warned, *Allow us to remind you, Alblaitor has never sat for a preffing session and these constructs are only inferential.*

Why remind her? Was E-P losing confidence in its work? "They'll do," she said, and when the pair of Zorannas had oriented themselves, the sim said, "Andrea, what is the meaning of this?"

"I wanted to know why you'd be willing to sell your company to Saul Jaspersen."

"Jaspersen? I would *never* sell to him." The sidebob agreed with the sim, and Andrea wiped them away.

"This doesn't track," she said. "Are you sure the pin came from Zoranna?"

From her hands to his, we're highly confident of it.

Andrea sat back as her car crossed the Copper River Valley below. Count on Jaspersen to reside beyond the reach of modern infrastructure, nearly four hundred kilometers from the nearest Slipstream station in Wasilla. Knife-edge ridges plummeted to ice-carved gullies. Water seeped from every cranny. Everything below timberline was a deep, vital green. Few signs of humans, no roads or power lines, no towers or relay stations, no strip mines, no forest clearings, and no flat places for her car to put down in case of emergency. She fretted for the continued purr of its engines.

After a while the car left the wilderness and entered a busy traffic corridor in a narrow valley. The second six-month term inside the quarantine space elapsed with no sign of trouble.

"Can we communicate with my sim?" she asked.

Not without breaking quarantine.

Andrea wasn't ready to do that, but neither could she let the mystery go. At the Wasilla tube station, she transferred from her taxi to her private Slipstream car. After the glory of the raw Alaskan landscape, the claustrophobic Slipstream tube was so bland that she returned to her always room. The room would make the four-hour trip tolerable at least, though her bones longed for the buoyant relief of her tank. "What if we went around the Jaspersen interface altogether and decoded and analyzed the pin ourselves?"

Assuming it didn't blow up, it could take months of realtime to decrypt it in quarantine. It's a very strong cipher.

"Can't you use the E-Pluribus processors?"

That would require taking our quantum lattice off E-Pluribus preffing work and quarantining it. That could seriously disrupt our core business. Is your sense of danger that great?

"I don't know. Better safe than sorry."

If something went wrong, we could lose the processors.

"Better than losing everything."

So E-P constructed a second quarantine space, this one containing an Andrea sim, the datapin clone, decoder algorithms, and three of the world's most powerful quantum processors. The lights came up in E-Pluribus preffing suites all over the UD, and patrons were asked to stand by during technical difficulties.

THE CAR WAS approaching the Bay Area when the quarantined processors went into standby mode. That meant the cipher had been broken. One of the processors started up again as the Andrea sim inside the quarantine space analyzed the data on the pin.

Andrea, meanwhile, waited in her always room, taking comfort in its well-ordered space. Outside her window, the sun was already setting.

After a half hour of sporadic activity, the processor cycled off and on three times—her sim's signal for all clear. At the same time she could feel the jostling of the Slipstream car as it rose from the intercontinental tube and joined the Bay Area traffic grid.

"Break quarantine and open a text channel to my proxy," she said. Soon a message came through:

BOOBY TRAP SET FOR JASPERSEN, NOT US. CLUMSY, LOW-TECH SLEIGHT-OF-HAND. DATAPIN FILLED WITH PROPRIETARY FINANCIAL RECORDS, AS JASPERSEN SIDEBOB SAID. PAINTED FALSE PICTURE OF APPLIED PEOPLE FINANCIAL WORTH MUCH ROSIER THAN JUSTIFIED. APPLIED PEOPLE BARGAIN OF THE CENTURY. NUMBERS RIGGED TO CHANGE BACK TO

AUDITED VALUES AFTER SALE COMPLETE
LEAVE NO TRACE OF DUPLICITY.
DIFFICULT FOR FORENSIC SLEUTH
TO PROVE OTHERWISE.

"Amazing," Andrea said.

We agree, E-P said. *Alblaitor thought she could sell Applied People to Jaspersen for far more than we would have paid, and it would have bankrupted him. Who knows, considering his lack of technical sophistication, it might have worked.*

"All our careful planning upset by a simple bait and switch."

Do you feel it safe now to reintegrate the processors into the E-Pluribus lattice?

Andrea thought about it. All her suspicions had melted away. There was no disconnect after all: Zoranna Alblaitor was acting true to her character. "Yes, it's safe."

She could feel the tube car's deceleration, and her sense of satisfaction was increased by the knowledge that she was less than twenty minutes away from her tank. She was about to leave her always room when she heard a strange sizzling sound behind her. She turned to see a thin yellow stain creeping up a corner of the room and spreading out across the walls.

"What is that?"

We are under attack. We are analyzing its nature.

The stain quickly crisscrossed the walls and ceiling, covering everything in a slimy yellow crust. Even the windows clouded over. Andrea's cheeks tingled, and her eyes itched, and she returned her POV to her Slipstream car afraid she'd find the real world also under attack. But all was normal inside her car. It was parked at a platform in the Oakland station. Commuters passed outside her windows.

"Give me a mirror!" she said, but no mirror opened. "Mirror! Mirror!" In desperation, she unlatched her pod harness and peered at her reflection in the window. No yellow streaks on her cheeks, though they burned. Nothing wrong with her eyes. A panic reaction?

"I'm going home," she said, making her way to the car door. "E-P?"

The infection is within my mind. The datapin was merely a catalyst that crystallized trojan elements already in place. I have no ready defense. I must isolate my mind while I can.

"Wait!" Andrea called. She stumbled leaving the car and nearly fell on the platform. "Save the Oship clones!"

*The teams aboard the ships have been independent since their creation.
They are safe for now. I must go.*

A pain greater than anything Andrea had ever experienced stabbed her
in the head. When she looked again, she was sprawled on her back on the
concrete floor. She had no idea where she was or how she had gotten
there. Mechanical bees were swarming all around, and a man in a gum-
mysuit like a stack of green jelly pillows was looming over her barking angry, meaningless words. She couldn't make out what he wanted or why he
was so angry. She sat up and shouted, "Go away!"

But the man didn't go away; he came closer. Andrea brought her knees
to her chest. Her knees were scraped and bleeding, but she hardly noticed.
She made a fierce face at the horrible green pillow man and screamed,
"Go away!"

Coin Toss

After Mary's last brainscan was complete, Meewee escorted her to the little
room that had served as a ready room during their brief stay. The small facility had a provisional feel to it, as though it had been assembled for them
alone and would be pulled apart once they left. Which Meewee suspected
was probably the case.

Mary leaned on him as they shuffled along the corridor. "That was ex-
hausting, so many memories. Did Ellen think that they were going to cure
me?"

"No, I don't think so."

Inside the ready room, Ellen was on the floor crying while Cyndee
and Georgine looked on impassively. They were further along than Mary and
had not spoken during the entire three days of their stay. When Mary entered, Ellen got up and hugged her legs. Mary merely looked down at the girl.
She had no comfort to give her.

"Well," Meewee said, "I suppose it's time to go. I promised Lyra I'd have
you in Chicago by now."

ARROW HAD CONFIRMED that it indeed still held the kill codes for
all Starke insiders, including Eleanor and Cabinet, and even including
himself. On his way from Chicago to the Mem Lab, Meewee wondered

idly how such a code would work in a biological body. Was it similar to the searing that the HomCom had once used to lock the cells of people exposed to NASTIEs? Or maybe there was a reservoir of poison hidden somewhere inside his body? He didn't pursue this matter and took the mentar's word at face value.

The real question, the one Meewee couldn't get out of his mind, was how Eleanor could place so much trust in that odd mentar and, by extension, in himself. Did she feel that she knew him so well that she was willing to put the fate of her whole universe into his hands? Or was she subtly manipulating him to always do her bidding? Whatever the case, it had worked in her favor thus far.

Whether or not helping her was a good thing was another matter altogether. Would he go down in history as humanity's traitor? As the man who ended history? Or as humanity's savior? Eleanor trusted his judgment over her own, apparently, and had put the final veto power into his hands. And yet, even as his car arrived at the Mem Lab, he didn't know who was right. Were brainfish really any better than Andrea? Why couldn't there be just people?

A CELEBRATION WAS in progress in the pond room. Momoko was there, and he went straight to her and took her in his arms and gave her a big greedy kiss. His own sense of entitlement startled him, he who had never had much interest in romantic love. But she kissed him with equal passion, and this startled him even more. Is this how you manipulate us, Eleanor? Or am I suddenly a romantic?

The room was roaring with laughter and music. Staff members from all the satellite mods were there in realbody or vurt, including russ guards and the two Els, who were a little bit drunk on champagne. Missing, Meewee noticed, was Captain Benson, the russ commander of the garrison. Was he already on board the *Hybris* in a cryocapsule?

"Bishop Meewee!" squealed an El; he couldn't tell if it was Elaine or Liz. Momoko put a champagne flute into his hand.

"What's this all about?" he said. "A going-away party?"

"Yes," Momoko said.

"And a victory celebration," said the other El who joined them. The Els were dressed in plain jumpsuits, one red and the other blue.

"What victory?"

"Haven't you heard? Where have you been?"

"Locked up in that autoclave you call a tube car."

The El in blue said, "An hour ago, E-Pluribus suspended all operations."

"At all their locations around the world," added her sister.

"And E-P has vanished from mentarspace!"

"And Andrea is in a private clinic."

The two young women clinked their glasses and chorused, "Ad astra!"

Eleanor's sim joined the group. She seemed happy but not so giddy as her younger sisters. "Oh, don't look so surprised, Merrill," she said. "I told you it would have to be done before the launch."

"Yes," he said, "but—"

"Don't worry about the ships," said the El in red. She cupped her ear with her hand and said, "Cur-chunk! Cur-chunk! What's that sound I hear?"

Her sister replied, "That's the sound of mentars rapturing."

The Els howled with laughter. Eleanor rolled her eyes and led Meewee by the sleeve to the side of the pool. The brainfish lined up for a pat on the head. "Dr. Strohmeyer tells me that your engram recordings of the evangelines are good," Eleanor said. "Their brainfish will be imprinted in a few days. Of course, they'll be kept in a separate facility."

"Good. Good," Meewee said absently.

"Did you tell them what it was for?"

"What? The evangelines? No. I thought it best that you do that."

She watched him for a little while and said, "So, have you made up your mind?"

"About what?"

"Don't play dumb with me, Merrill. I know that you know what's at stake here." She gestured toward the Els across the room. "We know what we are." At that moment, both Els turned to look at him. All three nodes of the posthuman woman, and all their fishy cohorts, were looking at him with intense interest.

"No," he admitted, "I have not. And I don't understand why you've put it on me to decide what you do."

"Then permit me to try to explain. Under the best of circumstances, a colony ship on a millennial voyage will be lucky to survive. If space doesn't kill it, its bickering human cargo will. Things will only get worse when they arrive and start colonizing their new home. They'll have a much better chance for survival with someone like me coming along, don't you agree?"

He nodded noncommittally.

"But what every human colony needs as much or more than someone like me must be someone like *you*."

"I don't follow."

"Look at it this way," she went on. "I've often thought of you as a modern-day Moses in the desert. Don't laugh, I'm serious. Moses brought his people to the gates of the Promised Land, but he was barred from entering it himself. It's the human condition, as I see it, the old belong to the old and may not cross over to the new. But we're not entirely human anymore, Merrill, and the old laws don't apply. Our new reality needs you. Come with us to our thousand new worlds and help us write our new commandments and put order to our new societies. We need your wisdom and judgment. Not to mention your *humanity*. Come with us, Merrill."

Moses? First he was a wild card, and now he was a mythological figure from the Christian Bible wandering in the desert? Meewee decided to test his powers. <*Arrow*> he said <*if I ordered you to kill all of the Eleanors and her brainfish and her Cabinet, could you do it?*>

<*Yes.*>

<Would *you do it?*>

<*Yes.*>

Eleanor made no comment, though she must have heard and understood. She merely gazed at him and nodded her head.

The Els came over and one of them said to him, "It's time to choose which one of us is going. Will you help?"

The hidden meaning of the request was not lost on him. They were forcing the issue, forcing him to decide. It was now or never, all or nothing, the status quo or the Promised Land. Momoko came to stand by his side and entwined her arm in his. She was trembling. The room grew still as others began to watch their little group. In the end, he knew there was no choice because there could never be a status quo; it didn't take the wisdom of Moses to see that. E-P and Andrea may be down for the count, but they or some other machine would try again and again until they succeeded.

"How can I help you choose?" he said.

"We want you to flip a coin."

Meewee said, "But I don't own a coin."

"My sister has one," said the El in blue.

"No, I don't," said the other. "I gave it to you."

"I distinctly remember giving it to you."

Eleanor quipped, "Well, so much for a shared mind."

The girls checked their pockets and the one in blue found the coin. She held it out to Meewee. "Will you?" It was a small copper-zinc disk that, even in its heyday, was the least valuable coin of the realm. Meewee accepted it from her. How fitting to decide the fate of a species with a penny.

"Listen up!" the El in red announced to the room. "We're choosing our first colonist." The music stopped playing, and the Mem Lab faithful crowded around.

Meewee turned the coin over in his hand. Heads or tails, mole or freckle, red or blue. "Winner goes on the *Hybris*," he said and tossed the coin over his head. "Elaine, call it."

A Ticket to Ride

Try not to think about it. Think about trying not to think about it. Try not to think about it. It was a short to-do list, but it was caught in a loop.

Fred sprawled on his couch not watching two holos running in his stateroom. One was of Mary's last FUS, still catatonic, still seated in her floral print armchair staring serenely into space. The other was a short tape loop depicting a donald dockworker floating serenely in the starry space beyond the buoys that marked the Port Clarke boundary. He wore only his dock overalls and was quite dead. An anonymous person had sent the clip to Fred. Fred had no doubt that the space-blown donald was the dockworker who had been clowning around during the hull breach emergency, and that Top Ape had both ordered his murder and sent the clip. It was an offering of appeasement. Top Ape probably thought that the insult to Fred was the reason he had not left his stateroom for the last few days, and the reason he hadn't swiped the latest shipment of Raspberry Flush. How frustrating it must be for them, to have a flask of heaven in their grasp but no way to open it.

Someone began knocking loudly on his door, kicking it actually. This had happened several times during the last day or so. There had also been shouted insults and threats by russ voices. Fred had ignored all this, but this time, just to mix things up a little, he pushed himself to his feet. Before he reached the door, a phone call arrived from Earth Girl with a floating red glyph pulsing EXTREME URGENCY.

Decisions, decisions, what not to do? Fred returned to the couch and said, "Okay, Earth Girl, what do you want?"

"Hello, Specialist Londenstane," the mentar's voice said. "So nice of you to take my call. You are signed up to depart on the ISV *Fentan* in ten hours. The ship will seal its hatches in four hours."

"Isn't that fascinating?"

The banging on his door continued, and the mentar said, "Do you intend to board the ship?"

"That's a good question. Anything else?"

The mentar paused, then added, "Yes, TECA authorities have asked me to inform you that if you intend to remain on emergency leave status but not return to Earth aboard the *Fentan*, you cannot remain in Wheel Nancy. We need the accommodations for incoming personnel. You will have to move to a civilian residential sector and be responsible for your own rent."

"Amazing."

The banging ceased and was replaced by scratching sounds.

"Is that all, Earth Girl?"

"Yes."

Fred ended the call with a swipe and went to the door. He made a fist and cocked his arm, intending to punch whoever was there in the face. But when he swung the door open, there was no one there. Someone had scratched a crude hangman's noose into the surface of the door, and Fred wondered idly how hanging would work in weightlessness as he shut the door and returned to the couch.

He was hungry, but the last time he'd gone to the commissary, even the dorises had shunned him.

THE THING ABOUT not thinking about things was that while you were busy not thinking about certain things, you were actually thinking about other things. So when the call from Marcus came, Fred took a break from not thinking and answered it.

"There's still time for you to board the *Fentan*," it said.

"That's very interesting."

Marcus refused to be put off and continued. "There have been sporadic incidents between russes and donalds out in the spars."

"Define incidents."

"Fights."

"What a shame."

"You have no intention of leaving the station, do you?"

"I honestly don't know, Marcus. I don't see what I would gain one way or another. For the first time in my life I don't know what to do."

"Perhaps I can help."

"Give it a shot."

"The Original Flaw."

"What about it? You going to tell me what it is?"

"Not I. In your present frame of mind, I doubt you would believe me anyway. The person responsible for sealing that information in the first place will tell you."

A third holo opened in Fred's crowded stateroom. It was a life-sized sim of Agnes Russ. She wore the old-fashioned pants and blouse, big hair, and kindly smile Fred remembered from Russ School.

"Mother?" he said, sitting up.

"Yes, Freddy, it's me. Marcus tells me you've made a mess of things up here, and he asked me to come up and straighten you out a little."

"Yes, Mother."

"First off, Tommy never diddled children, so get that out of your mind this instant. It's *garbage*, and it'll only poison you. Now, what I'm about to tell you is in the utmost, strictest confidence, and you must promise me you'll never tell anyone. Not even Tommy knew it, and it could only harm the rest of your brothers. Do you promise me, Fred?"

What else could he say? "Yes, Mother."

"Good." The sim gazed at him with a mixture of skepticism and affection. "Honestly, boy, how you could ever believe those disgusting lies is beyond me. You're so much like your father, worry and worry about every little thing until you've made a mountain out of air. It's what killed him in the end." She shook her head. "If you must know what was wrong with Tommy, I'll tell you. He was a congenital moron, or would have been. When I was carrying him, they had just started finding and fixing birth defects while the baby was still in the womb. A DNA scan discovered that my fetus had Gorman's Syndrome, a rare genetic brain disease. Marcus, explain to Fred what GS was."

"Yes, myr," Marcus said. "Gorman's Syndrome is the faulty expression of a cluster of genes responsible for manufacturing the calcium-calmodulin-dependent protein Kinase II. Its function in the pathway responsible for—"

"Thank you, Marcus. What the defect does is it makes it hard to learn things. To learn anything."

"Processing long-term synaptic potentiation, or LTP, into long-term memory," Marcus added.

"Thank you, Marcus. Anyway, it's a severe mental handicap. Children who have it never learn to speak. They can't tie their own shoes or hardly feed themselves. Even with the best care they rarely live beyond ten or so years. That's what my doctor told me.

"Your father wanted me to have an abortion, but my doctor told me about this new treatment. She said that GS was the result of only three defective genes, and they could try to insert normal ones into my fetus and maybe fix the problem in the womb. It was risky, but I loved you before you were born, and I decided to do it. It worked beautifully, and you— Tommy was born with normal intelligence.

"Your father and I were thrilled and very thankful, and we chose to seal Tommy's medical records so he could grow up as a normal kid without this condition hanging over his head everywhere he went. There was a so-called DNA Bill of Rights back then.

"Then he grew up and joined the Secret Service and died saving President Taksayer, and she picked him to be the first commercial clone donor, and nobody knew of his original handicap, or they surely wouldn't have picked him, no matter how heroic he was. But the genetic repair was stable and passed through to his clones and no one was the wiser, not even Applied People. Applied People still doesn't know. That's why you must keep this secret.

"It was only later, after your father died, and the first cloned lines were being so shamelessly exploited that I helped to found your Benevolent Brotherhood to protect you kids' rights. I turned Tommy's early medical records over to Marcus, including those covering the prenatal repair, but made him swear never to reveal them. It could ruin your germline, even today. Especially today.

"So, there you have it, Fred, the big secret. If we didn't fix Tommy, his life would have been a brief nightmare, and none of you would exist. But we had him repaired, and though his life was still too short, it was a decent, full, normal life. He had friends and girlfriends, was attentive to us, never got mixed up with bad influences, and he died serving his country. Your Original Flaw is a profound learning disorder, but it was permanently fixed."

"And I might add," Marcus put in, "that there is a zero probability of a 'clone fatigue' capable of reversing the repair in a mature brain."

"So, do everyone a big fat favor, son, and get over it already. Quit acting so self-destructive. Do you hear what I'm saying?"

"Yes, Mother."

"All right then. Be good; stay safe; I love you. Marcus, take me home."

"I love you too, Mother," Fred said as the apparition faded from sight. At first Fred felt such a rush of relief he fell back on the couch, drunk and dizzy, the happiest man alive. I'm not a bad man, he told himself over and over. Life was possible again.

After a little while, Marcus said, "There's still time to board the *Fentan*."

"Yes, of course," Fred said, jumping to his feet.

"You'll go then?"

The decision was suddenly easy. "Yes." He looked around his cluttered stateroom. "I'll just collect my things." His bag was still packed and ready to go.

"Good. You've made the right decision."

"Thank you, Marcus."

The mentar signed off, and Fred grabbed his travel bag and went to the door. But he stopped before reaching it when another thought crept into his mind, something Marcus had told him about the hoax russ metaverse, how a mentar could reconstruct all of human media in a day. Was it possible that Marcus had made a *counterfeit* Agnes Russ in order to manipulate him?

All of the goodness Fred had so recently reclaimed leaked away in a moment. If the Original Flaw was such a goddamn deep secret, faithfully kept for a hundred years even from Thomas A., why would they reveal it to him? Promise me, Freddy, you won't tell *anyone*. Yes, Mother. How brief his absolution.

Fred dropped his bag and just stood there, frozen in place again. After a while, when Marcus called back to check on him, he didn't answer but staggered to his couch, his mind stuttering like a faulty switch. Then out of the blue, a woman's voice spoke: "I suppose that in a dark room, even a dim bulb feels bright."

"Mary?" The FUS was active, Mary was watching him. Her surroundings had changed; she was no longer in her Starke suite. He recognized their apartment. "You're at home! Where have you been? Are you all right?"

She waved away his questions. "I only made this update to say good-bye, Fred. They wanted to biostase us, but we refused. I am mentally competent and so have the right to decide my own fate. My sisters and I have seen through the illusion of meaning. There is no meaning to life, Fred. There is no heaven or hell, no afterlife. And since we live in a society in which we are banned even from bearing children, there is no biological afterlife either. Knowing all this is killing my sisters, and it will take me, too, very soon."

"You're wrong! About there being no meaning, and about your mental competence. Obviously, you are temporarily insane, and as your spouse, I have the authority to—"

"You have no authority over me, Fred. I am my own person. Besides, you couldn't change things even if you tried. Stay up there and do your duty. That at least has meaning for you. This is good-bye, Fred. This is the end."

"Don't talk like that! Listen to me!" But she began to slip away again into her darkness. "You say you updated the FUS in order to say good-bye. Obviously, then, good-byes *mean* something to you. Your feelings for me *mean* something."

"If you must hold on to something, Fred, then hold on to that." With those final words, the FUS made a holo salute and withdrew into a passive state, and all of Fred's cajoling and arguments were so much noise.

The FUS holo showed a little of Mary's surroundings; a pair of legs intruded into the holospace, and Fred zoomed the view out as far as possible. Another evangeline was sitting there, Cyndee, who had helped them leave the prison. A third evangeline in the room was probably Georgine, who he had not met. They were placeholders, not active sims, as was a jenny nurse who moved in and out of the holospace.

Fred paced his room trying to come up with a plan. He picked up his travel bag, but set it down again. Think! He ordered his genetically repaired moron brain—Think! But thinking, like all his not-thinking, got him nowhere. His brain was the wrong muscle. He picked up his bag. Love was the only answer. Mary needed him. He wasn't helping her by staying; at least by going there was some minuscule chance of reaching her in time.

Someone knocked frantically at his door. Fred dropped the bag, made a fist, cocked his arm, and flung the door open. He threw a punch but pulled it back before it landed. Mando was at his door, in his service uniform, and it looked like someone had already punched him. His left eye was bruised and swollen half shut.

"Fred! Why are you still here?" Mando said. "Why aren't you aboard the *Fentan*?"

"I've been busy."

"Fred, Fred, Fred," Mando said, pushing past him into the room. He glanced all around, saw Mary's FUS and the spacefaring donald, spotted the travel bag. He picked it up and thrust it into Fred's hands. "We must hurry."

"Yes," Fred said, "let's go." Fred swiped away the holos, and they left the room. In the hall, the walls on either side of his door had been marked with hateful words and glyphs.

"Forget about that," Mando said and pulled Fred by the arm.

"Wrong way," Fred said. "The spokeway lifts are that way."

But Mando was insistent. "We'll take a utility lift to the hub. The main spokeways aren't safe." He didn't elaborate.

"Who hit you?" Fred said. "Was it a brother? Do you know his name?"

"It's not important. Getting you on that ship is important." He led Fred down little-used corridors to a service lift. They passed only a few startled dorises and aslams along the way.

"Wait a minute," Fred said as the elevator doors opened. "Why are you in a TECA uniform?"

"Because I am on duty."

"But why aren't *you* on the *Fentan*? You were supposed to board days ago." Then the truth hit Fred. "No one would sell you another homerun. You sold me your own ticket!"

"Yes, and if we don't hurry, it will all be for nothing. Come, my crazy friend."

He tried to pull Fred into the elevator car, but Fred stood fast. "What about Luisa? Don't you want to go to her? It's *your* ticket, not mine. How dare you put my heart before your own?"

Pain flashed across Mando's damaged face. "There is no time, Fred. When you are on the ship, call me and we will talk."

Fred shrugged him off. "We'll talk *now*."

"You are stubborn, my brother. Let us compromise and talk on the way."

"No!"

When Mando saw that Fred would not budge, he said, "I love Luisa more than breathing. But you, Fred, you and Mary. How can I say this? My brothers say you are sick, that you have the clone fatigue, and that is why you must humiliate us before the world. But I say they're wrong. You and Mary are special. What happens to you matters to all of us, to me and Luisa. If you or Mary die, we all die. You can't stay here any longer. Besides, I promised you a ticket, and a russ keeps his word. Now can we go?"

Fred joined him in the lift, and they rode it to the hub where they found a shuttle to the *Fentan*'s spar. They were silent the entire trip out, and Fred made a quick list of all his options. When at last they reached the *Fentan* gangway and processing station, Fred grabbed a handrail and halted himself.

"What's wrong?" Mando said. "Only a little farther."

"Not for me, my friend. I've been thinking."

"Fred!"

"No, shut up and listen. You are a true brother, Armando Mendez, and a true friend. You helped me see what I need to do. No, don't speak. I wish I could save all of us. I don't think I can, but maybe I can save a few." He shoved his travel bag into Mando's arms. "You're going back, not me. If they're still alive when you get there, do what you can."

Before Mando could object, Fred said, "Earth Girl, come in."

"Listening."

"Transfer my passage aboard the *Fentan* to Armando Mendez."

"You can't!" Mando said.

"It's already done."

FRED TOOK A cart to a spot near his old space gate. Top Ape was waiting for him in an EM shadow with two of the tamperproof cases. Fred swiped them and said, "Make all the bullshit stop."

Then he boarded a shuttle for the civilian port. He used his Spectre to send a message to Veronica TOTE to meet him at once. On his way to the Elbow Room he did some port traffic analysis and booked a room in a civieside rez wheel.

BY THE TIME Fred reached the stockroom, Veronica TOTE's proxy was waiting for him. "Smart decision, Commander."

"Wait until you hear my conditions."

If the real Veronica TOTE was as exhausted as her proxy looked, she hadn't slept in days. "By all means," she said, "let's hear your conditions."

"First, tell me if I'm reading the traffic data correctly. I see a lot of musical chairs with the cryocapsules. Have you changed your mind about the *Chernobyl?*"

A thin smile spread across the pirate's face. "Why, in fact, we have. We took your comments to heart and did a little research, and you were right about both the *Chernobyl* and the *Hybris*. When you're right, Commander, you're right. Fortunately, we're a nimble organization, and we should be able to handle the last-minute switch, especially now that you've returned to ride herd on our monkeyboys."

"About that. Tell me something: In this new society of yours, this new center of power in the universe, will there be room in it for clones?"

From the look on the proxy's face, this was a question that had never crossed Veronica's mind. "I doubt Applied People or Capias World or any other human resources agency will choose to operate there."

"I'm not talking about the companies. I'm talking about independent iterants, ex-commercial clones."

The proxy gave it some thought. "I suppose there could be a place for
runaway clones, but it's not something I could decide on my own."

"That's my first condition," Fred said. "After you take over the ship, you
will issue a public proclamation that all independent clones are entitled to
full citizenship and equal rights in your new colony." Then he remembered something Mary's FUS had said. "Including full unrestricted repro-
ductive rights."

"Clones having babies? That's a tall order."

"Watch it get taller. Second, you will immediately place into biostasis
my wife and her two sisters, Georgine and Cyndee. I can tell you where
you can find all three of them right now. You'll also biostase Luisa Mendez
of Cozumel, Mexico. I can give you a positive ID."

"They'll refuse. I understand that all 'leens are refusing that."

"I really don't care. You'll kidnap them if necessary and do it anyway.
Kidnapping is a TUG specialty, isn't it? Once that's done, you will hide
them from the authorities, but you will inform their spouses or designated
others and give *them* the decision of how and when to quicken them." Fred
paused to review what he had said, and he added, "And let the spouses
know it was me, Mr. Clone Fatigue, who so ordered it.

"Third, put Mary in a cryocapsule and smuggle her up here to the *Hybris* with your own stowaways."

The proxy was incredulous. "Anything else?"

Fred thought for a second. "No, that'll do. But when you take Mary, be
prepared; my wife keeps company with a diplomat-class bee."

The overtired proxy shook its head. "You know, Commander, there's
been a fair bit of discussion around the War Table about whether or not
you really have fallen out of type."

"Is that a fact? And what was the upshot?"

The proxy crossed its muscled arms. "You really want to know?"

"Why not?"

"All right. The Supreme Council thinks you're a bad apple, but whether
or not more russes will turn like you is an open question. In the meantime
we find you useful."

"Fair enough. Good to know." Fred began to swim to the door and
stopped. "What about you, Veronica? What do you think?"

"What do I think about you?"

"Yeah."

The proxy rubbed its chin. Even with her face unpacked, Veronica had a strong chin. "You have the clone fatigue, no doubt about it. You are ground zero for clone fatigue. You are the first robin of spring. I think that if we open our colony to runaway clones, we should expect a flood of you."

Fred grunted.

Epilogue

The Journey Begins

The journey of a thousand suns begins today. Meewee addressed a select audience of world leaders in the holo skybox as well as millions of Earthbound viewers on the Evernet. Five gleaming Oships floated in a ragged line within the Trailing Earth launch zone. Blue fire sparkled in their donut holes as their torus targets were energized.

Some may question whether the journey is worth the sacrifice and danger.

The skybox seemed to float within the launch zone and offered its guests a privileged close-up view of the ships. Among the VIPs in attendance were Cabinet, in its attorney general persona; Ellen Starke, who grew taller with each passing day; and Ellen's newly announced stepmother, Liz Starke. Liz had been cloned from the murdered Eleanor Starke's genetic material, according to news reports, and been granted a small portion of Starke Enterprises assets, including Heliostream. Also present were Saul Jaspersen, Zoranna Alblaitor and Nicholas, Million Singh, and other GEP brass. Noticeably absent were Andrea Tiekel, who remained hospitalized after a run-in with a NASTIE, and her mentar, E-P, who had mysteriously abandoned mentarspace and was presumed raptured.

To them I say that no sacrifice is too dear and no danger too great to ensure the very survival of our human species.

A second Eleanor clone, Elaine Starke, along with a Cabinet clone, attended the ceremony from the ESV *Garden Hybris.* All of the ship's illustrious plankholders not in the crypts had gathered before a giant holoframe in Nightlight, one of the four inhabited drums. Cabinet appeared as a fashionable young woman, the same age as Elaine; it was the old mentar's first new persona in fifty years. The clone of Million Singh, Seetharaman, was also present, as well as clones of Andrea Tiekel and E-P.

"Oh, this is going to be fun," Elaine whispered.

"Don't get cocky," warned her mentar.

What will we find when we arrive at our new homes? That's an open question. For a century, deep-space probes have reported alien lifeforms, but thus far none which we recognize as intelligent beings. Are we the only biological intelligence in the universe? Perhaps our definition of intelligence is too narrow, too specio-centric.

In the next *Hybris* hab drum over, and in the next few dozen more, in the core of the drums where it was weightless even under rotation, were the biostasis crypts. And in the crypts, among the inert colonists, lay thousands of secret soldiers of one stripe or another. Some were only slumbering, ready to answer their leader's call at once, and some were dry and brittle, like old paper, tucked away for the long haul.

In one cryocapsule crouched, not a human soldier, but a mentar with a rare tolerance for solitude. In its pasty brain festered schemes and plots of mass destruction.

For, are not trees intelligent, who know to shed their leaves at the end of summer? Are not turtles intelligent, who know when to bury themselves in mud under the ice? Is not all life intelligent, that knows how to pass its vital essence to new generations?

And among the sleeping soldiers and colonists in the crypts lay one apart, a woman who had forgotten the meaning of life.

While at Trailing Earth, a man in a bar attended to a conversation in his spex.

"What will you do now, Commander?"

"What do you mean? I'm coming aboard. You agreed to smuggle me aboard."

"Not yet. There's still some time. We suggest you return to Earth while you still can."

"I won't leave Mary alone."

"But you'll never be able to quicken her without a cure, will you? And you won't find a cure up here. Don't worry about Mary; we'll take excellent care of Mary."

Because half of intelligence resides in the body, be it plant or animal.

And on Earth, in a carton in the evidence room of the Chicago police department, among the physical clues of a triple kidnapping at the Lin/Wong gigatower, lay the smashed and lasered bits of a tiny blue mech. A timer switch inside the dead mech closed, and its noetics rebooted and released its millions of self-repair bots.

While under the Earth there pooled a slurry of quicksilver honey and pollen.

I now commend these brave colonists to the galaxy, to join their minds and bodies to the community of living beings they will encounter there, and to establish our rightful place among the stars.

Merrill Meewee swiped a control plate that sent a signal racing to a relay station orbiting the Earth that dispatched five invisible particle beams across space to the waiting Oships. The celebrants in the skybox milled about, drinking champagne and entertaining each other for 8.33 minutes as the beams found their torus targets, and another 8.33 minutes as pictures returned to Earth. Then everyone turned to the ships and cheered with one voice. The five hoops were encased in shivering energy that nudged them the first precious millimeters of their arrogant voyage.

Wet Epiphany

Mary gulped cold water and awoke in a panic. There were bubbles—bubbles!—streaming from her nose.